BLOOD ALLIANCE SERIES

Chastely Bitten
Royally Bitten
Regally Bitten
Rebel Bitten
Kingly Bitten
Cruelly Bitten

BLOOD ALLIANCE STANDALONES

Blood Day
Crave Me

COMING SOON:
Blood City
Frost Bitten

USA TODAY BESTSELLING AUTHOR
LEXI C. FOSS

CRUELLY BITTEN

BLOOD ALLIANCE SERIES

Editing by: Outthink Editing, LLC

Proofreading by: Katie Schmahl & Jean Bachen

Cover Design: Covers by Julie

Cover Photography: Wander Aguiar

Cover Models: Lucas Loyola & Sophie L

Published by: Ninja Newt Publishing, LLC

Digital Edition

ISBN: 978-1-68530-265-8

Paperback Print Edition

ISBN: 978-1-68530-315-0

For those who stuck with me while I finished the monumental task that was this book. Thank you for your support, love, and thoughtful words. I'm sorry this took so long, but I sincerely hope it was worth the wait.

Hugs to you all!
<3

CRUELLY BITTEN

CRUELLY BITTEN

Once upon a time, humankind ruled the world while lycans and vampires lived in secret.
This is no longer that time.

Ismerelda

The male I'm forever bonded to is now a monster. A cruel beast. A vampire without remorse and no memories of our previous existence together.

He has no idea who I am. What I mean to him. Who we used to be together. But I'm not giving up.

He will remember me. I vow it.

Cam

Except her. The female who refuses to bow.

I'm going to break her. Destroy her. Reform her. And when she's finally learned her place at my side, I'm going to end her.

Because I have no need for a disobedient pet. I'm meant to rule this alliance, and that's exactly what I'll do.

Welcome to the new reign.
It's filled with blood and broken alliances and littered with death.
My kingdom. My rules. My future.

Author's Note: *Cruelly Bitten* contains dark content. Please read the warning note inside. Also, while this story can be read as a standalone romance, this series is best enjoyed in order.

Once upon a time, humankind ruled the world while lycans and vampires lived in secret.
This is no longer that time.
Welcome to the future where the superior bloodlines make the rules.
Proceed at your own risk.

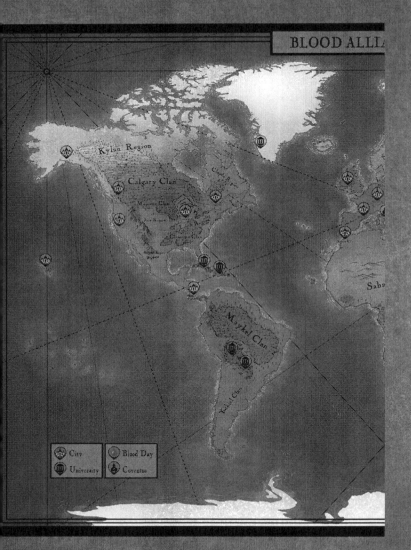

ANCE WORLD
Kostenka Clan
Stella Clan
Vladik Clan
ra Region
Lachlan Clan

THE BLOOD ALLIANCE

International law supersedes all national governance and will be maintained by the Blood Alliance—a global council of equal parts lycan and vampire.

All resources are to be distributed evenly between lycan and vampire, including territory and blood. Societal standing and wealth, however, will be at the discretion of the individual packs and houses.

To kill, harm, or provoke a superior being is punishable by immediate death. All disputes must be presented to the Blood Alliance for final judgment.

Sexual relationships between lycans and vampires are strictly prohibited. However, business partnerships, where fruitful and appropriate, are permitted.

Humans are hereby classified as property and do not carry any legal rights. Each will be tagged through a sorting system based on merit, intelligence, bloodline, ability, and beauty. Prioritization to be established at birth and finalized on Blood Day.

Twelve mortals per year will be selected to compete for immortal blood status at the discretion of the Blood Alliance. From these twelve, two will be bitten by immortality. The others will die. To create a lycan or vampire outside of this process is unlawful and punishable by immediate death.

All other laws are at the discretion of the packs and royals but must not defy the Blood Alliance.

PART I

CRUELLY BITTEN

A Note From

Izzy

Roughly ninety percent of the world's population was slaughtered after humans discovered the existence of vampires and lycans. The mortal governments tried to weaponize and enslave them.

That plan didn't work out well for humankind. Hence the massacre that followed.

The humans who survived were put into pens like cattle.

Many of them now serve as blood slaves. Others are chew toys for the lycans. It's the true meaning of dystopia.

And I've been living in this new reality for nearly one hundred and eighteen years.

However, I've held on to my hope, waiting for my long-lost vampire mate to return to me. He possessed a vision of respect, a way to govern humans without being cruel. He strongly believed in respecting the source of food that kept him and his brethren alive.

Cam.

The oldest of vampire kind.

There are many who once respected him. But the majority of the world thinks he's dead.

He's not.

I can feel it in my very soul. Because he's my mate. He's the reason I'm still alive. We performed a ceremony over a thousand years ago, binding our spirits together in a dance that's meant to last forever.

But he was taken from me.

Imprisoned.

Tortured.

And now… he's awake. Only, he's not the man I once knew and loved. He's a monster. He's cruel. And he has no memory of who I am to him.

He sees me as food. A toy. A fuck sleeve.

Which is the purpose of this note.

My story is not for the faint of heart. Cam is irrevocably broken. He's dark. He sees no problem with taking what he feels he is owed. Because he's been reprogrammed into an ancient being with no ounce of humanity left in him.

Apart from his link to me.

That's why I won't give up. I will fight for him until my dying breath, even if it's his hands wrapped around my throat.

Cam is destined to be king. *My* king. Just as I'm destined to be his queen. And you know what they say— the queen is always the strongest piece on the board.

He intends to make me bow and crush my spirit.

Meanwhile, I'll be searching for his soul. And when I

find it, I'll deliver a lethal blow. One that will bring him to his knees.

Unless he kills me first…

Trigger Warning: This book contains dark themes of dubious consent bordering on non-consent between the hero (Cam) and the heroine (Ismerelda). There are also instances of somnophilia, parasomnia, breath play, blood play, depressive thoughts, self-harm, and slave-like elements.

When I say this is one of the darkest books I've ever written, I mean it. There are certain scenes that truly broke my heart. And it took a while for Cam to mend it back together. But he does grovel. Eventually.

Love,
Lexi

CAM

THIS IS MY MATE? I THOUGHT, STUDYING THE BLONDE ON the bed. *Fuckable lips. Beautiful tits. Supple waist. Pretty face.*

I supposed I could see the physical appeal. But I felt nothing for her other than an urge to fuck her.

Well, that wasn't entirely true. I also wanted to drink her dry again.

Alas, I couldn't do either option because she was unconscious.

"Fucking mortals," I muttered, disgusted by her slow regeneration process. If only Lilith had succeeded in her attempt to create unbreakable human toys.

With a sigh, I returned my focus to my laptop and started a new log.

"My liege," Lilith's voice greeted, the tone grating on my nerves. I'd heard it far too often over the last ten days.

Unfortunately, it was required.

Too much had transpired over the last century while I'd slept, and with my failing memory, I relied on this high-pitched voice to update me on the world order.

"If you're watching this log, then you have decided it is time to announce your return to our alliance. I have prepared a few suggestions for you—"

"Have you?" I drawled, rolling my eyes. "And who is king here, hmm?"

I listened as she listed several ideas on how to approach my reemergence into society. None of them appealed to me.

This was my kingdom.

Therefore, I would run it my way.

She'd already set a meeting for three days from now, but thanks to Ryder's recent broadcast featuring Lilith's severed head, the various region royals and clan alphas were in distress.

I would need to deal with the errant rebel at some point. However, establishing order was a more pressing matter. Especially with the revolutionaries on the rise.

"You really did fail me," I said to Lilith as I turned off her log. "Perhaps I won't punish Ryder too harshly, as it's clear your death was well deserved." And not just for her failures as a leader, but for her irritating voice.

Did her voice always bother me like this? I wondered, wincing from the headache that followed her log. *Or is this just a residual reaction to sleeping for so long?*

Because every one of her logs seemed to splinter across my skull, leaving a dull ache behind. Which couldn't be normal. But I couldn't ask Michael or any of my other subordinates about it. Pain was a weakness. It made me no better than a mortal.

Like the delicious-smelling blonde on my bed, I thought, returning my attention to her. "I'm not sure why I've kept you for so long, Ismerelda. Maybe I'll let you explain it to me when you're awake."

Or, more likely, I'd just kill her again.

I was starved for her. I'd tried drinking from a few other humans, but their blood just didn't compare to her exquisite taste.

A fucking travesty, really. Because the female was disobedient with a penchant for speaking out of turn. I hadn't been impressed when she'd run toward me on the tarmac. And I was less than impressed now as she continued to sleep on *my* bed.

"I should put you in a cage," I told her. "Perhaps that would help you understand your role in life."

She didn't reply.

Didn't even fucking react.

Because she was still *recovering*.

With a growl, I set my laptop off to the side and stood.

It was time to send a communication to the leaders of the world—*Your king has returned.*

But first, I needed to move my pet to her quarters. I'd only put her in my bed because I'd hoped for her to awaken while I worked.

Alas, she remained comatose. Not my preferred flavor of female.

"You had better be ready when you wake up," I told her as I lifted her from the bed. "I'm going to destroy you." Because her scent was fucking killing me. That had to be why I'd chosen her as a mate—her addictive fragrance and taste.

I glanced down at her breasts again. *And probably that attribute, too.* My gaze traveled over her. *All the attributes, hmm.*

"Pity you won't wake up and give me a proper distraction." I carried her through my room to the bathroom area and the walk-in closet beyond it.

There was a little door at the back that led to the space I'd had made up for her. It was meant to be a private dressing room, but a small bed had been brought in to replace the furniture.

Nothing else existed here apart from a light overhead, which was controlled via a switch in my closet.

Just like the door had been redone to lock from my side, not hers.

I set her on the mattress and paused to admire the way her blonde hair flowed over the single pillow.

Very pretty, I admitted. *But still asleep.*

"Such a waste." I left her in the dark and locked the door before grabbing one of the many suit jackets hanging in my closet. The inky fabric paired well with my dark pants and my obsidian dress shirt. Mostly because it rivaled my mood—*black*.

Lilith had failed me. Not that I was surprised.

Oh, she'd been a faithful little pawn, following our cause all the way to the end. But she'd never been all that powerful. Her skills had resided in politics, her ability to persuade and manipulate others providing her with a strategic edge when convincing others to follow her lead.

But that was where her skills had ended.

She'd been naïve.

Arrogant.

Too caught up in her own glory to consider the brute strength of her elders.

Which had led to her demise, thus initiating the protocol to wake me up. Although, according to my assistant, Michael, she'd been considering stirring me from my slumber several months ago.

The rebels of our kind had started gathering forces. It wouldn't be enough to take down the Blood Alliance. But they would undoubtedly pose certain problems that I wanted to get ahead of.

Spilling ancient blood would be a waste of precious material.

Thus, we needed to find a way to collaborate. Form a middle ground. Or design a way to make the revolutionaries heel.

It would start with the mission I intended to deliver to the royals of my kind and the alpha lycans.

"My liege," Michael greeted with a low bow as I exited my room. He'd obviously been waiting for me, perhaps sensing my intentions through our Sire bond.

Because apparently I'd turned this male into a vampire as a gift to Lilith.

I had no memory of the act, nor did I feel all that connected to the man, but the records indicated I'd gifted him immortality shortly before the revolution. Michael anticipating my needs only bolstered the truth of our shared history.

His bright green eyes met mine for a brief second as he stood upright, his focus shifting to the female lingering near a door at the end of the long residential corridor.

Mira—the original lycan.

She remained alive while the rest of her kind always expired. That was what made her more of an equal than her brethren and why she'd joined our cause a century ago.

Or that was what Lilith's notes had stated.

Relying on her logs from the last century grated a bit on my nerves. Fortunately, though, I could still recall most of my oldest memories, which allowed me to remember my brief acquaintance with Mira.

We'd only met once, and she'd been just a pup at the time. She certainly wasn't the gangly teenager from three thousand years ago. Instead, she'd matured into a beautiful woman.

Alas, I found myself craving a very different blonde.

An unconscious one.

With delectable blood.

This was why the *Erosita* mating bond was dangerous to my kind—it made us infatuated with mortals. But once I'd indulged in my fill of Ismerelda's blood and her pussy, I would be able to tame this need.

I only wanted her because I'd gone over a hundred years without her.

And if she continued to insult me the way she had yesterday when she'd tried to run up and hug me after disembarking the jet, I'd be over her far more quickly than expected.

Besides, there was an entire array of blood virgins—a group of untouched humans with a unique blood type—upstairs waiting for me to stop by for a taste. I'd move on to them just as soon as I fucked Ismerelda out of my system.

"I'm ready to announce my return," I said, addressing both Michael and Mira. "We will be moving forward with the meeting in three days, but I'll be leading in Lilith's place for obvious reasons."

Michael nodded. "Of course, my liege. I'll go check our telecommunications connection to ensure we can reach all quadrants of the world for your announcement." He didn't wait for my reply, instead moving swiftly down the hall and through the door at the end in a shuffle of long legs and hurried steps.

"While he's doing that, I'll provide you with an update on Sota and Troph." Mira pushed away from the door frame, her arms falling from their crossed position against her chest to hang loosely at her sides.

"Have you been to see them?" I asked as I moved

toward her, my eyebrow arching up in curiosity. The two Blessed Ones were still in the process of rising, their mental states more ravenous than useful.

Fortunately, I had no memory of that part of my waking.

From what Michael had said, the feeding process hadn't been needed for me because I'd only slept a century.

Meanwhile, Sota and Troph had been resting for several millennia.

They'd been too weak to handle the gift Nyx had given them—immortal life with immortal children. The only cost was their inability to take a long-term mate.

For some of the Blessed Ones, they couldn't handle life without their former lovers and opted to sleep instead. But in Sota's and Troph's cases, they'd refused to accept their children's need for mortal blood. And rather than support their offspring, they'd chosen to hide in their slumber.

An atrocity, really. One that marked the two of them— and several others—as unworthy of their gifts.

However, Sota and Troph had been the first to choose their misguided morals over their children's survival.

Hence the reason we'd selected these two as our first subjects for the next phase of the trials—the ones Lilith had failed to complete during my century of rest.

"I brought them evening breakfast," Mira replied as she stepped out of my way through the threshold and followed my lead down the adjacent hallway.

The entire complex underground was riddled with corridors. It would be easy for one to get lost in the underground, but Michael had provided me with a map upon my waking, thus allowing me to relearn my way around.

I started toward the conference area where formal

communications were designed to take place. Lilith had fashioned the room to resemble the one often used in Lilith City, thus allowing her to keep this place a secret from all the royals and alphas.

That had perhaps been one of her more clever ideas.

"They're still ravenous for anything they can get their mouths on," Mira continued. "The intended lesson is definitely being conveyed."

I nodded. "As it should be." Blessed Ones didn't require the human essence to survive, which was partly why Sota and Troph had failed to understand the needs of their children.

But that misconception would soon be rectified.

Once Sota and Troph regained enough of their mental faculties to communicate, we'd show them the human bodies they'd devoured in their state of immortal hunger. Only then would they truly grasp the concept of survival and the fate they'd left their children to endure alone.

When a being is hungry enough, he'll consume anything to survive. Those were the words Michael had painted in blood above the mutilated corpses. And he'd been sure to write the statement in a script that the ancients would understand. We were just waiting for Sota and Troph to be cognizant enough to read it.

I turned left down another hallway, followed by a right and another left before reaching the elevator at the end. Mira watched as I punched in the necessary codes, then entered behind me in contemplative silence.

"I've been thinking," Mira started slowly, her ice-colored eyes bold as she met my gaze. She was an alpha wolf, used to subduing others with a stare.

However, her dominance was no match for my own, something I conveyed with a simple arch of my brow as I waited for her to finish her statement.

"I think we should wake up Fen next." The sound of the elevator reaching our desired floor punctuated her confident words. "His bloodline is slightly different, given that he's the father of lycans," she added as we stepped out of the elevator. "It would provide the researchers with another sample type for their trials."

"Technically, it would be your blood that would provide the varying sample type," I murmured, leading the way toward the conference room. "You're the only immortal lycan, after all."

"Yes, but if you bite me, I'll bite back. And I have sharper teeth." She flashed me a wolfish grin with her words, not at all afraid of challenging me as her superior. "Mortals are easier prey."

"Easier, yes. But they're not very durable," I returned.

"I take it your *Erosita* is still out of commission?" She gave me a pitying glance that I ignored, instead choosing to open the door to the conference area.

A massive round table took up the center of the room with more than fifty chairs encircling it. Most of the walls were composed of dark glass, just like the formal meeting room in Lilith City. Only that glass wall could be un-tinted to reveal the skyscrapers outside. These panes had hard rock behind them—rock that matched the wall with the door.

I moved toward the chair directly across the table and in perfect line with the entrance. There was a camera mounted just above the door, thus keeping the rocky wall out of view of the lens and making this particular spot in the room the central focus for filming.

"So…" I settled into my chosen chair. "You want to wake up your father and give him to the researchers."

It was a purposeful redirection of our conversation

because I had no desire to speak about my *Erosita* with Mira or anyone else.

Which was something I thought I'd made clear when I'd taken Ismerelda back to my quarters after Mira had recommended a room near the blood virgins.

Why the fuck would I keep my primary craving on a different floor?

No, Ismerelda would stay in the room I'd fashioned for her until I grew tired of her.

Then she could be moved.

Or killed.

But that was a debate for after she woke up.

And entirely irrelevant to this discussion.

"Fen's bloodline is likely similar to those of the other Blessed Ones," I continued as I steepled my fingers together on top of the granite tabletop. "He's not a lycan. We also already have two ancients in the process of waking. So why do we need a third one?"

She took over the chair to my right and met my gaze once more, her expression devoid of emotion. "Because Lilith failed," she answered flatly. "So now vampire kind is running out of time to develop an alternative blood bag."

Yes, because my brethren had been gluttonous over the last century. We weren't out of food yet, but we would be within the next decade if our trends continued. Hence the purpose behind the experiments—we needed to find a way to keep our food sources alive despite our feeding habits.

But I already knew all that. What I wanted her to explain was, "Why Fen?" I studied her emotionless expression. "Why do you think he's needed?"

"Because there's a chance his blood is different, and at this point, we need as large a sample as we can get."

"So by that logic, we should wake up all the Blessed Ones," I countered.

She shook her head. "Not at the risk of angering all the royals in existence."

Hmm. She had a point there.

"You chose Sota because you know Sahara will accept her father's fate as a justified punishment, just as Lajos would have—"

"Accepted his father's punishment as well," I finished for her. "Yes, I'm aware of why I chose Sota and Troph." Thanks to Lilith's records, anyway.

Because I possessed no actual memory of it, just like almost everything else.

"So you're suggesting Fen because there's a chance he's different and he wouldn't cause any issues with leaders of the Blood Alliance," I summarized.

"Yes. I would be the only one to protest his treatment, and I'm giving permission."

"Why?" I pressed. "I thought you were on good terms with him? Isn't that why you chose to rest with him in his crypt?"

Lilith had awakened Mira shortly before the revolution to bring her up to speed on what the human governments had attempted to do to lycan kind. That had made Mira's recruitment to join our cause relatively easy.

Mira studied me for a beat before relaxing into her chair with a sigh. "He abandoned me. Maybe not right away like Sota and Troph did to Sahara and Lajos, but that just means I endured more of his hatred than they could from their own fathers."

Her icy blue eyes met mine, betraying the first flicker of emotion. But it was gone in a blink, the stoic alpha returning to mask her features.

"My personal reasoning for giving permission isn't relevant. The point is, he might add a unique essence to the trials. And if nothing else, he's another body to experiment on." She lifted a shoulder. "I just wanted to provide it as a suggestion. You can decide if it's worth our time or not."

I considered her for a long moment while evaluating the potential of waking and experimenting on Fen.

Containing him would be easy. Because while the Blessed Ones were immortal and revered as the creators of vampire and lycan kind, they weren't supernaturally inclined.

They weren't abnormally strong or capable of hypnosis.

They couldn't shift.

They lacked the skill to phase, which was a rarer master vampire ability to teleport.

They were essentially human, just incapable of dying. Which was exactly what my kind needed all mortals to be for us to survive.

As for Mira, she just wanted a way to make lycans truly immortal. That wasn't something she'd admitted to me but was a note in her file regarding her allegiance.

Because if we found a way to make human life eternal, the same method could be applied to ensure lycan longevity—which would allow her to finally have a real pack that didn't eventually die.

That's why she wants Fen, I realized, still studying her. *Because his essence might provide the solution she's been salivating over. His actions created her, after all.*

"All right," I decided aloud. "Set everything up for the ritual and figure out where to house him."

I'd participated in the other two awakenings because they'd required a superior essence to satisfy the ritual. And as the eldest vampire, my blood was powerful enough to wake any Blessed One. But Mira was Fen's offspring, thus making her capable of performing the ceremony on her own.

"Thank you, my liege." Her chin dipped in a slight bow. "I'll make the arrangements."

"Let me know when everything is in place. I'll observe the ceremony and assist as needed," I said as Michael entered the room with an air of nervousness swirling around him. "What is it?" I demanded, his sickly sweet scent irritating my senses.

How is this weak male my progeny? Has no one taught him to control his emotions?

"It seems that our communications systems are down, my liege." Unlike Mira, Michael did not meet my gaze, his green eyes remaining on the ground while he spoke. "I have our technology team working on it right now, but they said it might be tomorrow before it's fixed."

My eyebrows lifted. "How the fuck did that happen?"

"They're not sure, my liege." He swallowed. "But they're looking into it."

"It's Damien," Mira muttered.

I glanced at her. "Damien?"

"Izzy's brother. He's a technological genius who also happens to be Ryder's progeny." Despite the irritation in her tone, a hint of admiration came through. "He's the one who has been fucking with Lilith's phone and helping the revolutionaries gain access to Lilith's former bunkers."

I snorted. "He didn't help them with anything. I let them explore the labs." It was all part of the protocol to help my cousin, Jace, and my progeny, Darius, understand what Lilith had been trying to achieve—an improved food source—during my slumber.

Alas, they didn't seem to appreciate it the way I'd intended.

They truly had been corrupted by my brother, Cane. If

the bastard weren't asleep in our father's crypt, I'd throttle him for brainwashing our cousin and my progeny.

"Regardless, Damien's the one sabotaging our communications now. He's probably trying to find a way to reach Izzy." Mira gave me a speculative look. "I warned you. She's headstrong and—"

"I can handle my *Erosita*," I interjected. "She's naked and locked in my closet. Her brother won't be able to reach her." I refocused on Michael. "Work with the communications team to fix this and contact me as soon as it's done."

"Yes, my liege." He bowed low before slipping out of the room without another word.

"Meanwhile, I'll go deliver a much-needed lesson to my *Erosita*," I added, a hint of a growl touching my words.

Because if this was Damien's doing, I'd be ensuring his sister paid for his interference.

You had better be awake when I get back to my room, Ismerelda, I thought at her.

Not that she could hear me. I had our mental connection locked down.

But that didn't stop me from adding, *I'm hungry and annoyed. And you exist for one reason*—to serve me. *Prepare to bleed.*

IZZY

Cold.

Dark.

Cam…

I shivered.

Why am I…? Where…? How did I…?

I groaned, my head pounding from the influx of broken questions. Everything felt… *wrong.*

What's…?

My fingers curled on a shock of pain, my arms too heavy to lift. I wasn't even sure what I'd intended to do. Palm my head? Massage my temples?

Ugh.

I attempted to pull my knees to my chest, but my limbs barely moved. *So dizzy,* I thought, a whimper escaping my throat. *Why do I…?*

A flinch ricocheted down my spine. *Cam… Is something…? No. No, he's okay. Mira said…*

My eyes flew open, only to abruptly shut on a wave of agony. *Shit.* I winced, my insides echoing in a scream of pain. *What…?*

Cam…

No.

I'm going in circles. Except I'm not. Just dizzy. Delirious?

I swallowed and winced again. *So dry.*

I feel like… like… like death…

My eyes opened again, causing another shock of sensation to flood my senses. I pushed through it, forcing myself to shove off the deep end of this ocean of agony and upward into the fresh, dark air.

I inhaled sharply, shooting spasms to my lungs and causing my heart to fly in a chaotic rhythm.

Death, I thought again. *I…*

Another pang ripped through my veins, setting my blood on fire. *This feels…*

A silent scream tickled my raw throat, my voice incapable of functioning. *Water… I need…*

But my hands… arms… they were still too heavy. Too… too… *dead.*

My eyes closed again, my world encased in perpetual darkness. *Is this a nightmare?*

I tried to pinch my fingers together, but they refused my command.

Another groan rumbled in my chest. Except it made no sound, just like my scream. *Was my first groan like that as well?* I couldn't remember.

I couldn't remember anything. Like how I ended up here. Why I felt… felt like *death.*

Cam…

I attempted to shake my head in denial. *I'm not feeling his death. He's okay. He has to be.*

Except no. That… that wasn't it.

Something about Cam…

My legs shifted this time when I called upon them to move, the heavy weights seeming to release my limbs to my mind. But it hurt. It… it didn't feel right. *It aches.*

Like death…

I shuddered as my knees finally met my chest, my arms slowly encircling my shins to hold myself in a ball on my side. Something soft existed beneath me. A bed, perhaps? But not my own. Because the smell was foreign. Musky. *Old.*

Tears dampened my eyes, the liquid a welcome kiss to my dry senses. Saliva pooled in my mouth, allowing me to swallow. But it all felt devastatingly wrong.

This has to be a nightmare. Maybe one of Cam's? Am I finally seeing into his mind? Is this where Lilith has kept him? In this perpetual state of torment?

More tears pierced my eyelids, spilling onto my cheeks. *Oh, Cam…*

I usually dreamt of our last night together. Or rather, the night over a hundred and eighteen years ago that had changed our lives forever.

The night Cam had erected a wall between our minds, mentally severing our link…

My eyes flew open as I felt Cam's intent, his plan taking

hold of my mind and sending my pulse into overdrive. I knew this might happen. He'd told me about the possibility.

But to feel it...

There has to be another way, Cam, I whispered into his mind. *You're sacrificing—*

It's my burden to bear, Ismerelda, he replied, his voice tired as though he was already in pain. *And mine to bear alone.*

Except you haven't been alone for over a thousand years, I wanted to say. But I couldn't form the thought, my heart breaking into a million pieces as I felt the wall between us solidifying.

Wait, I begged. *We have to talk about this.*

There isn't time to discuss it. I have to close off our link before it's too late.

Too late for what?

For me to protect you, he answered quickly. *I'm sorry, my love. I'm so fucking sorry. But this is the only way. I have to...*

A sharp pang cut through our bond, drawing a gasp from my throat. *Cam?*

I'm sorry, he repeated. *I love you. I'll always love you. No matter what.*

Cam!

Goodbye, Ismerelda. But only for now.

What? No! But I—

Agony sliced through my mind, sending a cascade of icy pricks down my spine.

And then I was engulfed in a deadly silence.

Cam?

Nothing.

Cam?!

Quiet. Peace. Solitude.

I sat upright in bed, my heart beating rapidly in my

ears as I searched the bedroom for the man I knew wasn't there. My Cam. My lover. My other half.

He'd left yesterday to meet with Darius and discuss a strategy for how to handle Lilith and her new world order. I'd begged him to let me go with him. But he'd demanded I stay with Luka.

"Where it's safe," he'd said.

But I didn't feel safe. Not now. Not with our link blocked and his fate unknown.

I pulled the sheets away from my sweat-soaked skin and slid out of the bed.

I needed answers. I needed to know if Cam was okay.

And more importantly, I needed to know if this was just a bad dream.

Please, God, let this be a bad dream, I prayed. Not that I believed in an almighty power. But I would if it meant Cam was safe.

However, I wasn't naïve. And I could feel deep inside that something was very wrong.

He'd mentioned this was a possibility, that he might have to cut me off to protect me. But he'd promised it would be a last resort.

Yet he'd severed our mental link without hesitation.

Because he's already hurt? I wondered.

I pulled on a robe to cover my silk pajamas and padded out of the room.

"Izzy," a deep voice said, the soft rumble one I rarely heard from the alpha lycan standing in the hallway.

"No," I replied, already seeing the bleakness in his kind light-blue eyes. "Tell me this isn't real. Tell me Cam is okay."

He merely shook his head in reply, his thick, dark hair falling across his forehead with the movement. "I won't lie to you."

"Then why are you here?" I demanded as I stalked up to him to poke him in the chest. "Why are you here, Luka?" But I already knew why. Just as I knew the sudden aggression I felt toward him wasn't fair or rational.

But he was here while Cam was not.

He was here to keep me safe.

No. Hold me *prisoner* so I wouldn't chase after Cam. Track down my mate. Demand that he lower this fucking wall between our minds.

There had to have been a better way! I screamed at him as I slammed a fist against Luka's firm chest. *You should have talked this through with me, not leave me in the dark. Alone. Here. Not with you. This isn't fair. This isn't fucking fair!*

My fist hit Luka again as tears clouded my vision.

Why are you doing this? Why do you have to be a martyr? Why, Cam? Fucking tell me why! I shouted at the closed door in my mind, my limbs shaking from the onslaught of my fury. My fear. My... my desperation for this not to be true.

"Why?" I whispered. "Why?"

"Because he didn't want to paint a target on your back, Izzy. It's best that Lilith and everyone else think you're dead," Luka told me, making me pause.

"What?" I blinked up at him, but his young face blurred before my eyes. "Dead?"

He frowned down at me. Or I assumed it was a frown, anyway. I couldn't really see, my world seeming to spin around me in a whirl of dizzying lights.

"Dead?" I repeated.

"You don't know?" Luka asked, sounding about as shocked and confused as I felt.

"I..." My knees wobbled. "I don't..."

He caught my hip as I started to sway. "I thought Cam told you the plan. But you don't know." He sounded mystified. "I... Izzy..."

"Cam just staged your death to get captured by Lilith," another voice informed me.

Female.

Alpha lycan.

Mira.

"He knows she won't kill him," she continued. "His blood is too powerful for her to waste. But he's hoping to talk to her. And he needs you to remain here where you're safe while he works."

I blinked over at the blonde female. I didn't know her well, but Luka had chosen her as his mate. So she'd been welcomed into the inner circle.

And she was the only one giving me the answers I needed now.

Answers I didn't want to hear.

Answers I required nonetheless.

"He cut me off mentally," I told her on a rasp of sound. "I can't feel him."

"To protect you," she reiterated.

To protect me, I repeated to myself. *To keep me safe.* Like I was some fragile toy he had to guard, not an equal. Not his *mate.*

Deep down, I understood. He couldn't focus properly if all his attention went into guarding me. But that knowledge didn't make it sting any less.

I shoved away from a still-silent Luka, aware that my legs weren't steady. However, I had to stand on my own. To prove that I was strong enough to handle this.

I'm a survivor, I thought. *Of all people, Cam knows that.*

Yet he'd kept me in the dark.

He'd… he'd faked my death and now…

"She might kill him," I said, my voice barely audible. "She's crazy enough to kill him."

And what then?

What happened to us?

We never even had a chance to say goodbye, I whispered to Cam. *Why would you do this to us after a thousand years? Are you truly that confident that you can change that crazy bitch's mind?*

But it was too late to ask questions.

Too late to change his mind.

Too late to do anything other than wait…

And waited I had for over a hundred years.

Until Mira had told me they'd found Cam.

My mind whirled with the memory of my relief, my elation, my nervousness.

I hadn't understood why our mental connection remained closed, but thought it might have to do with being away from my Cam for so long.

So many years of longing.

So many decades of worrying.

Over a century of solitude and waiting for my mate's touch.

I hugged my knees tighter to my chest, confused all over again by Mira's claims.

We got on the plane, I remembered. *I felt uneasy. But that was to be expected, right? I hadn't seen Cam in so long…*

I swallowed.

And then we landed.

The image of it was clear in my mind. *Cam.* He'd been standing in a proud posture off the tarmac, his dark hair longer than usual, fluttering just past his ears. But those striking blue eyes had been the same. As had his muscular build. That tall wall of strength.

I'd run to him.

Exuberant.

My heart bursting with renewed joy.

And then he bit me.

My hand flew upward to my neck, but the evidence of his bite didn't exist.

A dream, then?

Maybe.

Except…

He… he killed me.

My eyes widened as the final vestiges of reality settled over my mind. *Cam killed me.*

"No," I mouthed, my brow furrowing. *No. No, that can't be right. He wouldn't… Cam would never…*

He'd barely ever drunk from me during our millennium together. He… he'd only ever bitten me with permission or when he'd needed blood.

I touched my neck again.

But he drank until I died.

Unless…

Unless that wasn't really him.

That would explain why the mental barrier between us still existed. Maybe someone had created a Cam look-alike? *Is that even possible?*

I blinked for the thousandth time.

A fake Cam would make more sense than the real Cam killing me.

About as much sense as this all being a dream.

But then where am I?

This bed wasn't mine. There was only one sheet and a flimsy pillow beneath my head. No light. Just pure, cold darkness.

And that musky, old scent. My nose twitched. *That certainly smells real.*

I drew my fingers along the mattress, noting the thinness of the flat sheet. *Is there only one sheet on this bed?* I frowned, reaching the end of the mattress and hitting air. *It's small. Maybe a double bed. No nightstand on this side.* I rotated slowly and started searching the opposite way. *None on this side either.*

I reached above me, uncertain of whether I was in a small cage-like box or a proper room, but my fingers merely danced in the air.

Which meant it was safe to sit—

Blinding light had me yelping and curling right back into a protective ball as my eyes stung from the blunt intrusion. "*Fuck,*" I breathed, my throat still raw from *dying and coming back to life.*

Ugh!

I wanted to scream, but a shuffling noise—*the door opening*—had me freezing in the bed.

"Fuck," a male voice repeated.

A male voice that sounds exactly like Cam's.

"Yes, that's precisely what I want to do," he said, the sound of a belt being unbuckled punctuating his statement. "And then I'm going to feed."

IZZY

DEFINITELY SOUNDS LIKE CAM, I THOUGHT. *BUT IT'S NOT him. It can't be him.*

Cam would never speak to me this way.

However, that didn't stop my heart from reacting to his voice.

And now his face, I whispered to myself as my vision began to clear. *This man certainly looks just like him. Except crueler. Harder. Angrier.*

I swallowed, my gaze roaming over the man I hadn't seen in over a hundred years. *Same muscular physique. He's even wearing all black—Cam's favorite color.*

His belt slid through the loops to land on the floor with an anticlimactic thud.

"Get up on your knees. I want to take you from behind first," he demanded, making my eyebrows lift.

Excuse me?

I'd been so dazed from the light and then the presence of this male who resembled Cam that his words hadn't really registered in my cloudy mind. *He intends to fuck me, then feed from me.*

My thighs instantly closed. *No.*

This man isn't Cam.

This isn't going to happen.

This can't *happen.*

If I let him fuck me, my bond to the real Cam would shatter.

Absolutely fucking not.

No. No. No.

"Now, Ismerelda."

Fuck, he sounds just like him, I thought, dizzy. Except he'd never ordered me in that manner. Well, not in a long time, anyway. Things between us had started out a bit rough, but he'd always possessed a certain softness where I was concerned.

A softness this version of him clearly lacked.

His blue irises smoldered as he narrowed his gaze. "When I give you a command, you follow it."

"Or what?" I countered, my voice not nearly as steady as I desired. Not in the face of this imposter who reminded me of my lost mate.

What kind of cruel joke is this? I wondered. *Maybe this is a nightmare after all...*

His dark brow arched. "Or I'll fucking break you."

"By killing me again?" I asked, feigning a boldness I didn't feel as I forced myself to sit up on the bed.

"Perhaps for good this time," he threatened, making me snort.

Definitely not my Cam. Which both relieved me and terrified me. Because *my* Cam was locked up in a cage somewhere and incapable of coming to my rescue. And defending myself against a vampire of any kind was difficult.

Especially while naked—something I just now noticed as Fake Cam's eyes traveled down to my bare breasts.

Unadulterated hunger poured off him as he started unfastening the buttons on his dress shirt. "But I'm definitely going to fuck you first," he added, solidifying his threat.

My heart skipped a beat. *This isn't good.* Now that the light was on, I could see the room—which was more like a closet. No windows. Only one door. And he was standing in front of it. *Undressing.*

"I won't tell you again, *Erosita.* Up on your hands and knees or I'm going to take your ass first. *Raw.*" The growl in his tone sent ice shooting through my veins.

Because it reminded me of another time. A dark memory. *The night I met Cam.*

Which only further proved this version of Cam wasn't *my* Cam. Because he would *never* threaten me with that sort of punishment. Not after what fate he'd saved me from that evening.

Some dormant part of me had hoped I was wrong, that maybe this was just a fucked-up version of my mate. A fanciful part of me, perhaps. The hopeful dreamer in my soul that missed her other half.

But while this man might resemble my Cam in both physical form and with his familiar British tones, he was definitely an imposter.

And he wants to fuck me.

Anal sex might not destroy my bond with Cam. But vaginal sex absolutely would.

And neither option appealed to me in the slightest.

Not with him. Not with Fake Cam.

"I don't understand why you bothered to look like him if you weren't going to act like him," I said as I pressed one palm to the bed to pretend like I was obeying. "It sort of ruins the ruse."

He paused on the last button of his shirt. "Ruse?"

"Whatever this is." I gestured between us as I drew my feet up slowly on the bed, still pretending like I was going to turn over and go onto all fours like he'd demanded. "But you've made it clear that you're not *my* Cam. So what was the point of looking like him?"

I still had no idea if this was even real. I really hoped it was just some twisted dream. But I felt awake. And this was unlike anything I'd ever imagined before.

So how am I going to escape? I wondered. *He's standing—*

"*Your* Cam?" His other eyebrow lifted to match the one he'd kept cocked for the last several minutes. "You're *my Erosita*. I own *you*. Not the other way around."

"I'm not *your Erosita*," I told him. "I'm the real Cam's *Erosita*." *Which will become a false statement if I let this Fake Cam touch me.*

"The *real* Cam?" He gave me an incredulous look. "Did your brain not reset correctly when you woke up from your nap?"

"My nap? You mean my *death*?" I narrowed my gaze at him. "And I have no idea. I've never died before." But he did have somewhat of a point. *Maybe the biting was real and I'm still dead?*

No, that wouldn't explain this bizarre situation.

And the fact that *Cam* had killed me.

Except nothing about any of this made sense. Why pretend to be Cam just to act a completely different way?

Unless he doesn't know how Cam usually treats me. That means he doesn't know Cam. So who are you? I wondered.

"You've never died before?" He glanced over me and

grunted. "So my *Erosita* is a liar. Good to know." He unfastened the final button of his shirt, giving me a glimpse of the muscled torso underneath.

"You even got the abs right," I said, recalling every hard line in detail as he revealed his abdomen. "But not the personality. So I'll ask again, what was the point?"

"The point is, I'm going to fuck you. And if you don't stop talking, I'm also going to gag you."

He pulled off his shirt, giving me a glimpse of his chiseled shoulders and arms—a sight he ruined by beginning to roll the fabric into a makeshift rope.

"On your fucking hands and knees, *Ismerelda.* I won't say it again."

I swallowed. *This is bad. Very bad.*

He was still standing in front of the door, and the bed had maybe a foot of space on each side before it hit the wall. So I had to somehow get around the wall of muscle and out the exit into whatever waited beyond.

And do what? Run?

This was a vampire. Of that, I was certain. Which made him faster and stronger.

Even if I managed to get away, he'd catch me. And then what would I do?

He'll fuck me and I'll lose Cam forever.

My chest ached with the thought.

This can't be it. This can't be the end. I—

Fake Cam lunged forward and reached for my ankle. My opposite limb reacted, the heel of my foot slamming into his face and propelling me off the side of the bed.

I wobbled as I landed, my knees nearly giving out from the unexpected impact and my already weakened state.

A growl vibrated through the air, causing all the hairs along my arms to stand on end.

Fake Cam didn't speak, just moved with lightning speed

to slam me against the wall. No amount of sparring with lycans or vampires could have saved my head from cracking against the rock.

But my instincts fired, sending my knee upward to the sweet spot between his legs.

Only to be caught by a hard thigh.

I screamed and tried to shove him away, my need to escape taking over any amount of reason I could possibly fathom.

We won't end this way, I thought. *I refuse! I'd rather die!*

Fake Cam said something that I didn't hear over my shrieks, his fury hitting me like a whip. But I didn't care. I couldn't allow this.

Not my Cam.

Not this way.

Not fucking to—

The air whooshed from my lungs as Fake Cam whirled me through the air and slammed me into the mattress.

Right on my stomach.

Face down.

Legs spread.

I froze, my energy seeming to escape me on a wave as his much stronger form held me captive on the bed.

I'd never stood a chance. I knew that. But fighting was all I had, and I'd lasted maybe half a minute at most. Likely less.

Because he's a vampire intent on shattering my bond to Cam. And he wanted it to hurt.

Oh, God...

That's why he looks like Cam, I realized in the next painful breath. *He wants this experience to horrify me. To scar me. To leave a lasting wound.*

Does Cam know? Is he watching? Is this all about hurting him? Or both of us?

Fuck, I don't know.

The thoughts rolled through my mind, drawing a gasping pain from my throat as tears streamed into my eyes. I felt so weak and defeated. So crushed. Too utterly fucking helpless.

I don't want Cam to see me like this.

I'm sorry. I'm so sorry.

I shouldn't have trusted Mira. I should have followed my instincts. *You wouldn't have left me in the dark. You would have told me it was okay.*

Except that wasn't true. He'd shut me out all those years ago and chosen his own path without consulting me. He'd been trying to protect me.

And for what?

This?

I bit my lower lip to stop myself from screaming into the pillow.

I've forgiven him.

I understood his decisions.

We all made sacrifices.

But to have it end like this…

I trembled, a sob working its way through my core as I fought off a humorous laugh. Because it was almost poetic for this to be our end since this was all too similar to our beginning.

Only, Cam had slaughtered the men who had pinned me to the ground that day.

And I highly doubted he was going to show up now.

Why did Mira bring me here? Why did she betray us?

They were questions I might never learn the answers to because the imposter at my back was about to destroy everything I held dear in this world—*my ties with Cam.*

I fisted my hands against the pillow, barely aware of Fake Cam's grasp around my wrists.

He had me pinned.

There was no escape.

Just like that night.

And this time, I had no heroic vampire in the shadows stalking my attacker like prey.

CAM

What the fuck?

My *Erosita* was broken.

First, she'd spouted some bullshit about a ruse and how I wasn't "her Cam." All of which had made no bloody sense whatsoever and had given me just enough pause to engage her in the asinine conversation.

Then she'd fought me with a passion that had suggested she'd felt her very existence was in danger. Maybe because I'd threatened her. But something about her reaction had felt more desperate than a mere need to survive.

And now she was frozen beneath me.

Completely still.

Silent, too.

Exactly what I'd desired when I'd entered, only I'd wanted her on her hands and knees.

But this... this wasn't what I wanted at all. Her impassioned fight had made me harder than I could ever have anticipated. Just for her eerie quiet to deflate my interest in the next breath.

I didn't understand. I should be fucking her right now. Vampires thrived on intimidating and subduing their prey. Yet no part of me seemed to desire this.

Why?

Is it just this way with her? Is it a side effect of our bond? If it is, why have I tolerated it for so long? Is it my weakness? Is she *my weakness?*

I frowned. *No. If that was true, I would have killed her centuries ago.*

So why do I keep her?

She felt amazing beneath me. But there had to be another reason I tolerated this behavior.

Unless this wasn't normal.

"I've never died before."

Her words echoed through my mind, deepening my frown. I'd asked if her brain hadn't reset properly during her rebirth. Perhaps I was right. Maybe I'd broken my *Erosita.*

Then I'll have to kill her. For good.

I stared down at the back of her head, my brow furrowing even more. The notion of ending her before tasting her left me uneasy. She felt so good beneath me. So *right.*

Her tight little ass was pressed to my groin where I had her pinned to the bed, her slender wrists delicate joints beneath my palms as I held her arms over her head. *So breakable.*

And yet, she'd fought me with the spirit of a vampire. She'd just lacked the strength and speed necessary to take me down. However, each movement had been fluid and displayed evidence of her training.

Who taught her how to move like that? I wondered. *Me? Her brother? Another man?*

A growl taunted my throat at that last thought. *It better not have been another man.* This female was *mine.* My blood kept her alive. My essence thrived through her veins. My very being was tied to hers.

I could slaughter her almost as quickly as I'd made her.

But right now, I didn't want to kill her. I wanted to... to figure out why she was acting this way. Why she'd thought I wasn't real. Why she'd fought me. *Why she's so still beneath me now...*

It was as though she was barely breathing.

She still had her face pressed into the pillows, her body entirely unmoving.

The scent of terror wafted off her in an alluring wave that should have made me eager to fuck her, yet something about it all felt off. *Wrong.*

What the hell is going on?

I'd been hell-bent on destroying her when I'd walked in here, my cock rigid with the need to *fuck.* I'd been so damn *hungry* for this female, so intent on teaching her a lesson, on making her heel. But I was just as frozen as she was right now.

Stop this idiocy, I told myself with an inner growl. *Just use her the way she's intended to be used and be done with it.*

My thumbs skimmed her wrists as I fought my instincts, my inner beast growling in defiance as I forced myself to move the way I should.

She remained absolutely still while my hands slid down her arms, memorizing the silky texture of her skin all the way up to her shoulders. I sat up more fully, allowing myself a full view of her bare back. It was so much more beautiful now that she was breathing again.

She was more beautiful this way.

Alive. Pliant. *Mine.*

A possessive rumble reverberated in my chest, one driven by the predator within me. Only it sounded wrong. Too deep. Too territorial. Too... *angry.*

It caused the female beneath me to shiver in response. Goose bumps prickled along her previously smooth skin, and the scent of terror washed over me again. Except this time it was mingled with something else. Something even more potent. Something... I strongly disliked —*despair.*

Not arousal.

Not excitement.

But true anguish.

I should revel in that scent, force her to scream, and devour her pain. Yet nothing about her distress enticed me. It *repelled* me.

This isn't the way we play, I realized with a frown. *Or is this just a result of her rebirth?*

Her words echoed through my mind again.

"I've never died before."

Maybe she just needed more time to heal.

Or maybe time had destroyed whatever had previously existed between us.

I shook my head. *Why am I wasting my thoughts on this? She's nothing. Just a broken toy.*

And obviously no longer of use to me since I was more revolted by her than turned on now.

With another growl, I pushed away from her and the bed. *Fuck this.* I needed relief, and I clearly wasn't going to get it from her.

A blood virgin, then, I decided, wincing a little at the

memory of how that plan had gone the other day. All I'd wanted was fucking Ismerelda.

Well, I didn't want her now.

So I'd try again.

And if that didn't fucking work, I'd go for a run or beat someone up, or do something other than sit here and fret over *disturbing scents.*

I bent to grab my discarded shirt and headed out of the door, determined to forget the still-frozen female on the bed. She could die, for all I cared.

She means nothing to me, I vowed, ignoring the snarl inside me that vehemently disagreed with that statement.

This need to devour her came from that dark part of me, which made me wonder if that had been the real reason for my choosing to bond myself to her. Perhaps she had been the only one who could sate my inner predator.

I wouldn't know now since apparently *fear* wasn't my preferred flavor for her.

Stop. Thinking.

I ran my fingers through my hair and left my room in a burst of speed, unused to this sense of instability. *I'm a king. The eldest of vampire kind. The mastermind of the alliance. And I can't tame my feelings for one bloody human?*

My teeth ground together in frustration as I finally pulled on my shirt. I didn't bother with the buttons. They would take too long. Just like I'd left my belt behind.

Did I lock her door? I wondered. *Does it even fucking matter? Where's she going to go?*

If she managed to escape, someone would just drag her back to my quarters.

Or they'd lock her in a cell until my return.

Whatever.

She could rot there.

Fucking pain in my ass.

This was why my kind needed immortal blood bags. The *Erosita* bond was dangerous, as proved by the current of confusion flooding my veins now.

I can't let anyone see me like this.

But of course Michael was waiting by the elevator bay as I approached.

"You can provide me with an update when I return," I told him as I punched in the code to leave.

"Of course, my liege. Where will you be in the interim?"

I nearly growled at the intrusive question—I was the king here; why did I have to answer to him?—but a glance at his inquisitive features had me grating out, "Playing with blood virgins." *Or sparring with some of their guards*, I added mentally. *If they can even keep up.*

Michael's lips twitched in response. "Enjoy, my liege."

I won't, I thought as I stepped into the elevator. Rather than say anything in response at all, I pressed the requisite buttons and stared over his blond head as the doors closed.

This female is a problem, I decided. *A distraction I don't need. Once I get a handle on these asinine reactions, I'll end her.*

Then everything could proceed as planned.

And a new reign would officially begin—*my reign.*

IZZY

OH, GOD, THAT GROWL.

It reverberated in my head on repeat, making me wonder if Fake Cam was still growling or if it was all in my mind. I was too lost in the memories of my past, of a night when Cam had made that exact sound as a prelude to saving me.

Only, he hadn't been saving me at all. Not in the heroic sense, anyway.

He'd killed those men for standing in his way.

Because from the moment he'd first scented my blood, he'd wanted me.

And that was the night over a thousand years ago that he'd decided to take me. For good…

My father had always warned me not to walk alone in the dark. I should have listened. Oh, how I should have listened.

The weight bearing down upon me threatened to suffocate my very last breath. But still, I fought. Clawing. Screaming. Biting. I didn't care that there were four of them and one of me. I didn't care that my fight was futile. I didn't care that this only angered the men more.

I simply refused to let this be my end.

My skirts were bunched up around my thighs, the two men at my legs trying to pull them up to my waist. I tried to kick them, but their strong grips were too much for my plight.

Damien! I longed to shout. But I knew he wouldn't hear me. He was nowhere near home, having chosen to venture off to another part of the world with his new friends.

Friends he hadn't wanted anywhere near me.

Friends he'd claimed were too dangerous for his dainty twin sister to truly meet.

I knew why. I'd *known* since the moment I'd first seen them.

But I would take a night with all of his unsavory acquaintances over what was happening to me right now.

The men joked about who would ravage me first while another encouraged my fighting response, causing the others to chuckle in amusement.

"She's like a tiny bird determined to hold on to those

innocent wings," he mused. "I can't wait to pluck her apart."

I spat at them.

And a fist met my cheek, leaving behind a burn that radiated all the way to my soul.

"Don't bruise her yet," one of them snapped.

"She fuckin' spat at me," his friend shot back, his accent thick and suggesting he wasn't from around here.

None of them seemed to be, actually. But they spoke my language just to ensure I understood their intent. Or perhaps to provoke my fear.

But all I wanted was to kill them.

When Damien finds out... I started to picture what he would do to these men, just to be rudely interrupted by the sound of my bodice ripping.

Another scream built in my throat, only to be smothered by a far more ominous sound. A rumble of some kind. One that scattered goose bumps down my arms and caused two of the men to still above me.

The one had his hand on my bare breast; the other had his palm around my throat. It left me feeling exposed and undecidedly vulnerable. Yet fresh air seemed to renew my spirit as both of them shifted their attention toward the growl, their brows furrowing.

Foreign words followed from one of the men near my legs. The other replied in a fluent tongue very different from my own. And then a third voice followed, deep and hypnotic, causing an unnatural intrigue to blossom deep within me.

I shivered. I wanted to know the owner of that voice. To see him. Which was so entirely wrong in my current predicament. I should be screaming, begging for help, demanding that these men release me, anything other than marveling over a stranger's alluring voice.

More foreign dialogue followed, the two men at my legs leaving me abruptly to investigate the growl. I took advantage of their absence and attempted to pull my feet up to kick at the other two, but a smattering of liquid had me freezing on the cold, damp earth.

The male grasping my breast began to twitch, his head lolling forward.

I winced, my eyes closing as I tried to mentally prepare myself for the impact. Yet it never came. I blinked to find him gone and the other male beside me scrambling.

No, not scrambling, I realized. *He's... he's being dragged.*

And the other two hadn't left my legs to find the source of the sound; they'd been snatched away. Their heads were bent at awkward angles, their eyes unseeing.

I scrambled backward, only to hit a pair of hard legs. A yelp stalled in my throat as a rough hand wrapped around my mouth, the strength in the masculine grip sending my heart into overdrive.

"Shh," the male hushed, his lips suddenly at my ear as he crouched behind me. "You're mine now."

Strong arms engulfed me in the next breath, lifting me into the air and turning me around, thus allowing me my first glimpse at his beautiful face.

Too beautiful, my mind immediately whispered. *Too perfect.*

I reached for his jaw, my fingers moving as though tugged by a string.

His blue eyes widened in response, his nostrils flaring as I traced the edges of his flawless features. He reminded me of a few other men I knew.

Men I'd met through my brother.

Only they weren't men at all. They were blood-drinking demons who stalked the night for their prey. Prey they ripped apart much like this male just had.

Except he hadn't bitten any of them.

Thus his lips were pure with no trace of violence on them. But I suspected a pair of fangs were hidden inside—lethal, deadly, sharp points.

It was all instinctual on my part. I had no idea if I was imagining him or if I'd already died. But it didn't matter. Staring up into his ocean-like irises made me forget the last ten minutes of my life—the chase through the park, the eventual capture, the hands roaming my body, the fingers prodding at my delicate flesh.

I was lost to the male holding me.

Completely unfazed by the blood of the others staining my dress and uncaring of my exposed breasts.

There was just something so devastatingly right about this man. *A predator subduing his prey,* I thought with an inner sigh.

Most blood demons could hypnotize. Damien had never told me that. I'd just realized it after meeting his acquaintances. Actually, Damien had never even admitted what he'd become. He'd simply claimed to be taking a brief holiday with friends.

But I knew.

He was my twin.

There was very little he could hide from me.

Similar to this being staring down at me. His intentions were written clear as day in his beautiful eyes. He intended to devour me. Just like the other men.

"You didn't save me," I breathed as I admired his sharp features. He'd hushed me before saying, *"You're mine now."* I hadn't really considered what that'd meant, my mind too lost in the dreamlike state this man had pulled me into.

But I was beginning to understand now.

"You didn't kill them to protect me," I added, oddly in tune with this male I'd never met before.

"I'm not a protector, little swan. I'm a monster," he murmured, studying me just as intently as I studied him. "But I wasn't going to let them ruin you before I had the chance to taste you."

I nodded, somehow understanding and accepting that logic. Which probably made me crazy. I should still be screaming, demanding that this demon release me, trying to escape, anything other than staring into his eyes and accepting this cruel fate.

But some part of me had always expected this. Perhaps it was because my twin had been turned into a vile creature of the night. I had a strange sort of acceptance when it came to the supernatural as a result.

Damien had embraced his fate.

So why shouldn't I?

"You're not afraid of me," the handsome monster marveled, his gaze turning curious. "You're covered in the blood of four now-dead men—men I killed faster than you could blink—and your heart isn't even racing."

A growl underlined some of his words, the predator within him peeking out at me through his enlarged pupils. I traced the sharp cheekbone beneath one of his eyes, mesmerized by his beauty, his charisma, his lethal aura.

His fingers whispered up my spine to the back of my head, his gaze leaving mine as though inspecting me for an injury. Perhaps he was. Perhaps I was injured. Maybe even dead. I couldn't explain the unnatural calmness I felt in his arms or why his presence soothed my spirit.

Maybe being around Damien and his friends had numbed me to predatory threats. There was no one more threatening than Damien's friend Ryder. I suspected he was the one who had changed my brother into a blood-drinking beast. There was just something so incredibly old about him.

Similar to this being before me.

They both possessed ancient auras about them, their long lives evident in their gazes.

"Are you going to bite me?" I wondered aloud, likely proving even more that I had lost my mind. But I'd seen Damien do it once to a woman—one of the women in our village—and she hadn't made it seem all that painful. In fact, she'd seemed to enjoy it quite a lot.

I hadn't stayed to observe what exactly happened between them, but the woman had appeared to be in perfect health the next day.

Would this male bite me like that? My gaze dropped to his mouth. *Do I want him to?*

"Who are you?" the male asked on a breath, his gaze searching mine once more. "I only first caught your scent yesterday, but there's clearly more to you than a delectable fragrance. Tell me your name, little swan."

"Ismerelda," I replied, the name seeming to slip from my tongue as though enchanted by his very words. I wouldn't be surprised if that was true. I'd witnessed Damien compel that woman before biting her. That was what had drawn me forward to observe them, my need to understand what he was doing a compulsory pull inside me that had all but dragged me into the hallway to watch.

My father had always said my curiosity would get me killed someday.

It seemed he wasn't wrong.

"Ismerelda," the male repeated, his deep tones caressing the word and sending a delightful shiver down my spine. "I'm Cam."

"Cam," I echoed. "Are you going to bite me, Cam?" My voice held a breathy note to it that I should have been embarrassed by, but I couldn't muster up the necessary intelligence to react. I was too focused on this monster of a man and those perfect lips.

"I am," he promised. "I've been craving your taste since I scented you in the field yesterday. But I want to know how you know what I am."

"I really don't." The admission fell from my mouth, similarly to my name. "But I think you might be like my brother."

"Your brother?" His gaze swept over my face once more. "Who is your brother, little swan?"

"Damien," I told him.

"Hmm, I don't know a Damien. Perhaps I'm not like your brother at all."

"No," I agreed. "You're more like Ryder."

Recognition flickered through his features. "Ryder?" He glanced over me again, his gaze pausing briefly on my exposed chest before returning to my face. "Describe him."

"Intimidating. Lethal. Dark hair. Matching eyes. Pale skin. Blood-drinking demon…" I trailed off as Cam's nostrils flared.

In a blink, his hands were roaming over my body as he fixed my bodice and skirt, and suddenly I was already back in his arms, his movements too fast for my mind to even conceptualize before he finished. I wasn't even sure how he'd held me in the air through all of it, but somehow he'd managed.

Because he's not human, I reminded myself. Just like Damien and Ryder.

"You're going to tell me everything you know, Ismerelda," Cam informed me. "And in the interim, I'm going to reconsider what I had planned for you."

"So no biting?" I'd asked, feeling oddly disappointed.

"That'll depend entirely on you, little swan," he'd replied. "Now start from the beginning."

I'd felt compelled to tell him everything because he'd used his powers of persuasion on me. But part of me to this day knew I would have told him whatever he'd wanted to know that night regardless of his powers.

Because he was Cam.

My other half.

My soul mate.

I miss you, I thought at him. *I truly hope you're not watching me now, seeing me surrender to this horrible imitation of you. I'm sorry. I'm sorry I couldn't win.*

A sob threatened my chest, but I was too frozen to let it loose. Besides, I didn't want to give Fake Cam the satisfaction of...

My lips curled down. *Wait...* I blinked into the mattress, my back unbearably cold. *Is it already over? Did I miss him defiling my body?*

I'd been so lost in my memory of Cam that I hadn't been paying much attention to my surroundings. *Where is he? Why can't I feel him? Am I that numb?*

My legs twitched, searching for the sense of ache and dread I'd anticipated feeling. Only, my thighs were still touching. *Strange.* I also couldn't sense any dampness at all.

No blood.

No semen.

No signs of arousal or having been touched at all.

Is he playing the long game? Standing behind me and watching me squirm? Waiting for me to flip over? What?

I waited, my ears straining to hear anything and

everything in the too-silent space. But all I could hear were my own breaths.

He's playing with me, I realized. *Tormenting his prey.*

My gaze narrowed.

I didn't want to be a toy. Nor did I want to give him the satisfaction of my fear. Which was probably a bit too late, considering I'd shut down, but his mistake had been in giving me a few minutes to regroup.

He wanted to fuck with me?

Fine.

I'd fuck with him right back.

It didn't matter that I'd just lose again. At least Cam would get to see me fight once more.

Except, what if that hurts him? I wondered, pausing my inner need to retaliate. *Is that why Fake Cam is lurking and waiting for a reaction? To draw out the moment and upset my Cam even more?*

I swallowed.

I definitely didn't want that.

So what do I do? Just lie here and wait for the inevitable?

That would only make me nervous. And it would seem as though I were just giving in to the inevitable, which I'd essentially done when I'd shut down.

Would Cam want me to try to fight again or give up?

My brow furrowed. *Hold on… Shouldn't I be wondering if I want to fight or give up?*

My entire existence had been defined by Cam from the moment he'd first claimed me. Everything I'd done had been for him, including waiting in Majestic Clan for him to finally return to me. I'd tried to keep myself safe for him, knowing he needed me protected in order to focus on whatever he was doing behind the scenes.

However, his plan had obviously failed. He'd been in

captivity for over a century, which probably didn't feel like long to him, but it'd been hell for me. And while I knew he'd also suffered, it had been his decision to do this. Not mine.

But right now, the decision is mine, I told myself. *I can either fight or accept my fate. Which option do* I *want?*

Making decisions for myself and not for Cam had been one of my biggest struggles over the last one hundred and eighteen years. It had taken time for me to realize the importance of living for myself and not just for him, and it had required a lot of self-negotiation over the decades.

Even now, I was stuck between doing what was best for him and what I needed to do for myself.

I don't want to play this game, I thought. *I want to stand up for myself.*

Because no one was going to save me. Not in this dark world. My primary savior was locked away somewhere. And Damien was probably on the other side of the world.

Mira had claimed to have told him where we were headed, but I should have done it myself. I'd known something was wrong, and I'd ignored my instincts.

I'd trusted the wrong person.

Not that anyone would blame me. Mira had been a friend. Luka's mate. Part of our revolution. *So why did she betray us?*

Unless it's not her at all.

Unless she's a Fake Mira, too.

I frowned. *All right, but how are they making fake versions of lycans and vampires?*

Something isn't adding up…

I lifted my head, tired of my thoughts and this whirlwind of confusion befuddling my mind. "I'm not interested in whatever this is," I said, glancing over my shoulder in the direction of where Fake Cam was likely standing.

Except he wasn't there.

Just an open door.

IZZY

I STARED AT THE DOOR.

"Hello?" I asked, my brow furrowing.

Was Fake Cam inviting me into the other room for something even more nefarious? Or had he left to grab something?

I rolled onto my back and sat up, my knees drawing into my chest as I waited for him to appear. When several minutes of nothing passed, I started looking around my small white room. Now that the lights were on and I wasn't distracted by a Cam look-alike, I could properly evaluate my space.

Solid walls. A single bed with one sheet and a pillow. I studied the corners intently, then the high ceiling and the long light strip directly above me. *No signs of cameras anywhere.*

That didn't mean there weren't any listening or recording devices, though. Sometimes they were hard to see.

Damien had taught me that.

My twin had spent the last two hundred years mastering technology, and he'd shared a lot of his wisdom with me. Not many others knew that, though. I was often thought of as Cam's *Erosita* and nothing more. It came with a level of respect that I appreciated, but it also made my identity rather one-sided.

I gave the room a once-over again, then I slowly slid off the bed to peek beneath it. I wouldn't have been surprised to find Fake Cam there, waiting to pounce.

But no.

Just a stone floor like the rest of the room.

Hmm. I tiptoed forward to investigate the door. There wasn't a knob on my side of it, but since it'd been left open, I could easily step through the threshold. Which was where I found the switch that controlled the light to my chamber, as well as the exterior locks to ensure I couldn't escape the room.

So why did he leave the door open? I wondered. *A test? A game?*

I'd said I didn't want to play. But maybe I did. Being out here could offer more forms of escape, or even a weapon to use against him. And since immortal beings were always hell-bent on underestimating me, I could use that sense of superiority to my advantage.

The closet was filled with dark clothes—mostly button-down shirts and pants. *Definitely Cam's style*, I noted, fingering some of the fine fabric.

I pulled one of them off the hanger to glance at the label. It was a well-known Italian brand from before the revolution.

Cam used to wear these, I thought, slipping the shirt on over my head. It was unbuttoned at the collar, allowing me to easily pull it down over my body. Cam used to love it when I wore his clothes, mostly because his shirts fit me like a dress. And the buttons made it easy to remove.

I rolled the cuffs twice until they fit around my wrists, then I explored the rest of the closet. "Well, you may not have gotten the personality right. But you certainly know how he liked to dress," I told Fake Cam. Wherever he was.

I spent a few more minutes exploring the closet before moving on to the bathroom. The dark marble finish paired nicely with the stone floor—the same floor that went through the closet and into the room I'd woken up in.

Glass decorated a walk-in shower. No bathtub. Two sinks. Pretty standard as far as bathrooms went, but it possessed a distinctly masculine appeal. Perhaps because of the dark tones and lack of natural lighting.

Plush carpet met my bare feet as I wandered out of the bath area and into a bedroom. I half expected to find Fake Cam on the bed, but he wasn't there. Just a dark swirl of sheets and pillows, and something metal glinting off the low lighting.

A laptop, I realized as I crept forward.

I stared at it for a second, then surveyed the rest of the room, searching for Fake Cam.

He wasn't near the dark wood dressers, and they were too close to the wall for him to hide behind. I ducked to check beneath the bed—*clear.*

Frowning, I started toward the living area adjacent to the bedroom. There was a long sofa and a single chair with a kitchenette behind it.

No Fake Cam anywhere.

I opened the refrigerator. *Empty. Great.*

The cabinets had a myriad of red wine in one section,

then plates, bowls, and glasses. Another had some cooking pots and a drawer of utensils.

But nothing edible other than the alcohol.

Typical vampire, I thought, retracing my steps back into the living room. *So where did you go?* Because he wasn't anywhere in here, and I suspected the door across from me led to the exit. *Are you waiting beyond there for me? Hoping to catch me and punish me?*

I frowned. "What would be the point of that?" I asked aloud. "You already had me flat on the bed before. So why bother with this game?"

I assumed he would be able to hear me with his vampiric senses.

"I'm not going out there," I told him. "I'll just play with your laptop instead."

I half expected him to enter and say something like, "It's password protected." But nothing happened.

Shrugging, I decided to follow through on my threat. If it was connected to any sort of communication network, then I could reach out to Damien.

I settled onto the bed and pulled the computer into my lap, then opened the screen. It came to life without a sound, the password protection tied to a thumbprint.

It was a solid security measure, but Damien had taught me all the backdoor tricks. I lifted the device to check some information on the back, then held the start button down with another key.

My attention flicked to the door when the computer made a restart noise.

Still no Fake Cam. Fine. At least I had something to do with my time now. Better than just lying down on a mattress, awaiting my fate.

Keep underestimating what I can do, Fake Cam, I thought at him when a few more sounds followed.

"Pretty much all computers have an admin control—something to override the initial login. It's to help protect the device from the technologically illiterate," Damien had once told me. "Like Ryder."

The male in question had flipped him off in response. "Want to play with my favorite toys, Damien?" Ryder had drawled back at him.

"Always," my brother had replied, his lips curling into a smirk while his eyes danced across the screen in front of him.

I could hear him in the back of my head coaching me on next steps as a blue screen appeared requesting an admin key. He'd drilled the entire process into me after weeks of coaching while Ryder had observed with lazy interest.

"There are more important skills for her to master right now," Ryder had said. "Like how to fire a gun."

"I know how to fire a gun," I'd told him.

"We'll see," he'd tossed back.

Which, of course, had led to an evening lesson where I'd proved to him that I knew how to handle a firearm. My aim and precision were no match for his own, but very few were as skilled with weapons as Ryder was.

Still, he'd been impressed enough to allow Damien to continue his "new-age training"—a phrase Ryder had coined in reference to the changing times.

Both of them had done their best to distract me in the months that had followed Cam's disappearance and my notorious "death."

Alas, eventually it had become necessary for them to retire to their own areas—far away from me—to protect my location in Majestic Clan.

I'd used a lot of what Damien had taught me to maintain minimal contact with my twin via secret channels, but only sparingly. It'd been too big a risk to talk often.

Still, he'd managed to keep me mostly up to date on the changes throughout the new era of technology. I was nowhere near as knowledgeable as he was, but I knew my way around enough—as evidenced by the screen booting to life before me in admin mode.

I glanced at the doorway again, wondering why Fake Cam hadn't tried to come in and stop me yet. *Maybe his hearing isn't as good as other vampires',* I thought, shrugging.

Or, like all the others, he didn't realize what I could do.

Well, you're about to... I trailed off, my brow pulling down as I tried to access the network. *What...?*

I leaned forward to better read the details of the error.

No connection was essentially what it said.

Did someone leave this here to trick me? I wondered, opening up the control panel to dive into the computer host details. I skimmed through all the operating system jargon, my frown deepening along the way.

Some sort of simulation had been set up on this laptop, one that seemed to be controlled by another console.

I followed the path, typing in command codes in the script to dig deeper into the mainframe, searching for the source.

Only to stumble upon what appeared to be a data dump. *No, a server,* I corrected myself. *A server network. Except it's all internal and—*

"Oh..." I breathed as an array of screens appeared. It seemed to be a series of live feeds.

And one of them was of me.

On the bed.

In Cam look-alike's shirt.

With the laptop on my lap.

Shit.

I followed the line of sight to the corner and noted the strange texture in the ceiling. It was uneven everywhere in the room, suggesting we were underground.

Interesting that it wasn't smooth like the closet-like space I'd woken up in. But apparently this had all been intentional. To what end, I wasn't sure.

"So you actually put me in a glorified prison and just used the initial bed as a staging area. How inventive," I told the camera.

No sound came through the computer.

I increased the volume and repeated my statement.

Nothing.

"I see. You're only watching, not listening." *But why? And where did Fake Cam go?*

I started clicking through the different surveillance videos, deciding to learn more about my fancy little prison.

Dusty hallways.

More corridors lined with rocky siding.

A few random empty labs.

Some holding cells with all-white furniture.

And…

And the Coventus, I thought, bile forming in my throat as a room of kneeling humans appeared.

It's a classroom, I quickly discerned. *Oh, God.* The phallic tools in their mouths made it clear what they were learning, just as the vampires observing made no effort to hide their intrigue.

"Fuck," I breathed, exiting the feed and pulling up a blank hallway instead. "*Fuck…*"

I didn't need to see that. Nor did I want to see more. Not yet.

"But at least you didn't lie about where we were

heading," I muttered, my angry words directed at Mira. She'd said Cam had been found in the catacombs beneath the Vatican. It was an ancient site used by the Blessed Ones to rest while the upper floors were used for... *training.*

I shuddered.

So how deep underground am I? I wondered, staring at the empty hallway feed. There was really only one way to find out, but I wasn't ready to review the rest of those live videos yet.

Swallowing, I keyed in another command, looking for more details in the mainframe and searching for any way to break through the *no connection* block.

Maybe a back door to the primary control system...

I typed in a few more strings Damien had taught me, causing a few backend logs to blink across the screen.

Execute, I thought, adding the appropriate string to force the information to appear.

"Log year two, day thirty," a familiar voice said, making me frown.

Lilith.

I turned down the volume on the computer as the message played on.

"Hello, my liege," she greeted. "Unfortunately, I don't have positive news to report today."

"Liege?" I repeated, my frown deepening.

"The immortal challenge has not gone according to plan," Lilith continued. "We'd intended for the humans to fight for immortality and reward their efforts, but they are still banding together against our protocols."

"No shit," I muttered, recalling the incident.

"The Blood Alliance will be meeting later today to discuss the fate of the games. I suspect we will be voting to terminate all mortal participants," she concluded.

"Which you did," I said, glaring at the computer.

"Press the green arrow to proceed to next sequence log," a robotic voice declared.

"There is no green arrow," I replied, staring at the coding on the screen. "Hmm."

I typed in a few commands, trying to make the next *log* play, but nothing worked. Instead, I ended up in another mainframe littered with thousands of file names.

No. Not names. *Dates.*

"The logs," I whispered, my brow furrowing. "What even are these?"

I started another one dated in the year twenty-two and listened as Lilith explained the foundation of the first Immortal Cup.

"It felt momentous that we finally achieved success in creating worthy candidates, thus we rewarded six mortals this year. But we intend to move forward with your idea for two going forward. One lycan and one vampire."

"Whose idea?" I wondered aloud. "The Liege? Who is the Liege?"

I played a few more logs, all of them directed at the same unknown entity.

"Who is the Liege?" I asked again, trying to figure out the receiver of the logs.

Only then did I realize *I* was the receiver.

Well, not *me*, but this device.

They were all directed at the primary user of this laptop—*Fake Cam.*

I blinked. "What? Why?"

Is Fake Cam the Liege?

Wait…

What if…?

I blinked again. *No. No, that's not…*

I clicked several more keys, frantic now for answers. I

needed to understand, to know if it was possible... if maybe... if Fake Cam could be...

My Cam.

I entered another command, this one related to the history of the laptop and all the profile creations on the device.

Only one result came back.

Cam.

And the profile had been activated less than two weeks ago.

Which would have been around the time when Ryder had assassinated Lilith.

That bitch could have initiated some sort of protocol that led to this—to a laptop being created for Cam filled with logs addressed to *The Liege*.

But why would Cam even entertain this nonsense? He knew better. He'd gone into all of this with the intention of stopping Lilith.

Except she'd won. She'd subdued him.

By tapping into the Erosita *bond and destroying his mind,* I thought, my eyes widening. She'd attempted to do something similar to Ryder, but his mate had saved him by shooting Lilith.

Then Ryder had taken an ax to Lilith's head.

But from what Luka had told me, the pain Lilith had inflicted in that short time had been immense. Ryder hadn't been able to hear anything other than her voice. And she'd confirmed that she'd used the same device on Cam.

For the last one hundred and eighteen years.

Maybe our mental walls were permanently damaged because of her abuse. Maybe she'd managed to destroy that part of him entirely. Maybe her torment had led to memory loss.

And maybe…

Maybe Cam woke up and heard all these logs addressed to him— the Liege—and thinks he's the mastermind behind all of this madness.

My lips parted at the concept. Could Lilith have truly pulled that off? Made Cam into her puppet, even in death?

If Mira had been working for Lilith the entire time, then my location had been known from the beginning.

So why am I still alive? I wondered. *Why not just kill me?*

What's the plan?

Am I even right?

A brainwashed real Cam certainly made more sense than a look-alike Cam. Just like Mira having betrayed us all made a lot more sense than a look-alike Mira. From what I knew, that sort of technology didn't exist.

But a weapon that could destroy Cam's mind absolutely did.

However, I didn't understand why I'd been brought here. If anyone could fix Cam, it was me. So why risk us finding each other again?

Unless they were absolutely certain there was no way for me to bring him back.

Because maybe the change to his mind was permanent.

Or maybe I'm completely wrong.

I stared at the laptop again. *Was this left here for me to find? To confuse me? To give me false hope? Or does this actually belong to Cam?* My *Cam?*

It could all be a ruse. I'd been brought here for a reason.

And now I'd been left alone.

Why?

Where's Cam?

Is he really my *Cam?*

He'd killed me.

Then he'd nearly raped me.

That wasn't the Cam I knew. But it did remind me of the Cam I'd first met—the predator who had tracked me like prey.

I'd only dissuaded him that night because I hadn't been afraid of him.

He likely would have used me and killed me otherwise.

Just like he did after I got off the plane.

So did that confirm that he had no memory of me? Of *us*? And instead he'd been listening to these logs from Lilith, learning her way of life and assuming he lived in the same vein?

That would explain his behavior toward me.

But I had to confirm it somehow, to determine if this was truly what had happened.

And to do that, I needed to question Cam. Not overtly or in a direct way, just subtly so I could better evaluate the situation.

Then I'd have to figure out how to proceed.

Because if I was dealing with a version of Cam who didn't know me—and had been essentially brainwashed by Lilith—then I had to tread carefully.

Earning Cam's trust would be the key to everything. But to do that, I would need to convince him that I meant something to him.

Which might be rather difficult if Lilith had reprogrammed his mind to see me as nothing more than a fuck doll.

Bitch, I thought, my fingers typing in the commands to bring up the surveillance once more. Obviously, I needed to find Cam to eval—

A beep sounded, causing me to frown.

What…?

I searched the screen for the source, only to realize in the next second that it hadn't come from the computer.

But from the door.

Well, at least I know where he is now, I thought as I met Cam's gem-like stare from the entryway. *And he looks pissed. Shit.*

.

CAM

Ismerelda's escalating heartbeat sang to my inner predator, making me take a step toward her involuntarily.

But the door slamming behind me snapped me out of my instinctual pursuit.

As did her hitting a button on my laptop and closing the lid.

I stared at it, then glanced at the familiar shirt hanging from her shoulders.

"I see you've made yourself at home." My tone sounded calm to my ears, yet she must have seen through my facade because her pulse kicked up even more.

Her light green eyes followed my gaze to the shirt before blinking back up to me with a soft little frown marring her otherwise perfect brow. "You usually like me in your clothes. Has that preference changed?" Her voice lacked the bite in it from earlier, just as her scent seemed to have changed from that pungent note of despair to something else.

Something fearful, yet tinged with a hint of interest.

I inhaled deeply, testing my inner beast, curious as to how it would make me feel. My exhale left slowly, the tightening in my shoulders seeming to ease with the motion.

Hmm.

My focus returned to her chosen attire, noting the way she'd left the top two buttons undone, exposing a tantalizing glimpse of her creamy skin beneath. She'd also rolled the sleeves up to her dainty wrists, and the shirt covered just a little bit of her thighs. Perhaps it was longer when she stood, but it was bunched up now from her sitting on my bed.

"No," I said slowly, evaluating both her attire and her words. "My preference hasn't changed." Because I very much enjoyed the sight before me now. If I typically requested this, then I could forgive her for dressing without permission.

However, the laptop was another matter entirely. As was her comfortable position in the center of my bed.

Did I use to allow this, too? I wondered, studying her intently. *Why would I allow such freedom?*

There was so much I couldn't remember. But this female had known me for over a thousand years. What else could she tell me?

Hmm, but can I trust her to tell me the truth?

Mira had already warned me that Ismerelda was from a former time when humans were provided with more rights. However, Ismerelda had always been mine. Wouldn't I have been the regulator of those rights? Grooming her to be my version of a perfect little blood slave?

She hadn't tried to escape while I'd been gone, just dressed the way I apparently preferred and taken over my bed—a placement I imagined she'd been well acquainted with throughout the centuries. She also appeared to be in a more appropriate frame of mind now.

Perhaps she'd still been waking up from her death when I'd first approached her and that had been the cause of her bizarre behavior.

Now she was acting as though nothing had happened. She was just staring at me, awaiting further direction.

With my computer in her lap, I thought, eyeing the device again. "Do you typically touch my property without permission?" I wondered aloud.

She stared at me for a beat, her green eyes flickering with unreadable thoughts.

Well, that wasn't entirely true.

I could read her mind if I desired it, but there was a strong mental block between us that I'd clearly erected for a reason. So I wasn't going to risk taking it down just to listen to whatever words were flowing through her pretty head.

"You don't typically require permission for anything," she said slowly, her lips curling down. "It's password protected." She showed me the login screen. "And you know I've never been really good with computers anyway."

She stared at me for a long second, seeming to wait for my reply. Or perhaps she anticipated a reprimand. I really had no concept of our dynamic, only my inherent reactions to her words.

I'd initially been furious to find her sitting in my bed, especially after the last few hours of irritation I'd just endured due to my bizarre reaction to her behavior. But my mood had shifted almost immediately after her question regarding my preferences.

Now I felt almost relaxed in her presence. Content, even.

Which made no sense, given how freely she'd made herself at home in my space. But maybe that was typical for us?

And if it was typical, then perhaps I could finally satisfy the immense hunger lingering inside me.

Unless this is all a ruse of some kind, I thought.

Hadn't she accused me of not being her Cam? Or had that all been related to her death?

She'd said she hadn't ever died before. If that was true, her broken mental state would make sense.

"I'm sorry, my liege," she said when I didn't say anything.

Another pause followed.

"I… I was trying to pass the time until you returned." She gently closed the laptop lid, her expression thoughtful. "I would have cooked for us, like I did in the past, but there wasn't any food in the kitchen area."

Cooked for us? I repeated to myself. *Why would she cook for us? I live on blood. Specifically,* her *blood.*

But now I wondered what it was I would typically eat with her. Or what meals she'd usually prepared.

Maybe I could use this to my advantage, as it could help me determine if this was some elaborate lie or not.

I'd wanted to understand why I'd chosen her. Perhaps this would shed light on that as well.

"We don't have supplies for food," I told her, thinking through a plan quickly. "But I can order something to be delivered." Michael had provided me with a list of options shortly after I'd awakened and regained my senses. I hadn't paid it much attention, as my only craving had been for blood. Specifically, Ismerelda's blood. Which was part of the reason she'd been brought here—to satiate my hunger.

Obviously, that hadn't gone according to plan. Drinking her dry had only taken the edge off. Now I craved something *more*, something darker.

But first, we would play this game. Test her knowledge. See how well she actually knew me.

"Tell me what food I would like and I'll order it."

She studied me, her lips curling down into another frown. "You want me to guess what food you're in the mood for?"

I slid my hands into my pockets and arched a brow at her. "Isn't that what you would have done had there been food available in the kitchen to prepare?"

She shook her head, her confusion palpable. "Uh, no. You… you would have left the food you wanted in there for me. You know, like you did before…" She trailed off, her green gaze holding mine. "I don't normally *guess*."

Her pulse thudded unevenly, adding to the slight quiver in her voice. Something wasn't quite right. *Is she lying? Is it nerves? Is it something else entirely?*

"Um…" She cleared her throat. "We're in Rome, right? Well, Vatican City, but Rome?"

I stared at her. She already knew the answer to that, but I responded in the affirmative with a slight nod, curious as to where she was heading with this.

"Okay, well…" She swallowed, seemingly uncertain. But she appeared to come to some sort of a decision because she finally added, "Your favorite Italian meal is *parmigiana di melanzane.*"

Her Italian accent over those three words was flawless, making me wonder if she spoke the language. But I was too distracted by what it meant in English to comment on her potential linguistics knowledge. "Eggplant parmesan? My favorite Italian dish is vegetarian?" *Highly unlikely.*

But a sudden boldness overtook her expression as she

nodded. "Yes. But not the way Americans used to do it with all the breading. You like the eggplant bake where it's layered with tomato-egg sauce and parmigiano reggiano." She frowned then, her gaze suspicious. "But you know that. Right?"

I wasn't sure what that question meant, so I ignored it. I was too caught up in the dish she'd just proposed. "What else would I eat?"

She was quiet for a moment, observing me, then listed three of my supposedly favorite appetizers—all vegetarian. And followed it up with a brand of red wine she claimed was my favorite in Italy. "You like the French ones in the cupboard, but when in Italy, you drink Italian wine. And you usually sweeten it. With my blood."

Now *that* sounded like something I would very much enjoy. However, the general concept was too easy a guess.

Fortunately for her, she'd added the brand I supposedly preferred.

And several food dishes for me to try.

"What about dessert?" I pressed, beyond intrigued now with this game.

"Usually?" she asked, her eyebrow lifting. "You eat me."

My lips twitched. "That's too obvious."

"Obvious or not, it's true. But if you want me to name a food, then you like gelato. Cioccolato fondente, specifically."

Dark chocolate, I translated to myself.

"Hmm," I hummed, considering her responses. "And what about you, Ismerelda? What do I allow you to eat?"

"What do you *allow* me to eat?" she repeated, sounding surprised by my phrasing. "Whatever I want, usually."

"Do I?" That didn't sound right. Humans could alter their weight and size by eating too exorbitantly. And there were strict rules about that in the new world for a reason. However, her figure certainly appealed to me, so I decided to indulge her. "All right. In this case, what would you want?"

"Right now?" she asked, the question seeming to be rhetorical. "A pizza Margherita and some of the appetizers I already listed for you." Her eyes roamed over me. "And then you for dessert."

A coy response.

But it was a well-played move in this game.

"All right," I murmured. "I'll entertain this absurdity, Ismerelda. But if I decide you're wrong about any of my tastes, I'm going to do a lot more than just *eat you* for dessert."

She shivered. "I understand, my liege."

The term on her lips sounded odd to my ears. I couldn't exactly decide why, so I simply nodded in reply. Everyone referred to me as *my liege*. It was my due as king. And she, of all people, should absolutely address me that way. She was my *Erosita*. My toy. My immortal blood bag to fuck and devour as I chose. She should worship me.

That was the expectation, was it not?

So why am I entertaining this game with her? I wondered as I moved toward the bed and sat beside her.

I couldn't answer my own mental question, so I focused on continuing this little game by taking control of my laptop and logging in.

"Are you sure about this food order?" I asked, glancing away from my computer to admire her beautiful features.

She met my gaze without flinching. "Am I sure about your favorite Italian food from one hundred and eighteen years ago? Yes. Unless your palate changed while you were... away?"

"Asleep," I corrected. "And no." My focus shifted to her

slender neck. "I don't believe my *palate* has changed much at all."

"Asleep?" she echoed, her brow furrowing.

"Yes." I cocked my head at her befuddled expression. "Why does that confuse you?" It was an emotion I shouldn't entertain, but it was a bizarre reaction to something she had to know.

"I… I didn't realize you were asleep," she stammered, her pulse changing in rhythm.

Was that a lie? I wondered, trying to read her.

"How could you not realize that?" I asked, my attention entirely on her heartbeat now.

"Because you left without telling me what you intended to do, and no one fully explained to me what happened," she answered, an unexpected hint of irritation in her tone.

Her pulse evened out as well, the thudding sound back to normal despite her display of emotion.

Interesting.

That sounded like the truth. It also seemed like something I would do. "If I don't tell you something, it's because you're not worthy of knowing it." She served me, after all. Not the other way around.

But for tonight, I would indulge her in this meal and see how well she knew my food tastes.

As I couldn't remember the last time I'd eaten anything of consequence, it would be an entertaining experiment.

"Is your, um, *sleep*, impacting your food memories? Is that why you asked me for your favorites?" Ismerelda questioned slowly as I opened one of the icons on the computer.

I considered her query, unsure of whether or not I should answer.

It wasn't really her business—she lived to kneel for me and nothing more.

However, my faulty memory might become her burden, especially if I found her answers tonight to be true. Because if she proved to know my tastes, I'd likely require a few more details. Perhaps in regard to other pleasures of life.

"Waking from an immortal rest has some side effects." I looked at her again. "One of those side effects is the loss of inconsequential memories, such as favorite foods or details regarding meaningless relationships."

Which explained why I couldn't remember her or Michael but recalled Mira and others from my past.

"Meaningless relationships," Ismerelda repeated, flinching with the words. "Like ours."

"Like ours," I echoed.

And yet, I'd kept her for over a thousand years.

What did that say about me that I couldn't remember her or recall why I'd felt the need to maintain our bond for so long?

"It's possible that more memories will return in time," I said, repeating what the logs from Lilith had told me. "But only if they truly matter to me in some way."

"I see." Her tone lacked emotion, yet her eyes glittered like twin green flames. It was rather fascinating to observe. "I suppose that explains why your speech is still current and not like it was when we first met."

I blinked, surprised by that statement.

"And also how you know how to use a computer," she went on. "Those must be important skills you've recalled. But can you remember who taught you how to use a laptop?"

I stared at her. "Why would that matter?"

"Why indeed," she replied, her tone still lacking emotion despite the flames dancing in her gaze. "What was it Jace once said?" Her next words were ones from an ancient tongue, her fluidity in speaking them impressing me.

The phrase loosely translated to, *Memories are our foundation. But what happens when we have too many?*

"An accurate summarization," I murmured. "But my cousin didn't say those words. My father did."

"Cronus," she confirmed, her pupils flaring with the name.

"Yes." I studied her expression for another beat, again trying to read the meaning behind it. She almost appeared… relieved. But not quite. There were tears in her gaze, except they disappeared in a blink as she attempted to regain her composure.

"I'm surprised you're familiar with those words," I admitted. "I haven't heard them in a very long time." Not since my father had chosen eternal rest over life. And that had been well before my taking Ismerelda as a pet.

"You told me the phrase once. I just confused who originally said it." Her pulse fluttered again with the words, making me frown.

Does that mean she's lying?

But why would she lie about that?

Perhaps I was wrong and misread this female entirely.

Or maybe those fluctuations were what kept me so intrigued by her. *Is that why I erected this mental wall? Because my inability to read her amuses me?*

With those thoughts whisking through my mind, I pulled up the application that would allow me to call the kitchen—something I had yet to do since awakening. But Michael had shown me the protocol, just in case.

"Let's see how right you are about my tastes, Ismerelda," I said as I pressed the button to page someone in the kitchen. "I'm very much looking forward to *dessert*."

IZZY

It's Cam. My Cam.

Because there was no way anyone else could have known about Cronus's final words before resting.

Only *my* Cam would know that phrase. Or rather, who had said it.

Yet this man wasn't like my Cam at all.

"One of those side effects is the loss of inconsequential memories, such as favorite foods or details regarding meaningless relationships."

The implication in those words had resembled a knife to my chest. He'd essentially said I didn't mean anything to him and that was why he couldn't remember me.

But I knew deep down that wasn't true. There had to be another explanation. One that didn't involve *sleeping* since I knew that wasn't what he'd been doing.

However, he clearly thought that was the cause. He

obviously had no idea what Lilith had actually done to him.

And my assumption regarding his brainwashing seemed spot-on, given how little regard he appeared to have for me as his mate.

At least he was amusing me with dinner—a dinner I was *very* thankful he'd ordered preprepared.

Because I couldn't cook to save my life.

Okay, that wasn't true. I could cook. But not well. Which was something *my* Cam would know. My comments about being unable to prepare a meal as I normally would had been my way of examining his memory.

Although, it'd occurred to me while testing said memory that a Cam look-alike wouldn't have known the difference either. So I'd dug deep for something only my Cam would know.

And he hadn't even blinked.

This was my Cam.

But a Cam without memories of us.

Yet it was strange that he seemed to possess knowledge of modern dialogue patterns, computer skills—something *I* had taught him—and other current mannerisms.

So he wasn't stuck in the past, suggesting this wasn't a simple case of amnesia.

It was more targeted somehow.

More specific.

To me.

So again I wondered why I'd been brought here. If anyone could fix this, it was the one tied to Cam's mind.

Assuming I could convince him to break down the mental barrier, anyway. That wouldn't be easy, given that this version of Cam considered me to be inferior.

"If I don't tell you something, it's because you're not worthy of knowing it."

That statement had struck a chord with me. A dangerous one. One I'd tried to ignore for over a century.

A chord filled with resentment toward the man I loved.

Because that man *had* left me in the dark by not telling me his plans for Lilith or how he'd intended to return to me. And that had made me feel inferior to him. Like he hadn't been able to trust me with the information or valued me enough to share it.

I had fought those feelings since the day he'd erected the wall between our minds.

And he'd brought all of that to the surface with a few insensitive words.

I had to get a handle on my irritation before I said something I shouldn't. As it was, I'd already spoken my mind a few times in his presence. Particularly about how he'd left without telling me his intentions, but Cam hadn't reacted to my bluntness. He'd just dismissed it with his statement about my lack of worth.

I watched him now as he settled across from me at the small table in his kitchen area.

He'd left to take a shower while I'd decorated the table for dinner. He was back in another black shirt and matching pants, his hair damp at the ends.

His blue eyes surveyed the food I'd separated onto plates before settling on the wine glass. "Did you sweeten it?" he asked, his deepening accent sending a shiver down my spine.

"Not yet." I swallowed, uncertain of this next part because I didn't trust him not to hurt me. But I wanted to follow our usual ritual as well as I could. Because maybe, just maybe, it would inspire one of those *inconsequential memories* to arise. "You usually prefer to bite my wrist and sweeten it yourself."

His focus went to my neck and then my hand before

returning to his glass. "I think I'll taste the wine first, see if I agree with your assessment regarding my preferences."

"I didn't say you dislike the French brand," I reminded him. "Just that you prefer the Italian one when in Italy."

However, I also knew that this Italian wine was one of his all-time favorites.

I hadn't been surprised that the *staff*—or whoever that dark-haired human who'd delivered tonight's meal was—had been able to locate a bottle of this wine.

Vampires and lycans appreciated the pleasantries in life, which was why they'd relegated so many of the service industry workers—who were literally mortal slaves that had been assigned the service designation on Blood Day—to farms and vineyards to maintain the quality of food they'd enjoyed from previous eras.

Lilith had thought of everything when she'd created this new world order. She'd found a way to psychologically pit humans against each other by forcing them to fight for immortality, and she'd been able to satisfy her fellow vampires and lycans with certain camps that fit their specific needs.

Harems for vampires.

Moon chase victims for lycans.

Blood virgins for vampires.

Breeding farms for lycans.

It was disgusting. Cruel. Completely fucked up.

And my Cam seems to agree with all of it now, I thought, watching as he elegantly tasted the wine. *Worse, those videos I'd played appeared to refer to him as the Liege, which meant he might even think he orchestrated all this madness.*

"Hmm," he hummed, drawing my attention to his full lips. "This is exquisite wine, Ismerelda."

I said nothing, my brain waiting for the *but* that seemed

to be lingering on his tongue. *This is his favorite Italian wine,* I told myself. *If he says otherwise, he's—*

"But..."*And there it is...* "You're right. It does need to be sweetened."

My heart practically leapt into my throat. I was equal parts relieved that he hadn't denied the flavor and terrified that he was about to bite me again.

Because the last time he'd sunk his fangs into my flesh, he'd killed me.

And he'd done it while ensuring I felt every painful second.

I swallowed, my arm rising of its own accord toward him, just like I would have done a hundred and eighteen years ago.

Only this time, I wasn't filled with expectation born of repetition and routine. Because I didn't know what he would do. The uncertainty unfurled inside my stomach in a fluttering sensation sending a slight shiver up my spine. It reminded me of the night he'd first bitten me, when I hadn't known exactly how it would feel.

Will it hurt?

Will I like it?

Will it be like before?

Will it be new?

His long fingers wrapped around my own, pulling my hand across the small table, his hungry gaze holding mine. Another quiver worked its way through me, causing my thighs to squeeze as my wrist inched closer to his alluring mouth.

He might kill me again, I reminded myself. *But what if he doesn't? What if he—*

His incisors bit into my flesh before I could finish that thought, sending a jolt of heat through my veins meant to entice and subdue. *Pleasure.*

It was so unexpected that I moaned, my eyes falling closed at the sensation I hadn't experienced in far too long.

Cam hummed in response, the sound going straight to my core. It was as though he had my clit in his mouth, sucking and nibbling and drawing me closer to climax.

Ohhh, how I missed this... My stomach clenched around an inferno of passion, bringing me to the brink, only to dissipate in the next breath as Cam released my wrist.

My eyelashes fluttered, reality slowly settling in around me as I realized that only a few seconds had passed.

Those blue, hungry orbs caught and held mine, Cam's soul seeming to speak to me directly through his gaze as he let my blood flow into his glass.

My throat worked as I attempted to swallow, my world having whirled in the wrong direction, taking me into the past and making me want to beg him for more.

But this wasn't my Cam. Not really. Not until I broke through the mental barriers between our minds and ensured that he remembered me. Remembered *us*.

His fingers deftly moved across my hand as he guided my wrist away from his glass and back to his mouth. Lust and need brewed in his alluring eyes as he licked the wound closed, all while he held my gaze.

I shuddered, my insides fully primed for more, my thighs tense with desire, and my nipples pulled taut in anticipation of another bite. *There. On my breasts. Please...*

His focus shifted downward as though he'd heard my request. The Cam I knew had only rarely indulged in biting me there. He'd preferred my neck and my wrists, mostly because he'd feared other places might hurt me.

Which made it rather strange that I'd imagined him nibbling the sensitive area between my thighs. He'd never done that, too afraid of the pain it would inspire.

But something told me this version of him wouldn't care at all about my discomfort.

He kissed the inside of my wrist and released me.

"You're going to make that sound again for me later while I fuck your mouth," he said. "That'll be your dessert." His attention went to the food. "Assuming this all impresses me, of course. Otherwise, we'll be doing something much less enjoyable. For you."

I shivered at the threat as well as the insinuation that me sucking his cock would be my *dessert* only if he approved. *So what will he do if he disapproves?*

Cam picked up his fork and brought it to a plate of caprese—one of the appetizers I'd suggested.

"I rewarded you for the wine." He glanced at my wrist and then my lips. "Let's see if I feel like rewarding you for the food, too."

I remained still as he brought a tomato up to his mouth, his expression thoughtful as he chewed.

After he swallowed, he gathered another bite, only this time he lifted it for me to try.

I wasn't sure if this was his way of *rewarding* me or making me taste the food with him. But I stopped caring when the explosion of flavors touched my tongue, and I groaned in approval.

"Hmm, I think you like that more than I do," he mused. "Which is saying a lot because I rather enjoyed the taste myself. But the sounds you're making intrigue me more."

He fed me another forkful of deliciousness before moving on to another appetizer—bruschetta.

Rather than try it himself first, he cut off a piece and brought it to my lips. "Open."

I obeyed. Not just because I was starving but because this reminded me of *my* Cam.

He watched while I chewed and swallowed, his sapphire gaze following the column of my throat before taking his own piece.

"I prefer the other one more," he admitted after finishing his bite. "But this is decent."

My lips twitched. "You've said that before."

He arched a brow. "Have I?"

"You have. But you still always order bruschetta."

"I wonder why," he murmured as he gathered up another bit of caprese on his fork.

"You like the way it pairs with the eggplant," I told him, glancing at the main dish.

He considered it as he enjoyed another tomato. Then he shifted gears to his entrée and cut an adequate piece off to try.

His expression didn't change at all while he ate it, his blue eyes more focused on me than on the food. But when he picked up a piece of bruschetta to eat with it, I knew he was satisfied.

Thankfully, I'd been truthful about his favorite food. I'd considered lying in case he asked me to prepare it—which would have been a huge problem—but this had worked out okay.

And I had some answers about Cam.

My Cam.

Because he was here. In front of me. Eating Italian food.

My heart skipped a beat as I allowed the realization to settle over me, my insides warming with excitement.

We're finally together.

It wasn't the way I'd anticipated us meeting again, nor was it ideal, but I'd accept this over never seeing him again.

"You may eat your pizza, Ismerelda," he told me, his gaze still holding mine.

"Thank you, my liege," I replied, playing into the obedient act he obviously expected of me.

Because of Lilith mindfucking him, I thought sourly while taking a bite of my pizza.

I needed to find out exactly what Lilith had done so I could attempt to reverse the damage.

Or perhaps it's as simple as breaking down the mental wall between us.

Well, *simple* was an understatement. Nothing with Cam could ever be *simple*.

Cam was the most stubborn vampire I'd ever met, his decisions resolute and unapologetic. Once his mind was made up about something, it was basically impossible to convince him otherwise.

And I had no doubt this version of him was exactly the same.

Which meant I had to coax him into coming up with the idea himself rather than blatantly suggest it.

That would take time, something I hoped we had a lot of but likely didn't.

"You don't seem to be enjoying your pizza as much as the caprese," Cam said, his focus shifting from my mouth to my eyes while he spoke. "Does it taste all right?"

It tastes fine, I thought. *But I'm rather distracted at the moment thinking about how to fix you and not all that concerned with the food as a result.*

But I couldn't say that.

So once I finished swallowing, I gave him another truth. "It's a little dry, but it's otherwise okay." It had probably been in the oven a little too long, or perhaps hadn't been in the right type of oven. Which was a shame, considering we were in Italy, but we were also somewhere underground and I had no idea where they'd prepared all this food.

He considered me for a moment. Then he reached for my plate and swapped it with the caprese, setting the appetizer directly in front of me and the Margherita in the center beside the bruschetta. "Finish eating that instead. I prefer your moans over silence."

My lips threatened to curl at his words, but the dark hunger in his gaze kept me from showing my reaction.

Because he looked ready to devour me.

And I wasn't sure if that was a good thing or a bad thing. Or a bit of both.

Rather than lose myself in my thoughts again, I picked up my fork and shifted my attention to the caprese salad. It really was a lot better than the pizza, the flavors bountiful and pure. I could tell good olive oil had been used, as well as a handful of fresh spices.

"Much better," Cam murmured, his gaze on my mouth.

I hadn't meant to moan again, but apparently I had. And I didn't bother to hide my enjoyment as I continued eating, something he seemed pleased by.

When he finished his meal, he simply watched me eat, his pupils flaring with ominous warning. He resembled a predator preparing to pounce on his prey.

Goose bumps trailed down my arms. *What will he do after I take this final bite? Make me suck him off for dessert?*

I shivered at the thought.

It'd been so long since I'd been properly touched by this man.

Except this wasn't my Cam at all.

This was a male brainwashed into thinking of me as beneath him. Not his mate, but a blood bag. Which was why he'd bitten me so freely yesterday, allowing me to die.

And why he'd walked in earlier with the intent to fuck me regardless of my mood or willingness.

Did I want to entertain that sort of a man in my bed?

Was it wrong to do so? What would *my* Cam think after his memories returned? Would he feel betrayed?

I swallowed, the caprese feeling heavy in my throat.

That last question had evoked a visceral response deep within me, one that said Cam *should* feel betrayed.

Because the notion of being taken by this version of my mate left me feeling uneasy... but also intrigued.

What would it be like to be touched as though I weren't breakable? To be taken with the true power of his spirit? To be bitten in places my Cam would never have considered because I was too fragile to accept it?

It was wrong to ponder. A *betrayal*. Because this wasn't my version of Cam. This was... a broken version. A dark figure of the male I'd once loved.

But maybe sex will help him lower his shields.

Intimacy had typically brought us closer together, our minds marrying in the oldest of ways as our bodies consummated our love for one another. It had fed our souls, bolstered our bond, and—

"Ismerelda." Cam's silky tone drew me out of my mind and into the present as he set his empty wine glass on the table. "I'm ready for dessert."

CAM

A BEAUTIFUL FLUSH STOLE OVER ISMERELDA'S FEATURES, creating a crimson invitation I longed to accept.

This was much better than before, her scent far sweeter now and serving as a beacon to my inner predator rather than a deterrent.

I inhaled deeply, noting the scent of subtle arousal that accompanied her hint of fear.

Perfection, I all but purred in my mind.

The meal had been surprisingly pleasant. Ismerelda's food choices were unlike anything I could remember eating, making me wonder what other cuisines she'd recommend.

But first, I felt a strong desire to reward her. She'd pleased me in a way I hadn't expected, which I imagined was related to why I'd kept her all these years. She'd also been beautifully subservient throughout our meal, waiting for permission to eat and thanking me when I granted it.

And those moans…

Fuck, I'd nearly shoved all the dishes to the ground just so I could bend her over the table and drive into her.

Her scent now told me she'd be ready.

And tight, too, I thought with a mental groan.

Ismerelda hadn't been fucked in over a hundred years. Her unused cunt would feel almost as good as a virgin pussy, squeezing and pulsing around my eager cock while I pounded into her without remorse.

It would hurt. But she'd take it because she had to. She was mine.

And fuck if that knowledge didn't make me even harder for her.

It'd been too long since I'd felt the pleasure of sliding into a woman. Gods, I couldn't even remember the last time, just that it'd been euphoric. Unworldly. *Addicting.*

Once I started fucking Ismerelda, I likely wouldn't be able to stop. She'd probably die with my cock lodged deep inside her, begging me to slow down or grant her a reprieve.

But I wouldn't be able to. Not with the savage hunger riding my predator right now.

Not with her sweet scent curling around me and that delectable blush teasing her neck.

A growl slid from my mouth, making my little *Erosita* shiver. There was no doubt between us as to what dessert I intended to devour.

However, I still wanted to praise her in some way. Perhaps grant her a sliver of pleasure before I destroyed her with my needs.

Maybe that would ensure she woke up properly next time.

"Clear the table," I told her. "Then I'm going to *eat you*, just like you said I would."

Because chocolate gelato certainly didn't appeal to me the way her sweet arousal did.

I'd spread those athletic thighs—which I admired now as she stood without a word to do what I'd demanded—and properly taste her. Lick her deep. Bite her. Mingle her pain with her pleasure and drink every drop.

Her natural perfume seemed to bloom with every step she took, her interest an intoxicating aroma thickening the air between us.

Goose bumps pebbled down her legs, an intriguing display that confirmed she was both turned on and scared.

A beautiful combination.

She bent over the table beside me to pick up her discarded pizza, causing my shirt to ride up a little more along her thighs.

My fingers itched to explore her creamy skin, but I held myself still, even as she straightened and allowed me a tantalizing glimpse of her hardening nipples beneath the thin fabric.

She had not been wrong about my wardrobe preference. Because she definitely wore my shirt better than I did.

I admired her movements as she retrieved the last few plates, setting dirty dishes in the sink and storing the minimal leftovers in the refrigerator.

My wine glass was the final item, something she walked over and hand-washed before slowly returning to my side. Her eyes were lowered in clear submission, her cheeks still boasting that alluring pink shade.

"Have a seat," I said, gesturing to the table in front of me. "And spread your legs."

She swallowed, her green eyes flickering up to mine

before lowering again. "Yes, my liege," she whispered, her earlier confidence seeming to have fled.

That reaction suggested she was used to my particular brand of brutality.

Good.

Because I was feeling ravenous for her and I would not be holding back, something she obviously knew and accepted.

I leaned back in the chair as Ismerelda slid onto the table, her legs appearing even longer as she positioned them off the edge and allowed them to dangle on either side of my thighs.

"Wider, Ismerelda. And pull up my shirt."

Her pulse jumped at the sound of my voice, her eyes briefly skipping up to mine before lowering once more. Rather than verbally reply to my command, she skimmed her palms up her thighs to the edge of the fabric and higher to expose her bare sex.

I'd already seen it earlier when I'd stripped her before bathing her—a task I would have given to someone else, but I hadn't wanted anyone else to touch her. Not when I'd been so hungry for her.

Alas, she'd been unconscious through the experience. Mostly dead, truly.

However, now she was very much alive.

Which meant I could ask her a question I'd considered before yet hadn't been able to voice because she hadn't been alive enough to answer.

"Did you keep yourself groomed for me?" I couldn't imagine who else she would have been prepared like this for, but a possessive part of me felt the need to confirm her intentions.

"No. I did it for me," she replied softly, her answer

surprising me. "I kept it trimmed for centuries, but shaving everything is… freeing." Her pretty blush spread down her neck to the sliver of skin revealed by my shirt. "It makes things more sensitive."

"Hmm," I hummed, intrigued by her claim. She widened her legs, allowing me an unfettered view of her slick heat.

So wet and ready.

So very much mine.

"Let's see just how *sensitive* you really are, Ismerelda." I gripped her thighs and forced them even farther apart before leaning down to inhale her addictive fragrance.

Her pretty eyes met mine, allowing me to see the flicker of uncertainty mingling with interest in her dilated pupils. She had no idea what I intended to do to her. And I had no desire to define it.

This was my playground. My rules. *My fucking blood slave.*

"Lean back and balance on your palms," I told her, my grip going to her hips. "And try not to—"

My wrist buzzed with an incoming notification, stirring a growl from my chest. Ismerelda trembled in response, her needy pussy a mere centimeter from my lips.

Fuck. "This had better be important," I snapped as I accepted the call on voice-mode only. I didn't want anyone else seeing my *Erosita* like this. She was *my* dessert, not theirs.

"You asked me to notify you when the preparations for the ritual were done," Mira replied, her tone flat. "I'm ready to begin."

I straightened, my gaze still on the delectable sight before me. There really wasn't a choice on how to proceed here despite my wishing I had one. But I'd wasted most of the night taking out my aggression on lesser vampires and indulging Ismerelda in a meal.

And now I was paying for delaying my gratification.

I blew out a long breath and closed my eyes. "I'll be there in five minutes. Don't start without me." I ended the call before she could reply and refocused on Ismerelda. Lust shone bright in her gaze, her interest palpable and very welcome.

Just a few hours too late.

"I expect you to be naked, wet, and waiting for me in my bed when I return," I told her. "Don't disappoint me, Ismerelda." I moved before she could reply, my lips meeting her thigh on my way to her clit, where I bit her. *Hard.*

She screamed in response, her pleasure-pain receptors overwhelmed by the sudden onslaught of endorphin-laced venom from my incisors.

Vampires could severely hurt their prey. Or we could introduce a victim to a new realm of ecstasy.

I chose the latter, mostly because I wanted to hear one more delicious moan before I left. My darling slave didn't disappoint me. She *sang*, her body convulsing on an orgasm I envied and wished to replicate for myself.

Alas, I had work to do.

But once I finished, I would return.

And I would do a lot more than simply bite Ismerelda; I'd annihilate her.

"I'll be back soon," I said against the wound I'd left on her pretty pink flesh. Blood mingled with her arousal, providing me with the perfect dessert, but I only allowed myself one long lick—a lick that sent her spiraling into another climax, her prone form devastatingly primed for my brand of fucking.

Rather than heal her, I left her exposed. The residual

ache would resemble my own, punishing her right along with me while I delayed the inevitable between us.

My immortal blood running through her veins would ensure she recovered quickly; it just wouldn't be as immediate as me closing the wound.

"Soon," I repeated, my tongue sneaking in one final taste before I phased away from her toward the door.

I didn't turn around to observe her or make sure she followed my commands to be naked and ready for me in bed. I knew she would obey me. She was mine, after all.

I savored the flavor of her as I made my way down the hall, all the while commanding my dick to calm down. But having her essence in my mouth didn't help.

All I wanted to do was turn around and fucking devour her. Pound into her for hours. Release all this pent-up lust into her soaking wet cunt and smother her in my seed.

I'd take her every way I could on repeat until I tired of her.

Then I'd probably do it all over again tomorrow.

Fuck.

I ran my hand over my face, the scent of her still fresh on my palm. And that hadn't even been from her pussy, just her skin.

This was why I'd kept her around. It had to be. She was bloody addictive.

I closed my eyes and forced myself to focus, then phased the rest of the way down the corridor to the elevator.

Where I found Michael waiting for me like he always seemed to do.

Fuck off, I wanted to say. I wasn't in the mood for formalities. I just wanted to turn around and destroy my *Erosita*.

Instead, I raised a brow, waiting for him to speak.

"My liege," he greeted, bowing low and making me roll my eyes. "The technical teams have informed me that we should regain control of our communications console within the next six to twelve hours."

Well, that's at least useful information. "Did they determine a cause?"

"Not yet, my liege. But it's very likely Damien's interference, like Mira said. He's probably trying to locate his sister."

A sound theory, except... "If he had the power to infiltrate our systems previously, why didn't he do it after acquiring Lilith's phone? Why wait until now?" Because that didn't make sense to me at all. He'd been fucking with our systems for nearly two weeks. What had allowed him to break through our security now?

"I'm not a technical expert, but I feel the better question is: What's changed that suddenly granted him access to finally hack our systems?" Michael countered. "I agree that he had initial access through Lilith's phone, but he didn't fully breach our communications server until your *Erosita* arrived."

I studied his expression and deciphered the true context of his words. "Are you trying to imply that Ismerelda has something to do with his ability to break through our security walls?"

"She is one of the changes," Michael pointed out. "It could be that she was the inspiration he needed to push his way into the system or, more likely, there's something she's done that has allowed his interference."

I stared at him. "She was dead and locked up when he breached our systems, Michael. She's not helping him, if that's what you're implying."

"Well, perhaps not knowingly or actively," he

rephrased. "But there could be a chip implanted in her that's allowing—"

"A chip?" I repeated.

"Yes, as in a small technical device that could be implanted under her skin," he clarified. "One that could be used to track her, or perhaps as a way to remote into our system based on proximity."

Similar to how I instinctively knew all about computers, I also already knew what a chip was and hadn't been repeating it for a definition, but more of an incredulous inquiry.

"I highly doubt her brother has implanted her with a *chip*, Michael. But if you have a scanner or some sort of tool to check her with, then I can use it on her later." And if we found one, we'd remove it. "Now, I need to meet with Mira."

I turned toward the elevator bay once more.

"Or I can check her while you work with Mira?" Michael suggested.

I glanced at him. "No."

His brow furrowed. "But if she has a chip inside her, we need it removed immediately. Otherwise, Damien will simply thwart our efforts and continue holding our communications abilities hostage."

"You said your team hasn't discovered the true cause," I pointed out. "If you can prove it's Damien, then I'll re-prioritize scanning my blood slave. Until then, I need to oversee Fen's reawakening."

"But if she has a chip, then we'll know it's Damien," he argued, his manner and change of tone surprising me.

He was directly questioning my authority, and while he had somewhat of a point, it wasn't good enough for me to allow him near my naked *Erosita*—a fact my inner predator immediately agreed upon by growling deep in my chest.

"Who is liege here, Michael?" I asked as the elevator arrived. I ignored the opening door and faced him fully instead.

He swallowed and bowed his head slightly. "You are, my liege." A low response, almost grating in sound because his teeth were grinding together over the words.

"I am the Liege," I echoed. "And I am telling you to find me a device to use on Ismerelda when I have time. In the interim, work with the technical teams in determining a cause. If you can prove it's Damien, I'll escalate your request."

Because no way in hell was I allowing him to go in there and put his hands all over my impassioned *Erosita*. She was my present to devour later, not his.

"Do you understand me?" I pressed, the elevator closing behind me as I stared the other man down. Or rather, the top of his head since he wasn't strong enough to look at me.

He swallowed again. "Yes, my liege."

"Good." I punched in the code one more time. "Now get back to work."

"Yes, my liege," he repeated, that grating quality still underlining every word. But fuck if I cared. He'd questioned my command. He was *my* progeny and *my* assistant. It was best he remembered that and left me to handle my *Erosita* on my own.

I stepped into the elevator and waited for him to join me. There was no reason for him to remain on my floor now that I'd ordered him to stay away from Ismerelda.

He followed, but I sensed it was a begrudging movement.

Fortunately, he said nothing and simply selected the floor I needed as well as the one right above it. I didn't speak as he left, simply allowed myself one final private moment with Ismerelda's sweet taste on my tongue.

Then I focused on the task at hand when I arrived at my destination.

It was time to wake another Blessed One.

Fen.

IZZY

A Few Minutes Earlier

"Soon." The word vibrated across my slick heat, followed by the kiss of a hot tongue right against my throbbing clit.

And then the source was gone, the sound of a door closing echoing through the room as my heart pounded in my ears.

Oh, God…

I could barely breathe. I couldn't even think. I… I just existed. I lived. I shuddered. I nearly came again.

Everything was so *hot*.

Cam's venomous kiss had left me delirious. *How many endorphins did he push into that bite?*

My legs were still quaking, my insides churning with

the intensity of being forced into an orgasm by a vampire's fangs.

How…?

Why…?

Ohhhh… I squeezed my legs together as another jolt speared through my senses, the agony of where he'd bitten me dancing with the residual ecstasy swimming through my veins. It was a dizzying sensation. Unnatural. Debilitating. *Damning.*

Because *my* Cam had never done *that.* Oh, he was a master with his tongue, having brought me to climax countless times.

Just never in that manner.

Never so quickly. No, not even that. *Immediately.* He'd sunk his fangs into my clit and sent me immediately spiraling into a vortex of intense sensation.

It had been unlike anything I'd ever experienced.

And part of me hated this new Cam for that. He'd… he'd introduced me to a pleasure I couldn't ignore.

I'd wondered what it would feel like to be bitten there, had pondered the notion of being treated as unbreakable rather than fragile…

And now I knew.

Only, I didn't *want* to know.

I wanted to be true to my Cam. To be faithful to his memory. To not give in to this villainous version of him.

It was wrong.

It made me feel dirty, like I'd disrespected him by… by *enjoying* the experience. Yet there hadn't been a choice. I hadn't even known what this Cam had intended to do. He hadn't given me a moment to think. He'd just thrown me into the deepest depths of oblivion without a life raft and left me there to drown in an unending current of rapture.

My legs tensed once more as another jolt shimmered down my being, settling right between my thighs.

He didn't heal me, I realized. *He wanted me to feel the agony mingling with the residual aftershocks of my orgasm.*

No. Not singular. *Plural.*

I'd come at least twice. Maybe more. All in the span of what felt like seconds.

I carefully curled into a ball on the table as I rode out the remaining spasms in my core, my heart racing unhealthily in my chest.

Thank God Mira called him away. Because I would not have survived these sensations with him doing whatever else he'd intended.

Death by climax, I mused. *Not a horrible way to die. And yet...*

I sighed.

This isn't my Cam.

I needed to find a way to trigger his memories.

Which meant doing something proactive, like getting off this table. Only, to do that, I needed to not be a squirming mess of overwhelmed nerves.

I moaned as my knee touched my chest, every part of me incredibly sensitive.

Deep breaths, I coached myself. *Inhale. Exhale. Repeat.*

Oh, but it burned...

The spot between my legs. My lungs. Even my throat.

Because of my screams, I thought. I closed my eyes and focused on calming my heartbeat by breathing properly. It hurt. My insides protested.

And my clit... *pulsated.*

I bit my tongue to keep from groaning.

Come on, Ismerelda. Get up. Grab the laptop. Focus on finding out more about Cam.

And the... the ritual *she mentioned.* I frowned. *What ritual? What preparations? What are they doing? Why is Cam...?*

My eyes opened as I finished my thought. "Why is he involved?" I whispered to myself, blinking. *Does it have something to do with why they brainwashed him?*

I forced myself to sit up again as another shock of pleasure-pain jolted my system. Cam's bite pulsed between my legs, serving as a symbol of his brutal claim. But I forced myself to ignore it.

Something important was happening.

Something I... I needed to... *to see.*

I glanced at his discarded laptop. He'd left it on the bed in full view of the camera.

But he hadn't exactly said I couldn't use it. Instead, he'd bought my lie about being computer illiterate—which had been one of my first tests. If he'd been the real Cam, or in this case, a Cam with all his memories intact, he would have scoffed at my comments.

However, he hadn't. He thought I hadn't even been able to log in despite having been on his computer for a while in front of that camera. Did he think I'd just been guessing passwords the whole time?

Or had he not seen me at all?

I considered the camera and then the laptop again.

Maybe he'd been too busy to check the feed. Which meant he might be too busy to look again now.

But why would he have a camera in his own bedroom if he's the one monitoring the video? I wondered, frowning again. *That seems... odd.*

Granted, nothing about this made sense. Cam's memory loss. My being taken here. Why Lilith had brainwashed Cam. Mira's betrayal.

I slid off the table and winced at the pang between my legs. I was absolutely going to bruise down there. But at least my immortal ties to Cam would help me heal faster.

With awkward and careful steps, I made my way over

to the bed and climbed into it while my lower half protested.

Ow, ow, ow, I chanted in my head as a moan slid from my mouth. It was such a contradiction, but I couldn't help the sensations flowing through my blood.

Why has Cam never bitten me there before? I wondered as I settled against the pillows. *It hurts, but it's also...* I trailed off as I squirmed, another jolt of ecstasy flooding my veins. *Sooo good...*

I swallowed, my eyes closing briefly as I fought the urge to climax again. It would probably be more painful than pleasurable at this point. And it felt wrong to take advantage of the situation, especially knowing my Cam would never have bitten me like this.

But now I sort of wish he would, I admitted to myself. *Which probably makes me a terrible mate.*

I cleared my throat and grabbed the laptop, determined to do better. To make my Cam proud. To respect his true memories. To be the mate I'd vowed to always be.

Even when he—

No. Don't go there.

I entered the password that Cam had used earlier, the keys having been in plain sight when he'd logged in to order dinner.

A blue screen came to life, followed by a series of applications. I searched for one that might be linked to video feeds, hoping that maybe I could find Cam and see where he was heading and what he was doing.

But there didn't appear to be anything related to a security system anywhere. No surveillance programs. Nothing streaming-related. And no video icons.

"That's odd." I clicked through every program

available and found them to be not only minimal but also useless.

Logs was one of the final items I tried, and I flinched as Lilith's face appeared on the screen.

"Log year one hundred and twelve, day one," a voice said. It sounded like Lilith; however, her lips didn't move until she added, "Hello, my liege."

"Yeah, no, thanks," I muttered, minimizing the screen. While her *logs* might provide some insight into Cam's behavior, it wasn't what I was looking for right now.

I backed out of the current screen to survey the list of videos in this folder. They were all dated like the ones I'd seen behind the scenes, only these had Lilith's face attached to them in thumbnail form.

Not current surveillance. Hmm.

I exited the application and selected the remaining few, one of which was a communications panel that had the words *Not Connected* scrolling across the screen.

There wasn't a password or anything, so I assumed it referred to the lack of an external connection to whatever network this system used.

Still, if I could call Damien…

I clicked on a few buttons to try, and each time, an error message popped up with the same words: *Not Connected.*

Blowing out a breath, I went back to searching for the live feeds.

They're definitely not here. Which was strange since the videos were housed on the internal network—something I knew since I'd been able to pull them up via a device connected to the system.

So why can't Cam see them? Does he not have access?

That could be why he hadn't commented on me being on his computer for so long—he hadn't known or seen me use it. That might also explain why he had a camera in his own bedroom.

Does he even know it's there? I frowned as I glanced up at the camera in the ceiling.

If I was right about Cam not having access to these feeds, then he likely didn't know they existed.

So who are you? I asked the unidentified observer, aware that he or she couldn't read my mind. *Mira, maybe?*

Well, whoever it was, the person clearly wasn't concerned about me being on Cam's laptop. Maybe because the watcher assumed I only had access to the same files as Cam.

Which suggested my backdoor method from earlier likely hadn't been detected.

Or whoever is in charge doesn't care.

I considered the camera once more, then shrugged and went to work. If the watcher cared, perhaps he or she would reveal his or her identity.

Meanwhile, I'd do some investigating into this *ritual* and see what Cam and Mira were up to.

Another spasm shot up from my center, making my thighs clench as a wave of heat rolled through my being. I swallowed, the pang not quite as rapturous as before. Maybe because I was starting to heal, thanks to my ties to Cam's ancient immortal genetics.

It was a blessing and a curse because it expedited the process, which could sometimes result in higher degrees of agony.

Is that why you didn't heal me? I wondered while I worked on logging in via the backdoor protocol on his laptop. *Is this some sort of twisted foreplay?*

Cam had always been gentle with me, his touches reverent more than passionate. But this version of him almost felt predatory. Beastly, even. Like he wasn't holding back his baser instincts at all and allowing me to witness his darkness.

Is this who you always were deep down? Or is this a result of our time apart? The way you woke up? The way Lilith tortured you? There were so many questions, so many possibilities, none of which I could respond to.

But the biggest query of them all lingered at the forefront of my mind, the one I wasn't sure I wanted an answer to. *Is this version of you permanent?*

What if I couldn't make him remember me?

What if his memories were lost forever?

What would that mean for us?

I shivered, my mind racing into the land of "What Ifs." It was a dangerous train of thought, one I forced myself to derail from as the administrator panel appeared on the screen.

The script cursor blinked, awaiting my typed command. My fingers flew over the keyboard, all too eager to engage in a distraction from my mental roller coaster.

A series of backend file names appeared next, taking me through a catalog of surveillance feeds. I clicked through them, searching for Cam.

I found myself in one, just like last time, and ignored the image.

Since there only appeared to be one camera in this room, it was impossible for anyone to tell exactly what I was doing on the screen unless they attempted to remote into the computer. And if that happened, I should be notified of it since I was lurking in administrator mode already.

Moving on, I found several more of the infamous Coventus. There were girls and boys in various rooms, some alone, some in groups, all being taught about their future lives as blood slaves. The feed made my stomach twist, bile rising in my throat as a sadistic-looking vampire bent one of the older matrons over a table to provide a hands-on demonstration for a classroom of young females. His beady black eyes observed them all with interest, showcasing his proclivities in a dark light for all to witness.

Monster, I thought, memorizing his face. If I ran into him here, I'd do my best to drive a knife through his heart.

Too bad I didn't have Lilith's infamous dagger handy. Apparently, it hadn't been found on her corpse after Ryder had killed her. Probably because she hadn't wanted it to be near him on the off chance he'd be able to grab hold of it.

Unfortunately for her, he'd improvised by taking an ax to her neck.

A poisoned blade would be much easier for me to handle, as I doubted I could repeat Ryder's actions very easily. That sort of act required supernatural strength and expert precision when dealing with an immortal.

I clicked off the screen, not wanting to see how the demonstration ended, and kept searching for Cam.

There were various hallways—most of them vacant except for a guard stationed here or there. Two more bedrooms appeared, both empty.

However, the visual that followed had several people in it. A mountain of them, it seemed.

Dead humans, I realized with a flinch.

My fingers moved to select another feed, only to freeze as my eyes caught on the wall behind the mutilated pile of flesh.

There appeared to be a message written in red—*no, that... that's blood*—on it. Except it wasn't in a language I could read. It was something archaic. A script Cam could probably decipher.

Or write...

Did… did he paint that on the wall? I wondered, swallowing. *For what purpose? Is it related to the ritual?*

My lips curled down as I scanned the room—which was really more like a cell—for any signs of Cam. *Is there another angle? Another viewpoint?*

I selected the next feed and found another view of a hallway.

Hmm.

I shifted forward a few more, wondering if it would return to the—

My eyes widened. *Oh. Oh, God…*

The display before me had my jaw dropping in utter shock. There were two naked men chained to what appeared to be thrones made of… of *human flesh and bones.*

I lifted the back of my hand to my lips to keep from gagging at the sight. It was unlike anything I'd ever seen.

They were clearly starving. Yet they were being fed by two others holding human sacrifices up for them to devour.

"*What the…?*" I muttered into my hand. "Why? *Why?*" And who were these two obviously insatiable men?

A hint of script on the wall told me this was from the same room as before, suggesting that pile of corpses was their doing. However, they didn't appear to be satiated at all. They were half-mad with starvation. I could see it in their eyes, the way they were glowing with hints of insanity as they bit into the necks of their new victims.

I couldn't hear anything, but I suspected they were growling like untamed beasts.

And the vampires feeding them… were… *smirking?*

They were amused by the sight.

But why? What is this? Who are they?

I tried to study their features, their gray skin and long white hair unfamiliar and decidedly inhuman. They had their hands free, allowing them to better grip their victims.

Their nails resembled talons, overgrown and unkempt. Although, they almost appeared brittle.

Actually, most of their appearance seemed fragile in nature. Like they were too weak to truly be alive.

Like mummies, I thought, my brow crinkling and then flying upward. *Like. Mummies.*

"No," I whispered as an unsettling realization disturbed my mind. "No way. No fucking way."

Except the proof of it was on the screen with eyelashes that resembled ash, irises that lacked pigmentation, and skin that had clearly not seen the sun or any other element for quite some time.

"Ancients," I breathed.

We were in Vatican City. *No, we're beneath it… where the Blessed Ones rest.*

Blessed Ones who could only be awakened by a ritual.

A ritual that required royal blood to be activated.

And there was one vampire whose blood could be used to wake every Blessed One in existence.

The eldest of vampire kind.

Cam.

IZZY

Is that why this is happening? Why Lilith brainwashed Cam into believing he's the Liege? To make him cooperate with this madness?

But why am I here? What purpose am I meant to serve?

And why are they feeding humans to the Blessed Ones?

Blessed Ones didn't drink blood. They were immortal without having to imbibe mortal essences. All vampires knew that. Yet these two were devouring these humans like food.

What. The. Fuck?

I searched for a way to zoom in on the camera feed, wanting to see if I could pinpoint any defining traits that would identify these poor souls.

There were twenty Blessed Ones in existence.

All of them were men.

And they would all resemble these mummified states after being awoken from rest.

Although, there were also some vampires who'd chosen eternal rest—vampires like Cam's brother, Cane. Which meant these two could be vampires, not Blessed Ones.

No. That couldn't be right. Because if they were vampires and they'd devoured all the bodies in that pile, then the blood should have helped them heal by now.

So why are they giving Blessed Ones blood? I wondered again, my frown deepening.

I'd witnessed the ritual when Cane had chosen to sleep. It hadn't required any human sacrifice, just the essence of a higher-ranking royal or a Blessed One. As Cam was the oldest royal vampire in existence, his blood had been more than sufficient for Cane's ceremony.

Just as it would be more than sufficient for the requisite waking ceremony. Or that was my understanding, anyway. Cam had told me they were similar processes, going as far as to teach me the ancient words involved just in case I ever had a need to orchestrate such a ritual.

Not that my blood would be sufficient.

But another royal's would be.

However, nowhere in that conversation had Cam mentioned *this*.

Why are they—

The lights shut off around me, pitching me into darkness with the laptop providing my only source of light.

I blinked.

What—

A blaring alarm sounded, making my ears ring.

"Ow," I breathed, my hands flying upward just as the screen shifted to a weird red tint. Then it went dark. Now red. Pitch black again. More red.

I stared at the scene as movement flickered in the

strange lighting, the two ancient beings climbing off their macabre thrones and moving out of sight.

What happened to their chains? I wondered, my gaze trying to focus on the image. But the strobe lighting made it too difficult to decipher any details.

I jumped as a body flew across the live feed, the crimson color creating a grotesque scene of brutality. More body parts appeared next, making me gag.

Enough of this. I switched the video, my ears still ringing from the alarm. More red strobe lights lit up the screen, stirring a dizzying sensation inside my mind.

I can't keep watching this in the dark.

I quickly keyed out of the admin mode and made sure I was logged off of Cam's profile, but I didn't close the lid. Because if I did, the room would go completely dark.

So the alarm sounds in here, but not the crimson strobes.

Maybe because it was Cam's room and not one of the main areas? Of course, that cage holding the two ancients was probably more of a cell than a public space. Just as some of those classrooms resembled a prison-like setting more than anything else.

I shook my head to clear the images from my brain. I needed to focus. *Cam's here to help wake the ancients.*

So again I wondered, *Why am I here?* While I understood the customs, my blood couldn't help with the rituals. Thus, it couldn't be for that.

Perhaps whoever is in charge brought me here as a way to control Cam?

No, that couldn't be right. He didn't remember me. And the wall between our minds prevented him from knowing me as well.

Unless that was the concern—that he might try to locate me if he couldn't talk to me in person.

I frowned. *Then why not just kill me?* I was the best

opportunity Cam had to remember everything. Surely that went against—

The sound of the door opening made me freeze, the glimmer of the login screen my only source of light.

Shit… I swallowed, my exhale seeming to halt in my throat. No other noise followed. No footsteps. No clothes rustling. Not even the faint hint of someone else breathing.

But predators could be silent. And they didn't require light to see.

I waited. *So quiet. Too quiet. And dark…*

My lungs burned with the need for air, forcing me to inhale sharply. Goose bumps trickled down my spine, the feeling of being stalked a visceral fear that held me captive on the bed.

"Cam?" I whispered, wondering if he'd returned during the blackout.

No reply.

Just an eerie silence that left me uneasy, making my neck prick with awareness.

The laptop screen fell asleep, casting me in a sea of perpetual darkness where I continued to sit still. Some morbid part of me thought perhaps that would mark me as less interesting prey.

Which was just ridiculous.

I was a human. My blood was ideal for every monster lurking in the darkness beneath the Vatican.

Stop sitting here and do something, I told myself, irritated by my innate reaction to my stark surroundings. I had a perfectly good light on my lap that could confirm whether or not someone stood nearby; I simply had to use it.

Rather than overthink it, I hit a key and angled the computer toward the open door.

Vacant.

A quick flicker around the room showed there was no one standing near the bed either.

Of course, they could be hiding somewhere, given that it'd taken me so long to intelligently respond to the situation, but a measly laptop wouldn't prove to be much of a defense against someone wanting to spook me anyway.

Rather than dwell on it, I slid off the mattress while holding the laptop against my chest with the screen facing outward like a bulky flashlight.

I crept toward the door, my ears listening for any possible movement around me, and paused just at the threshold.

Is this some sort of test?

I frowned at the thought. A test wouldn't explain what I'd seen on the monitor with the Blessed Ones in the catacombs.

Unless that had all been some sort of bizarre setup. But for what purpose? Why let me see something so grotesque?

No, this couldn't be a test at all. Something was happening here. Something I wasn't supposed to know about. Something that required Cam to think he was the Liege.

Something involving waking ancient beings.

I stepped into the hallway and hit a key to keep the screen awake. It wasn't exactly bright, but it was enough to cast a glow in front of me.

Unfortunately, that glow made the rock walls appear rather daunting in nature. *Like living in a cave.* Although, the texture appeared smooth, which reminded me more of concrete than a standard boulder.

So more like a prison, then, I decided as I turned right and meandered forward.

There were no other doors along the corridor this way,

just a lot of vacant wall space until it ended. I turned and wandered in the opposite direction, passing the entrance to Cam's quarters and ending in a spacious area with a set of elevators and a single open entryway.

I used the laptop to peer through the latter and found that it led to a set of stairs. My eyebrow arched upward. *Definitely feels like a test now.*

But I didn't understand the purpose.

And even if I took the stairs, where would I go?

I'd been in the catacombs once—when Cane had opted for eternal rest—and I hadn't exactly taken myself on a tour. Besides, that was several hundred years ago. Would I even know my way around down there?

Or is it up there? I wondered, noting that the stairs went both up and down.

Who knew what Lilith had changed beneath the Vatican? Clearly, she'd built a residence quarter for Cam. *Is this where she kept him all these years?* Somehow, I doubted it. His accommodations were too luxurious for that.

So did she keep him upstairs or downstairs?

I recalled the day I'd witnessed Cane's ritual and how deep underground we'd ventured for it.

The catacombs had resembled an ominous cave, the crypts all made of aged rocks and bound by precious metals. It'd been a tomb designed for royalty, but without the usual upkeep. At least at that time, anyway. Lilith had probably remodeled it into a glorified throne room centered around her overly inflated ego.

Bitch, I thought, narrowing my eyes. Thank God Ryder had killed her. I only wished I'd been there to witness it.

So up or down? I pondered. Because test or no, I intended to explore. If Cam found me, I'd just say I was looking for him because of the blackout.

Shrugging, I stepped into the stairwell. The cold, hard

floor instantly reminded me that I was barefoot, and the slight draft up my legs tickled the bare skin beneath Cam's shirt. Another jolt speared through my being, courtesy of Cam's bite.

I winced but forced myself to ignore it as I moved toward the steps.

Down it is, I decided, tiptoeing along the cement stairs while keeping the laptop facing outward.

I ventured two floors down before I discovered another open door. Peering out of it, I spied a corridor similar to the one I'd just vacated.

This was probably another residential area, something I assumed since Cam's quarters were about two stories tall. It seemed likely that all the rooms were that large. Not that it made much sense with the lack of windows and furnishings.

I kept moving and stumbled upon another similar hallway about two floors down again.

Hmm. I took a few more steps, then paused to listen. *How far down does this go?*

My ears told me nothing.

No alarm echoed in the distance. No sign of footsteps. Not even the murmur of voices.

Glancing over the banister, I shined the light downward to try to locate the bottom and jumped backward when I found a pair of glowing red eyes staring right up at me.

The laptop nearly tumbled out of my hands, but I managed to clutch it to my pounding chest at the last second.

A scream lodged in my throat as the red-eyed being appeared in front of me, his speed indicating his otherworldliness.

Vampire, I realized on a gasp. *Lycans have yellow eyes because of their inner wolves.*

Although, now that he was close, I could see his facial features in the dim lighting. His eyes were no longer a red glow, but a vibrant green. And he had long blond hair to his shoulders.

My lips curled down. "Michael?" I'd met him once, well over a century ago. Shortly before he'd *died*.

"Ismerelda," he returned, his tone flat. "Trying to escape?"

I blinked at him. "What?" *Why would I try to escape?* But that wasn't the most important question. "How are you here?" *You're supposed to be dead.* Humans had killed him. That was part of what had driven Lilith to want to essentially enslave humankind.

Or that'd been the theory, anyway.

But if Michael's alive...

"I see our Liege hasn't broken you of your vulgar habits yet," he drawled, his voice holding an arrogance that reminded me of Lilith. He snatched the laptop from my hands and closed the lid, cascading us both into a sea of perpetual darkness.

I instinctively tried to reach for it and came up against nothing but air. My balance shifted with the movement, my hands searching for something to hold on to and finding nothing of substance.

I attempted to grasp behind me, my arms spinning as my feet shifted to try to remain on the stair, but I couldn't see.

Fuck!

The world tilted.

I tucked my chin and covered my head as I gave in to the fall, aware that there was no stopping it now. Harsh cement bit into my knees first, then my elbows, stirring a cry from my lips as I twisted and whirled, only to land unceremoniously on my back.

The air halted in my lungs, my chest momentarily stunned and forgetting how to function. Then I gasped and curled into a ball of agony, the throb starting between my legs and echoing up my spine to join the cacophony of intense sensations swimming through my nerve endings.

I'd clearly ripped open the wound Cam had left behind, only now there were no pleasant residual effects. Just pain.

So. Much. Pain.

"Oh, I'm sorry. Did the overconfident mortal fall off her high horse?" a taunting voice mused far too close to my ear. "Such a shame."

A sharp pang radiated up from my ankle as a heavy weight pressed down upon it.

Is that his hand or his foot? Rubber ridges bit into my skin in the next moment, answering my mental query. *Definitely his foot. Covered by a boot.*

I gasped, the pang morphing into a crushing sensation that had me forgetting about all my other injuries and focusing entirely on my lower limb.

"Humans have no rights in this world. Even humans owned by the supreme being of our kind. If you intend to live, you need to learn that lesson. And quickly."

A scream clawed at my throat as he applied even more pressure.

"Otherwise, you'll be easily replaced. Especially as we're in a bunker full of blood virgins. I doubt Cam would even miss you. I mean, it's not like he remembers a damn thing about you."

He twisted his boot, shooting agonizing sensations up my calf. But his words hurt more, and the implication behind them.

I'm expendable because Cam doesn't remember me.

He… he could replace me.

"Ah, there it is," Michael mused. "You're beginning to understand. Excellent. Now be a good little blood whore and tell me how you're helping Damien dismantle our technical operations."

His boot dug into my skin, forcing me to bite down on my lip to keep from crying out. I refused to give him the satisfaction. Just as much as I refused to speak. I didn't owe him anything, least of all an explanation.

Although, I'd love to know how the hell he was still alive.

The pressure on my ankle increased to an excruciating level, forcing another scream to build in my throat.

Don't let him win. Don't scr—

"Tell me how you're helping Damien. If I like your answer, I might just let you crawl up the stairs and return to Cam's quarters in one piece."

He released my ankle, making me want to curl into myself even more as renewed agony shot through my veins. But his fingers in my hair suddenly grasped my attention as he tore at the roots.

"Speak, blood whore." His breath was hot on my face, confirming his nearness.

I blinked into the darkness, only to fiercely shut my eyes as all the lights came on at once. It was blinding and cruel and unexpected.

But Michael didn't give me a second to acclimate, his fingers tangling harshly in my knotted strands. "Answer me, Is—"

He released me suddenly, making my world spin once more, almost as though he'd thrown me down another flight of stairs. But only my head seemed to whirl, not my body.

My stomach heaved in response. *No, no. Not now.* I

covered my mouth, forcing myself to swallow as discomfort threatened to overwhelm me.

I felt broken.

Bruised.

Wounded.

"What the hell is going on here?" Cam's voice cut through my mind, filling me with a wave of immediate comfort and safety.

Until the hard edge of his words filtered through my thoughts.

He sounded irritated. No, more than that. Lethal intent lurked beneath his question. A command that required a response.

But I was too disoriented to explain.

"My liege," Michael murmured, his reverent tone nothing like the sinister voice from seconds—*or was that minutes?*—ago. "I was tracking the source of our technical disturbance when I found your *Erosita* trying to escape."

I frowned. "I wasn't escaping." The words came out gravelly, everything feeling disoriented and wrong. I tried to open my eyes, to find Cam, but the brightness caused my head to ache and sent me into a downward spiral once more.

Why am I so dizzy? I didn't hit my head during my fall.

Unless...

Did I?

Ugh, I don't know. It just hurts.

"Why is my *Erosita* bleeding?" Cam asked, that sharp quality in his accented tones still prevalent.

"She tripped and fell down the stairs in the dark," Michael explained. "Apparently, in her hurry to escape, she forgot her mortality and inability to see without light."

His description made me want to growl. "I was not

escaping," I repeated through my teeth, again trying to open my eyes.

"And why do you have my laptop?" Cam inquired, ignoring me entirely.

"Because it's the source of our technical disturbance. I found your *Erosita* carrying it, which confirms she's working with Damien. They clearly caused the security breach."

What? That doesn't make any sense. I'd tried and failed to access an external network. Only the internal system seemed to be working. So how was I even communicating with Damien?

And why would my brother be hacking into their system?

Well, I supposed he could be trying to locate me and Cam. But—

"I see." Cam's voice pierced through my mental ramblings, his easy acceptance of Michael's words causing my brow to furrow even more. "And you have proof that my laptop is the issue?"

Okay, maybe he hadn't accepted his explanation entirely.

"I will once I get this to the tech team," Michael replied.

"And they'll be able to confirm that Ismerelda is the one who helped Damien gain access?" Cam pressed. An icy note underlined his words, causing a chill to sweep along my spine.

I opened my mouth to deny the accusation, but Michael was already saying, "I'm not sure, my liege. I was trying to question her when she fell. But she never responded."

"So it's still possible that she has done nothing wrong."

"It's possible, yes. But unlikely, given that I caught her

trying to escape with your computer," Michael pointed out, again making me want to snarl at him.

"Why would I escape by going down?" I snapped, my eyes finally seeming to focus on my surroundings.

It was a little blurry, and very bright, but I could make out Cam standing on the platform a foot in front of me. Michael appeared to be a few steps down, his body hidden by Cam's impressive form.

"We're under the Vatican," I continued before either man could disregard me again. "If I wanted to escape, I'd go *up*."

Neither male replied, but I sensed a shift in the air. Something subtle. Something that left me… uneasy.

"She has a point, Michael," Cam murmured, his body rotating toward me as he slid his hands into his pockets. "So what were you doing, Ismerelda? Why were you carrying my laptop in the stairwell?"

CAM

IT TOOK PHYSICAL RESTRAINT NOT TO REACT TO THE injured female on the ground.

My nose had led me to her the moment I'd stepped off the elevator onto my floor. For whatever reason, those had begun working before the lights had flickered back on.

I'd been on my way to check the door to my quarters when Ismerelda's alluring scent had led me toward the stairwell instead.

Her fresh blood had been like a beacon, calling to my inner predator and taking me downward.

Where I'd found her crumpled on the floor with her ass exposed, thanks to my rumpled shirt.

Not that she seemed to have noticed her precarious position. She'd been locked up in the fetal position, her pain evident.

Her skinned knees and elbows flavored the air with her

essence, but that wasn't the heart of the aroma that had called me to her.

No. The source of my intrigue rested between her thighs and the alluring blood seeping from the bite I'd given her earlier. Her tumble down the stairs—if Michael's description of the accident was to be believed—had likely worsened the wound.

"Everything went dark, and the door to your room opened," she said, drawing my focus to her lips. "I grabbed your laptop to use as a flashlight and went looking for you. But there was nothing on your floor other than the stairs, so I started wandering downward."

She uttered the words with the conviction of a queen, her pain seeming to take a back seat to her need to explain herself. It almost made me proud, which was a strange reaction. Her ingrained forwardness was something I had to break, not praise.

And yet, it came in handy in this situation.

"So you didn't fall in the dark?" I asked, arching my brow.

I suspected Michael hadn't been entirely forthcoming, mostly because he'd been interested in interrogating Ismerelda only an hour ago. And I'd told him to stay away from her, yet found them alone in a stairwell.

"I did," she replied, her gaze boldly holding mine. "I fell after Michael abruptly took the computer away and blinded me in the middle of the staircase."

"Because I wanted to end whatever game you were playing with your brother," my progeny stated flatly. "Which obviously worked since the lights came on not five minutes after I closed the laptop."

That was a suggestive piece of evidence. *However…* "Have the technology teams confirmed that the system intruder lost his connection? Or did they successfully remove him?" I faced Michael again. "And have they confirmed it is, in fact, Damien hacking our network?"

The tic in Michael's jaw confirmed his answer before he voiced it. "No, my liege, they have not. But they sent me up here to track the source using this." He pulled a square device from his pocket. "And it led me to your laptop."

"Is that a scanner?" I asked, eyeing the item in his hand.

"It's a tracker that pulses with color," he explained. "The techs told me what floor the breach appeared to be coming from and sent me up here to investigate. The closer I came to your laptop, the brighter the flash got."

"It isn't very bright now," I said, still looking at the unassuming black box in his palm.

"It turned off when I closed the laptop."

"I see." I shifted my attention to the computer in question. "Then I suggest you take that to the technical team and ask them to conduct a thorough review."

"Yes, my liege." He tried to glance around me. "And what about her?"

"Ismerelda is mine to handle," I told him, my tone brooking no argument.

"But this is proof she's working with Damien, my liege."

"I fail to see how her using my laptop as a flashlight is proof of anything other than her being resourceful while exploring areas she shouldn't." Which was technically my fault, as I hadn't explicitly told her to remain in my room. I'd simply implied it.

"Maybe she doesn't know that she's helping him," he said, his tone urging me to reconsider. "I found a scanner, my liege. I can bring it to you. At least then you can be certain Damien didn't implant a chip inside her."

He must have been very serious about this accusation to have found a scanner in such a short amount of time.

Alas, he wasn't exactly wrong to make these assumptions. He simply wanted to protect the operation, and someone—possibly Ismerelda's brother—was making that very difficult at present.

Whoever had hacked the system had allowed the Blessed Ones to escape their cages, as well as over a dozen other research subjects.

Mira and the others were still deep underground, chasing them all down.

I'd left them to clean it up since it was their faulty systems that had allowed this mess to occur. Because if a lone hacker could wreak this much chaos, then the team who'd built this facility deserved to learn from their own ineptitude.

My final words to Mira had been "Find me when everything is in proper order to house our experiments. Only then will we wake Fen."

The last thing we needed was the unequivocal father of the lycans to add to this catastrophe.

"My liege," Michael started, interrupting my thoughts. "I—"

"Take my laptop down to be inspected and bring me back the scanner. If Ismerelda has a chip, I'll find it and we can go from there," I told him. "But I still want proof that this is Damien."

Which perhaps the chip would demonstrate.

However, I highly doubted we would find anything. Mostly because there hadn't been any notice that Ismerelda would be taken here. Implanting a chip required foresight, and I very much doubted anyone had seen this coming.

"Of course, my liege," Michael replied, bowing deeply. "I shall return."

He left without another word, but I caught a whiff of his satisfaction on the wind.

I ignored the irritating scent and rotated toward a far more intriguing one—Ismerelda's blood.

She had moved to brace her back against the wall, her legs tucked at an awkward angle. Tears glistened in her pretty eyes, her jaw tight.

A fighter, I thought, compelled by the sight of her refusing to let those treacherous emotions fall despite the agony she clearly felt.

I took in her form, noting the scrapes again on her knees and elbows. She had more on her forearms, but the primary source of her sweet fragrance still came from between her thighs.

That drew my attention to her legs, the beast inside me longing to spread them and devour a splendid meal of pussy and blood.

Only the bruising on her lower leg momentarily distracted my inner predator, drawing out a growl of a different nature. Primal. Vicious. *Furious.*

I crouched before her to get a better look and noted the bruising on her ankle. Her other blemishes were clearly from landing on a step or perhaps on this cement platform. They were smaller. Round. Blistered with blood.

But this one... this one was longer. With imprints digging into her skin. *Imprints that resemble a boot print...*

"What happened here?" I demanded, my fingers flexing with the need to touch her delicate skin and trace the foreign marking. It was definitely going to form a ghastly bruise, marring her otherwise flawless features.

Only I can mark her, I thought. *And never like this.*

I blinked, the reaction so deeply profound that I barely recognized my own mental voice.

But Ismerelda didn't give me time to reflect as she replied, "Michael wanted to remind me of my place in this new world."

My jaw clenched. "What?" Oh, I'd heard her just fine. But I needed her to say it again.

She blew out a breath. "Michael used my ankle as a reminder of my mortality. Or maybe it was his way of proving his own immortality." She lifted a shoulder and winced. "The last time I saw him, he was human. And I thought he was dead. I guess he didn't appreciate my curiosity."

I reached for her ankle, giving in to my need to touch her.

And almost instantly regretted it when she flinched away from me with a hiss that ended in her clamping down on her lower lip.

Another hint of her essence warmed the air, taunting my taste buds and making me long to lick the blood away from her mouth.

But a stronger part of me needed to fix her.

To heal her.

To *avenge* her.

Because how fucking dare Michael touch her. Especially after what I'd said to him a mere hour ago.

Ismerelda was mine to punish. Mine to control. *Mine to protect*.

I swallowed and pushed away that last thought. This need to possess her, to *claim* her, all came from the bond between us.

Which was why I'd tasked Lilith with finding a better alternative to taking an *Erosita*. These possessive instincts were dangerous and distracting.

Still, I couldn't deny my desire to heal Ismerelda.

I didn't want to risk losing her to death and her bizarre waking state again. Not when I had yet to fuck her properly.

She was my toy.

My primary source of sustenance.

And I couldn't thoroughly enjoy her in this condition.

Rather than think on it further, I lifted her into my arms—just barely managing to ignore her sharp intake of breath—and phased up the stairs to my floor, then directly to my room.

It was maybe two or three seconds of travel total, but it was enough to have her biting her lip again and drawing more blood as she fought the urge to react to her injuries. *And what had to be excruciating pain between her thighs.*

I'd bitten her clit to keep her in an aroused state.

Clearly, that had backfired.

I'd remember that for the future.

"You shouldn't have gone wandering," I told her as I laid her on my bed. "If something like this ever happens again, wait for me here."

She swallowed and lowered her gaze. "Yes, my liege."

My lips threatened to curl downward at the sign of her submission. Which was strange because she should be submitting to me, just as everyone else did. But I'd rather enjoyed her warrior-like display in the stairwell. It'd been much more alluring than this docile appearance.

Interesting. The female I'd witnessed on the landing had been one I'd consider changing into a vampire, if nothing more than because her spirit was obviously superior to most humans.

However, this version of her was weak and exactly what was expected of inferior beings.

Maybe this is why I've kept her as a blood slave instead of making her my queen, I thought. *And perhaps I've kept her all these years because I saw the potential for more.*

Yet this display proved she couldn't handle true immortality.

Because a queen would never bow this easily. Not even to her king.

Sighing, I lifted my wrist to my mouth and bit down. "Drink," I told her as I placed the open wound against her lips.

Glittering green eyes glanced up at me, the emotion shrouded beneath a veil of unshed tears. For a moment, I thought I caught a hint of surprise in her watery gaze, but it was gone in the next blink as she obeyed my command.

My opposite hand went to the back of her head, holding her to me while she fed. I'd intended for it to be a way to control how much she drank, but her knotted strands distracted me from the task.

Her hair appeared tousled. Like someone's fingers had roughly tangled with the strands.

Or another man's hands.

I narrowed my gaze. "Did Michael touch you here?"

Those pretty irises found mine again as she slightly dipped her chin in confirmation.

I took my wrist away. "Why were his fingers in your hair?"

Her throat worked over a final swallow, her cheeks crimson in color—not out of embarrassment, but from the excitement provoked by drinking from a vampire's vein.

"He was questioning me about Damien," she said, her voice confident once more. "He asked how I was helping my brother."

"And what did you say?"

"I didn't get a chance to reply." She stared at me. "But, for the record, I'm not helping Damien do anything. I would need to be able to get on some sort of external network to be able to reach out to him, and I haven't had an opportunity to do so."

"You've had access to my laptop," I pointed out, studying her as she continued to boldly hold my gaze. "And, according to Michael, the technical team traced the interference to that laptop."

She shrugged. "I can't explain that. I also couldn't tell you what purpose it would serve me to open all the doors *and* turn off all the lights while underground. I can't see in the dark. Obviously."

A fair point.

I also couldn't determine what she would have to gain by letting the Blessed Ones out of their cages. She probably didn't even know they were awake.

But she clearly knew we were beneath the Vatican since she'd mentioned it in the stairwell.

"Have you been here before?" Because if she had, she could already know her way around.

However, she'd gone down instead of up.

Which, as she'd said, made no sense if she were trying to escape.

And why would she want to escape anyway? I was her immortal lifeline. Her mate. She'd literally run toward me on that tarmac, not away from me.

Her pupils flared as she replied, "Yes. With you. When Cane chose eternal rest."

"Hmm." I didn't remember that at all. "We attended his ceremony." It wasn't a question but a statement.

Because of course I'd attended the ritual. I would have participated in it to ease my brother into his chosen sleep. But it was surprising to learn that Ismerelda had been there with me.

"How long ago did my brother pick eternal night?" I

hadn't read about it in the files. But it probably wasn't very relevant to our current world since my brother had chosen to rest through it all.

"About four hundred and fifty years ago. So I only visited the catacombs where the ancients are kept. Not"—she waved around the room—"this."

"And you witnessed the whole ceremony?" I pressed, still hung up on the notion that I'd taken her with me.

"Yes."

I narrowed my gaze. "Prove it. Tell me part of—"

A knock interrupted my demand. *Michael.*

My gaze narrowed as my fingers left Ismerelda's hair. I hadn't even realized I'd still been holding her, my mind too captivated by our conversation to consider the actions of my hand. Touching her had felt normal. Expected. Soothing, even.

With a shake of my head, I stepped away from my bed and went to the door.

"The scanner, my liege," Michael said by way of greeting, his head bowed.

I considered him for a long moment, the beast within me warring with the strategist inside my mind.

He touched my female.

He's my assistant.

He hurt *Ismerelda.*

He only wants to protect our mission. If he had interrogated anyone else, I wouldn't care.

Ismerelda isn't anyone else.

"My liege?" he prompted when I didn't immediately reply. "Would you like me to demonstrate how it works?"

Hmm. Part of me wanted to take the device from him and use it to bludgeon him.

Yet the more intelligent side of me had another thought.

135

An idea of sorts.

One that developed into a plan that didn't quite appease the animal roaring inside my mind, but it quieted the feral beast enough to allow me to continue. "I imagine I simply roll that device along her skin, yes?"

"Correct, my liege. You just flip this switch"—he pointed to a toggle on the side—"and proceed. I recommend you scan every part of her, just in case Damien chose an, uh, *inventive* location for a tracker."

I nodded, understanding what he meant—he was saying Ismerelda should be naked for the exam.

Which I'd already anticipated.

"You can remain while I examine her, Michael," I told him, causing my inner predator to snarl with disapproval. But knowing why I intended to allow Michael's presence throughout this intimate procedure pacified most of my possessive instincts.

Michael's lips curled, more of that satisfied scent wafting off of him. "Of course, my liege."

I stepped aside to allow him entry into the room.

Then I faced my *Erosita*.

It was time to find out if my instincts about her were correct. Or if I'd somehow been blinded by the millennium-old bond between us.

IZZY

"REMOVE THE SHIRT, ISMERELDA," CAM SAID AS HE TOOK the device from Michael.

I shivered, the intent behind his words settling deep inside me. *He wants me to disrobe. To be naked. Exposed. Vulnerable. In front of another man.*

My Cam would never have allowed this, let alone even considered it. But in this world—the new one created by bloodthirsty vampires and lycans—humans were cattle.

And *this* Cam intended to remind me of that.

Just like Michael had tried to in the stairwell.

Fine. If these two powerful beings wanted to make me submit, I'd play along. Just like I did every time I referred to Cam as *Liege*.

I just have to find a way to make him remember me, I thought as I started unbuttoning my shirt. *Which is something I can't do in front of Michael.*

I had to indulge in this behavior, treat it like a game, and find his vulnerable heart beneath all that hardened vampire exterior.

And if that doesn't work? a part of me wondered. *What then?*

Then I make him fall in love with me again, I decided. *He's my soul mate. That can't be erased, can it?*

I refused to allow the cynical voice in my head to answer that and finished unbuttoning the shirt.

Cam's eyes trailed down over my torso as I removed the fabric from my shoulders. Rather than let it drop, I folded it on the bed beside me and waited for his next command.

Will he ask me to stand? Because I wasn't sure if I could right now. While I'd swallowed enough of his blood to begin the healing process, it had only just started to work— as evidenced by the tingling sensation in my ankle. It would take me another hour or two to feel whole again. Maybe a little more.

I bit my lip as the apex between my thighs began to sting again. *Definitely not a fan of being bitten* there, I decided. It'd been enjoyable at first, euphoric even, but now... now not so much.

I absolutely do not want to stand. But if Cam demanded it, I wouldn't have a choice.

Instead, he merely admired my breasts for another moment before lowering his gaze to the mark he'd left on my sex. His nostrils flared and he stepped closer, the scanner in his palm.

Rather than speak, he sat beside me on the bed and used his free hand to comb my hair away from my face.

"It might be easier if she stands, my liege," Michael

said as he moved closer to us. "Just to ensure you can scan every inch, I mean."

Cam considered me for a beat, his gaze flickering between my mouth and my eyes. I held my breath, waiting for him to issue the command and hoping I could find the balance to follow it through.

"Easier, yes," he murmured, his blue irises swirling with a darkness that had me shivering beneath his perusal. "But I prefer a challenge."

"Of course, my liege," Michael replied.

Cam continued to study my face, his fingers untangling my hair with gentle pulls. His gaze seemed to burn into mine, his power a whiplash to my senses that revitalized my veins and caused my heart to beat faster.

Something about this felt dangerous.

Hypnotic.

Terrifying, yet arousing.

His scanner wouldn't reveal anything. I knew that. But there was a violent undertone to his movements that left me uncertain of what would come next.

I fear this version of Cam, I realized. Which made sense, given everything he'd done. But to feel this way about my mate, about the love of my existence, was perplexing. Both upsetting and invigorating.

Because I couldn't anticipate his next move.

He wasn't the version I knew and trusted. He was an ancient being with a reprogrammed sense of humanity. Or lack thereof. He didn't care about me or the mortal race.

Yet he continued to pet me with a tenderness that reminded me of my Cam. Only, the male I loved would never have allowed another man to see me this way. To degrade my sense of privacy. To force me into submitting so thoroughly.

I swallowed as his fingers ventured downward to my

neck, his thumb brushing my racing pulse. "Hmm, you're afraid." He canted his head. "Because I'm about to find out you've been lying about working with your brother?"

"No." I was positive he wouldn't find anything at all.

"Then why is your pulse racing, little mouse?" he asked, his voice whisper-soft and filled with lethal intent.

But I was too hung up on the nickname to allow the threat underlying his tone to disturb me. *Little mouse?* I mentally repeated, my lips curling down a little. "You usually call me *little swan.*"

He stared at me for a beat. "Little swan?"

"Or sweet swan," I told him.

He focused on my mouth, his palm encircling my nape. "I suppose you have some swan-like features." His attention shifted to my neck as he squeezed slightly. "If you tell me where to scan you first and help speed up this process, I may be inclined to lessen your punishment."

I narrowed my gaze. "You're going to have to scan every part of me, my liege. Because I'm not hiding anything."

Well, that wasn't entirely true. I was technically hiding a whole history from him. But that wasn't my fault. Lilith had done something to his mind, making her the culprit instead of me.

And I couldn't just blast him with the truth. At least not under these circumstances. He wouldn't believe me. I was just a toy to him right now.

One he seemed very intrigued by at the moment as he ran his gaze over me again, his lips curling just a fraction. "Do you hear that, Michael? She insists she's done nothing wrong."

Michael grunted. "Our current technical issues suggest otherwise."

"Is that why you attempted to interrogate her?" Cam

glanced over his shoulder at the blond man standing near the bed. "Because I don't recall you bringing proof that the interference is Damien's doing yet."

"I asked her a few questions, my liege. After foiling her escape attempt. It was an appropriate reaction to her actions."

My jaw clenched, but I didn't bother correcting him again. Michael knew I hadn't been trying to escape. He'd just wanted to lord his immortality over me.

"Then I suppose we'll see if your *reaction* was justified," Cam replied, his attention returning to me as his hand moved from my nape to my throat. Violence danced in his sapphire gaze, making me swallow against his palm.

He fully expected to find something embedded inside me.

I could see it in the way he studied me so intently, like he couldn't wait to wring my neck for defying him.

This was a side of Cam I'd never witnessed before— the true predator beneath the skin. He'd typically hidden that part of himself away, choosing his human mask over his vampiric side.

Now he appeared more feral. In touch with his hunger. No longer caring that the mortals around him might fear his true nature. Demanding all those beneath him to *bow*.

Somewhere inside you is my *Cam*, I thought at him, my gaze boldly holding his. *I will find a way to bring him back to life. I vow it.*

His lips curled as though intrigued by my mental promise, but I knew he couldn't hear me. A barrier existed between our minds—one he controlled, not me.

However, I'd know if he took down the wall because I would be able to hear the words feeding that dangerous look on his too-handsome face.

Which meant that block between us was still very much in play.

"A swan, hmm?" he mused, his thumb brushing my pulse as he referred to the nickname I'd mentioned. "That's interesting. I suppose it fits your more delicate traits." He glanced over me. "But your eyes are much more feline than avian right now."

He squeezed my throat, preventing me from replying—not that I knew what to say—and abruptly released me.

"Pull your hair up," he commanded, his thumb switching on the scanner. "I'm starting with your neck."

I gathered my errant strands up into a ponytail, my *feline* gaze holding his.

Since when am I feline? I wondered. *Cam always saw me as a swan.*

"So fragile, yet beautiful," he'd often said.

Never once had he described me as *feline*.

Nor had he ever called me a *mouse*.

Hearing those endearments—or *insults*, maybe—from his mouth almost made it seem as though this male was possessed.

Or that I never knew Cam at all.

But that wasn't true. We'd been together for a thousand years before his capture. I knew him better than anyone else.

Yet this version... I thought as he placed the scanner against my throat. *This version I don't recognize at all.*

His pupils flared as he focused on the device sliding across my skin, the low hum of electricity the only sound between us.

He moved slowly, thoroughly checking every inch of my neck before shifting the item upward along my nape and into my hair.

I held my ponytail in a single fist, frozen beneath his

ministrations. He worked around my hand, checking the top of my head and the sides before saying, "Let go and press both palms to your thighs."

I obeyed while studying his still-dark expression as he continued his path along the back of my skull.

The electric hum vibrated my ears, sending a shiver down my spine. Then he started on my face.

I refused to close my eyes, not that he'd asked me to. He held my gaze for a long moment, that twitch in his lips happening once more before he shifted focus to my shoulders and upper back.

He used one hand to pull me forward by my nape, his chest pressing against my bare arm as his opposite hand scanned my spine all the way down to the top of my ass.

I expected him to tell me to shift onto all fours, just like he'd done when he'd wanted to fuck me before, but he said nothing. Instead, he essentially held me against him while he examined me, using his hand to maneuver me as needed.

He checked my sides and my arms, then continued on to my torso before sweeping back up to my breasts.

It was all very clinical, and yet, there was something undeniably sensual about the way he moved me around to meet his needs. His touch wasn't harsh, just sturdy. Confident, even.

But as he reached my legs, he seemed to falter a little. Mostly when he brought the scanner near my inner thighs.

The blood from his wound had dried against my skin, my body having mostly healed the bite, thanks to his essence running through my system.

He studied it for a long moment, hunger seeming to darken his irises into a deep, oceanic blue. I wondered if he wanted to lick me clean, and I couldn't stop myself from imagining it.

His tongue against my clit. His mouth warming that intimate part of me. His fingers...

I swallowed, the thoughts making my lower limbs clench just as the device dipped between my thighs. But the metal wasn't what I craved. It wasn't what I needed or desired at all.

And the slight twitch at the corners of Cam's mouth told me he knew it, too.

He slowly scanned my intimate flesh, drawing me deeper into a strange state of need.

This shouldn't be turning me on. I... I don't want to enjoy this...

My throat worked, my mind seeming to splinter between remembering my reality and losing myself to the touch of my mate.

But he's not my Cam. He's... he's someone... something....

His palm grasped my hip before drifting down my leg to continue guiding me around like a doll. Each touch was purposeful and efficient, but as he neared my hurt ankle, his grip lessened.

His fingers brushed the skin, making me flinch slightly because the featherlight stroke tickled. "Does it hurt?" he asked, his voice deceptively soft.

I considered my ankle, surprised to find that it no longer ached. "It's mostly healed," I admitted. Which meant he'd been scanning me for a lot longer than I'd realized.

Given how thorough he was being, that made sense. I was more surprised by how easily I'd fallen under his spell and forgotten exactly what it was we were doing.

Rather than verbally reply, he nodded and finished examining my lower limbs.

The device hadn't made a single sound, just like I'd

expected. Which made it extremely satisfying to hold his stare when he finally looked at me again.

"Straddle me, lioness," he said, his choice of nickname almost surprising me as much as his demand. "Now."

He twisted his body away from mine, his feet planting on the floor.

The action forced me to crawl around him to settle onto his lap, something I normally wouldn't have minded, but the action reminded me of Michael's silent presence. He stood a few feet away from the bed, giving him a full view of my naked form as I parted my legs over Cam's muscular thighs.

Goose bumps pebbled along my arms, my back feeling utterly exposed to the other man's view.

But then Cam wrapped his palm around my nape again and suddenly he was the only one I could see. His beautiful irises. Chiseled jaw. Cruelly handsome lips. So full and perfect. His defined cheekbones. His thick, dark hair.

I could feel his strength beneath me, his soul tethered to mine.

I'm safe.

Except I wasn't safe at all. Danger practically poured off of him in dark, toxic waves, drowning me beneath a sea of malice.

I didn't understand. I'd passed his test. I'd done nothing wrong.

And yet I could sense his intent to punish. To hurt. To *kill.*

His grip tightened, pulling upward and forcing me to balance my weight on my knees as he exposed my backside entirely to Michael.

A shudder ran through me, grounding me in reality and making me wonder what he intended to do next. *Offer me to the other man? Allow him to beat me? What did I do wrong? Why is he—*

Metal touched the back of my upper thigh.

The scanner. I blinked. *He's checking my ass for an implant. Oh.*

That was the last place for him to examine. *Of course.*

I took a deep, calming breath and focused on the sharp contours of his face while he worked. The intimidating lines defined his features, his ire palpable. He seemed to want to punish me, yet the device didn't make a sound.

Because I'm innocent. At least, partly.

Had I been able to reach out to Damien, I would have. But I'd had no reason to set off those alarms or open doors or do whatever else had happened in that short breath of time. What would I have to gain?

And why would I try to escape?

I'd spent over a century pining for my lost mate. He might not be the man I once knew, but he was still Cam. I had a responsibility now to save him and make him remember his own mind. Leaving would accomplish nothing.

He released my neck and tossed the scanner onto the bed beside us. "She's clean, Michael." Cam's hands went to my hips as he pulled me off him to land near the device on the mattress. I winced a little at the manhandling, but it was his tone that really snagged my attention.

Because he sounded unbelievably calm. It didn't match the darkness swirling in his gaze or the rigid way he moved as he stood.

Something is coming, my instincts whispered. *Something bad.*

"That doesn't make her innocent, my liege," Michael replied, his long face void of emotion. Either he was oblivious to the hostility simmering beneath Cam's serene facade, or he knew it wasn't meant for him.

I shivered. *Can I only sense it because of our bond?*

Cam had never been a very angry man, even when he'd been faced with Lilith's proposed changes for society. He'd always been strategic and composed, choosing to use words to deal with matters rather than fight.

But this version of him didn't seem opposed to the latter.

Unless I'm reading this entirely wrong, I thought.

"She could still be working with Damien," Michael went on. "I traced the interference to your laptop. It's quite possible he taught her how to reach him, or how to orchestrate the hack from inside the compound. She needs to be thoroughly interrogated."

"Is that why you took it upon yourself to begin questioning her?" Cam asked, that eerie calmness still prevalent in his words.

"I started questioning her when I found her wandering the stairwell with your laptop, my liege. She wasn't forthcoming."

"Perhaps because you chose violence first." Cam slid his hands into his slacks as he moved in front of my field of view, blocking Michael from my line of sight. "That is why you decided to crush her ankle, yes?"

Michael snorted. "She twisted it in the fall. I just applied a little pressure to get her to speak."

"And did it work?"

"No. She refused to give me anything, which further proves she's guilty. Or, at the very least, she's hiding something."

Well, he wasn't wrong there.

"So you think she's capable of using laptops and taking down our security system?" Cam pressed. "You think she's the one who released Sota and Troph?"

I stared at his back while I repeated those names in my

mind. They were two Blessed Ones. Fathers to Sahara and Lajos. *Is that who I saw in the video feed?*

"What would she have to gain by disrupting their lesson?" Cam added, his tone slipping just a little to reveal the darkness. "Are you suggesting she's here to dismantle the entire operation? That would imply she even knows what we're doing. Is it public knowledge?"

"Well, no, but——"

"Why would *my Erosita* choose to defy *me*, her liege?" He took a step forward. "Are you suggesting I've not properly trained her to serve me?"

"O-of course not, my——"

"So then again I ask, what would she gain in this situation, Michael? Why would she try to take down our operation?"

"Because she doesn't want to be replaced," Michael said quickly. "The whole purpose is to manufacture immortal blood bags. When that process is perfected, you won't need to tie yourself to her anymore."

My lips parted. *What? That's... that's what they're...? But... but how?*

I blinked, my mind quickly providing an answer with what Michael had just said—*by creating more Blessed Ones.*

Blessed Ones didn't require blood to survive, only their children did. And yet, Blessed Ones were immortal.

That made them the perfect food source for vampires.

Because they can't die.

And then... *then Cam will no longer* need *to tie himself to me.* His *Erosita.* His mate. His immortal source of blood, but with a spiritual tie.

Oh, fuck...

CAM

THE SHARP INTAKE OF AIR BEHIND ME TOLD ME EVERYTHING I needed to know. Still, I glanced over my shoulder to take in the shocked betrayal coloring my *Erosita's* features, mostly to ensure Michael could see it, too.

"Does her expression look like that of a woman who already knew of our intentions, Michael?" I asked flatly. "Because she certainly appears surprised to me."

Michael cleared his throat. "She could be acting."

I scoffed at that. "Doubtful." Those tears in her eyes were too genuine to be fake, something I only knew because of the way they tugged at my soul.

Which was ironically why I needed to cut ties with this human.

Ismerelda inspired irrational desires within me, such as the one still riding my spirit even now. The one that told me to *kill* Michael for touching my *Erosita*.

"You're... creating... and replacing..." Ismerelda trailed off, her eyelashes fluttering as she tried to harness her emotions.

I arched a brow, waiting to see if she'd try to say more. But my darling lioness had disappeared behind a cloud of doubt, the confident feline part of her no longer in control.

A shame, really.

I'd been incredibly intrigued by that part of her while using the scanner. She'd been bold and assertive, her gaze holding mine without flinching as she told me without words that she hadn't betrayed me.

Then a few careless words from Michael had chased the fierce lioness away, leaving the *swan* behind.

Such an intoxicating conundrum, I marveled, still staring at her. *This must be why I keep her—her complexity.*

Well, that and her delicious essence.

And maybe for sex, too. Although, I hadn't experienced that part yet.

Soon, I thought. *After I finish dealing with Michael.*

"So what other reason would she have to interfere in our plans?" I asked, refocusing on the male in question. "Because she clearly wasn't aware of our goal until you mentioned it."

Michael's green eyes narrowed slightly. "Her brother is a known player in the revolution, and he's technologically savvy."

"I'm aware," I drawled.

"And she"—he pointed at Ismerelda—"is his sister and has been living with a clan that's also known to be against our principles. It makes sense that she would help her brother try to take down our operations, regardless of our goals."

That was a much better reason to accuse her of

assisting her brother. *Except...* "We still don't know if Damien is the culprit."

"Whoever it is clearly wants to sabotage our work here, and the only ones with motive for that are members of your cousin's revolution." Michael folded his arms across his chest. "And these problems started after she arrived."

"While unconscious," I reminded him. "Which means she couldn't have hacked into anything to open a communication channel with her brother, yet he—or someone else—gained access to our systems during that time."

Michael's jaw ticked, but he didn't otherwise speak.

Which was good because I wasn't done.

"I used the scanner on her, and she's clean, thus disproving your theory that Damien implanted a chip, which he then in some way used to connect to our systems."

Michael still didn't comment, nor did he nod in acknowledgment. He merely stared, waiting for more.

"So even if Ismerelda somehow miraculously connected to Damien tonight, using my laptop, it still doesn't explain how someone hacked into our system initially," I went on. "Nor does it explain why she suddenly needed to help him tonight."

Because, again, there wasn't much motive other than wanting to dismantle our operations.

However, Ismerelda had to know that harming our goals would hurt her as well. She was mine. If I failed, she failed. It didn't make sense for her to try to fight me when I already owned her.

"Maybe she reached out to him tonight to provide an update and that's why the tracker led me to your laptop," Michael proposed.

"My laptop had no external communication abilities

due to the hacking issue," I pointed out. "Unless you're suggesting she knows a workaround that our entire technical team has failed to contrive?"

That seemed pretty fucking unlikely to me. I glanced back at her, curious to read her expression, and startled at the fierce gleam in her eyes.

The lioness is back and she's pissed, I marveled. *Excellent.*

"Do you know more about computers than you led me to believe?" I asked her.

"Are you going to replace me with an immortal blood bag?" she countered, apparently still stuck on that revelation.

"Not today," I told her. "Or anytime soon, given that Lilith failed me entirely."

She snorted at that, the noise one I strongly disliked. It was both rude and unacceptable.

I faced her fully. "Are you forgetting your place, *little swan?*" I took a step toward her. "Shall I force you to your knees and remind you of your purpose here?"

The feline danced angrily in her gaze, making me hard in an instant.

This female wasn't broken at all. She was full of fire and life, making her more intriguing by the second.

No wonder she's mine. A thousand years and she still looks at me like this? With all this passion and confidence?

And she'd proved to know when to bend, too. How to submit.

So exquisite.

I wanted to bite her. Master her. Make her mine and hear her *roar.*

"I know a little bit about computers, my liege," she said, startling me from my hungry thoughts. "Enough that, yes, I could log on after you showed me your password. But you had no connection to an external network, so even if

I'd wanted to send my brother a note, I wouldn't have been able to."

"So you admit to logging in to his laptop?" Michael pressed, interrupting the moment and forgetting his place in this room.

"I logged in to see if I could send an email just to let Damien know I was okay," Ismerelda replied, her gaze still on mine.

"Without my permission?"

She frowned. "You've always been okay with me talking to him before. I didn't realize I needed permission."

"Because you've yet to learn your role in this new world," Michael grumbled behind me.

Yes, speaking of roles…

I turned toward him once more.

Time to let my beast loose.

"Ismerelda is my *Erosita*, Michael. Not yours." I took a step in his direction. "I've already stated that *I* will be the one to handle her. Not you."

He shuffled backward. "Of course, my—"

"No," I cut in. "That response isn't acceptable, Michael. Because you've already demonstrated that you don't respect or understand my position."

I phased forward and grabbed him by the neck before he could try to reply, the force of my movement sending him back into the wall beside the door.

His eyes widened, his lips moving soundlessly as I squeezed. Unlike how I'd handled Ismerelda moments ago, I didn't bother controlling my strength with Michael. He deserved to feel my power, to realize whom he'd crossed with his careless actions.

"Ismerelda might be human and therefore beneath you in rank, but it isn't your job or your right to train her. She's *mine*. If I want her disciplined or interrogated,

I will handle it. Never you. Because *she is not yours to touch*."

I lifted him up against the wall, causing his legs to dangle.

"I warned you earlier to stay away from my *Erosita*, yet you left marks on her delicate skin. Bruises with your imprint. All because you felt it was your right to do so."

He started to shake his head, which only infuriated me more.

"I saw the imprint, Michael. There's no denying what you've done, nor is there an excuse for it. I made myself clear and you disobeyed me."

His hand came up over mine, his eyes beginning to water from the lack of oxygen. But there was also a lack of grief in his expression, no hint of remorse or a plea for leniency.

Instead, all I saw was rage. Likely because he couldn't believe I'd punish him over a human. It was belittling and cruel, but that arrogance was precisely why this needed to happen.

"She isn't just a human," I reminded him. "She's *my* human. My pet. My charge. That makes her superior in ways other mortals are not because *I am your king.* And you do not touch a king's property without permission."

I released him just before he would have passed out, his pained gasp echoing through the room as his knees gave out beneath him.

He crumpled to the floor and started coughing, his long blond hair covering his face.

"Do not touch her again, Michael. Or I will take away your immortal gift faster than you can blink."

I trapped his ankle under my leather shoe and pressed down with all my strength. He shrieked, the sound raspy and broken and nowhere near as loud as the snap of his bones.

But my inner beast wasn't satisfied.

I needed *more*.

He'd disobeyed me. Touched my female. *Marked her*.

I shattered his other ankle in the next breath, then leaned down to grab hold of his neck and opened my door with the other.

"Consider this your one and only warning, Michael. Do not disrespect me again by touching my property." I dropped him in the hallway and slammed the door.

It was that or end him.

Alas, he'd been particularly helpful these last few weeks while I'd awoken from my prolonged sleep. Thus, I was willing to give him this one chance.

Although, it would be short-lived if he so much as looked at Ismerelda again.

Running a hand down my shirt, I faced the female in question and found her feline gaze watching me intently.

There was a hint of something in her features that I couldn't quite define. Not fear or disgust, nor was it born of shock or surprise.

I tilted my head, curious. "You're not afraid." Not a question, but a statement. "But you're staring at me strangely. Why?"

She said nothing for a long moment, making me want to remind her of our roles here. But in a very different way from how I'd just put Michael in his place.

I took a step forward, ready to begin a new lesson, when she said, "You just reminded me of the night we first met."

"The night we first met?" I repeated, frowning.

Her lips curled a little. "Yes."

"How did we meet?" I wasn't sure why this mattered, but I found myself eager to know.

"You saved me from being gang-raped," she replied, shocking the hell out of me.

"I what?" My brow furrowed. "That doesn't sound like me at all." I wasn't a hero. I also usually avoided human interactions, leaving them up to their own devices whenever possible. "Why the hell did I do that?"

She laughed a little and shook her head. "Because you were hunting me and they were about to taint your intended meal."

"Oh." That sounded much more reasonable.

"But I wasn't afraid of you," she went on. "And that intrigued you."

I stared at her. *Of course. Because I saw the lioness in your gaze.* The same one I'd noticed tonight.

"I already knew about vampires because of my brother," she continued. "So I knew what you were, too. Or what I thought you were, anyway. Then I mentioned Ryder."

I moved closer to the bed while I listened, enthralled by this encounter I had no memory of.

"And that changed everything," she concluded.

"Because I didn't want to potentially harm another royal's property," I surmised, aware of how I would handle a similar situation now.

It didn't matter that I was older and therefore higher ranked in the bloodlines than Ryder. Altercations with other royals were time-consuming and bloody. I wouldn't have wanted to risk something like that over a meal.

"Yet I obviously kept you." I slid my hands into my pockets as I paused next to the bed, my thighs a mere inch away from the mattress. "So what happened next?"

"I told you about my connection to Damien and Ryder.

And then I begged you to bite me." Her cheeks reddened a bit with her words. "I wanted to know how it would feel."

"And I obliged you?"

She snorted, the sound irking me less than before. "Barely. I think you took two pulls from my vein before you insisted that I drink from you to cure myself."

"Why would I do that?"

She shrugged. "Because you were terrified of injuring me."

"I see." I must have been afraid of repercussions from Ryder. He'd turned her brother, making her essentially a relative to his family tree. He would have been quite protective of her.

Hell, he probably still was despite her being mine.

"Then you stayed with me for months while we waited for Ryder and Damien to return. It was a time before technology existed, so we didn't have much choice."

"I stayed with you?" That was surprising. Perhaps I'd wanted to discuss something with Ryder.

"You did. And we kept exchanging blood, which led to other things." Her light green eyes danced with intimate knowledge. "And you eventually claimed me."

"Before Ryder and Damien returned?" I guessed.

"Yes. About three weeks before they came back for a visit."

"How did they react?" Because I could imagine that Ryder had not been pleased.

"Like overprotective big brothers," she muttered. "They still act that way."

Which implies that killing her in front of them would be a suitable punishment for everything they've done.

Of course, that might hurt me as well.

Hmm, I'd have to revisit that notion later. Preferably *after* I'd properly enjoyed Ismerelda.

I admired her bare breasts before taking in her svelte waist and continuing on down to her shapely thighs. My blood had healed her quickly, just as it should, leaving behind a refreshed female, waiting to be ravaged.

But how should I take her first? I pondered, my inner beast purring with malicious intent. She hadn't imbibed much of my essence, but she had enough running through her to keep up with my demands.

Hopefully, anyway.

She swallowed, drawing my attention to her delicate throat and back up to her eyes. The dilation of her pupils confirmed that she could sense my mounting hunger. And the sweet scent of fear-induced arousal told me she anticipated it, too.

I'd told her what to expect when I returned for her. It just happened to be sooner than I'd expected, with a slight detour involving a disobedient progeny.

He touched her, I thought, furious all over again. *He touched* my *female.*

Well, now I would just erase him entirely.

Repossess every inch of her, inside and out.

Fuck her until she couldn't walk.

Make her scream for hours on end until she was hoarse.

I wanted to taste her tears. Revel in her pleasure. Force her to come for me even when she no longer could.

And then I wanted to destroy her.

Fill her with my very being and ensure she could never be touched by another again.

Only to do it all over again until she suffocated on my cock, drowned in my seed, and awoke with me buried inside her. Fucking her. Taking her. *Claiming* her.

It was a visceral need that I allowed her to see in my

expression, the predator within me ready to take on his desired prey.

This would hurt.

Because I had no intention of holding back.

"Up on all fours, Ismerelda," I told her, ready to begin. "And you'd better be wet for me. Because ready or not, I'm going to take what's mine. Right fucking now."

The jarring change in conversation and tone didn't seem to affect Ismerelda. Because she simply obeyed, presenting me with the alluring view of her shapely ass as she balanced on her hands and knees.

I admired her from behind while I unbuttoned my shirt, my mouth salivating for a taste of her. My cock, too.

The fabric whispered across my torso as I pulled it from my shoulders and allowed it to drop to the floor. My shoes were next, then my belt, but I paused when I reached the button on my trousers.

Something isn't right.

The position was perfect and exactly what I desired. She smelled exquisite—like fear-induced lust. The glimpse of her pussy told me she was glistening for me, too.

Yet there was a strange pull in my gut that held me back from removing my pants.

It didn't make sense. My beast was practically panting for her, my cock hard and ready, but that sense of wrongness nagged at my instincts.

I took a step to the side, taking in her body from a new angle.

Her tits were firm and full, waiting for me to grab on to them. Those nipples were ripe and rosy, too.

Definitely turned on. So very different from the first time I'd demanded that she take this position. Which was good because I wanted her eager to be fucked. Eager to be mine. Eager for my *bite*.

I kept moving, circling her as a predator should, and paused when I reached the opposite side of the bed.

Her eyes.

That was what I needed.

Those beautiful green irises, so feline in nature and filled with calculative intent. Almost as though she knew something I didn't. Some sort of secret.

No, not a secret.

A *challenge.*

One her gaze told me she fully intended to win. Only, I didn't know what game we were playing. But I was intrigued to find out.

"Come here and take my pants off," I told her, wanting her eyes on me almost as much as her hands.

She crawled forward and sat back on her heels with her knees slightly spread. I admired her thighs and the hint of her shaved mound before shifting my attention up her flat stomach to her tits.

And ended my perusal with those addictive irises.

I felt hypnotized by her, utterly enchanted by the cunning glimmer lurking in those emerald depths.

How did I miss this earlier? I wondered, enthralled by her gaze now. Not even her fingers on my trousers could distract me. *So enchanting…*

This was why the *Erosita* bond was dangerous. Why it had to be destroyed. It weakened even the oldest of beings, including me.

But Ismerelda wouldn't win this match between us.

I'd remind her of her place—*beneath me.* And I'd stare into those alluring eyes while I did it.

The sound of my zipper inching downward sent blood rushing to my groin, making me impossibly harder for the female before me.

Definitely dangerous. Addictive, too.

I hadn't been able to touch another woman since waking. Ismerelda was the only one I craved. And it wasn't for a lack of offerings underground. I had an entire buffet of blood virgins to pick from, and not one of them had appealed to me the way Ismerelda did right now.

Part of it was our link. But I suspected it went much deeper than that. I'd chosen this female for a reason. And I couldn't wait to find out why.

She inched forward, her hands on the sides of my pants as she pushed them down to my thighs, revealing my throbbing cock to her view. Yet her eyes remained on mine, her athletic form moving to the floor to kneel at my feet while she worked.

Fuck.

The sight of her kneeling before me like this was far more appealing than her being on all fours, primarily because I could see her face. Her expression. *And those incredible eyes.*

It was as though I'd been drugged, my obsession with her heightening by the second. The cure was simple— fuck her.

But I didn't want to rush it. I wanted to savor this. Indulge in my cravings to the fullest. *Finally feel alive.*

The anticipation was unexpected but welcome. As was Ismerelda's soft touch against my lower limbs while she pulled my dress pants away, along with my socks.

My focus went to her mouth, causing me to visualize those plump, damp lips wrapped around my shaft. She'd suck me deep while staring me down with those catlike irises. *Yes. Yes, I want that.*

However, I also wanted to taste her. Properly this time. Not just a bite, but a thorough sampling.

We have the rest of the night and all day, I thought, my hand finding her head to pet her soft hair. *There's no need to expedite anything. I can fuck her to my heart's content in every way imaginable.*

And I never had to stop.

She was mine.

My toy.

My eternal source of blood.

My *Erosita*.

"You still owe me dessert," I told her, deciding that was the best place for us to start. "I want to devour you until you can't walk." And in return, I'd give her something to swallow. "Get back up on the bed, little lioness. I want you to straddle my face."

IZZY

My THIGHS CLENCHED, MY BLOOD HEATING IN MY VEINS AS I absorbed Cam's words.

"I want you to straddle my face."

In all our time together, Cam had never said anything like that to me before. I hadn't even realized I'd like it until he'd uttered the command.

Now I couldn't stop repeating it in my head as he slid onto the bed. His muscles flexed as he moved, providing me with an alluring display of athletic man.

So much strength and prowess.

So much beauty.

So much *lethality*.

And he wanted me to press the most delicate part of me to the most brutal part of him.

I swallowed.

He absolutely intended to bite me again. I could see it in his hungry expression as he positioned his head against the pillows.

Will he make this hurt? Leave me to heal on my own again?

"I want to devour you until you can't walk," he'd said.

A shiver traversed my spine. *How far would he take this?*

Would it be enough for me to find a way to break down the mental barriers between our minds? I doubted it.

But what choice did I have?

He plans to replace me. My eyes narrowed. *Because that's what Lilith programmed him to do.*

Well, I would just reprogram him and make him remember me. Even if it hurt to do so.

I stood and placed my knee on the bed, my gaze holding his. *You're going to be mine again. I vow it.*

His lips twitched at the edges, almost as though he found my thoughts amusing. If only he could actually hear what I had to say, I'd completely blow his mind.

Which was why I had to do this—to try to break down the barriers between us, to find a moment of weakness in the throes of passion and force my way through.

His expression told me it wouldn't be that easy, the predator already preparing his battle against me when he didn't even know what fight we were about to experience.

He could easily destroy me. I knew that. But I refused to accept his current state. My Cam existed somewhere inside this man, and nothing would stop me from finding him.

His gaze lazily tracked my movements as I crawled toward him on the bed. I felt very much like stalked prey, fully aware that I was about to be *devoured* by a vampire with sharp teeth.

My pulse sped up with every inch forward, my palms

slick with sweat. I couldn't tell if I was aroused or afraid or some crazy combination of both.

I paused beside him, determining the best way to straddle him.

One perfect eyebrow inched upward as he said, "Nervous, *little swan?*"

That endearment had always sounded sweet on his lips, yet somehow this version of him made it resemble an insult.

Or maybe he meant it as a challenge.

I grabbed the headboard above him and started to move, but his hands on my hips stopped me. "Other way, Ismerelda. You're going to suck my cock while I drink from your pussy."

My hands landed on the bed on either side of him as he pulled my lower half upward. I automatically spread my knees over him, the pillows cushioning my stance. But none of that paused the erratic thudding of my heart.

Cam had never handled me like this.

He'd always given me time to acclimate, to be comfortable, to—

His tongue traced the seam of my sex, causing me to jolt in surprise. "Fucking delicious," he murmured, making my knees weak.

This was like being with a new man. Someone I'd never met before. *A stranger.*

Does it count as cheating? I marveled, stunned above him. *No. It's still Cam. Just… not the version I know.*

"Hmm, maybe you really are a swan." The words were a breath against my clit as he forced my legs to part even more, making me well and truly straddle his mouth. "A lioness would be sucking my cock by now."

He palmed my ass and slowly ran his fingers up my spine.

"Shall I guide you?" His low tone held a subtle taunt to it that felt even more threatening with his mouth being so close to my intimate flesh. "Is that what you need?"

My fingers dug into the bedding on either side of his abdomen as his touch continued to drift upward toward my shoulder blades.

This isn't new, I told myself. *We've done this before.*

Only, I'd trusted Cam not to hurt me then. Now... now, I wasn't so sure.

However, something about that excited me. Maybe because it felt so fresh and new. The uncertainty of our situation lit a fire within me, made me want to experience this new side of Cam and embrace his darkness.

To be treated as someone strong, not delicate.

To be an equal.

A crazy notion, given his age and supernatural existence, but here—in the bedroom—I could hold my own. I could bring this *king* to his knees.

Because he was actually allowing it, not dictating our pace or ensuring I felt okay every step of the way. This version of Cam told me what he wanted and didn't mince words.

I found his directness almost comforting, even while terrifying.

He wants my mouth on him, I thought as his palm reached my nape. *I can do that.*

And I would blow his mind wide open in the process.

I leaned down before he could force me to move, my lips grazing the tip of his thick length before drawing my tongue all the way to the base.

His body flexed beneath mine, his fingers clamping down around my neck as he growled against my pulsing center. *"More."*

I grinned, the need in that single word emboldening my confidence.

This I knew how to do.

Because while Cam might not be himself right now, his body was one I'd mastered thousands of times before. And it'd been over a century since he'd experienced my touch, my tongue, my *teeth*.

I nibbled his hard flesh, drawing a hiss from him—one I felt right against my sensitive nub. His grasp tightened even more, his anticipation fueling my movements and desire. I could feel myself dripping into his mouth, my body ready for more despite the pleasure he'd inflicted upon me not hours ago.

It'd been so long. *So, so long.*

This might not be the reunion I'd craved and fantasized about, but that didn't stop my body from reacting to its mate.

My Cam.

I drew my teeth along his shaft, back to the head, and licked the precum waiting for me there. His taste was familiar, his groan even more so.

From this angle, I couldn't see the cruelty lurking in his gaze or the foreign expressions on his too-beautiful face. So I imagined the looks I knew and adored, the ones that told me I belonged to him, forever and always, no matter what.

That devotion stoked the fire within me, making my thighs clench around him. He hadn't bitten me yet, just continued to breathe against my soaked skin, teasing me with the promise of more.

I took him into my mouth, deciding to up the ante in this game. Cam's resulting curse vibrated my slick folds, making me moan against his hard length as I swallowed him deep into the back of my throat.

Yes, I thought, reveling in the natural motion, one I'd done so many times before.

Cam had always fit me perfectly. Or maybe he'd simply taught my body to accept his. Regardless, I knew this— knew *him.*

And I proved it with each stroke of my tongue.

"*Fuck,* Ismerelda." His fingers knotted painfully in my hair, his opposite hand going to my ass as his mouth sealed over my clit.

I gasped around his thickness, my body jumping in response to his hot kiss. I'd been anticipating it, but it was nothing compared to *feeling* it.

He didn't hold back, suckling on me as though I were his own personal dessert. It was rougher than usual, *intense,* and punctuated by the threat of his fangs.

His grip tightened even more in my hair as he forced me to take him deeper, his eagerness and need palpable. There was no care here. No concern over hurting me. Just pure, unadulterated *lust.*

This was the side of Cam that he'd hidden from me, the monster inside he'd worried would hurt me.

Unleashing that cruel part of him should have terrified me, but all I could do was embrace it. Embrace *him.*

I allowed him to shove me down on his cock, taking him past the point of comfort and trying not to gag around his hardness.

Being at his mercy felt… natural.

Like we'd always been meant to fit this way, for me to give him control and follow his lead.

Yet this was unlike anything we'd ever done before, that feeling of newness stirring a tingling sensation deep within me.

A tingling sensation that Cam deepened with every swipe of his tongue.

My thigh muscles went taut, my focus dividing between pleasuring him and the rapture he was unleashing upon me.

"You're addicting, little lioness." His words reverberated against my center, sending a pulsing throb through my veins.

How am I already close? I marveled.

Then I remembered his blood.

Oh, God…

Vampire blood amped up human senses, making mortals ultrasensitive to *everything*. No wonder I was on fire for him. It wasn't just how long it'd been since I'd last experienced this, but how primed and ready my body was to explode for him.

"I'm going to spend all night fucking your mouth." He drove upward to punctuate his point, causing me to nearly gag around him. "Then I'm going to take your cunt." His fist tightened, pulling my hair sharply at the ends. "And after that, your ass."

He nipped at my clit, stirring a yelp from me—one that came out muffled against his hot arousal and silenced as he thrust deep again.

"Every part of you belongs to me," he panted, his hips lifting off the bed as he forced my head down, fucking my mouth just like he'd said.

I relaxed my throat as best I could, determined to take him, to tempt him into falling apart. Because I knew how fragile his mind became in the throes of climax, how open our connection could be.

Come back to me, Cam, I whispered to him. *Fall apart for me and remember me.*

His teeth skimmed my core. "You'd better swallow, Ismerelda," he purred. "Even while you scream."

He barely gave me a second to breathe before his fangs

sank into my delicate flesh, sending me spiraling into an orgasm headfirst as his cock jerked in my mouth.

Oh, God, I'm... I'm going to... to drown...

There was nothing compassionate about this. It was animalistic. Fierce. *Violent.* Because he kept driving into my mouth as he came, leaving me with no choice but to swallow while ecstasy stole my vision and thoughts.

I couldn't do anything other than take it, riding a high unlike anything I'd ever experienced before. Because this... this was not us. Not what we did. Not how we made love.

This is how his beast fucks.

The predator I've never truly met.

The vampire deep within his soul.

My lungs screamed as I continued to swallow, air nonexistent. There was no way to inhale, his head suffocating my throat with each punishing stroke. His hand held my head as his hips shot upward, my eyes pooling with tears.

I was blind.

Lost in a cloud of oblivion.

And drowning in a sea of sin.

Cam, I breathed, trying desperately to get through the wall between us. But it was too thick, too impenetrable.

This isn't... We don't usually... I sputtered, only to be forced to swallow more.

He was still coming.

As was I, his fangs lodged deep into my flesh and demanding that I submit to *more.* Another climax. Deeper penetration. No oxygen.

My vision swam.

My lungs burned.

My stomach convulsed as rapture seduced my very being.

Nothing made sense, my control having fled the

moment he'd taken charge. I was merely a toy. A being for him to fuck. To use. And he was an animal releasing over a century's worth of *need*.

I gasped as my back hit the mattress, my world having shifted unexpectedly. My chest immediately wept with glee at the newfound life source, my throat greedily working over each harsh inhale. But then everything shifted once more, my head going upside down…

No, not upside down. Not quite.

Just over the side of the mattress.

I don't…

Cam's cock nudged my mouth again, wedging inside and shortening my breaths once more.

Fuck… He had me hanging over the side of the bed, his feet on the floor as he fucked my mouth with renewed vigor.

I choked, the angle too much, my body not ready yet for more.

But there was no stopping him, not even my nails biting into his thighs—something I hadn't realized I was doing until now. If anything, that only made him more aggressive, his voice trailing over me as he uttered everything he wanted to do to me.

"You're going to swallow more," he told me. "So much more." His mouth was on my sex again, causing me to squirm in protest, my insides not ready. "And so am I." His fangs bit into me again, sending me spiraling into a deep pool of obscurity.

It… it felt good.

It hurt.

It was too much.

Yet not.

His blood, I thought deliriously. *His blood is curing me even while he's killing me.*

It kept me conscious. Aware. Torturing me with licks of extreme gratification followed by exquisite agony.

I tried to say his name, to beg him for a minute to recover, but it came out garbled around his long length, his head lodging deeply in my throat with each punch of his hips.

This would kill a normal human, I thought. *Or at least shatter something inside them.*

But I... I wasn't a normal human. My soul was tied to an ancient being, and that ancient being had given me some of his essence an hour or so ago.

That tainted everything.

Made me more durable.

However, that didn't stop it from hurting.

It didn't stop me from being afraid, worried about what terrible ways this male could truly harm me. *He's not my Cam even if he is my Cam.* It was a drugging notion, one that left me dizzy as his cock began to spasm again.

Already? I marveled. *Or has that much time passed?*

I couldn't keep track of our movements, my mind lost in an orgasmic cloud. Still, I tried to swallow. Or I thought I did. My body didn't have much choice. It was that or drown in his seed.

Cam...

Still nothing—that wall... it was... *never going to be breached.*

I'd spent over a hundred years trying to get through, to talk to my mate. But nothing had worked.

Not even this.

A tear escaped my eye, this one born of emotional pain rather than physical. However, it disappeared among the others, my face a mess from crying while he used my mouth like it was an endless hole, heedless of the fact that I needed it to *breathe.*

My limbs felt numb from the lack of oxygen. Or perhaps from his violent drinking.

Can I bleed out this way? I wondered. He wasn't feeding from my artery, but he was certainly taking his fill from between my thighs.

I could no longer feel my clit.

A blessing, I supposed.

Except that this was Cam. The love of my existence. The one who was supposed to protect me. Cherish me. Make me feel like a queen.

But there was nothing *queenly* about this.

He's killing me again. Would his blood allow that? Or would this take me to the brink and force me into a harsh recovery while awake?

I shuddered at the thought, my eyes falling closed and envisioning the morbid possibility.

Everything felt cold. Overwhelming. *It hurts.*

My lungs resembled ice, the air trickling through sharp spikes of pain that had me wincing with each inhale. Then something warm touched my throat.

Cam's coming again? I guessed, disoriented and bordering on broken.

I'd wanted to find a way into his mind. Instead, he'd simply fucked with mine. Making me think it would be that easy to inspire his memories of me, pull *my* Cam out of whatever pit Lilith had buried him in.

I was wrong. So, so wrong.

Maybe it was seeing him hurt Michael that had inspired my confidence. He'd stood up for me in a way, shown his possessive side for just long enough to spark a hint of optimism in my heart.

But that optimism was gone now.

Lost in the sea with my dignity.

I'd find it again, assuming I survived.

The numbness had taken over entirely, cascading me into a world of darkness. *Yes, he's definitely killing me.* I had maybe a few more minutes left before the end.

Then I'd wake up.

Just to experience this hell again...

CAM

"YOU ARE EXQUISITE," I MURMURED, MY FINGERS BRUSHING through Ismerelda's hair while I held my opposite hand near her mouth, my open wrist pressed against her lips.

She couldn't hear me, mostly because I'd coaxed her into a sleeplike state to aid her in her healing.

I wasn't sure why I'd felt compelled to do that, but it seemed right. Ismerelda didn't deserve to suffer, especially after the immense pleasure she'd just bestowed upon my being.

There was also the benefit of her recovering faster so we could continue fucking—which was the reason I kept telling myself to console the part of me that worried about being too easy on my *Erosita*.

She was mine for a reason.

Ensuring her thorough rehabilitation made sense, as it

benefited me. The healthier my *Erosita*, the more I could play with her.

That it also made me feel good to heal her was neither here nor there.

"I should have given you a minute to catch up," I admitted, analyzing our initial reunion and determining where I'd made an error. "It's been a while since I last fucked a human. Obviously. And I forgot how vulnerable your kind can be."

Had Ismerelda been truly mortal, I would have killed her with some of those thrusts, either by breaking her neck accidentally or making her suffocate on my cock.

I'd done it several times, long ago in my youth. Before I'd learned how to harness my strength.

But it'd been too long since I'd experienced the pleasures of a female, of *my* female, and the control I'd had over my beast had snapped the moment I'd entered her mouth. I'd needed to brand her from the inside out, pour my essence inside her and demand that she take everything I had to give.

Which she had.

"Because you're perfect," I mused aloud. "That's why I've kept you." The fact that she could handle my brand of brutality again and again. "A true lioness."

I pulled my wrist away from her mouth, certain that I'd given her more than enough blood to speed along her recovery.

"Sleep," I murmured, my command lulling her into a deeper state of unconsciousness.

I'd purposely kept her on the edge of awareness to ensure she'd swallow my essence without choking, but now I wanted her to truly rest.

At least until my blood did its job.

After that, I'd fuck her again.

And again.

Until she couldn't walk.

Sliding from the mess of blankets, I wandered over to the kitchen area to pour myself a drink. The red wine lacked Ismerelda's special touch, causing me to glance back at her on the bed.

I'd manufactured a room just for her, and yet I had no desire to demand that she use it. Strange how a day could change my perspective. But she looked good in my sheets, her blonde hair strewn over the black fabric, her creamy complexion blushing with the effects of my blood.

Mmm, good enough to eat, I thought, admiring her exposed breasts. *Heal faster, little lioness. I'm hungry for—*

A knock echoed through the living space, the source coming from my front door.

My lips curled down at the intrusion. I'd been very clear with Michael—*no disruptions.* So either my progeny possessed a death wish or someone else had decided to brave my presence.

Setting my wine down, I wandered back toward the bed to retrieve my boxers from the floor and put them on. Then I pulled the blanket up over Ismerelda's breasts, not wanting anyone else to enjoy the view.

As I started toward the door, my nose twitched with the familiar scent of the female waiting in the hallway.

Not Michael.

But I wasn't sure if the intruder lingering was much better.

I opened the door to reveal Mira. My eyebrow arched in question, my mouth flat. I'd told her not to follow up with me until she had a new security plan in place to guarantee that the Blessed Ones couldn't escape.

And I highly doubted that plan was already enacted.

I leaned against the door and folded my arms, my stance making it clear that Mira wasn't invited inside.

"I'm sorry to bother you, my liege," she began. "But we need to discuss the meeting Lilith scheduled. It's in three days, and, to be blunt, my king, we're not ready to address the alliance. Not with all the security issues and connectivity problems."

Well, at least she'd gotten straight to the point of this interruption. "I assume you have a suggestion?"

"I do, yes. I think you should pre-record an announcement regarding your return and let the alliance know we're rescheduling the meeting to next week. I'll personally take that message to Lilith City, where it can be disseminated to the alliance."

"I see." I considered her for a moment, her logic not quite computing in my mind. "Is there a plan in place to fix our current security concerns?"

Because I highly doubted that had been accomplished in the last few hours.

Hell, they probably hadn't even finished catching everyone who had escaped during the blackout. And even if they had completed that part, they would still be busy trying to resecure them all.

Mira's jaw ticked. "No, my liege. There are no protocols in place for this failure, as it wasn't anticipated by the previous management."

"You mean Lilith."

"Yes." A blunt response, one tinged with a hint of annoyance.

Probably because I'd tasked Mira with cleaning up the other female's mess.

Or perhaps she was just as irritated by Lilith's failings as I was.

"But that's why I'm suggesting we postpone the

meeting," she continued. "Given everything I've witnessed downstairs, we're not ready to address the alliance."

Normally, I would point out that it wasn't her place to make that decision. But in this case, I happened to agree with her. And I appreciated her frank assessment.

However, I disagreed with one point. "Why do you need to go to Lilith City to disseminate the message? Surely you could work with Helias, Sofia, or Hazel, yes?"

All their regions bordered former-day Italy, making them much closer than Lilith City, previously known as Chicago.

She appeared thoughtful for a moment, then nodded. "Yes, I suppose I could." She uttered the words slowly, causing me to arch a brow.

"You sound uncertain."

She shrugged one slender shoulder. "I've spent over a century playing a role as Luka's obedient mate. It didn't really occur to me that I could venture into another royal's territory on your behalf, or that I could allow my real identity to become known."

Hmm, I thought. "They all think you're just a normal lycan."

"They do, yes." She frowned. "Although, word of my true nature is likely being spread now that Jace and Darius uncovered my secret."

"Another one of Lilith's security failings," I muttered, thinking of how easily Jace and his new *Erosita* had breached the security protocols in the various bunkers.

Of course, Damien had been helping them. But he'd primarily succeeded because he'd been able to hack into Lilith's phone.

Which suggested her protocols hadn't been all that robust.

Or he's just that good.

Regardless, it confirmed that Lilith's operations had weaknesses.

And I did not like weaknesses.

However, given that there hadn't been much I could do about her failings, I'd opted to use the situation to my advantage and had allowed Jace's curiosity to play out. I'd hoped it would help him understand our purpose here, perhaps sway him to our side.

Except he'd allowed *Calina*, his *Erosita*, to direct their search.

The female had mainly focused on her origin story— the one that informed her she'd been the product of Michael's sperm and Mira's egg, thus making her a unique breed of immortal human.

Too bad Lilith hadn't been able to replicate that experiment in other trials.

Something about the golden-blood female surrogate had been key in birthing Calina.

Alas, my brethren had killed all the remaining golden-blood mortals in the world. The only humans left with a similar genetic disposition were the blood virgins.

Tasty, yes.

Appropriate candidates to birth immortals, no.

Hence the reason we'd moved on to the Blessed Ones.

"If I go above ground, I may be able to connect to a satellite and open up communications with one of the nearby royals. Would you like me to do that?" Mira asked.

"Which royal would you contact?" I queried, curious as to who she would deem as *trustworthy* in this situation. I had my own opinions based on Lilith's logs, but Mira might have a refreshing perspective.

"Helias," she responded without hesitation. "He'll appreciate the stroke to his ego."

"And Hazel?" I pressed.

"Hazel has never approved of Lilith's reign," Mira replied. "I wouldn't trust her with this."

"What about Sofia?"

"She's an unknown. Similar to Khalid and Naomi."

I nodded. That matched my understanding of Lilith's reports. Of course, I would need to meet with all of the other royals to properly evaluate their loyalty. Only Kylan's, Ryder's, and Jace's allegiances were truly known, their ties to the revolutionary mindset absolute.

The lycans would require another evaluation entirely.

Including the one in front of me, I mused, my gaze roaming over Mira's athletic form. Rather than comment, I pushed away from the door and stepped inside, leaving the entryway open for her to follow.

She'd proved to be somewhat useful, her outlook and approach rivaling mine. *Perhaps I'll test her a bit more,* I thought, wandering into my kitchen to pour myself another glass of red wine. It was the brand Ismerelda had claimed I'd like, and, well, she wasn't wrong. It had a nice smoky undercurrent that I favored.

Although, it was nothing compared to her blood. That was a different flavor entirely. *Sweet. Intoxicating. Mine.*

Sighing, I brought the glass to my lips and glanced at the alluring blonde on my bed. Her even breathing told me she was still resting, but I sensed a slight change in her heartbeat, one that suggested she was on the edge of stirring.

Good. We can continue where we left off.

But, in the interim, I'd play a game with the lycan standing in my living area.

"Have you prepared a speech for me?" I asked her, referring to the message she'd proposed we disseminate to the alliance.

Mira's light eyebrows pulled down, her icy eyes

narrowing. "No. I only came up to voice my suggestion, my liege. I would never presume to speak on your behalf."

Hmm. "Indeed," I murmured. "However, Lilith would."

The lycan bristled at that. "I'm not Lilith."

"No, you're most certainly not Lilith." I took another sip of my wine, my gaze holding the lycan's as I considered our current situation and her potential worth.

Thus far, she'd proved herself useful. She'd kept my *Erosita* safe and had delivered her upon my request. Mira had also managed to keep her allegiance a secret for over a hundred years, feeding Lilith worthy details of the growing rebellion while maintaining her position without fail.

And now she stood quietly in my living area, awaiting direction like a good little soldier.

Yet I could see the calculating glint in her icy gaze.

Something about her itched at my instincts, making it difficult to trust her despite all the favorable evidence indicating her unquestionable loyalty.

Hmm. How truthful will she be with me? Will she be direct or play word games?

Only one way to find out...

CAM

"Give me your frank assessment of the operation here and what you would do differently." I voiced the words as a demand, not a request.

Mira didn't react to my slight change in subject, her expression instead turning thoughtful. "Well, the infrastructure is solid."

I arched a brow. "Meaning?"

"Meaning it was smart to build all the research tunnels under the catacombs. Not only is this considered neutral territory, but it's also sacred. No one would think to look here. And, even if they did, it would be difficult to physically break in without anyone noticing."

"True," I agreed. It was a strategic location, but also a meaningful one since it was where all the Blessed Ones rested. But we weren't here to celebrate their eternal sleep. We were here to ensure our eternal existence.

Still, it was a symbolic location, one founded in power.

Thus, it made sense for us to make this our research headquarters.

"That all said, Lilith employed human Vigils." Mira voiced the statement with a hint of annoyance.

I sipped my wine, waiting for her to continue while the predator within me monitored the heart rate of the *human* in the room.

Ismerelda's pulse had escalated just a tad bit more, confirming that I'd been right about her beginning to stir. I could compel her to continue sleeping, but I wanted her aware sooner rather than later.

Because—awake or not—I fully intended to fuck her the moment Mira left the room.

I made a gesture for Mira to continue, eager to hear her full assessment. Quickly, preferably, as I had more intriguing plans to get to.

Mira gave me a look that told me she thought her statement should be more obvious. And while it was, I wanted her to explain it anyway.

"I understand using the Vigil position to give mortals a competitive goal to reach for," she stated slowly. "But humans are too fragile to use as guards at the bunkers and here in the heart of our operation."

Rather than agree, I simply finished my wine.

"Additionally, the enterprise is too technology dependent," she added. "As we're finding out, that technology can be easily manipulated. It can also reveal too much. I mean, every facet of the infrastructure is being recorded in video logs. What if Damien has accessed those?"

"We still don't know it's Damien," I reminded her.

"It's Damien," she replied, her tone confident. "I'm sure of it. But *who* it is doesn't actually matter. The heart of the issue here is how reliant our security is on the technology to function correctly. And how reliant we are on *humans* to guard appropriately. It's a huge shortcoming that needs to be overhauled."

Hmm. Definitely a logical assessment. And frank, too.

"So what would you suggest, Mira?"

"Lessening the surveillance, for one," she responded immediately. "Monitoring the blood virgins makes sense. Monitoring our experiments on the Blessed Ones does not. That's a secret we don't want to let out too soon. So why are we recording it? Why make ourselves vulnerable in that way?"

"Because Lilith documented everything." Primarily to keep me apprised when I awoke, but Mira certainly had a point about the vulnerability of relying on technology to safeguard our secrets.

"Maybe she shouldn't have documented everything," Mira muttered. "If those videos of what she was doing to the lycans get out…"

I nodded, aware of what she meant. "It will make for a very stressful meeting with the alliance."

Of course, Jace and Darius had already seen some of those recordings. It would only be a matter of time before they shared them with others, something that would likely lead to further rebellion.

Unless I could convince them to support our cause, anyway.

A feat that will require some persuasion.

Fortunately, most of my vampire brethren wouldn't care about the lycan experiments. The wolves, however, would absolutely care. And they would be furious.

Which would result in a need to remind the lycans of their place in our supernatural hierarchy.

"You asked me for my assessment and what I would

do." Mira locked her gaze with mine. "I would lessen the surveillance, specifically around our more sensitive experiments. I would stop relying solely on technology to provide security. And I would bring in additional trusted supernatural resources to help guard the facilities."

Those were all good ideas, except... "That last point won't be easy to do until we properly vet our allies."

She inclined her head in agreement. "Yes. And to acquire those allies, we need to present them with positive findings."

"Which we don't have."

Another dip of the chin from the lycan. "Unfortunately, I don't think that's going to change in the next few days. We also can't wake Fen until we have a suitable cell to put him in—one that has a real door, not one that's controlled by unsecure technology."

I agreed with everything she was saying, but rather than show it, I moved into my kitchen to set my empty wine glass in the sink.

"All of this is why I recommend postponing the meeting. We need a stronger presentation for the alliance, my liege. One that will help explain some of Lilith's more unsavory experiments."

"Like the lycan trials," I translated.

"Yes." A blunt response, yet that single word held a hint of disgust. "We need something to show them, something that will validate our efforts here."

"Something that they can support, even at the cost of lycan lives," I translated. "Yes, I agree."

"Then you agree a video message should be disseminated?"

"I don't think a video is required. A simple written communication should suffice." It would inspire curiosity and fear, two emotions that would suit well for my reunion with the alliance. "Just send out a notice that the meeting has been postponed a week. That'll give us ten days to resolve our issues here. Unless you think we need more time?"

"Ten days should be sufficient to bolster our operations, but I doubt we'll have a viable solution to the human immortality issue by then. However, it'll give us time to present our findings in a more constructive manner."

"Or we won't present them at all," I countered. "The meeting's focus will be on my awakening and return to power. I could simply state that I'm still reviewing Lilith's work in my absence and will present her efforts at a later date."

"And how would you handle the rebels, like Ryder and Jace?"

I smiled. "I've been handling my cousin for millennia. As for Ryder…" I glanced at Ismerelda. "I suspect his relationship with my *Erosita's* brother will provide me with an edge where he's concerned."

The female on the bed didn't move or respond, but her heart rate had escalated a little more over the last few minutes, confirming that she was on the edge of waking.

Time to go, I thought as I returned my focus to Mira. "Is there anything else you wish to discuss?"

She considered me for a moment, her gaze telling me there were several items on her mind. However, she smartly shook her head. "No, my liege. I'll wait for your communication, then I'll arrange a visit with Prince Helias."

"Good. I'll draft something for you by midnight. Plan to leave then." That would give her half a day to make arrangements while I reacquainted myself with my *Erosita*.

An announcement regarding a date change wouldn't take much thought to prepare.

Which meant I could spend most of the day fucking Ismerelda.

"As for our procedures here, kill the live feeds monitoring the Blessed Ones, and reallocate our vampire guards to protect our assets. The Vigils can watch over the blood virgins and ensure they stay in line. Just keep a few of our kind in place to oversee the operation."

It wasn't a perfect solution, as we didn't have many vampire guards, but it would have to suffice for now.

I started toward the bed, dismissing Mira without another word. Only, the lycan lingered near the doorway, her scent irritating my inner predator. Mostly because I wasn't in the mood for an audience. I wanted to play with my *Erosita* in private.

"Yes?" I asked, pausing next to the beauty tucked beneath my covers.

"I have… a query." The curiosity coloring Mira's tone had me rotating partially toward her, my eyebrow inching upward in silent interest. "Our operation's goal is to create immortal blood toys who can replace the *Erosita* bond. And I know you spent some time with the potential candidates —the blood virgins—shortly after awakening."

I leaned against the post of my bed, waiting for her to get to her supposed *query*.

"So now that you've reacquainted yourself with your *Erosita*…" She trailed off, her focus shifting from me to the blonde on the bed. Perhaps because she'd heard the slight intake of air like I just had—a tell that confirmed Ismerelda was either awake or beginning to stir to awareness.

About time, I thought, her pulse having been steady for what felt like an hour now.

Mira cleared her throat. "Well, I'm wondering, how do the blood virgins compare to your *Erosita*? Sexually, I mean."

That had my eyebrow inching up even higher. "You're curious about my gratification?"

Ismerelda's heartbeat escalated even more. *Definitely awake. And likely now thinking about our* mutual gratification *from an hour ago.*

"No." Mira's full lips twisted to the side. "I'm curious as to if the blood virgin program is adequate or if it needs improvement. They're trained to excel beyond an *Erosita's* skill set. So I'm asking if the blood virgins you tasted meet or surpass your *Erosita's* capabilities, or do they need work?"

Ah. That made more sense.

Unfortunately, I couldn't provide a reasonable answer, as I hadn't actually tasted the offerings last week. I'd merely used the blood virgins for sustenance, not sex. They hadn't appealed to me.

Not like the beauty in my bed did, anyway.

It was likely a consequence of our ancient bond. My body appeared to be incapable of physically performing around anyone other than Ismerelda.

Alas, I couldn't exactly admit that aloud.

My attraction to my *Erosita* was a weakness, one I intended to kill. Just not yet.

Which meant I had to tread carefully now, as I couldn't afford for anyone to find out about this flaw.

"I'm still evaluating," I told Mira. "Once I've thoroughly *reacquainted* myself with my *Erosita*, I'll let you know how the blood virgins compare."

Mira considered me for a moment and nodded, seemingly satisfied with my response. "Please do. In the interim, I will get to work with our technical and security teams to make the appropriate changes."

"Good." I dismissed her again in favor of the blonde in my bed.

This time Mira didn't comment; she simply let herself out.

I waited for Ismerelda to move, but she remained absolutely still.

"Hmm," I hummed, intrigued by whatever game she was trying to play. She seemed to be pretending to sleep. But I had no idea why.

"I can hear your heart beating," I murmured as I removed my boxer shorts. "I know you're awake."

Silence.

My lips curled. "Do you want me to prove just how awake you are, *little swan?*" I asked as I slid onto the bed behind her.

Still nothing. Not even the taunt in my tone when I uttered that ridiculous—or perhaps, *appropriate*—nickname provoked a reaction.

I pressed my growing erection into her backside, loving the way her natural curves cushioned my hardness. *So fucking perfect.* I couldn't wait to take her here. Bend her over, own every bit of her, reclaim her as *mine.*

But first I wanted her pussy.

In so many damn positions.

From the back. From the front. *From the side.*

If she wanted to pretend to be asleep, I'd allow it. Because making her scream would be that much more exhilarating.

"Let's see how long you can keep quiet," I whispered into her ear, my hand going to her hip. "The longer you pretend, the more I'll reward you."

My lips trailed down to her neck, my sharpened incisors skimming her now-thundering pulse.

The scent of fear warmed my senses, making me want to bite. Taste. *Mark.*

There was something else in that aroma. Something sharp. An emotion I couldn't define. Not quite arousal, but close. Passionate. Intense. *Alluring.*

I inhaled deeply, my eyes falling closed.

Holding her like this gave me so many ideas. Taking her while she slept. Waking her with an orgasm only to fuck her into oblivion once more.

Gods, I needed this woman. It *hurt*, this desire so overwhelming that I almost wanted to give up control and let my beast out to dominate.

She's mine, my inner predator seemed to whisper. *Let me have her. Let me fuck her.*

I nipped Ismerelda's raging pulse, my cock stiff and ready against her ass.

Preparing her would be futile. Her body was made for mine, enslaved to my needs, molded to take my brand of aggression.

Besides, we'd already indulged in a warm-up with our mouths.

Now it was time to *fuck*, to feel her from the inside, to win this silly silent battle by making her scream.

I slipped my arm beneath her and reached up to palm her throat while my opposite hand slid from her hip to her slick heat. She was already wet for me, her endless orgasms from earlier leaving her primed and ready for my cock. Just as she should be.

Her pulse sang beneath my mouth, yet she didn't otherwise make a sound. She didn't even move.

I tested her resolve by pressing my thumb against her

clit. Her ass flexed subtly against me, but other than that, she didn't react.

My inner predator growled in approval, this game reminiscent of seeking prey. Hunting a mark. *Coercing* a reaction. Dining on the fear and arousal of a victim.

Gods, I was so damn hard for her. Ready to take. Mark. *Claim.*

Everything about her called to me, from her scent to her delectable curves, to the way she seemed to crave defiance to her pleasant subservience.

I was drunk on her.

So dangerous.

Too consuming.

I have to kill her.

But not yet...

I could play. Taste. *Fuck.*

I'd indulged in her for a thousand years already. What was a few more days or weeks or months? Nothing, really. Just a way to rid her from my system for good.

And potentially use her to teach Ryder and his progeny a lesson.

Keeping her was practical. A decision that afforded me some pleasure in the interim while also serving a purpose in the long term.

I drew my hand away from her sex to grab her thigh, pulling her leg back over mine.

"Time for you to roar, little lioness," I whispered to her, my hips shifting against hers to line myself up with her weeping entrance.

Her pussy resembled a hot kiss against my shaft, causing my balls to tighten as I thrust inside her, the sensation one that dangerously threatened my self-control. Feral instincts clawed at my restraint, urging me to let my inner predator free.

Let me have her, that beast growled. *Let me take what's mine.*

Her cunt felt so good. *Too* good. I couldn't think. I could only *be*. I could only *claim*. Deeply. Thoroughly. *Exquisitely.*

And *fuck*, she was tight. Molded perfectly for me. Squeezing my dick with an aggression I admired. Owning me entirely. Allowing me to feel at peace for the first time since I'd awakened.

This has to be why I've kept her, I marveled, utterly lost to the pleasure zipping up and down my spine. I was barely even moving, just embracing the heat, indulging in her flawlessness.

I buried my head against her neck, my lips pressed firmly to her now-raging pulse.

If Ismerelda had flinched when I'd entered her, I wasn't sure. I'd been too consumed by our intimate connection to notice. But other than a small gasp, she'd remained quiet, her taut form pressed firmly to mine.

Her thigh clenched beneath my palm. My lioness wanted me to move, to feel my power, to lose ourselves to a pleasure we hadn't experienced in over a hundred years. I could sense it in the way her sheath clamped down around me, demanding action.

Demanding that I perform.

Demanding that I own her. Mark her. Remind her of her place in my life. Rekindle our bond. *Take her.*

My incisors skimmed her tender skin, my hand still clasped around her throat while my opposite held her leg. "This is going to hurt, Ismerelda."

Because once I started, I wouldn't be able to hold back.

I pressed my lips to her ear, adding, "But I promise to reward you for taking it."

And then I let my beast free.

To fuck.

To mark.

To do whatever the hell he desired.

Because this female belonged to me. She was built for this as my *Erosita*. My immortal blood toy. *Mine.*

IZZY

My palms hit the mattress as a scream escaped my throat. That scream was almost immediately smothered by a pillow meeting my face.

Violent hands grabbed my hips, forcing them upward as Cam drove into me, his movements bordering on feral.

I dug my nails into the bed, my limbs straining to hold myself in the position he'd roughly manhandled me into.

"This is going to hurt," he'd warned. "But I promise to reward you for taking it."

I hadn't been given time to consider what that meant before he'd rolled our bodies and forced me into this submissive position on the bed.

My teeth sank into my lip as I tried futilely not to whimper, my heart a shattered mess in my chest.

I'd woken up to voices. A conversation about our

location. The security. *Technology and cameras.* Something about lycan experiments.

At first, I'd thought it was a dream. Then reality had slowly settled around me, a memory of Cam fucking my mouth nearly making me bolt upright.

But then I'd recognized Mira's voice.

"It was smart to build all the research tunnels under the catacombs. Not only is this considered neutral territory, but it's also sacred. No one would think…"

Her voice had faded then, unconsciousness stealing over me for a long moment before allowing me to resurface.

Although, I'd been so utterly focused on the details regarding our location that I hadn't thoroughly listened to their conversation, only picking up pieces of it until the very end.

"I'm wondering, how do the blood virgins compare to your Erosita? *Sexually, I mean."*

Those words had pierced right through my chest and anchored deep within my mind.

Why would Cam know that? I'd wondered.

Only for Mira to essentially answer me less than a minute later.

"I'm curious as to if the blood virgin program is adequate or if it needs improvement. They're trained to excel beyond an Erosita's *skill set. So I'm asking if the blood virgins you tasted meet or surpass your* Erosita's *capabilities, or do they need work?"*

I'd stopped breathing at that moment, and I hadn't been able to inhale properly since.

Cam had tasted the *blood virgins.*

And I knew Mira hadn't just meant their blood, but *sexually.*

Cam slammed into me, grounding me in the moment

and demanding that I pay attention. But how else could I fucking feel?

Betrayed? I thought. *Broken? Livid?*

His hips met mine, his cock lodged deep.

He was inside someone else.

Another woman.

Maybe multiple women.

This bond between us didn't require his fidelity, only mine. I'd never understood the magic, just that it existed. And there were rules.

Rules I had followed.

Rules I'd taken to heart.

Rules that had felt natural and right.

But Cam...

I swallowed an agonized scream as his fangs bit into my throat, the endorphins flooding my system and cascading me into an unwelcome climax.

Cam growled in approval, his palm having shifted from my throat to my nape. The pillow beneath my face threatened to suffocate me, my ability to breathe constricted by the silky fabric.

It was all too much.

Too overwhelming.

Too *wrong*.

This wasn't how Cam and I made love. *Because this isn't my Cam.*

He'd choked me with his cock.

And now he was going to break me in half with his harsh thrusts.

My hip was bruising beneath his hand.

My insides ached.

My heart... *pounded*.

Because some forbidden part of me seemed to thrive on the sensations his brutality stirred within me.

This isn't right. This isn't my Cam.

He betrayed our bond, a sharp voice snapped in my head. *My* voice.

And yet another part of me argued, *He doesn't know who we are. His memories of us are gone. He didn't mean to hurt us.*

Tears burned in my eyes, my emotions warring as pleasure licked across my skin and set my veins on fire.

"You feel amazing like this," Cam whispered against my ear. "I'm going to force you to come all day while I fuck you. Make you so tight that it'll be a challenge to push my way inside."

God, when had Cam ever spoken to me like this during sex?

Hearing him now, feeling him like *this,* I… I started to wonder about our past. About why he'd kept this part of himself hidden.

Did I even really know him?

But of course I did. We'd been together for a thousand years. I knew him better than anyone else.

And yet… I'd never experienced this side of him at all. He'd kept it buried inside, locked away where I couldn't reach him.

How fulfilling had life actually been for him if he'd needed to fight this part of himself?

Or did this part not usually exist around me?

My head spun with uncertainties, making me dizzy.

I'd wanted to provoke him into letting go, to make his mind vulnerable to mine, and somehow I'd ended up even more conflicted than before. Even more *wounded.*

"*Fuck,* I might just live inside you forever." Cam's breath was hot against my neck. "You'll fall asleep on my cock and wake with me taking you. Over and over again."

He panted the words, his body hard and dominant over mine as one hand continued to hold my hip captive. But his other palm was moving, going from my nape to throat once more, then up to my chin.

"Kiss me," he demanded, his grip rough as he tugged my head to the side and leaned over me to claim my mouth.

It gave me a break from the orgasm ripping through my being but wrenched my head back at an uncomfortable angle—one I worried might end in him snapping my neck.

Only, his tongue was almost reverent against mine, his movements slowing slightly as he pulled almost all of the way out of me.

Then he drove back in with a strength that had me yelping against his lips.

He smiled, repeating the motion and hitting that spot deep inside. I clenched around him impulsively, my body reacting to his savage strokes.

I felt owned.

Possessed.

Trapped.

All emotions I hadn't really experienced before with Cam. Owned, maybe. But not the others.

This… was new. And I hated how it made me feel. *Aroused. Ready. Begging for more.*

I'm broken, I decided. *This version of Cam has broken me.*

I can't let him win this battle. I have to fight.

For what?

For our future. For the sake of humanity. For our bond!

My mind warred with itself as my body succumbed to the hot maelstrom brewing inside me.

So good. So intense. So overwhelming.

His tongue danced with mine, his grasp on my chin unrelenting as he forced me to take all of him. Deeply. Thoroughly. Hitting my aching center.

I nearly bit down on his tongue, the urge to scream riding me hard.

It would be born of frustration and agony. *And pleasure.*

Such a fucked-up mix.

My mate was unfaithful.

He doesn't realize what we mean to each other.

Does that make it any better?

It explains it.

Fuck. That. Fuck. Him. Fuck. This.

I needed him to fall apart, to allow his mental walls to crumble. Sucking him off hadn't worked, but maybe this would. Maybe coming inside me would weaken his mind enough for me to access his thoughts.

A few memories were all I needed.

He would understand. He would realize his mistakes. *He would be mine again.*

Not some blood virgin's.

Mine.

We'd always been faithful to each other. Always been a pair. Partners.

Until he ran off to face Lilith, I remembered darkly, the incident threatening to consume my thoughts.

Stop. There's no changing the past, only the future.

Which, ironically, meant I needed Cam to recall the past.

Fuck.

I winced as he angled my hip to seat himself even more firmly inside me, his length surprising me. It was like he'd grown.

That's impossible.

Unless this was never Cam.

No. It's Cam. Just not my *Cam.*

Fuck, stop thinking, I commanded myself, my need to focus on Cam overriding everything else.

I wanted him to explode. To be overcome by his orgasm. *To let me in.*

My tongue met his as I sought to take over for the first time since he'd kissed me.

He growled, the sound reminiscent of his earlier approval, and immediately mastered me with his mouth.

Not good enough, I thought, anger fueling my rebellion. *You played with another female. Likely more than one. I'm going to remind you why* you *are* mine.

I didn't share. And neither did he.

Whether it was his lack of memories or not, his body should have known that. But since he clearly needed the reminder, I'd demonstrate the full extent of our bond.

My teeth sank down on his tongue. *Hard.*

And then I froze.

Because *that* hadn't been what I'd meant to do.

We didn't fuck like this. We made love. Yet he'd bitten me so many times today that I'd simply… reacted.

I was just so… so… *furious.*

How could you? I wanted to demand. *You want to replace me? What the fuck is wrong with you?*

But I already knew the answers to that. *Lilith* was what was wrong with him. She'd messed up his head.

Because Cam went to her on his own in an attempt to reason with her.

He abandoned me to play hero.

He *did this to himself.*

No. Don't think like that. Blaming—

My vision spun as Cam roughly rolled us on the bed, causing my back to connect with the mattress. I barely had a moment to breathe before he slammed into me again, this time with even more strength and force than before.

I yelped as he bit my lip, the sting quickly replaced by his tongue.

And then he was devouring me. Owning me so severely with his mouth that all I could do was take it.

Just like my body was his to use.

The bed creaked with the movements, his hips beating into mine as his palm closed around my throat once more. His opposite hand was on my breast, squeezing my flesh and tweaking my nipples.

A moan left me without permission, this violent version of him taking me to heights I'd never known existed.

It was like being fucked for the first time, and not just by Cam.

He wasn't gentle or coaxing. He was harsh and demanding.

I grabbed his shoulders and dug my nails into his skin, needing to mark him. Claim him. Leave something behind that said *mine*.

Those blood virgins couldn't have him.

There would be no replacing me.

And *fuck* what Lilith had done to his mind.

This male belonged to me, and I would break through to him. I would find a way to remind him of us, our past, our promised future.

He might have made a fateful decision without me—one that had changed everything between us—but fuck if I would allow it to happen again.

I wasn't the meek female of his past. I'd grown over the last one hundred years. And I would not sit by and wait for him to solve all of the world's problems.

You. Will. Remember. Me. I etched those words into his mouth with my tongue while my nails drew blood. *You. Are. Mine.*

He snarked in response, his grasp on my throat tightening as he pulled back to stare down at me. "Fucking beautiful," he hissed. "Come for me right now, little hellcat. I need to feel your cunt squeezing my shaft."

Hellcat was new. Just like *lioness*.

But I didn't care.

Both sounded a lot more fierce than a swan.

If that was how this version of Cam saw me, then good. Because I wanted to be fierce. A force to be reckoned with. *His mate.*

This whole operation beneath the catacombs was going down. Lilith might be dead, but I'd be damned before I let her legacy survive.

"*Now*, Ismerelda," he growled, his mouth going to my neck.

He thrust deep just as his fangs sank into my neck, the combination of sensations and forced endorphins sending me spiraling into a sea of dark bliss.

Rapturous waves flooded my veins, coercing me into a black whirlpool with no end in sight.

My lungs burned.

My legs went numb.

My insides clenched.

My body was no longer my own.

Cam released a thunderous sound that was more beast than human, his body destroying mine as he fucked me without restraint.

I could feel my inner thighs bruising while my legs remained jelly-like in response.

I was a toy. A doll to be taken. Abused. *Used.*

All the while, I continued to drown in an endless pit of ecstasy.

I clawed at his back, desperate for breath, to resurface, but he wouldn't stop drinking. Each pull pushed me deeper into that dangerous vortex.

His name left me on a voiceless whisper.

He's killing me. Again.

And he showed no signs of stopping.

How am I supposed to get into his head if I keep dying?

My fingers were going cold, my nails no longer secured in his skin.

I need him to come.

My hips were aching from the onslaught of his thrusts.

Please, Cam. Come for me. Come back to me!

My arms fell to the mattress, my hands resembling ice.

Fuck... this is... starting to hurt...

He wasn't stopping. He didn't even seem aware. Or maybe he didn't care.

Cam...

He roared, his fangs finally leaving my delicate skin. However, not because he'd heard me.

There. He's... he's coming.

His seed should have felt hot inside me, but I couldn't feel it. I couldn't feel him. I could no longer see.

Cam! I shouted, desperate to get into his head.

Except a wall of silence met my efforts. Dark. Cold. Alone.

Cam!

Nothing.

Just a dead bond. One he'd cut me off from.

I screamed in my mind, furious at him for this situation, for everything he'd decided without me, for everything he'd now done because he no longer knew me.

I won't give up. I can't give up.

And yet, I wasn't sure what to do now.

Fuck him again? Try to break through once more?

What else can I do?

I shivered, lost in the dark spell of death. Only for a hint of sensation to warm my inner thighs.

A tongue?

No. Too… firm.
A finger?
No. It's too thick.
Cam's…?

My eyes flew open to reveal the room around me. My head was on a pillow, and Cam was behind me again with my leg strewn over his thigh.

My throat was dry, reminding me of starchy cotton. But other than that, I felt fine. No agonized lungs. No pain. Just the subtle pressure of his cock gliding in and out of my damp heat.

"Time to roar again, little hellcat," he told me, his lips against my ear.

IZZY

Oh, God.

How long had I been out?

And had he really just woken me up by sliding into me?

His words from earlier came back, his threats about making me sleep with him inside me swirling in my mind.

Had he done that? Had he been keeping his dick warm while I'd been recovering?

I shuddered, then moaned as he bit me *again*.

Tears clouded my vision as an orgasm overtook me without warning, throwing me into a pit of delirious despair.

I wasn't ready.

I couldn't do this.

I... I needed... *rest.*

But he'd clearly fed me his blood because I was fully healed.

Which meant he could start over again. Just like he'd told me he would.

And take me he did. Carnally. Without care. From the back and then the front.

Drinking me dry.

Dragging me into another coma.

Only to wake me once more, this time with my bottom half hanging off the mattress while he stood and took me with significant thrusts.

I passed out before I could come.

Just to be awoken by his fangs and a vicious climax that blanked out my mind.

I fought through the fog, determined to find him—*my Cam*—but continued to wake up to this predatory version of him.

Days seemed to pass.

Or maybe hours.

But he'd left a few times. Once to deliver a message—something I only vaguely recalled from his cold conversation with Mira.

Another time he'd returned with a new laptop, which I didn't even bother to touch because I was just too exhausted to try.

The cycle continued on end, leaving me more and more lost every time I passed out.

He finally noticed after… I wasn't sure how long. He set a vial of blood down and asked me to drink it.

I did.

That happened a few more times but did little to assuage the pain echoing inside me. It wasn't just emotional, but also physical.

When was the last time I ate or drank anything?

I'd ended up voicing a version of that concern aloud sometime later, after Cam had mentioned my waning energy.

"You're beginning to bore me," he'd said. "What happened to my lioness?"

His words had lit a fire within me. Because hell if *I* was going to be blamed for not *performing* adequately. "Even lions need food," I'd muttered. "Or have you forgotten that I eat?"

It'd come out snippy, my annoyance of being used like a fuck toy shining through.

I'd half expected him to bend me over and fuck me in response. But instead he'd canted his head for a thoughtful moment and then nodded. "Would you like the same food from last week? Or shall we try something new?"

Last week? I'd repeated to myself. *Fuck...*

I'd agreed to the Italian because I was starving.

Then I'd only eaten part of it because my stomach had been too small to fully empty the meal.

"You proved with this meal that you know my more modern tastes," Cam had said after we'd finished. "Educate me on some of my others, starting with evening breakfast. Tell me what to order for tomorrow."

I'd been momentarily surprised by his request, a hint of hope warming my heart. *He wants me to remind him of the past.*

But once I'd finished listing foods, he'd simply placed the order on his new laptop and dragged me off to the shower to fuck me against the wall.

I'd woken up again with him inside me, his appetite insatiable.

But at least he'd begun to feed me.

Although, he'd made me his personal dessert after every meal.

I'd come countless times over the last—*seven? Maybe eight? Or was it nine?*—days. But the experience hadn't been for me; it'd been for him and his pleasure.

He liked making me tight. Making me wet. Making me moan.

While it felt amazing, it wasn't. Because each climax pushed me a little bit deeper into a pit of despair.

I couldn't break through his mental walls. They were impenetrable. And sex wasn't helping.

Not even when he let me stay awake long enough to watch him fall apart.

Like now.

He had me straddling his lap, his movements penetrating me sharply with each upward punch of his hips. His fingers were locked in my hair, his mouth owning mine while his opposite hand palmed my ass.

I was sore.

Tired.

Used.

But he'd woken me with his cock, followed swiftly by his hands and a demand for me to ride him.

I'd obliged in a daze, my last memory of him fucking me into the mattress.

Days of sex weren't exactly rare for us; Cam had always enjoyed long hours and nights in the bedroom. However, this was something else entirely.

It felt as though I'd been thoroughly introduced to my mate's predator side.

No limits. No rules. No holding back. Just a beast taking his female in every way imaginable.

His fangs skimmed my lip, his bite imminent. It was his favorite way to force me to come. Not only did it feel good for him, but it also gave him an excuse to drink from me.

Which then left me with no choice but to imbibe more of his blood in return.

He'd started leaving vials of it for me on the nightstand. Other times, he'd fed it to me while I slept. Or I assumed he had, anyway. That was the only explanation for how quickly I'd regenerated.

I waited for his bite, my heart hammering in my chest, aware that it would wring every bit of energy from my veins, rendering me useless all day.

Again.

Except… the sting never came.

Just his tongue.

A gentle kiss.

A trick, I thought, confused by this change of pace after what felt like an eternity of being *bitten* and *fucked* to the brink of death.

His palm slid along my ass to my hip before slipping between us. I jolted as his thumb found my sensitive nub, his touch unexpected and so very desired.

Which I hated.

I *hated* how I reacted to him. Hated how I loved his soft strokes. Hated how he set my blood on fire with a few simple touches.

My body had belonged to this male for so long, my heart and soul his in every way.

Even when he broke my trust.

Even when he hurt me.

Even when he no longer acted like the man I knew.

I still wanted him. Craved him. *Loved* him.

Tears collected in my eyes as I slowed my pace above him, our session revolving into a blissful memory of passion and tenderness. *This* was how we embraced one another, how we showed our emotions and adoration.

Is he starting to remember? I wondered, a spark of hope flaring inside me. *Is he finally coming down from his mating high?*

It was as though he'd fallen into a strange sort of rut, his instincts demanding that he *take* instead of *give*.

But now… *this*… it… it felt like… *my Cam.*

He sat up, causing his muscles to flex against me, his body all feral, hard male. "Wrap your legs around me," he whispered against my mouth.

I obliged, reveling in the angle of this position. It was one of my favorites. I relished the closeness, the way the embrace made me feel cherished.

His arms encircled me, his mouth reverent as our bodies danced in hypnotic shifts.

This. This is my Cam.

I nearly sighed, contentment filling my being.

God, I've missed this, I thought at him, wishing he could hear me. *I've missed you so much.*

I've missed you, too, he murmured, his voice in my head making me freeze.

Cam?

He smiled. *Who else would it be?*

I pulled away to search his face, only he chased me with his mouth, his lips hot against mine.

Wait—

Shh, he hushed me. *Let me love you.*

My lips curled down. That sounded so much like my old Cam. But how could he just revert without a conversation? Without even addressing what he'd done? What we'd been through?

I attempted to move again, but his arms held me tight against him, his mouth even more demanding. Almost as though he was desperate to keep me here. To hold me for eternity. To make me his again.

I grabbed his shoulders, conflicted and elated at the same time.

My Cam... He's—

I gasped as his fangs sank into my lip, my eyes flying open.

What...?

I was no longer straddling him, but on my back. My thighs were cradling his hips. My nails were digging into his shoulders.

And his irises resembled dark pools of intense need.

I jolted as he slammed into me, his pace brutal, his tenderness nonexistent.

Because none of it had been real.

It was a dream.

This is my reality.

I trembled, my heart shattering in my chest as Cam fucked me with a vengeance.

There were no soft words or tender touches. No mental thoughts of love. No kindness.

Just a predator taking his prey.

I wanted to scream. To hit him. To *fight.*

But his mouth claimed mine in the next breath, his tongue issuing sharp commands for me to surrender. To embrace him. To let this happen. To accept the new version of my mate.

No! I shouted. *I won't accept any of this. You. Are. Not. My. Cam.*

He growled against my lips, his movements becoming even more feral. "I love how you fight me, lioness," he praised. "You're fucking perfect."

How is any of this perfect? I wanted to demand. *This is a disaster.*

But I couldn't deny how good it felt to have him inside

me, how the bite from his endorphins lit a fire within me that only burned for him.

I hate this.

I love this.

I hate him.

I love him.

So fucking conflicting. So messed up. So damn wrong!

He made a noise of maddening approval as my nails cut into his skin, his thrusts brutal and constant as he drove us both toward a dark oblivion of pain and pleasure.

I held on, my broken heart hammering an unsteady rhythm in my chest.

Please don't bite me. Please just let me be aware a little longer.

But the pleas were futile. Cam would do what he wanted because this was about him and not about me.

So different from our past when he'd always put me first.

Or did he? I wondered. *He abandoned me to save the world, and now look at us.*

I shoved the thoughts away, irritated at myself for blaming him for such a selfless act. But being in this position with him now made it hard for me to respect his choice.

Because that's what it was—his choice. Not our choice.

I growled in annoyance, which earned me a snarl from the predator above me. He'd completely misunderstood the sound, instead translating it as arousal and fucking me even harder.

My hips were going to shatter beneath him. Not that it mattered. He'd just heal me with blood.

How the fuck am I supposed to fix this? I wondered dizzily. *How do I get my Cam back?*

His tongue stroked mine, his hands on my waist as he maintained a furious pace. He grabbed my breasts.

Tweaked my nipples. Nipped my tongue. My lips. Then buried his face in my neck.

I braced myself.

But he didn't bite me.

Instead, he suckled my neck, teasing the skin, and continued his ministration below. Only, his hand slid between us, his thumb finding my clit. Similar to my dream.

Did he do this to me while I slept? Is that why I dreamt about it?

I shuddered, the extra sensation exactly what my body craved.

"Come for me, little hellcat," he demanded against my ear. "I want to feel you squeeze my cock with that delicious pussy of yours."

I swallowed, his words adding fuel to the flames dancing within me.

It didn't matter how upset I might be, how lost I was, or how defeated I felt. My body still responded to his. It always would. Even when it hurt.

I arched up into him, my insides clenching beneath an onslaught of sensation as my heated center spasmed around him.

A curse threatened my tongue, tears clouding my vision, my limbs strung tight.

It was right there. So close. So intense. So *consuming*.

I whimpered.

And Cam... pressed his thumb... *down*. Hard.

I screamed.

It was... too much. Too exhausting. Too beautiful. Too wrong.

I swam in a turbulent sea rippling with waves of agony-induced ecstasy.

None of it made sense. My brain no longer functioned. My lungs wept. My heart beat too wildly. My limbs were nonexistent. My body resembled a vessel meant solely for Cam's pleasure.

His seed warmed my insides, his passionate growl vibrating my chest.

My head fell automatically to the side, aware of what would come next. *A bite that would send me back into my endless slumber.*

Yet all he did was kiss my throat.

I waited.

Then I frowned.

And eventually, I glanced at him. He was still inside me, his upper body braced on his forearms.

But rather than stare at my neck like it was his favorite food, he watched me.

I gazed up at him, noting the varying shades of blue in his eyes. It wasn't a deep ocean color anymore, but layered in a way that reminded me of the shoreline. Dark to light. All ringed around his black pupils.

"I need to prepare for tomorrow's meeting with the alliance," he told me quietly. "So I will be gone most of the night."

My brow furrowed. *He's talking to me about his plans?*

And he's going to meet with the alliance?

"I need you to drink two vials of my blood in preparation for when I return," he continued. "Because I suspect I'll be in a brutal mood and I don't want to accidentally kill you before I'm finished with you."

Oh. If there was any question as to which version of Cam I was dealing with, those final words confirmed it was new Cam.

The vestiges of my dream melted away into my heartbreaking reality.

Those walls in his mind were as impenetrable as ever,

even with him lodged deep within me and having just fallen apart.

How am I going to break through? I wondered for the thousandth time. *Is it even possible?*

At least our bond was still intact. That much I could feel in my soul.

Which means he's definitely Cam and not some dangerous clone of him, I thought to myself with a sardonic snort. *Silver lining and all that.*

"Come," he said, slipping out of me. "I want to fuck you again in the shower before midnight breakfast."

CAM

I'M ADDICTED TO THIS FEMALE.

Her curves.

Her moans.

Her *eyes*.

Fuck. It didn't matter that I'd just taken her twice before midnight breakfast. Simply seeing her in my button-down shirt at the table had me hard all over again.

I wanted to devour her for dessert, which I'd done several times over the last week.

But I couldn't tonight.

There was too much to do before tomorrow's meeting with the alliance. We needed to explain Lilith's research and the purpose, while also ensuring everyone understood what was at stake.

Our blood supply was on a downward trajectory. Our only solution was to find a way to immortalize our food.

Anyone who didn't understand that didn't deserve to be part of the alliance.

Alas, I needed to present our findings in a thorough and appropriate manner.

Which required preparation, including reviewing the findings some of our researchers had documented in regard to the blood of our recently awakened Blessed Ones.

Ismerelda set her glass of water down, then took another bite of her French toast—a food she'd introduced me to the other evening.

American cuisine.

While I could remember bits and pieces of the formation of the United States of America, I couldn't recall many details. But Ismerelda had reintroduced me to some of the meals she claimed I'd favored a hundred or so years ago.

And one of those meals was French toast with fruit and Canadian maple syrup.

It was all rather decadent, but I couldn't deny the appeal. Actually, everything she'd suggested over the last few days had more than satisfied my taste buds.

Of course, nothing compared to her blood.

Or her, I mused, my gaze tracking down her neck to the collar of my shirt. She'd left the first two buttons open, allowing me to admire a sliver of her creamy skin.

Gorgeous.

Talented.

Mine.

My obsession with her was unhealthy. I really should task her with training a few replacements. It would be cruel. But it was needed.

I can't keep her forever.

She stood for everything my mind sought to correct. No one wanted to be tied to emotional burdens.

Yet I couldn't stop considering what she would be like as a vampire. An equal. A true mate.

Why haven't I turned her?

It would make so much sense. But maybe I hadn't found the right replacement for her blood.

That would explain my disinterest in the blood virgins. They were supposedly the most delectable humans in existence, but none of them compared to Ismerelda.

I'd bitten a few of them for sustenance, yet it hadn't been enough. I'd longed for more but not from them.

And now that I'd more thoroughly experienced Ismerelda, I understood why.

She was my weakness. My ultimate craving. My everything. No one else compared.

Killing her will be the hardest task I've ever taken on, I decided. *But I don't have to do that yet.*

Not until we figured out how to solve this immortal-blood problem.

I finished my coffee—the dark liquid flavored with a hint of my lioness's essence. I hadn't taken much from her, my desire to give her a day of healing superseding my own needs. She'd given me everything, just as I'd required.

Some part of me wished to please her in return, and I'd sensed her exhaustion even with the constant intake of food and blood I'd provided.

Ismerelda needed true rest.

"There are some bath salts under the sink," I told her. "Use them for a bath."

She blinked at me. "A bath, my liege? For your return?"

I shook my head. "No. For you. I want you rested and ready for me tonight. And baths are relaxing, yes?" I'd taken them a millennia ago before showers existed. However, that had been in a tin-like tub.

The large one in my bathroom suite was far more advanced with mechanisms that actually moved the water. I hadn't indulged in the experience, but I suspected the jets would provide massage-like sensations against my *Erosita's* sore muscles.

My hands itched to do the task themselves. Alas, I couldn't trust the instinct. Mostly because it would end with Ismerelda on her back once more.

And I really needed to get to work.

"Yes," she said quietly, agreeing with my statement regarding baths.

"Would you like me to have food delivered to you as well?" I asked.

She studied me for a long moment, almost as though she was trying to understand the question.

She really is exhausted, I realized. I'd been hard on her, my cravings dark and depraved. I hadn't realized how starved I'd been for her, and now it seemed I would never be satisfied.

Replacing her right now was not an option.

No wonder those blood virgins didn't appeal to me.

"Do you mean for dinner?" Ismerelda's tone held a note of confusion to it, making me realize that the agenda for this evening might not be clear.

"Yes. I likely won't return until close to dawn, so the night hours are yours today. Is there something I should order for you to eat?"

I learned my lesson the other day about how to properly care for my *Erosita*. She'd waned considerably, even with my blood in her system. And it had taken a snarky remark from her to tell me why.

My human requires sustenance to thrive.

I'd taken the discernment seriously and had prioritized her meals ever since. It'd served a dual purpose to also reintroduce me to modern cuisine, which had allowed me to justify the amount of time I'd devoted to sharing food with her.

In truth, I'd just enjoyed her company.

But I'd never admit that aloud.

"Um." She cleared her throat. "Maybe a pizza? I could keep it warm for whenever you come back…?" She trailed off, her light green gaze searching mine. It was bold. Alluring. *Queenly*.

Mira had warned me that my *Erosita* hadn't conformed to this new world, that she'd essentially refused to bow to her superiors.

A human with a backbone of steel.

When she'd first arrived, I hadn't been able to fathom why I'd allowed such a rebellion to exist. But now I was beginning to understand my choice.

Ismerelda intrigued me. She might be human, but she possessed a powerful soul. That was how she'd survived me this long, how she'd been able to match me in the bedroom, and why I'd indulged in her for over a millennium.

She's destined for so much more, I thought.

Mira wouldn't have known that. I wouldn't have told anyone my true intentions where Ismerelda was concerned. But there was absolutely a reason I'd demanded that she be kept safe.

And thank fuck those orders had been followed.

The last nine days had been more pleasurable than any of my existence.

Any that I could recall, anyway.

How strange that I don't remember this female, I thought, still holding her gaze. *I should. I want to. I could…*

All it would take was to remove the mental walls between us and delve into her mind, read through the memories of our past, see if I might be right about her being my intended partner in life.

The recollections would be from her point of view, but I should be able to glean the details I needed to paint a proper picture of our history.

Later, I told myself, my watch buzzing as though in agreement. "I have to oversee some of the trials with the Blessed Ones tonight," I murmured, glancing at the message scrolling across my wrist. "Then I'm meeting with Mira and Michael to prepare for tomorrow's presentation. And…"

I paused to skim Mira's words about our meeting confirmation for five o'clock in the morning.

"And then I have a call with Helias. Assuming that goes well, I'll be back soon after." I flicked Mira's message away from my wrist. "But I suspect something won't go as planned today, which is why I'll likely be delayed until closer to six or seven. You can eat without me."

I opened my new laptop to key in the order for a pizza.

"Any toppings?" I asked her, aware that she was still staring at me. Probably because I'd just outlined my day to her. But if she was going to be my queen, she would have to become used to such schedules.

Because I would expect her to join me.

Or lead them on her own.

I didn't want arm candy. I wanted a partner.

And while it hadn't been something I'd ever really considered or sought in my previous life, it seemed I'd potentially found it over the last thousand years.

In Ismerelda.

It was the only thing that made sense. Why else would I keep a human tied to my soul for so long?

And why else would I feel so intrinsically protective of her?

Yes. I may need to pull those memories, I decided once more. *But when I have more time to sift through them.*

"Pepperoni," she replied. "And olives. Preferably green."

I arched a brow, then keyed in the preference. "Anything to drink?"

She mentioned a white wine rather than a red, then gave me a backup brand in case the kitchen couldn't find the one she desired.

"I'll have it delivered at five," I told her.

"Thank you."

My lips curled. "You can thank me properly later, little lioness."

She swallowed, her expression seeming to go blank. A strange response to my innuendo, but she was probably too tired to consider another round right now.

Poor darling had been overworked.

Yet another reason to make her immortal. Her appetite would be as voracious as mine, perhaps even more intense. And then we could indulge in a whole new world of fun and pleasure.

Decisions, decisions, I mused, closing my laptop.

I really didn't want to have to kill her. Keeping her would be so much more fun. Besides, she seemed to have earned it.

She would be a far better progeny than Michael, too.

And Darius for that matter.

All I needed to solve was the immortal-blood-bag issue.

Which I'm not going to do by sitting here, admiring my Erosita, I told myself.

Clearing my throat, I pushed away from the table. "Take a bath. Rest. Relax." I leaned down to press a kiss to her head, the action strangely intimate yet it felt incredibly right. "I want you ready to play later." Something that required her to be pleased and content, not stressed and sore. "Enjoy your evening, Ismerelda."

I didn't wait for her to reply, instead heading toward the door.

But I heard her whisper, "You, too, my liege," just before I entered the hallway, her voice nearly giving me pause.

She sounded... sad?

No. It's the exhaustion.

I'd been too rough. I supposed that was to be expected after a century of sleep. However, I felt a niggling of guilt at how I'd used her. Endlessly. Tirelessly. It was my due. But I wanted her to enjoy it, too.

Fortunately, she had today to recover. By the time I returned, she'd be back to her lioness-like state.

Then I would reward her just like I'd promised.

Well, technically, I'd said I might be in a mood to hurt her later.

But given how I felt right now, that seemed unlikely. I'd much rather fulfill the vow I'd made initially about rewarding her for taking my brutality.

She made me feel light. Alive. *Pleased.* And now I wanted to return the favor.

It would be a fun surprise. A passionate one. *The perfect gift.*

Yes. Tonight, I would pleasure my *Erosita.*

Then I would delve into her mind and retrieve some of our shared memories.

And if my instincts proved right, I just might ask her how she felt about becoming a queen.

IZZY

I NEED A NEW PLAN.

When Cam had suggested I take a bath and rest, I'd almost sensed a hint of care in his words.

Then he'd dismantled that false hope by telling me why he wanted me rested.

"I want you ready to play later."

For more fucking.

More domination.

More endless orgasms for his pleasure rather than my own.

My legs crossed, my muscles tightening in protest. Cam had never pushed my body like this, taking me to such an extreme over and over again.

Who knew it was possible to come this much? This often?

I shuddered, my stomach clenching.

I need more than an evening off. I need a week.

No. What I need is to fix Cam.

But how?

I pressed my palm to my head, my thoughts spinning with doubts and questions and painful realizations.

The mental wall between us was too strong. Sex hadn't helped. If anything, it'd just made all this worse.

Cam saw me as nothing more than a fuck doll.

He might have offered me a bath and some food today, but it wasn't for me. It was for him. Just like everything else.

I swallowed hard, my eyes falling closed. *What am I going to do?*

He was off preparing for tomorrow's meeting, reviewing test results or whatever. Trying to perfect the concept of immortal blood bags.

All to replace me, I thought sourly.

My fingers curled into fists.

This was unacceptable. All of it. Including me sitting here, wallowing in my sorrows.

Which I'd been doing for at least an hour now.

Shit.

I ran my hand over my face and glanced at the camera in the ceiling.

A vague conversation trickled through my mind. Something about turning off various live feeds and no longer relying on technology for security.

Cam had said to move all the vampires to the labs, thus leaving the Coventus to be guarded by humans.

And the catacombs, I considered, my lips curling down. *They're probably leaving that unguarded, too.*

It was sacred ground. No one would think to go there. And everyone was asleep anyway.

Except the Blessed Ones who had recently been awakened.

Too bad Cronus isn't one of them, I muttered to myself. *Or Cane.*

They would fix Cam in a heartbeat. Not only would he remember them, but he'd also respect them and their opinions.

Blowing out a breath, I stood from the dining table and busied myself with the breakfast dishes. I'd let them sit a bit too long, but I welcomed the tedious task, as it gave me something to do while I pondered my options.

I could try his computer again. It's probably been overhauled with some sort of monitoring security, though. And who knows if the network—internal or otherwise—is even working?

My lips twisted.

But if I could get a message to Damien… I trailed off. *What would I even say? What would I expect him to do?*

The alliance meeting was tomorrow. Maybe they already had a plan in place. Jace and Ryder would be there.

Will they be able to save Cam?

I set the dishes to the side, my heart skipping a beat.

What if they can't save him?

Surely he would listen to them. He'd known them for thousands of years. Unless he thought they were brainwashed by the enemy.

Lilith had royally fucked with Cam's mind. Who knew what she'd written and recorded about her opposition?

Did she paint Cane and Cronus in a similar light? I wondered, frowning. *Or would they have been exempt because they were sleeping?*

What if Jace and Ryder aren't even invited to the meeting?

I paced the kitchen and dining area while my mind spiraled with questions.

If Jace and Ryder weren't allowed to attend the meeting, they wouldn't be able to even try to reason with

Cam. Which meant I couldn't rely on that possibility at all.

I had to do something myself. Something *here*.

But what?

All this version of Cam wanted to do was fuck me. And that had proved to be unhelpful in terms of breaking down the walls between us.

So what else can I do?

I glanced at his laptop on the table. I'd already tried that avenue, and that was before Michael had done whatever he'd done to it.

My gaze ventured to the door. *Escaping would be counterproductive.* Cam's passion might be cruel, but he didn't exactly scare me. And leaving wouldn't save him.

No. I needed some way to fix him here.

Or maybe someone, I thought, my steps slowing. *Someone Cam will listen to that's already here.*

Someone like Cane.

I rolled my shoulders back and headed toward the bathroom where Cam had left the vials. *Could it be enough blood to wake Cane? Would it even work?*

I knew the ritual from when Cam had taught it to me, and he'd suggested at the time that my ties to him as his mate would likely allow me to perform the ceremony, too. But he hadn't been sure. And we hadn't exactly tested it. However, he'd shown it to me just in case I ever needed to know how to do it.

In an emergency situation, I thought. *A situation like this.*

Why hadn't I considered this earlier?

Probably because I'd been certain of my ability to bring Cam back on my own.

Well, I wasn't so certain now. Not after these last few days. Or however long it'd been.

Cam's memories were either gone forever or locked

deeply within his mind, and I needed to do something drastic to yank him out of this.

If it's even possible.

I swallowed and pushed that pessimistic idea to the back of my mind. No time to fret. I had a plan to form.

Cam had told me to relax today. But he hadn't told me I couldn't go for a walk. He'd only told me to wait for him here if a blackout were to happen again, which I supposed implied he didn't want me to leave his rooms. However, I could use an excuse similar to the one I'd given him about his laptop—he'd never put me on a leash before. Why would he start now?

I would just play the ignorant card if he found me wandering around.

Of course, that would be harder if I was in the middle of the ritual. But I'd just have to make sure there was no one around when I started.

Or any cameras, I thought. *Although, it sounded like they were turning a lot of those off.*

I chewed on my lower lip as I went into Cam's bathroom and closet to prepare myself. I couldn't exactly go out in just his shirt again. I needed shoes for the stone floors of the catacombs—shoes would also confirm that I'd just wanted to go for a walk—and pants to cover my legs.

Unfortunately, he had very few options for me to choose from as he mostly had suits.

Okay, maybe I'll wear some boxer shorts instead of pants, then, I decided, grabbing a black pair. *They'll fit me like shorts anyway.*

The shoes were another issue entirely.

He had a pair of sneakers, but they were way too big.

Sighing, I selected two pairs of socks instead and layered them on my feet. *It'll have to do.* If he found me, I'd tell him I'd improvised since I didn't have access to my wardrobe. Maybe he'd react the same way he had when I'd pointed out that I needed food and would get me some fresh clothes.

Or he'll be furious and fuck me to death.

Considering that was probably his plan for later anyway, I didn't give the deterring thought much credence.

I ran a brush through my hair and left it down—there were no products for me in this bathroom, just items for Cam—and gave myself a once-over in the mirror.

Exhaustion stared back at me.

Exhaustion with a hint of devastation, I admitted numbly.

I'm not giving up. Not yet. Not now.

I closed my eyes and blew out a breath, then I grabbed the blood vials and tucked them into the band of my shorts.

Right, then. Let's go.

While I knew the catacombs were above the research bunker area, thanks to Mira's conversation with Cam, I had no idea how many levels above me they were or if I would even make it far enough before being caught.

There are cameras everywhere, I muttered to myself as I glanced at the one in Cam's living area on my way to the door. *Hopefully, I'm right about what I overheard and the majority of them are turned off.*

Of course, the one in Cam's suite was probably still on.

Which meant whoever was watching him had definitely witnessed all of our intimate moments. *Awesome. Another item to worry about later.*

Because concerning myself with that frivolity now would just slow me down.

I was determined to do something, *anything*, to snap Cam out of this.

Squaring my shoulders, I grabbed the doorknob and twisted.

Unlocked.

This was either a good sign or a sign that I'd just engaged in a trap.

Regardless, I stepped into the hallway.

There were no guards or any signs of life, similar to the last time I'd entered the corridor. Except the lights were on this time, which helped.

The stone floor was hard beneath my socks, but bearable.

Cool air touched my calves as I started moving, sending a slight shiver up my spine. I embraced it, focusing on the chilly temperature out here—it had to be ten degrees colder than Cam's room—instead of the very real likelihood that I was going to get caught doing something I shouldn't.

I paused outside the elevator. While it would be helpful to see if there were any labels on the buttons inside, it would also probably set off an alarm if I tried to call the elevator.

Stairs it is.

I opened the door and glanced down and up the cement steps. No one was waiting for me.

Hopefully, that was a good sign.

Act confident, I told myself. If caught, then Cam would need to believe that I'd thought this was a perfectly normal thing to do.

I straightened my shoulders once more and started up the stairs, my head held high.

No one stopped me.

No alarms blared.

Just quiet stillness and the soft whisper of my sock-clad feet meeting the cement.

A door appeared after two floors. I opened it and found a hallway that looked just like Cam's did.

Bypassing it, I went up another two flights and found the same thing.

How far under the catacombs is Cam's room? I wondered.

Seven stories, I answered myself after finally reaching the top of the stairwell. At least, I assumed this was the level I'd intended to reach.

A peek outside the door confirmed it, the scent of dust and stale air tickling my nose.

Wow. The research bunker obviously went deeper than seven stories, making me wonder how Lilith had built it all. She'd essentially created a small city beneath the Vatican.

I quietly stepped into the eerie catacomb underground, my neck prickling with awareness. *So much ancient energy. Just like the first time I came here.*

Swallowing, I let the door close, then quickly checked to ensure it hadn't locked. Not that I was sure what I'd do if it had, but fortunately I didn't need to find out.

Right, I thought, glancing around. *So where am I?*

The catacombs were a maze, the lighting barely existent.

Well, it looked similar to what I remembered, just with a few enhancements. Like the various electric-based lights situated at certain points throughout the tunnels.

The stairwell seemed to be in a corner of the underground tunnels, making it potentially easy to return to. Assuming I didn't get lost in here.

My fingers flexed, the urge to curl them into a fist hitting me hard. *Keep. Moving.*

With a deep breath, I crept forward in an attempt to acclimate myself.

When I'd visited with Cam, he'd done all the leading. And we'd entered via a secret tunnel that led to the surface, not the corner staircase behind me.

Hmm. Two choices—left or right.

I opted to go right, my steps slow and steady as I wandered the unfamiliar space. The limestone walls were still very much intact, the tunnel-like surroundings seeming to go on and on.

Which they did.

But the Blessed Ones were in a very specific tunnel, one that had been protected by vampire kind for thousands of years. I'd met two of them when I'd visited with Cam, their roles having been to hide the Blessed Ones from humankind. They'd used compulsion to safeguard their secrets, forcing mortals to forget that certain areas of the catacombs even existed.

Now I just have to find that specific tunnel.

There were several entries to other tunnels to my left as I walked, the right side seeming to be one solid wall of limestone.

The Blessed Ones are kept in a similar-looking location, I thought, recalling how it had felt like we'd reached a solid wall of the underground. *It would make sense for the stairwell to be close to the Blessed Ones, too, right? For ease of access to the research labs?*

Of course, vampires were fast. Some could even phase, which was akin to teleporting. So location really wouldn't matter.

Good thing Cam is busy tonight, I thought, deciding on a random tunnel to my left. *I'm going to need some time to figure this out.*

Hopefully, no one would come looking for me.

He'd mentioned meeting with Michael and Mira, so they should be otherwise occupied.

And the guards, from what I understood, were sparse.

Just pretend to be going for a stroll, I told myself. *You're mated to a vampire. Why wouldn't you choose the catacombs for an evening walk, right?*

Besides, I'd already told Cam he'd brought me here. Perhaps this was what we did. How would he know the difference?

I swallowed, my steps starting to pick up pace a little. Because despite my self-assurances, time wasn't really on my side.

All right, Cane. Where are you?

IZZY

I HAD NO IDEA WHAT TIME IT WAS, BUT THE ACHE IN MY feet told me I'd been walking for a long time. The uneven ground might be part of it, too. However, I'd definitely been roaming for hours.

Not only had I not found the Blessed Ones yet, but I'd also completely lost sight of the stairwell that would take me back to Cam's rooms.

My jaw clenched. *So much for that restful evening.*

At least I hadn't found anyone else lurking down here. No guards. No wandering vampires. *No cameras.*

Well, none that I could see, anyway. If they existed, they were well hidden.

I walked up to a limestone pillar near the entrance to this tunnel and drew an *X* in the dust gathered on the edge.

I'd started doing that after my third row as a way to

mark where I'd been. It had helped me not venture down the same path twice, but it hadn't assisted my sense of direction at all.

And nothing, I thought after several minutes of exploring. *Next aisle.*

I blew out a breath, repeated the *X*, and headed down another row. I wasn't actually finishing them, the tunnels too long to examine completely. One could spend a week down here, maybe more, and still not see everything.

I just needed to find something familiar. Then I could retrace the steps from my memory.

Not here.

Not there either.

I'm definitely lost now.

Hmm. Nope. Nothing familiar here.

Cam's probably going to have to come find me in this maze. That'll go over well, I'm sure.

Ugh, my feet hurt.

More Xs.

And another X.

At this rate, I'm never…

That last thought trailed off as a staircase appeared before me. *Hold on…*

I crept forward, the steps leading up to a solid door. It was a nondescript set of metal steps, one I distinctly recalled from my memory.

Cam and I had met a vampire here, the entrance one humans didn't know existed, thanks to vampiric compulsion manipulating their minds and visions.

I walked up the stairs and turned around to survey the catacombs, my brain immediately igniting with a vivid recollection.

"This area primarily consists of human remains," Cam

had told me. "But over there is the entrance to our ancient crypt."

I closed my eyes and recalled where he'd gestured to, then descended the stairs to follow that path.

My memory led me to a nondescript part of the catacombs, the crypt closest to me lacking an *X*, which meant I hadn't yet wandered down this aisle.

Swallowing, I stepped forward and shivered as a chill kissed my exposed skin. *It's in my head,* I told myself. *Just the past and the present combining in this warped version of my reality.*

Unfortunately, that didn't dispel the unease trickling down my spine. Maybe because I knew if Cam found me here, he'd be suspicious of my intentions.

I need to make this fast.

I had no idea what time it was or how I was going to make it back to his room, but if I could at least wake Cane…

Well, hopefully, it would do something. Or at least be enough to give Cam a reason to think.

This has to work.

I didn't want to consider what would happen if it didn't.

My hands clenched, my palms sweaty despite the cool air. Cam's family crypt was in the middle of all the Blessed Ones, forcing me to pass several other resting places before I found the one I needed.

Unlike the other areas of the catacombs, these crypts had doors, all of them marked by their family crests and other shiny adornments. Cam's family crypt had obsidian diamonds encrusted into the design, their crest topped with a crown to signify their leadership.

While all Blessed Ones and their progeny were considered royals, Cronus's line was seen as the true monarchy.

Which probably explained the opulent gold etchings around his family crypt.

A fancy space for someone to sleep.

The vampires hadn't bothered to invest in air-conditioning or heat but had put significant energy into installing lights and other comforts. And the craftsmanship was exquisite, something that was decidedly evident when looking at the beautiful caskets inside Cronus's tomb.

Three, to be exact.

One was meant for Cam should he ever try to rest.

Did Lilith have you wake up here? I wondered as I slid into the room. *Is that how she convinced you that you were asleep? Or did she keep you here the entire time? Trapped in that endless mental torture?*

It seemed like such an obvious place for her to have hidden Cam. Why hadn't we even considered looking here?

Because it's sacred and shouldn't be touched.

Of course, that logic wouldn't have applied to Lilith. She'd fancied herself to be a goddess, allowing her to break the rules as she saw fit.

Bitch.

I had never been a particularly violent person, but if she were still alive, I would absolutely enjoy killing her. Painfully.

Focus, Izzy, I thought at myself as I gently closed the door behind me. *Time to wake up Cane.*

I would wake up Cronus, too, but I doubted I had enough of Cam's blood to pull it off. Hell, I wasn't even sure I had enough to wake up Cane.

"It doesn't take much," Cam had told me as he'd held his wrist out for Cane to drink. "Our blood is powerful and old. A few drops should do."

I had no idea how much Cane had actually imbibed,

though, since it hadn't been measured out. However, he'd only been attached to Cam for thirty seconds or so before he'd let go and lain down in his coffin.

"I'm ready," Cane had said, his accent similar to his brother's. At least at the time, anyway.

Cam's lilt had evolved over the last few centuries, and it had oddly been the same today despite his lacking memories.

Although, I supposed when Cane woke up, he'd have a thicker English accent, perhaps even a different vocabulary entirely.

Cronus would be even worse. *Would he even know English?*

I wasn't sure. I'd never met the ancient; he'd been asleep for well over a millennium. But Cam had always spoken highly of him, and he'd slept because he'd wanted to maintain his connection to humanity.

I approached his casket first, noting the crest etched into the ornate marble. It matched the one on the door, just as it rivaled the ones decorating his sons' coffins. Only the names along the ribbon at the bottom differed. This one said *Cronus*. The one beside him read *Cam*. And the last one belonged to *Cane*.

All of them had that crown on top and an infinity symbol in the middle, along with two flags and various other details to form the entirety of the family emblem.

These crests weren't commonly seen outside of the vampire community, the royals having kept them close to the chest for millennia.

Fen's was perhaps the most notable with his wolf and claw mark embellishments.

Johan's contained a scale, which made sense for his lineage—Jace had always been notably fair in his judgments.

Meanwhile, Relios's was a tree, which didn't exactly

match his son, Ryder. But I could probably make some sort of profound statement regarding roots and Ryder being a sturdy presence in my life.

Not that I had time for that right now.

No, I needed to focus on Cane.

The caskets weren't sealed, but the marble tops were heavy. Or I assumed they were, anyway. Solid stone couldn't be *light*.

I glanced around for something I could use to perhaps pry the top open and found a crowbar near the door, almost as though someone knew I'd need it. But I suspected each tomb had one for this very purpose.

Or it was there from when they "woke up" Cam.

Rather than ponder over it too much, I grabbed the tool and headed back to Cane's resting place. There was a slight gap between the top and the side, allowing me to slip the slender iron inside to create a lever of sorts.

With a deep breath, and a quick glance at the door, I pushed on the metal handle. The rock grated as it shifted slightly, my efforts only moving the slab a few inches.

It took four more tries to create a larger gap up top.

I held my breath, almost anticipating some sort of decrepit stench to hit my nose.

Yet nothing came.

Just air.

Slipping the bar down a little, I continued my ministrations until the top slab was a few inches off the tomb.

Only then did I peek inside, half expecting to find a decayed corpse.

But that… that would have required a body.

What the fuck?

The coffin was empty.

Just lined with fine silk.

And no Cane.

How….? I pressed on the lever to move the marble another inch. *Shit. This isn't good.*

"What the hell is going on here?" I wondered aloud, my voice barely a whisper.

"Took the words right out of my mouth," a deep voice drawled, drawing my attention to Michael in the entryway.

He'd opened the door without me hearing him, likely because I'd been too focused on opening the tomb.

Had I opened the wrong one? Was he asleep in Cam's coffin? Did Lilith do something to him?

I had a thousand questions, none of which I could ask or voice.

Because Michael was sauntering toward me.

And his expression resembled pure evil intent.

Izzy

I took a step back, but Michael was faster, his hand reaching out to snag a fistful of my hair. He yanked my head back hard as he spun me around and pushed me up against a wall.

"What the fuck are you doing in here?" he demanded.

My jaw clenched. No way in hell was I telling this asshole a damn thing.

His grip tightened, his own jaw ticking. "You still don't get it, do you? Cam's gone. You mean nothing to him now. And you're going to mean even less when I tell him where I found you. Humans don't belong on sacred ground. A fuck toy like you being here is an insult to all of vampire kind."

If that's true, then why did Cam bring me here before? I wanted to demand.

Instead, I said nothing.

Mostly because I was a bit too preoccupied with how the new Cam might react to my presence here.

I couldn't exactly tell him I'd been out for a walk now. I'd purposely disturbed Cane's tomb.

But he isn't in there.

Does Cam know?

If not, then maybe that information would distract him from negatively reacting to my—

A ringing sounded in my ears, silencing my mind and grounding me in the present.

A present where a sadistic vampire now had a hand wrapped around my throat.

And my feet were no longer touching the ground.

It all happened too quickly, my brain slowly processing the situation in pieces.

He hit me, I realized. *Hard.*

Now… now I can't… breathe…

I swallowed. Or I attempted to, anyway. His grip around my throat thwarted the movement.

Michael was saying something, but I couldn't hear him, the echoing in my head too loud. "Weak" was the only word I seemed to understand.

That's rich coming from someone who used to be human, I muttered in my mind.

Or I thought I'd said it to myself, anyway. But I must have spoken the words aloud because Michael growled and threw me to the ground.

His foot hit my stomach, knocking the wind from my lungs as he berated me for my disrespect.

"I earned this position. Meanwhile, you're just an immortal blood bag. He'll kill you as soon as he can find a worthy replacement."

My head burned as he caught my hair up in his fist once more, my vision spiraling with flickers of color amidst a sea of darkness.

"What do you think he's been doing all week while you slept?" Michael demanded. "He's been grooming your replacements, Ismerelda. And after this little stunt? He'll probably take a temporary one without a second thought."

I gritted my teeth. There was no way Cam had been *grooming* anything or anyone this week. Not with how many hours he'd spent inside me.

"He doesn't remember you," Michael went on. "And he will *never* remember you. Lilith's fail-safe made sure of that."

My heart skipped a beat. *"Lilith's fail-safe made sure of that."*

No.

No, I refuse to believe that.

He'll remember me. Cam has *to remember me.*

"Lilith won," Michael whispered against my ear. "You mean nothing to Cam. And even if—and that's a pretty strong *if*—he ever realizes the truth, it'll be too late. The damage is already done."

I tried to shake my head, but his grasp held me firmly in place.

"Where do you think he is right now?" Michael asked. "Because I can tell you... Or maybe I'll just show you."

He yanked me upward, causing pain to shoot up my spine. *Fuck!*

That time, the thought didn't escape my mouth. Probably because I was too busy groaning for coherent words to escape me.

Space whirled around me as Michael dragged me through the catacombs by my hair, my feet moving on autopilot despite the agony swimming through my being.

He's compelling me, I realized as my legs moved without my permission. *He's making me run to keep up with him.*

My lungs protested, my muscles cramping.

But I didn't have a choice.

He was tugging me along without thought or care as to my mortal condition.

Another way to make me feel inferior, I realized. *To prove that I'm* weak.

A growl worked its way through my chest but lost its momentum before it could leave my mouth. All that came out was a soft gasp, my body trembling as Michael started down the stairs.

My feet weren't really touching the ground now. It was mostly my toes, skimming the surface as he maintained his grip on my hair, his compulsion still working magic on my legs.

This is bad.

Very, very bad.

My knees buckled.

My scalp spasmed.

My vision darkened.

Something hard hit my back. *Another wall.* A palm met my face. Michael's lips were at my ear again, his words cruel as he commented on my fragility.

"He'll never turn you," he told me. "And not just because he can't remember you. A millennium is a long time to keep a mortal pet. He obviously never wanted an equal. He just wanted a toy."

You don't know anything about who we were to each other, I wanted to say. But I didn't have the energy to try.

A small part of me also softly admitted, *If Cam had turned me, I wouldn't be in this situation right now.*

He'd kept me human because of our bond. He hadn't wanted to change it. And neither had I.

But now that uncertain voice in my head wondered if I

hadn't wanted to change because of Cam. If I'd been appeasing him instead of myself.

The world shifted again as we continued down the stairs for an inconceivable number of flights. I couldn't focus beyond the pain, my skull pounding from his manhandling.

"He's been down here for hours, too preoccupied to even notice you were missing."

The insinuation in his statement wasn't lost on me.

And the cause for it became evident as he pulled me into a room with half a dozen naked women in it.

I wasn't even sure when we'd left the stairwell or how I'd ended up in this sterile space so quickly, but one minute, I was focused on hating his words, and the next, I was staring at the cause of them.

Blood virgins.

They were too perfect to be any other type of human. And too meek to be vampires or lycans.

Their heads were bowed, their hands loose at their sides.

Michael shoved me to the ground before them, forcing me to kneel. "Ismerelda. Meet your replace—"

"What the fuck are you doing?" Cam's tone echoed throughout the space, his voice sending a chill down my spine.

He was here. With them. Doing… doing…

I couldn't finish the thought, my stomach twisted in knots.

"I found her in your family crypt," Michael said, wasting no time in informing Cam of my actions.

"So you brought her here?" Cam's shoes appeared in my line of vision, making me realize that I'd been staring at the floor. But I didn't want to see whatever state of dress he was in, or lack thereof.

Although, it's a good sign he has on his shoes, right?

"She demanded to see you, my liege," Michael replied.

My eyes widened. "I—"

"*Silence.*" Cam's demand cut through me like a knife, rendering me speechless.

This is too much.

Too… too… hard.

I swallowed, my throat tight from Michael's ministrations. Or maybe it was due to the emotions threatening to choke the life out of me.

I failed.

Michael caught me.

Cam's been busy… doing… I don't want to know.

He played with blood virgins before Mira brought me here.

He's treating me like a sex slave.

His memories are never coming back…

My heart fractured in my chest, stirring an agonizing sensation deep within me.

I didn't want to believe Michael. I didn't want to give up. And yet… *and yet…*

"Mira. Take her to my room. I'll deal with her later."

"Of course, my liege." Mira's silky voice had my hands curling into fists.

She brought me here.

She lied to me.

She betrayed everyone.

The bitch in question grabbed my arm, her nails digging into my skin. "Time to go, Izzy."

My teeth ground together, only for another sharp pang to dismantle my ability to think.

Shit. Michael had hit me hard. And the compulsion to run had turned my legs to jelly.

But unlike last time, Cam didn't intervene. He didn't

even acknowledge me. "Michael. Stay for a moment," he said instead. "We should talk."

The violence underscoring those three words caused my stomach to churn. It was almost sensual. Probably because Cam was in a certain mood, thanks to his *replacements.*

That was the term Michael had been about to use.

My replacements.

The immortal blood virgins destined to serve vampires for eternity without the complications of the *Erosita* bond.

Cam had been here all evening doing what? Testing their aptitudes? Tasting their skill sets? Selecting a new toy?

Maybe he intended to parade them in front of the alliance as some sort of offering.

How has it come to this?

"Lilith won," Michael had said, those two words repeating through my thoughts now.

Because I worried he might be right. That there was no coming back from this.

Maybe I can't save Cam.

Maybe... maybe this is our life now. For the rest of eternity. Until I die...

I said nothing as Mira escorted me to the elevator.

There were several choice things I would have remarked on a week ago that failed to matter now.

She obviously didn't care about her mate or her daughter. Why bother asking?

Why bother even trying to plead with her over anything at all?

If Cam couldn't access his memories, then how could I change his mind?

I could keep trying to knock down the mental wall. Alas, after tonight's stunt, I doubted he'd be all that willing to listen to me, let alone allow me to access his thoughts.

He believes he's superior, that he created all this.

He thinks he doesn't want an Erosita, *that he desires an immortal blood doll instead.*

He's convinced that this is his lifelong dream, his goal for the alliance.

My chest pounded with each thought, my steps heavy, my soul… breaking.

I felt… lost. Broken. Incapable of more thought. Because why did it matter? What would I achieve in pondering over this situation for hours on end?

No.

I would just… wait for him to return.

Maybe I would drink the blood still tucked into my shorts and heal. Or maybe I would simply remain in this state.

Does it matter? Cam's probably going to kill me anyway.

Would he even ask for an explanation? Give me a minute to speak? To tell him about Cane?

My throat worked in an attempt to swallow, every part of me exhausted and overwhelmed and… *finished.*

I was too tired to keep doing this.

Perhaps I should have rested today after all.

"You reek of dejection," Mira muttered as we reached Cam's floor.

She stepped out, her grip still on my arm, and took me to the mouth of the hallway that led to Cam's room.

"Go shower it off before Cam gets back," she added, releasing me. "He needs you to be strong right now. *Push him.*"

Those last two statements were much softer than the previous one, her words more of a whisper under her breath.

I glanced up, confused, but she was already walking away.

"Don't wander off again, Izzy. You won't like what happens if you do."

With that lingering threat, she stepped into the still-open elevator. Only then did she turn to look at me.

Her face was emotionless.

But her eyes... her eyes were all wolf.

And for a brief second, I swore I saw a hint of sadness in their depths.

Then the door closed.

Leaving me alone once more.

What just happened? I wondered, baffled by her conflicting statements. *Did I mishear her? Daydream what I saw?*

I blinked.

Then I shook my head and hobbled back to Cam's room.

Hope was a fickle emotion, one I wasn't sure I wanted to indulge in right now.

But I would take Mira's advice and shower. Maybe it would help wash away Michael's touch.

Or maybe I'll just drown.

CAM

A Few Minutes Earlier

"DR. WAGNER, TAKE THE TEST SUBJECTS TO THE LAB NEXT door. You can proceed with the physical examination and blood draw there."

"Of course, my liege," Wagner replied from behind me. We'd been discussing some of his research results in the adjoining room when I'd sensed Ismerelda's presence.

I had no idea why she'd been wandering in the catacombs, or how she'd found my family's crypt, but I was more interested in Michael's audacity at the moment.

Not only had he touched my *Erosita*—again—he'd brought her here, to a room full of blood virgins about to enter a research compatibility trial.

My teeth ground together as Wagner led the test

subjects out of the room. His movements were methodical and stoic, just as they'd been each time I'd spoken to him.

He was one of Lilith's successful immortal creations, just like Jace's new *Erosita*, Calina. Both Wagner and Calina had been created using a golden-blooded surrogate and a mixture of other supernatural genetics.

Unfortunately, my brethren had killed all the known golden bloods in the world, leaving the blood virgins as the closest available blood type.

Wagner was testing all of them to see if any of the females had close enough markers for a potential surrogacy trial involving the Blessed Ones.

So far, none of the candidates had proved viable, something Wagner had been saying when Michael had barged in with Ismerelda.

The door whispered closed, leaving me alone with my progeny. He'd claimed he'd brought Ismerelda here because she'd demanded to see me, and while that might have been true, he shouldn't have been with her to begin with.

"You should have called me the moment you realized where Ismerelda was," I said as I faced him. "Instead, you took it upon yourself—*again*—to discipline my *Erosita*."

Because there'd been no question as to her injuries or how she'd acquired them.

The bruise forming on her face had been fresh, and I'd sensed her exhaustion, too. I had no idea what he'd done, but I fully intended to find out once I spoke to her.

"I found her in your family crypt." He uttered the words like they were an explanation. No, not just an explanation, a *validation*.

"Which is when you should have called me so I could have handled the situation," I returned.

"I had to stop her, my liege. She was in the middle of opening up your brother's tomb."

I frowned. That was a strange thing for her to be doing. "Did she tell you why?"

"No. She insulted me, then she demanded that I take her to you. That's all she said."

My nose twitched as Michael's scent sweetened. It did that often, something I was beginning to think might be a tell of some kind.

A tell that he's lying to me.

"How did she insult you?" I asked, curious as to if that was the source of his changing cologne or if it was the latter half of the statement.

Because the bruises I'd seen forming on my *Erosita's* throat had suggested Ismerelda hadn't been given much of a chance to speak.

"She reminded me of my mortality," he bit out, causing my eyebrow to arch.

"And?"

"And she said it with a sarcastic tone." He folded his slender arms. "She has no manners, my liege. She doesn't understand her place. And she talks to me like I'm her lesser, not her superior."

Because she should be my queen, not my Erosita, I thought.

The fact that she'd taken it upon herself to wander today spoke volumes of her strength and courage. She didn't act like a weak human. She acted like a vampire.

But why go to my family crypt?

She'd mentioned that I'd taken her there before—to witness Cane's resting ritual—but we'd never finished the conversation.

Was there something she wanted to find? Maybe something tied to an old memory? I pondered. *But then, why not just ask me to go with her?*

"She's a problem, my liege," Michael continued. "We might not have proof of her tampering, but I don't trust her."

I snorted. "She's not here for you to trust, Michael. She's also not here for you to *touch*. Which I thought I made clear to you already, but apparently my lesson wasn't thorough enough."

Michael took a step back, his eyes widening. "I found her opening Cane's tomb, my liege," he repeated. "I reacted protectively. That's sacred ground, and she was threatening to defile it."

"How did you even find her up there?" I asked him. "I sent you to retrieve my laptop. You should have returned and told me she was missing, then let me handle it."

He ran his fingers through his light-colored hair and blew out a breath. "When I realized she was missing, I followed her scent. I was... I was concerned. And you were busy. I was trying to help."

"By laying your hands on my *Erosita*? After I expressly told you *not* to?"

"She refused to come with me, my liege. She was being particularly difficult." He held up a hand before I could comment. "But I see now that I should have contacted you first."

He should have done a hell of a lot more than that. Starting with letting me know she was missing the moment he'd reached my empty room.

I'd sent him to my room as a test of sorts to see if he would leave Ismerelda alone.

He'd failed that test.

However, the circumstances weren't what I'd anticipated, either.

"If I may be bold, my liege, your *Erosita* is acting above her station because you're giving her too many liberties.

She's been spoiled by Majestic Clan's philosophies and hasn't truly embraced your vision for the future as a result. Being stern with her is the only way to correct her behavior."

I stared at him, incapable of comprehending how he could think *this* was the appropriate time to give me a lecture on *my Erosita*. It was as though the male failed to comprehend that she was *mine*, not *his*.

And her *behavior* wasn't his to correct.

"She should be locked in the room you created for her," he continued, obviously oblivious to my growing ire. It'd already reached a peak before he'd started speaking.

Now, it was erupting in silent waves of hot fury that prickled the hairs along my arms, flowing all the way to my fingers—fingers that itched to wrap themselves around this man's throat and *squeeze*.

"At the very least, you need to lock your door," he went on, his survival instinct clearly obsolete.

How the fuck is this male my progeny?

"But I personally don't think she should be allowed to live after what she's done. She desecrated sacred ground by setting foot in the catacombs, then further violated the area by trying to pry open your brother's tomb." He shook his head, his fingers running through his hair again. "She's broken, my liege. Unfixable. In my opinion."

"In your opinion," I echoed, my voice lower than before. Lethal, even.

"Yes," my ignorant progeny replied. "I can handle the task for you, if you'd like. I know you're busy and she's not really worth your time."

Why would I choose to turn this male and not Ismerelda? I wondered, baffled as to how I could ever have found this imbecile worthy of my blood.

"Do not touch Ismerelda," I told him, violence

underscoring each word. "In fact, don't go fucking near her again."

"My liege—"

"No," I bit out, my hand wrapping around his throat as I slammed him against the nearest wall—which was a good fifteen feet away. However, phasing allowed me to cross that distance in less than a second.

Michael's pupils flared, his eyes blowing wide.

"I warned you not to touch her, Michael. I told you what would happen if you disobeyed me."

My grip tightened around his windpipe, the urge to rip his head off causing my inner predator to grin with malicious excitement.

"*She is not yours to punish. Or to fucking touch.*" The snarl of words left my mouth on an infuriated hiss of sound, one that chilled the air between us.

A shadow fell over his features, his heart thudding loudly in his chest.

Yes. You sorely misunderstood your predicament, I thought at him. *But you understand now, don't you?*

"Ismerelda may have misbehaved today," I told him. "However, I will speak to her about it privately. Only then will I decide if a punishment is warranted."

Because, frankly, I was more curious about her actions today than angered by them.

Very unlike how I felt about Michael and his incessant need to interfere where my *Erosita* was concerned.

"Your blatant disregard for my demands is a problem," I went on as his face began to change color due to the lack of oxygen. "A problem that I'm not sure I can allow to live."

He grabbed my wrist, his nostrils flaring.

"If I can't trust you with a simple *no touching* policy, then how the fuck am I supposed to trust you to do anything else competently?"

His nails dug into my skin, his other hand coming up to my shoulder in an attempt to shove me away.

I didn't move.

I was much older, much *stronger*, than this worthless excuse for a male.

"You may fancy yourself superior to my *Erosita*, but she's *mine*. That makes her an extension of who I am. And *I* am your fucking Liege."

He started to squirm, his legs kicking out at mine, his fight instincts beginning to take hold.

Because he seemed to understand that I wasn't just going to choke him until he passed out and then let him wake up.

No. I fully intended to rip his head clean off.

He hurt my lioness. Twice.

Never again.

I didn't care if it made me appear weak or obsessed or possessive. I was the fucking king. If I wanted to take a mate, then I would take a fucking mate.

If I wanted to turn Ismerelda, then I would fucking turn her.

And no one—especially not *Michael*—would influence my choices.

"I forgave your initial insult. I even gave you another chance, yet you deliberately ignored my—"

My watch buzzed with an incoming call, Mira's name appearing on a holographic screen beside me.

Fuck. I'd told her to escort Ismerelda to my room. Which meant there could be only one reason Mira was calling now.

"Don't move," I told Michael as I released him.

He partly disobeyed me, his knees buckling and

sending him to the ground. Fortunately, he remained mostly still after that, his only sounds ones of wheezing and coughing.

My inner predator grinned with dark satisfaction.

Meanwhile, my practical side focused on my watch.

"Answer," I growled at it, my gaze narrowing at the image floating in the air.

Mira's calm features appeared, her icy irises vivid on the screen. "My liege," she greeted. "Helias is here."

I blinked. "What?"

"His jet just landed. Apparently, the humans running the flight towers assumed he was here for the Coventus and assisted with his arrival. Not that they could refuse him, anyway. He's a royal, my liege. The royals and alphas are treated as royalty among the humans."

"I'm aware," I muttered, her explanation frivolous and unneeded. All Helias would have had to do was announce his arrival and the humans would have bowed to the request without question.

It was as it should be—vampires and lycans were superior. Humans were lucky just to be alive.

But if that's all true, if this is truly my desire, then why do I enjoy Ismerelda's bravery? I wondered. *Why did her courage make me feel proud?*

I should want her to kneel. To bow. To *beg* for her life. To thank me for choosing her. To make her crawl and supplicate and obey.

Yet I didn't.

Instead, I wanted to reward her with immortality for proving to be stronger than the rest of her kind. For proving to be courageous. For proving to be opinionated and challenging and very much unlike the other humans in this world.

However, Ismerelda came from a world where her

behavior was normal. A world where mortals had equal rights.

Vampires and lycans had stripped away those rights and enslaved the human race.

For what purpose? I asked myself. *How is any of this logical? To want to praise Ismerelda for her bravery but also squash it at the same time?*

"My liege?" Mira prompted, drawing my focus back to her. "How do you want to proceed?"

"On what?" I asked, momentarily confused. *On Ismerelda? On the plan for this world? On——*

"Helias, my liege," she said, her brow crinkling just the slightest bit. "Should I tell him to fly home?"

Right. Helias.

Focus, Cam.

I cleared my throat. "Did he say why he changed the parameters of our call?"

"Yes. He said that video and audio can be manipulated, while an in-person meeting cannot."

My lips curled down. "Is he implying that we intend to record him?"

"No, my liege. I believe he's saying he wants proof that you're alive."

I stared at her. "And he thinks that can be faked with a video call?"

"Yes." A single word with no elaboration.

"I see." I'd read in Lilith's files that several royals suspected I might be dead; it seemed the revolutionaries had spread that rumor to undermine me.

Apparently, Helias had concerns that those rumors might be true.

I could tell him to fuck off, but it would likely benefit me later to appease him now.

One never knew when an allegiance might be needed.

"Bring him to the Coventus's conference room," I told Mira. "I'll meet with him there."

She bowed her head. "Yes, my liege."

The screen disappeared in the next beat, leaving me with Michael still cowering at my feet.

Clearly, I had more important things to handle right now. And I wasn't in the mood to make Michael's death quick.

Assuming I still want him dead, I thought. *He did react the way anyone else would in finding a human roaming around in the catacombs.*

Only, Ismerelda wasn't any normal human. She was *my* human.

"Stay the fuck away from my *Erosita*," I told him. "And go help Dr. Wagner with his labs."

I'd figure out what to do with him later.

I had an old friend to greet.

IZZY

I ENDED UP DRINKING CAM'S BLOOD, MY NEED TO HEAL trumping every other thought in my mind. I also took a shower.

But I didn't bother drying my hair.

I left it combed and wet and just put on one of Cam's dress shirts, then paced his room while I waited for him.

The absence of pizza meant either it'd come and gone in my absence, or it wasn't time for dinner yet. I had no concept of the hour, the lack of a clock leaving me very much in the dark. I couldn't even try to peek at Cam's computer for an answer because it was no longer here.

Is that how he knew I wasn't here? I wondered. *Had he come back for his laptop, realized I was missing, and sent Michael to look for me?*

I shivered, his ire a palpable presence that still lingered on my skin.

What is he going to do to me?

Something painful, surely.

Something sexual, too.

Or maybe he'd just discard me for one of those blood virgins.

God, how was I supposed to fix this? To fix *him*?

"He will never *remember you. Lilith's fail-safe made sure of that."*

Michael's words reverberated around in my head, each one threatening to dissolve the last strands of hope in my mind.

Cam's memories are gone.

This is who he is now.

And I… I'm just his immortal blood bag.

I wrung my hands in front of me as I paced, my teeth grinding together. *I can't give up. But I… I don't know what to do.*

Waking up Cane had been an epic failure. He wasn't in his coffin. And even if he had been, I wouldn't have had time to do the ritual.

"Lilith won. You mean nothing to Cam."

I winced, Michael's voice echoing in my thoughts on repeat, the finality of his statements continuing to chip at my resolve.

If Cam's memories were inaccessible, then I had to win him over in his current state.

A state whereby he'd been brainwashed by Lilith to hate humanity. To think of me as property, not a person. To care only about his vampiric satisfaction and nothing else.

Even if I could get through to him, would we be able to move on from this? He's playing with other females… Because I'm not enough for him?

After over a thousand years of faithfulness, of being by each other's sides, his body still allowed him to indulge in someone else.

No, not just someone—*someones*.

I didn't want to hold it against him, and I knew it wasn't really fair, but how could I just let that go?

My hands flexed, then curled, and then flexed again as I drew my arms around myself. *What can I do?* I asked myself on repeat. *How do I fix this?*

I continued to pace, my body healed from Michael's treatment—and my endless walking earlier—yet exhaustion tugged at my psyche.

No amount of Cam's blood could alter my feelings. He could give me a temporary high, a taste of euphoria, but the moment reality settled, my mood plummeted.

"I love you, Ismerelda. Always. Forever. For eternity."

I closed my eyes as I pictured Cam's face, the earnestness in his features, the adoration in his gaze, the warmth in his touch…

My throat tightened.

"I love you, too," I'd whispered back to him.

How many times had we engaged in that exchange? A hundred? A thousand?

A promise to always be there for each other. To always care for one another. To always be together.

Except, he's not that Cam anymore. And he'll never be that Cam again.

To give up on him would be worse than his infidelity. He needed me now more than ever. But how could I help him if he didn't want my assistance?

Without his memories, he was a completely different person.

Is this who he would have been without me? I wondered. *Was he always destined to be this cruel monster? And I just distracted him from that path? Or were there other aspects of his life that made him who he used to be?*

Had I altered fate? Was this fate correcting itself?

My jaw hurt from clenching it so hard.

I hated this. Hated Lilith. Hated Michael. Hated *fate.*

"He'll never turn you. And not just because he can't remember you. A millennium is a long time to keep a mortal pet. He obviously never wanted an equal. He just wanted a toy."

I swallowed, those last two sentences repeating in my mind.

Is he right? I wondered. *Is that why Cam never turned me?*

I shook my head. *No. He... he just wanted to preserve our bond.*

But why? I whispered. *Was it really because he didn't want our connection to end? Or because he needed my blood?*

I palmed my forehead, my eyes burning behind my closed lids.

These brimming uncertainties were going to drive me mad.

I knew Cam. He was my mate. The other half of my soul. He wouldn't... he wouldn't just *use* me.

And yet, this version of him did.

This version of him—the one that was essentially like the male I'd met a thousand years ago—had no problem seeing me as a doll meant for his pleasure alone.

So how did I change him then? Why can't I do it now?

Because the element of surprise was gone.

That element of surprise—the moment when I'd given him pause because I knew what he was—no longer applied.

Humans were fully aware of the existence of vampires and lycans now.

Humans were also enslaved to them.

There was nothing extraordinary enough about me to make Cam take a few steps back, to truly evaluate the potential of our situation. Instead, he was hungry. Demanding. *Sexually charged.*

I wasn't unique to him. Hell, I probably didn't even taste as good to him as the blood virgins did. All I had to barter with was my body, which clearly hadn't been satisfying enough to keep him entertained for long.

My knowledge of his current likes and dislikes might prove useful, but nothing more. And once I divulged enough information to appease his curiosity, then what?

I pinched the bridge of my nose and blew out a breath.

He'd told me to relax today. I was very much the opposite of relaxed. A bath would do little to dispel the tension tightening my shoulders and neck. Besides, he'd probably try to drown me in it when he returned.

And I did not want to die that way.

What am I going to say to him? I wondered. *Can I distract him with news of Cane being out of his tomb? Or does he already—*

A male voice echoing down the hallway had my head snapping up, my gaze focusing on the door. *Cam.*

No, I thought in the next beat. *Michael.*

"Are you sure, my liege?" he was asking. "Because there's no going back."

"It's the way she should have died a thousand years ago," Cam replied, his English accent more prominent than usual. Or maybe it just felt that way because of the words he was saying.

What does he mean, "It's the way she should have died a thousand years ago"?

He couldn't possibly be talking about the night we met... right?

He... he wouldn't... He couldn't... He didn't even remember...

Except… Well, I'd told new Cam about it. Not every detail, but enough for him to… to…

No.

No.

"Seems fitting enough to me," he concluded, causing the hairs along the back of my neck to stand on end.

Fitting?

"If you're certain."

"I am." Two crisply spoken words that sent a chill down my spine. There was a hint of finality there, a whisper of *goodbye*. "Get it over with."

This… no.

No fucking way.

He can't—

"As you wish, my liege," Michael murmured. "Consider it done."

"Good. I have more important things to tend to."

"Understood, my liege."

The door to Cam's suite opened, but not all the way. "Do what Michael says, Ismerelda."

My lips parted. *What?* He wasn't even going to give me a chance to talk to him?

"Are you fucking kidding me?" I breathed out. "No. No!" I ran to the door, prepared to go through it and grab him by the shirt.

But he was already at the end of the hall, his suit-clad back all I could see before he disappeared into the elevator.

"Cam!" I shouted.

The doors shut without him even bothering to turn around.

"I'm sorry, Izzy, but I warned you," Michael said, his shoulder braced against the wall across from me. "He's done. Which means *you* are done."

I stepped backward as he pushed off the wall, my head

shaking back and forth. "No," I said. "He just needs to let me explain."

"There's nothing to explain. You're a glorified blood bag who has proved to be incapable of respecting her superiors. He's already found one to replace you. One who, what did he say exactly?" He glanced upward and snapped his fingers. "Right. A blood virgin who knows how to properly perform in the bedroom."

I narrowed my gaze. "I've been his mate for over a thousand years."

"Yes," he agreed. "But the man you mated died over a century ago. This is the new and improved Cam, and he no longer needs his blast from the past."

Michael grabbed me by the back of the neck, his movements lightning fast.

"Walk with me, little blood whore," he demanded. "I've been given very specific instructions to let you die the way nature originally intended for you to die."

He uttered the words as he dragged me into the hallway. I tried to stop him, to anchor my bare feet to the ground, but my legs moved against my will, suggesting he'd silently compelled me to cooperate.

Or maybe Cam did that when he ordered me to do whatever Michael said, I thought, shuddering.

"The Liege said he finds it *fitting*," Michael mused, repeating the statement I'd already overheard. "I suppose it's his way of correcting a wrong and resetting fate on the appropriate path."

"That's only because he doesn't know who I am," I snapped, furious and terrified that my legs were still moving without my permission.

"And he never will," Michael returned. "Lilith's protocols fried the part of Cam's brain where the *Erosita* bond exists. All his memories of you were erased as a result, and there's no way for him to get them back."

I ground my teeth together. "There is if he looks in my mind."

"That would require him to actually care enough about you to try," Michael drawled as we entered the elevator.

He selected the number thirteen, causing the lift to spring into action.

"You've had roughly ten days to convince him of your true importance, and you've failed. Why? Because he's no longer the Cam you knew. Instead, he's the Cam he was meant to be—a king destined to rule the alliance and bring all the rebels to heel."

"He never wanted any of this," I argued. "He stood against it."

"For you," Michael murmured. "But as Lilith predicted, without your mortal influence in his mind, he's a proper vampire. We just had to be sure of that before we unleashed him on the world."

I frowned. "What?" I asked as the doors opened to a new floor. "Sure about what?"

"Sure that he was officially cured of your influence," he replied. "Bringing you here was the ultimate test. His decision to break his ties with you is the passing grade."

My blood went cold. *This whole thing was a way to see if I could... if I could still influence him through our bond?*

"Thanks to you, we now know losing the memories is key to curing those with longstanding infatuations." Michael sounded pleased. "So thank you for your participation in this study. Your services are no longer required."

He paused outside a door, a truly evil grin gracing his full lips. He knocked once on the wood, his palm finally leaving my nape.

"You're going to go in there and offer yourself up as dessert," Michael said. "And die the way fate intended you to die."

He took a step closer to me.

"The best part is, you have no choice but to enjoy it, because I'm telling you to." His green eyes flickered with ominous intent. "You're going to moan with delight while they rip you apart, all the while begging and crying in your mind where no one can hear you scream."

I stood frozen as he leaned forward to brush his lips against my cheek.

"I'd say it's been a pleasure, Izzy, but that would be a lie. The pleasure will be in watching you die."

CAM

I SAT AT THE TABLE, MY FINGERS DRUMMING AN IMPATIENT rhythm against the wood tabletop.

My gaze flicked down to my watch, my eyes narrowing. I'd been in this damn conference room for the last ninety minutes, waiting for Helias to arrive.

What the fuck is taking so long?

Rome was practically abandoned apart from the Vatican, making it rather easy to navigate the streets. From what I understood, Lilith had renovated the once famous mortal city to meet her needs, which included installing a much closer airport.

Thus, Helias should've been here by now.

I pulled up Mira's name on my watch, half tempted to call her. Perhaps I shouldn't have come directly up here after leaving Michael with Dr. Wagner.

Had I known it would take this long, I would have gone by my room first to have a word with Ismerelda.

Why were you in the catacombs? I wanted to ask her. *What were you trying to do to my brother's tomb?*

The temptation to link to her mind to question her was strong, causing me to prod a bit at the mental walls between us.

Hmm. It seemed the blocks in place had deteriorated over the last week, indicating my growing curiosity regarding our bond and our true history.

The inclination was only natural to want more information, particularly as my memories didn't appear to be coming back. *Why can't I remember her?*

Something about it didn't feel right. I'd suspected it was due to her not meaning much to me, but that logic didn't match my decisions. Why would I keep an *Erosita* for over a thousand years if she didn't mean anything to me?

No, the more time I spent with Ismerelda, the more connected I felt to her. A lot of it was likely a result of the bond, but there was something else here.

Her behavior only deepened my interest, especially the incident today.

My lips flattened as I checked my watch again, my impatience growing. I'd much rather be questioning Ismerelda.

Hell, I'd much rather be doing a lot of things to my *Erosita* than sitting in this empty room.

A king waits for no one, I thought, my gaze narrowing. *So why am I waiting for a lesser royal? One who chose to show up unannounced at that.*

My jaw ticked.

I didn't have much experience with this emotion —*impatience*. Mostly because I'd lived too long to care much for the passing of time.

An hour was nothing for a vampire my age. Mere seconds, really.

So why did this feel like an eternity?

And what the hell is this sensation in my chest? I wondered suddenly, my palm covering my heart to rub at the ache forming there. *A physical response to my growing irritation?*

No, that didn't seem quite right.

Why would irritation stir pain?

Why am I feeling pain at all?

I frowned.

Something is very wrong here.

I glanced at my watch again, as well as Mira's name hovering over my wrist. I hadn't minimized the translucent screen. My finger itched to touch the Call button, but an instinctual part of me held back. A part I didn't quite understand.

A part linked to that odd pang stirring inside me.

I returned my hand to my chest, my fingers pressing into the muscle in an attempt to alleviate the pressure. Yet it only seemed to be growing, the intensity warming my veins and sending shocks to my nerve endings.

My brow furrowed. *What is this?*

A particularly painful spike sliced through my being, making me wince. Then I gasped as my lungs suddenly fought for air.

It felt like I was dying.

Like I was losing the will to live.

What the fuck is happening? I shoved away from the table, my predator instantly searching for whatever threat was doing this to me.

But I sensed nothing.

Because it wasn't coming from an outside source; it was coming from within me.

Ismerelda, I realized, my brow coming down.

What the hell are you doing? I demanded, my words slamming through the barrier between our minds as the shield I'd created long ago crumbled to pieces. *Why are you…*

I trailed off, my spine straightening as Ismerelda's psyche washed over me.

Devastation.

Despair.

Hopelessness.

She… she was reliving some sort of memory. A horrific one. One where she was surrounded by several men, all of whom intended to harm her.

Only for a shadow to appear. *Me,* I recognized in the next breath. *The night we met.*

She'd mentioned something about this, about how I'd saved her, but seeing it in her mind… it… it added credence to the story.

Except the memory seemed to be blending into something else. Something horrendous.

Don't, she told herself. *Focus on real Cam. Remember him. Only him.*

I blinked, not understanding what she meant.

He's gone, she whispered. *I tried. I failed.*

"Lilith's protocols fried the part of Cam's brain where the Erosita bond exists. All his memories of you were erased as a result, and there's no way for him to get them back."

Michael's words echoed in her mind, the statements not current, but a memory.

When was this? Is it real? I followed the strand in her thoughts, her conversation with Michael unfolding before my eyes.

I could see him from her point of view, feel her pain as he lashed out at her with his claims.

And then I felt her utter defeat as he… as he…

My eyes widened. *Fuck!*

That was the reason for her thinking of the night we met. The bastard had led her to a similar fate, one she seemed to think *I* had demanded.

What the hell? I phased out of the room and to the elevator, my mind locked on Ismerelda's as I dug through her memories to figure out exactly where Michael had taken her.

She'd paid just enough attention for me to follow her.

Come on. Come on. Come on. I thought at the slow-moving lift. *Fuck this!*

I burst into the stairwell and phased to the thirteenth level of the underground. The door practically fell off the hinges as I ran onto the floor.

Ismerelda's scent—*fear and desolation*—drew me right to her.

To a room.

A room full of vampires.

Several of whom had their fangs in my *Erosita.*

Draining her. Killing her. *Touching* her.

She was naked. They were naked. Hard. Ready to fuck.

One was already in her mouth. Another... positioning between her legs...

Red.

Everything. Went. *Red.*

My inner beast *roared*, my hands and legs moving without thought as I painted the room in deadly shades of *red*.

Bloodcurdling screams rent the air, followed by the violent thuds of heads rolling across the ground.

It all happened in a split second, my speed and strength far superior to every supernatural in the room. They'd been too lost in their feed, in their intended *rut*, to even sense me coming.

And Ismerelda... *my lioness*... fell limply to the ground.

I went to my knees beside her, my bloody hands moving over her, searching for... for... for a way... *fuck.*

A way to what? To make this okay? To make this right?

I...

How the hell did this even happen?

It was like a bad dream.

A bad dream made worse by all of Ismerelda's thoughts infiltrating my mind.

She'd shut down entirely, choosing to lose herself in her mind rather than allow my compulsion to win.

What compulsion? I wondered, only for the response to slam into me in the next moment.

New Cam can't have this, she'd told herself. *He may have compelled me to obey Michael, but I refuse to give them the satisfaction of hearing me* enjoy *my death.*

It'd been an act of defiance on her part. A final *fuck you* to me and Michael.

Why do you think I did this to you? I demanded. *Why would I hurt you in this way?*

She didn't reply, her psyche locked in some sort of memory spiral. A safe place. One she'd created in a moment of despair and closed herself within.

I swallowed as more events played out in her mind. Nights of lovemaking. Passionate words. Promises. A world of love and admiration and respect.

"I love you, Ismerelda. Always. Forever. For eternity."

"I love you, too."

"It's the way she should have died a thousand years ago. Seems fitting to me."

My brow furrowed as memories seemed to overlap in her thoughts, one an ancient vow and the other... I followed the words, ones she recalled me saying, and watched her recollection of events.

This was today. Maybe thirty minutes ago. It's what led to this.

But that man wasn't me.

A realistic hologram, maybe? Lilith's technology was advanced enough to pull it off. That was why Helias wanted the in-person meeting—he didn't trust this technology era.

I cleared my throat, my hands still fluttering uselessly over my *Erosita.* The fact that our bond was still in place confirmed that none of the men had penetrated her vaginally, but she… she was definitely…

"*Fuck.*" I wanted to kill everyone in the room all over again.

There'd been six of them. *Six.*

Why the fuck would Michael do this? And all those things he'd told her…

Is it…?

I cleared my throat again as more of Ismerelda's mind melded into mine.

She hadn't been surprised at all by Michael's revelations because she'd known something about it already.

A truth I wasn't sure I understood.

Lilith won, she kept lamenting, her heart seeming to break with the admission. *That bitch won.*

By fucking with my mind.

That seemed to be the consensus.

Ismerelda's frame of events did not match mine.

Yet she'd kept them to herself all this time, aware that I would never have believed her. Never have trusted her. Never have even considered listening to her side of events.

She'd tried to win me over in other ways.

With sex.

Only, that had backfired.

He doesn't care about me. This is all for him. Even my pleasure… is for him.

This isn't how we make love.

This isn't my *Cam.*

Please come back to me… I… I miss you…

"Gods," I whispered. "What the hell have I done?"

I'd… There were no words. I… I couldn't…

"Fuck, Ismerelda." I pulled her into my arms, her sweat-soaked hair clinging to my suit jacket.

I need to get us out of here, I realized.

It wasn't safe here.

No one could be trusted. Nothing was what it seemed.

I needed answers. Answers only Ismerelda seemed to have. But she was catatonic in my arms, lost so deep in her own psyche that she was barely breathing.

I bit my wrist and pressed it to her mouth, mentally compelling her to drink. But she was too far gone to obey me.

Shit.

There wasn't time to snap her out of it here. We needed somewhere to hide. A place where no one could find us. Only then could I begin to try to fix this. To apologize. To… to *grovel.*

Later, I told myself. *Focus on getting out.*

Michael had said he would be watching Ismerelda die, which made it likely he'd seen me slaughter the entire room of vampires.

Fortunately, not much time had passed. Maybe five minutes. Not nearly long enough for him to amass enough vampires to take me down.

Unless he has whatever device Lilith used to incapacitate me before. I could hear whispers about it in Ismerelda's memories, something about how it was connected to the part of the mind where the *Erosita* link resided.

*He'll never remember me. He's irrevocably changed. My Cam…
is dead.*

Her thoughts resembled daggers against my chest, each
one pricking my insides in a way I'd never experienced.

Her pain was my pain.

Her heartache was my heartache.

And her damaged soul… was my damaged soul.

I'll fix this, I promised her, not that she seemed to
hear me.

But first, I needed to get us the fuck out of this bunker.

Hold on, my queen, I whispered to her. *Just, please, hold on
for a little longer. I'm going to make this right. I vow it.*

PART II

ETERNALLY BITTEN

CAM

THIS PLACE IS A BLOODY MAZE.

Endless corridors. Stairwells. Crypts.

While I knew my way around the underground tunnels that Lilith had built beneath Vatican City, I hadn't been to the surface much. My few visits to the Coventus hadn't counted.

But now I needed a way out.

An escape.

Somewhere to take the unconscious woman in my arms.

My *Erosita*.

My *mate*.

Fuck.

Her mind revealed so many truths, so many *memories*, that I could barely hear my own thoughts.

She was reliving the night we'd met on repeat, thinking

about how I'd saved her from being gang-raped. That recollection blended with the present as the word *fitting* echoed in her head.

"Seems fitting enough to me."

My voice echoed in her mind, only I'd never said those words. I'd told Michael to leave her the fuck alone, not drag her off to a room full of low-level vampires.

"You're going to moan with delight while they rip you apart," he'd told her.

If I saw him on our way out of here, I'd be ripping him apart instead.

What the fuck was he thinking? I wondered as I phased up several flights of stairs to the catacombs.

There were numerous staircases throughout the underground compound; I'd chosen this set because I wanted to avoid the Coventus—which was in the heart of the former Vatican at ground level.

I didn't know who I could trust down here. And I didn't want to risk running into anyone.

Ismerelda's memories warned me about some sort of weapon Lilith had used to incapacitate me.

Impossible, I kept thinking. But there was no denying the validity of the claim in Ismerelda's mind.

The same weapon had been used on Ryder. Yet he'd been saved by his *Erosita.*

And then she helped kill Lilith, I marveled, gathering the truth from Ismerelda's recollection of events. Ryder had finished the job with an ax, but his hybrid mate had immobilized Lilith first.

Fascinating.

I lost myself in her memories once more, her psyche possessing a wealth of information from my lost time on earth.

Everything I overheard conflicted with everything I thought I knew.

Lilith's logs had depicted me as the Liege, the creator of this new world. It'd been my vision for lycans and vampires to rule. For humans to be treated no better than cattle. To create a superiority system based on blood. *To rid our kind of our* Erosita *links.*

Gods, what a fool I'd been to believe a voice on a computer. But Michael had played his part well, too. Pretending to be my assistant. Feigning subservience.

Fuck, was he even my progeny?

How deep did the lies go? What was the truth? What was fiction?

Ismerelda's mind held so many answers—answers I skimmed while trying to focus on my surroundings.

There wasn't time to properly evaluate her or her memories. I had to get us somewhere safe. A place where I could take my time absorbing a thousand years' worth of knowledge and experience and figure out what the hell was really going on here.

A location where we could be alone and heal.

Ismerelda had locked herself away in her head, her body completely limp as I carried her through the catacombs. Talking to her in this state would be impossible, even with my ability to speak into her mind.

Instead, our psyches seemed to be weaving together, my internal questions sparking answers from her thoughts and providing memories to go with them.

Like now as I navigated the underground, I pulled the memory of the last time we'd been here together.

There was a staircase that led up to ground level, the door one humans had never known existed, thanks to vampires manipulating their minds.

Instinct drove me toward that exit. Mostly because I didn't trust what I knew—or what I *thought* I knew.

There were cameras everywhere.

Including in my room, I realized as another one of Ismerelda's experiences graced our link. *She found the camera in the ceiling near my bed, saw the footage from it on my laptop.*

I would ask her why she'd never told me about it, but I already knew the answer—I would've never listened to her.

She was a human. A glorified pet. A slave meant only for blood and sex.

Yet some part of me had already begun to acknowledge her as my equal. A potential partner. *My queen.*

I'd wondered why I hadn't turned her. Unfortunately, that part remained unclear.

But this female had obviously been mine in every way.

Why did I block you from my mind? I questioned. *Why would I cut off our link?*

The response hit me on a wave of agony as Ismerelda recalled my choice to build that impenetrable wall, how I'd taken it upon myself to face Lilith alone and hadn't involved my *Erosita* in the decision at all.

"I thought Cam told you the plan. But you don't know," Luka had said after telling her about how I'd apparently staged her death. "I... Izzy..."

"Cam just staged your death to get captured by Lilith," Mira had added. "He knows she won't kill him. His blood is too powerful for her to waste. But he's hoping to talk to her. And he needs you to remain here, where you're safe, while he works."

Is that really what I said? I wondered. *Or is this another lie?*

Michael had told me that Mira had served as my *Erosita*'s babysitter, ensuring Ismerelda had remained safe and content while I'd slept. It'd also served a dual purpose of spying on Majestic Clan and their known associates—vampires and lycans who might not be acclimating to the world changes as well as the others.

That appeared to be true for the most part, but was the explanation accurate? Had I truly left Ismerelda behind just to talk to Lilith?

Why the fuck would I do that?

A recent memory answered my question.

"He never wanted any of this. He stood against it." Ismerelda's voice had been insistent. Angry, even.

"For you," Michael had returned. "But as Lilith predicted, without your mortal influence in his mind, he's a proper vampire. We just had to be sure of that before we unleashed him on the world."

The recollection turned into Michael admitting why she'd been brought here—to test the theory.

He'd claimed I'd *passed* because I no longer cared about her, as evidenced by me leaving her with those monsters.

Fuck. If I could shred them all again, I would. Especially hearing Ismerelda relive it again and again, the juxtaposition between the event and how we'd met wreaking havoc on her thoughts.

I wanted to force her to stop. To make her *wake up*. But I couldn't. Not here. *Not yet.*

The staircase I'd seen in her mind finally appeared, the area around it dark and vacant. No signs of life. Just dust and the scent of ancient limestone. Still, I ascended carefully, my senses on high alert, waiting for someone to step into my path.

Michael had mentioned a *we*. Had he been referring to himself and Lilith? Himself and Mira? Or was there someone else in charge here? *Maybe a puppet master I haven't seen yet...*

Regardless, I needed to be prepared for everything and

anything. And whatever weapon Ismerelda kept thinking about inside her mind.

The weapon that had disabled me. *Destroyed* me. My mind. My love for her. My soul.

I'm going to fix this, my queen, I promised her as I stepped out into the night, my focus on the shadows of the stone-paved courtyard.

Nothing moved or breathed, including me. I didn't trust the silence, not after all the details I'd discovered in the last few moments.

Michael had said this was a test—one I'd passed. But I hadn't. As was substantiated by the unconscious woman in my arms. She still wore the blood of the vampires I'd killed, their essence sticky rather than dry.

Because only a handful of minutes had transpired since I'd found her.

Which meant Michael might be coming after us now.

Try it, I thought, my jaw flexing.

Except the unknown weapon chipped at my confidence. From what Ismerelda's psyche told me, the device manipulated the section of the mind connected to a vampire's *Erosita*.

Ismerelda had suspected that might be the cause of my memory loss. It would make sense as to why every event tied to her no longer existed in my head, yet I could recall other things.

Such as this courtyard.

I've been here before. An obvious deduction, given that Ismerelda had shown me this in her mind, proving we'd been here together.

But I'd also been here without her, because there were details I recalled that I hadn't picked up on from her thoughts. *Like the courtyard's only exit.*

I phased over to the archway that led to an old side

street, my senses sweeping up and down the cobblestone alley, searching for potential threats.

Nothing.

Because we were outside the Vatican City walls here.

And all the vampires were deep inside the bunker, protecting other immortal assets.

That part I knew was real—the lack of supernatural personnel on-site. Lilith hadn't trusted many of our kind with our—no, *her*—secrets. Thus, the primary security I should face up here would be human Vigils.

At least until Michael deployed the others to come after us.

Assuming they're even chasing me.

There wasn't time to ponder Michael's intentions or what-ifs; I needed to put distance between us and this place. *And the weapon that rendered me useless.*

I phased down the alleyway to another main street, my moves driven by ancient recollections of what Rome used to be.

Unfortunately, it was nothing like I remembered.

Quiet. Abandoned. *Desolate.*

The buildings weren't crumbling or destroyed, just *empty*. Dust settled in the air around me, the small flecks disturbed by my teleporting down vacant streets.

I need a car, I decided, seeing none in sight.

But I knew from my trip to the airport the other week that there were several automobiles and bikes near the compound.

And even more near the city border—which we had crossed to reach the airfields.

Everything had been guarded by humans. No vampires or lycans.

That gave me an advantage.

Lilith wouldn't have trusted mortals with a potentially

lethal device against her own kind. She'd only given them weapons to use against other humans. And she'd taught them to be subservient to vampires.

What else did she teach them? I wondered as I teleported Ismerelda and myself along a familiar street. It was the same route I'd taken with Michael to the airport, the road as vacant as all the alleyways and buildings around us.

Gods, I'd been so irritated that day, the concept of having to drive to my *Erosita* feeling degrading and below me.

"She should be coming to me, not the other way around," I'd said to Michael. "Why the fuck am I standing here, waiting for a fucking toy?"

"Because she insisted," Michael had told me. "I warned you, my liege. She's not conforming like the other humans. She seems to think she's some kind of queen."

I'd been disgusted by the concept, and even more turned off when she'd run toward me on the tarmac.

All that hope in her eyes...

That happiness...

I swallowed, glancing down at her now. Blood and other fluids marred her pretty features, her naked body lifeless in my arms.

No more hope. Definitely no happiness.

No life.

My teeth ground together as I phased us another mile ahead. I paced myself, primarily because I was carrying Ismerelda. I didn't want to risk hurting her. Not any more than I already had, anyway.

Fortunately, it didn't take long to reach the city blockade—a fancy set of gates that had been installed on the road to force cars and bikes to stop upon entry.

Many of the other roads leading into Rome had been

demolished or blocked by residential developments that housed Vigils and other mortal servants.

It served two purposes: a way to operate as a place for humans to sleep and a means to force anyone venturing into Rome to halt their process.

Vampires and lycans assumed it was in place to regulate access to the Coventus—and the sensually trained blood virgins housed within.

They were half-right. But their lack of investigation or questions caused them to miss what was hidden beneath it all.

A lab full of immortal experiments. At least I knew that part was true. Everything else remained to be seen.

Five humans leapt into action upon my arrival, their shock palpable.

Two of them instantly bowed.

One gripped his gun a little tighter.

And the other two gaped at me before remembering their roles and mimicking the bow the first pair had executed.

A chorus of "Sire" filled the air, the Vigils clearly uncertain of what to do.

They were meant to protect the city limits and report any arrivals—which likely always occurred by automobile or limo, not by foot.

"I need a car," I told them. "And a phone." I had no idea if the latter would even work—*were the network issues a lie, too?*—or what number I'd dial, but a communication device seemed like a sound idea.

Unless it would also be equipped with a tracking mechanism.

Fuck. What if there's a tracker inside me? Michael had been so obsessed with the possibility of Ismerelda having one. Was that why? Because he knew I had one?

If that was the case, I needed to put as much distance between myself and this city as possible.

We need to cross a boundary. Go into a territory that Michael and Mira won't dare enter.

Hazel Region, I decided in the next instant, recalling what Mira had said about Hazel.

"Hazel has never approved of Lilith's reign."

It could be a lie. However, searching Ismerelda's mind now, I didn't pick up on any hint of dislike toward the ancient royal.

Very unlike Ismerelda's response to thoughts of Mira and Lilith.

My little lioness was downright feral when it came to the now-dead "Goddess." She was both excited and jealous that Ryder's *Erosita* had been the one to take Lilith down. She wanted to kill the cunt all over again. Make the pain last. *Bleed her dry.*

I growled in approval inside, my own desire rivaling her own.

But we had more pressing matters to see to, such as the fact that none of the humans had responded to me yet.

"Was I not clear?" I asked, arching a brow. Not that any of them could see it—they were all staring at the ground, including the one with the gun. "I need a car and a phone. I also need a human who can help me make a call."

Primarily because I had no idea what numbers to dial to reach anyone. Michael had helped me call Jace a few weeks ago, and the external connection had been unavailable since.

I would need to phone Hazel first, inform her of my intention to cross into her region.

Unless the calls will be monitored.

But Michael would likely be sending someone after us regardless. *And we might have trackers embedded in us somewhere.*

Which meant I needed these humans to start moving. *Right fucking…* "*Now.*" I uttered that final word aloud, my impatience underlined by the bark in my voice.

"Keys," the one with the gun breathed. "*Keys.*"

My brow furrowed. "Yes, keys would be useful."

But the moron started shaking his head, his resulting tremble making me question why this Vigil had been trusted with a gun. "N-no, you—"

"He's paging me," a deep voice said as a dark-skinned male appeared in my peripheral vision. He stood in the doorway of one of the new residence-style buildings, only this one was actually a security depot.

"My unit calls me *Keys*," he continued as he walked toward me. "I'm Vigil One, manager of this checkpoint. How can I help you, Sire?" He bowed his head on that last part, his reverence a little delayed. At least according to new customs.

"I need a car, a phone, and a human who knows how to operate both," I told him. "And I need all of that done right now."

He raised his head, his brown eyebrows lifting. "Only two of us here know how to drive, one of whom is me. And I'm the only one who has been trained on communication devices."

"Then I guess you're who I need right now, *Keys*." I stared at him expectantly.

While my brain might be a riddled mess of truths and lies, the hierarchy of our reality was certain—vampires and lycans ruled and humans served.

I'd just thought the whole concept had been my idea, thanks to Lilith's mindfuck.

Keys cleared his throat. "Right. Yes. This—"

A blaring alarm cut him off, his shoulders hunching as he visibly flinched. The other humans reacted similarly, all of them standing at full alert, their gazes surveying the boundaries for the cause of the disruption.

My senses flared as a buzzing sound filled my ears, the source of it coming from Keys's wrist.

He responded nearly a second later, his human reflexes much slower than mine. I caught his forearm before he could answer the incoming call, Ismerelda's weight shifting unsteadily against my chest.

"Ignore the alarms. Remove your watch and drop it on the ground. Then focus on finding me a car and a phone." I laced each word with compulsion while sending a blast of power out to the humans around us, knocking them out with a mental command to *sleep*.

Not many of my kind contained this level of vampiric persuasion.

But I wasn't an ordinary immortal.

I was the oldest vampire in existence.

The one who should be king.

The rightful fucking Liege.

"Yes, Sire," Keys answered with a swallow, his gaze flitting over the bodies lying all around us as he removed his watch.

"Ignore them," I instructed him. "Focus on my tasks."

I readjusted Ismerelda in my arms, then stomped on his watch before dropping my own—and stepping on that one, too.

It didn't serve a true purpose, but it soothed the anger brewing within me. At least temporarily.

"This way, Sire," the human said, his voice devoid of emotion as he adhered to my commands.

I followed him while the alarm continued to blare from the watches of the humans we'd left behind us. The sound echoed in the distance as well, telling me more humans were being dispatched to our current location. I swept my senses in a half-mile radius, dropping every mortal I touched to the ground and putting them in a temporary coma-like sleep.

There weren't many humans—maybe three dozen.

And my senses didn't pick up on a single lycan or vampire.

They were all either still deep underground or not bothering to come after me.

At least, I assumed the alarms were for me and Ismerelda.

Not that there was much an army of humans could do against me. Except maybe shoot me to temporarily knock me out. But that required them to be awake and aware and brave enough to try.

There are flaws in your system, Lilith, I thought at her dead soul. *So many flaws.*

Keys led me to the house where he used a card from his pocket to digitally open a steel cabinet built into the wall just inside the door. "What car would you like, Sire? We have—"

"I want the fastest car you have that will travel the farthest distance without needing to stop."

He nodded and plucked a set of keys from the top row. "This one is fully charged to go fifteen hundred kilometers and maxes out at five hundred kilometers per hour."

My eyebrows threatened to rise. "Really?" That was… impressive. Technology had clearly continued to advance while I'd slept. "That'll do."

Rather than respond, he bent to find the second item I'd requested. "Satellite phone," he said as he held it out toward me. Then he rattled off a series of digits, saying it was the code for an external call.

"Hold on to it and take me to the car," I told him, not accepting the phone.

He dutifully obeyed, his steps languid instead of rigid. Almost as though he was enjoying my compulsion, not hating it.

When we reached a sleek black sedan, I nodded toward the back door. "Open it."

He obliged without me having to compel him.

Hmm. I gently set Ismerelda on the soft leather interior, her bloodied and bruised form causing me to move her slower than I usually would. I just didn't want to risk hurting her more. "Do you know the number for Hazel Region?" I asked Keys.

"I know the number for their checkpoint at the border, yes," he replied.

"Good. I want you to call it and let them know we're coming." I straightened to look at him. "And tell them you'll be driving."

CAM

Keys made the call.

Then he slid into the driver's seat, pulled up a navigation panel to direct us to Hazel Region—something I verified by watching him closely—and began driving.

Three hours later, he was still silent, his gaze on the road as we entered former-day Bologna. He was making good time with this car yet driving at a slower pace than I would behind the wheel.

However, we didn't appear to have anyone tailing us.

So I let him continue on our path while I observed from the back seat.

I'd taken off my suit jacket to wrap it around Ismerelda, her head resting in my lap, her eyes closed. She hadn't stirred at all, my darling queen having locked herself deep within her own mind. I wanted to coax her out, but to do that, I needed to understand her. To understand *us*.

Thus, my focus shifted between our surroundings and her memories. *Our* memories. Memories I might never experience for myself.

How had I become this male? I kept wondering, confused by how softly I'd treated Ismerelda. She'd been my own little porcelain doll, a beautiful being I'd been too afraid to hurt. Hence, I'd left her on this untouchable shelf and had done everything in my power to ensure no one and nothing could harm her.

Had I not noticed the lioness lurking in her gaze? Perhaps I'd been too blinded by my heart or too scared to lose her to focus on anything other than protecting her.

But at some point, I'd lost sight of who she could be. What *we* could be.

I'd left her in the care of another male—a *lycan*—and run off to save the world without her.

What an arrogant and selfish thing to do.

Nothing should have mattered to me more than Ismerelda's life. Yet I'd abandoned her for everyone else. Put the fate of humanity over the fate of my *Erosita*.

Perhaps *selfish* wasn't the right term. Yet it felt that way.

I'd put my own purpose—my own *goal*—above my relationship with Ismerelda. I hadn't asked for her input. Hadn't treated her as an equal. I'd just... acted.

She harbored some resentment toward me for it. However, that resentment was riddled with guilt.

Because she didn't want to fault me for my decision. She understood it. She even wanted to commend me for it.

But deep down, she was hurt. Angry. *And scared.*

That sort of decision had required a conversation. Yet there hadn't been one.

I'd simply cut her off.

And disappeared.

I ran my fingers through her knotted strands, my throat working as I continued skimming through her mind, learning more about our history, about *us*.

Most of it felt wrong, like I was observing a past that belonged to her, not to me. Which I was in a way. Except all her recollections featured a man who looked exactly like me. *Dark hair. Blue eyes. Chiseled jaw. Straight nose. Muscularly lean. Tapered waist. Fine ass.*

Her descriptions of me rolled through my mind, causing my lips to curl in amusement.

She might hate me when she woke up, but part of her would still want me. Just as she had all week.

Although, thinking of that had me hearing her mental distress—something I'd entirely missed while lost in her sweet pussy.

She'd been miserable.

Ecstatic at points, too. But overall… *broken*.

Which had led to her current state.

"Fuck," I breathed, rubbing a hand over my face as her thoughts and memories rushed over me, the heat of them searing my heart rather than my groin.

She'd enjoyed what I'd done to her, all while hating it at the same time. Because I'd treated her like she'd meant nothing. A toy to be fucked. *Someone I didn't know or respect.*

Ismerelda wasn't wrong.

But she wasn't exactly right either.

I'd handled her roughly because I knew she could take it. More than that, I knew it would intensify her pleasure, which it had.

However, she'd been too distraught to truly enjoy it.

She was used to a male who treated her like a fragile object, not an equal.

That's a mistake from my past self, I thought at her. *One I will be rectifying.*

Ismerelda wasn't a docile doll; she was so much more.

You're my queen, I whispered to her. *Why have I never turned you?*

The answer didn't reveal itself, her memories not touching much on the topic of her not becoming a vampire.

Did we never discuss it? I wondered.

Had I kept her human for her blood? Or had I kept her human because I preferred to keep her weak?

The former would be a practical reason. The latter... a selfish one.

Sighing, I focused on our surroundings again, noting the wildness growing alongside the roads. Vines and other greenery had taken over the vacant storefronts, gas stations, and various other structures. It was clear this area hadn't been inhabited in well over a hundred years. And other than the road, nothing else had been looked after.

"Is it like this everywhere?" I asked Keys. "The run-down buildings and out-of-control greenery?"

The human blinked up at the mirror before refocusing on the road. "I... I don't know, Sire. The airport is the farthest I've been from the Coventus. Other than my time at the Blood University, anyway. But that... hadn't been like this."

I considered him for a moment. "What had it been like? At the Blood University, I mean."

"Cold," he replied without missing a beat. "There was ice everywhere."

"Hmm, one of the Nordic schools, then," I guessed, recalling the map of Blood University locations.

There were ten scattered across the globe, some of them on random islands and others in locations vampires and lycans didn't want to claim—like lands covered in snow.

"You were either in Svalbard or Greenland," I told him. "Not that those names mean anything to you now."

He said nothing, just focused on the road, but I caught the subtle interest in his features—the flare of his nostrils, the way his throat worked as he swallowed, his gaze chancing a glance at me in the mirror once more.

"You have no idea who I am, do you?" I asked, the realization yet another punch in the gut.

Lilith's logs had claimed the humans were taught about royals and alphas, our identities well known and revered.

But Keys hadn't mentioned my name when he'd made his call earlier.

I hadn't thought much of it, my concern having been on getting the fuck out of Rome.

However, now I grasped the fatal error of that conversation.

"Hazel has no idea I'm coming," I mused aloud, the human seemingly frozen in the front seat. "Did the checkpoint personnel not ask for an identity?"

"You're a vampire, Sire," Keys said slowly. "It's not our place to ask for a name."

I nearly laughed. "Of course." *Because humans serve in this world.* "But you don't know me at all. My name. My reign. My royal status?"

The human's shoulders went rigid, his gaze returning to the mirror long enough for the car to swerve.

"Focus on the road, Keys," I told him conversationally. "I'm not upset." Well, not at him, anyway. "I'm just… absorbing the information that you have no idea who you're driving to Slovenia."

His lips curled downward.

"Sorry, *Hazel Region*," I clarified. "The border for her

territory begins in Slovenia, a country from the olden world. I assume you've never heard of it?"

He stiffly shook his head.

"Because all you know are regions and clans," I presumed aloud. "That's all they allow you to know." I ran my fingers through Ismerelda's hair again, another sigh escaping me. "It's strategic. Keeping mortals in the dark makes them easier to control. Lilith had me convinced that it was all my idea."

Which made sense because, intellectually, I understood her decision.

But hearing Ismerelda's mind made me realize that there'd been a key piece missing from all of this—my humanity.

You're the reason I feel, I thought, looking down at the angel in my lap. *You keep me grounded. Help me remember my human nature. Ensure I don't become a complete monster.*

And I'd rewarded all of that by abandoning her on a quest to save mortal kind.

Fascinating, I marveled. *Fascinating and infuriating.*

"My name is Cam," I told Keys, my attention returning to the barely breathing human in the front seat. I needed him to calm down and focus on driving safely. While I'd absolutely survive a car accident, Ismerelda might not.

Oh, she'd wake up eventually.

But we didn't have time for any of that.

And she would lose her memories like she did when I killed her, I thought, frowning once more. *Fuck, I'm an asshole.*

She'd been so relieved to see me alive, so enthralled by my presence, and I'd... *bled her dry.*

Her mind filled in the memory for me, only from her perspective, showing me the pain of that moment. Her heart shattering in her chest. How she'd thought it wasn't me, that Lilith had somehow created an evil look-alike.

Not my Cam, she'd often thought. *He's not* my *Cam.*

Except I was her Cam, something she'd soon learned. That moment appeared to be almost as agonizing as the one where I'd sucked the life out of her. Perhaps it was even more excruciating.

It was hard to say.

Ismerelda had a lot of distressing recollections from the last two weeks.

Because of me.

I bit the inside of my cheek, my fingers threatening to curl into fists.

This was all so fucked up. *I* had fucked up. *Fucking. Lilith.*

"A-are you a new royal?" the human asked from the front seat, his question catching me off guard and distracting me from my mental tirade. "If you are, I apologize for not recognizing you, My Prince."

I snorted. "I'm more than a royal, Keys. I'm the fucking king. The oldest of vampire kind. But you can call me *Cam*. I'm tired of false platitudes."

Keys's hands tightened on the steering wheel, causing his exposed forearms to flex. Given what he'd revealed about his university assignment, I wasn't surprised by his choice to wear sleeveless fatigues. This region of the world probably felt like hell compared to the Arctic.

"The oldest?" he repeated, his brow furrowing in his reflection in the mirror.

"I take it they didn't teach you that fact in your vampire politics courses?"

"They taught us all the royal names and pertinent details. Kylan was noted as the oldest of vampire kind." He swallowed. "I… I don't recall learning about you…"

His hesitation didn't seem to be about disbelief so much as nerves, like he was afraid he'd just failed a test or something.

"No, I imagine not. It seems my existence has been kept a secret." Which wasn't what I'd been led to believe at all.

Yet another lie in a field of untruths. *Shocking.*

"I'm older than Kylan, just not by much." A few centuries, maybe. I wasn't quite sure. "Time becomes irrelevant after so many millennia."

Time, among many other things, I thought, my fingers still lost in Ismerelda's hair. *My humanity was nearly lost when we met. You helped restore my faith in humankind.*

Or that was what I'd gathered from her mind.

Perhaps you restored it a little too well.

Why else would I sacrifice everything for human lives?

"What else did the university teach you about the world?" I wondered aloud, curious as to what mortals really thought today. "Take me through an average day at school and what you were taught."

Keys cleared his throat, his fear a pungent scent in the air. I nearly commented on it, but he seemed to squash it himself in the next breath, his shoulders squaring as he refocused on the road and began speaking.

He took me through his average day, which included sexual training, physical training, and world preparedness courses.

Vampire politics—as previously mentioned.

Lycan hierarchy.

Service industry tutorials.

General education classes—math, written communication, verbal obedience.

History.

I asked him more questions about that last one, my amusement growing by the minute.

"That's utter bollocks." Everything he'd been taught about the formation of the world had been a lie. "Humans used to rule. Vampires and lycans fought back after the mortal governments tried to weaponize the shifters."

I wasn't sure why I was bothering to tell him all this.

Maybe I just needed something to pass the time on this drive. Perhaps it was because he'd impressed me along the way. Other than my initial compulsion, he hadn't required any persuasion. He'd simply obeyed. And he hadn't been all that afraid.

At least not until he'd realized who I was.

But even now, he was relaxed again and taking all of the information in stride.

"Are you used to vampires talking to you?" I asked him. "As you're the lead Vigil for your unit, I imagine that happens often."

He lifted a shoulder. "I typically meet with one or two a week. But our conversations only last five minutes at most. Nothing like this."

"Then you're oddly at ease with this situation."

"I learned long ago that there is no sense in living my life in constant fear of what might be; it's better to just embrace what is, instead."

"A wise approach," I admitted. "One that goes against Lilith's goals, I assume. But she would have been too blind to realize that."

Keys didn't reply, but I caught the way he flinched at my tone. Or perhaps it was the mention of *Lilith* that bothered him. He'd probably been taught to only address her as *Goddess*.

I nearly grunted at the concept.

No wonder her voice irritated the fuck out of me, I grumbled to myself. *Because she'd been torturing me with it for over a century.*

My gaze returned to Ismerelda, my attention shifting into her psyche again as I sifted through more memories. More truths. More *pain.*

She was cowering somewhere deep within the recesses of her mind, refusing to come out. Like she'd given up on life. On existing. On *us.*

I'd tried feeding her some of my blood when we'd settled into the car, but she'd refused to swallow. My essence still lingered on her lips, her body rejecting mine.

You can't hide in there forever, my queen, I whispered to her. *I'll find you and drag you out if I have to.*

Which was probably the wrong way to approach this. But I needed her to wake up. We were about to enter another vampire's region in a world I didn't trust or know. Ismerelda was the only one I could rely on.

I also wanted to… *apologize.*

The term made me frown. I couldn't remember the last time I'd felt the need to *apologize* for anything. Granted, the last millennium was a bit fuzzy, but my memories prior to meeting Ismerelda were very much intact.

Maybe Cane? I thought, my frown deepening. *Is he the last one I apologized to?*

I'd accidentally killed his human pet. Not directly, but indirectly. She'd offered me a vein. I'd accepted, and then I'd left her for him to heal.

Only, he hadn't been the one who'd found her nearly drained in her hut.

Another man had.

And he'd taken advantage of her weak state before slitting her throat.

A gruesome scene, one I'd felt an inkling of remorse about. However, Cane hadn't truly cared. He'd shrugged and found a new pet a week later. Still, I'd felt the need to voice my regret. Thus, I had.

But *this*, with Ismerelda, sparked far more than an *inkling* of guilt.

I'd hurt her in a way that burned my very soul. I owed her far more than a mere apology.

"Who is sh…?" The words were a whisper of sound from Keys's mouth that he tried to cover up with a cough.

I arched a brow at his reflection in the mirror. "Were you about to ask about my *Erosita*?" My fingers were still stroking through her blonde strands, the knots long gone despite the blood sticking to some of her hair.

She needed a bath.

A long grooming session.

Food.

Compassion.

"*Ero…*?" Keys started to repeat.

"*Erosita,*" I said again. "It's a fancy term for a vampire's human mate. Very rare. Mostly because my kind gets bored easily. However, I've never grown tired of Ismerelda." Something that wasn't just evident in her memories, but also in the way I'd become obsessed with her in a very short time. "She's mine."

Keys glanced up at me, then back at the road, his expression carefully blank.

His ability to mask his reactions was impressive, really. And perhaps a bit sad. Mostly because I could only assume this discipline had been beaten into him.

Lilith's regimen for humans had been all about turning off their emotions and molding them into silent and willing blood bags. Well, silent when outside of the bedroom, anyway.

I'd witnessed a bit of that with the blood virgins.

The Blood Universities probably maintained similar training methods.

"You can speak and react freely around me, Keys," I told him. "It would actually be rather refreshing after all the lies I've been told."

His grip tightened on the steering wheel like it had before, his biceps bulging. It was the only tell he displayed to convey his discomfort.

"This isn't a test," I added. "You can't fail. And I won't hurt you." If anything, I might just reward him.

Assuming things go smoothly in Hazel Region...

I'd met Hazel several times in my very long history, but I had no idea what kind of vampire she'd become while I'd been indisposed. "Tell me what you know about Hazel, Keys."

Because I would use all the help I could get right now. Even small details could be useful.

Such as whether or not Hazel seems to support this new way of life, or if she appears to oppose what this world has become...

CAM

"Princess Hazel runs Hazel Region," Keys informed me, his statement fucking obvious and a complete waste of time. "She has five sovereigns, two—"

"I don't care about the politics, Keys. I'm asking about Hazel as a vampire. Is she kind? Cruel? One of Lilith's former minions? A cunt? What's her personality like these days?"

Keys froze again, a hint of shock rolling off him in a tangible wave. "I... I don't know how to answer that, My Prince."

"Preferably bluntly," I told him. "And don't call me *My Prince* again, or I'll consider leaving you stranded here while I take the car."

I wouldn't actually do that. Despite barely knowing the human, I rather liked Keys. Perhaps because he was helping me when I needed it.

Not that he had a choice.

But he wasn't exactly fighting it, either.

"I don't… I don't know Princess Hazel." His words came out on a breath, his emotions peeking at me from beneath his veil of stoicism.

"Surely you all discuss the royals in private? Share rumors?"

He shook his head. "No, My…" He coughed again, attempting to mask the words he'd been about to say. "It's against the rules to discuss such matters. Besides, I have no one to discuss those things with."

"What about the men in your unit?"

He blinked in the mirror. "Our focus is on security, not talking."

"Don't you need to communicate to do an effective job?" I pressed.

"Our discussions are limited to what we see. When not on shift, we train, eat, or sleep."

"No socializing," I translated.

"Socializing is forbidden," he parroted at me, the statement sounding more like a repeated rule than his own personal mantra.

"I see." I hadn't spent a lot of time reviewing files on the Blood Universities; I'd only studied high-level curriculum details, not the actual execution of said curriculum.

"We are also permitted to pray three times a day," he added. "Typically before a meal, to thank the Goddess for all she does."

I laughed. "Praying three times a day? To Lilith?" She'd mentioned assuming the role of *Goddess*, as per *my* supposed recommendation. "Fuck, that's rich."

Now I understood Ismerelda's feelings on Lilith's death.

I, too, was jealous that I hadn't been the one to rip the bitch apart.

The car swerved a little, another burst of surprise chipping at Keys's mask.

"She's not a Goddess," I informed him. "She's a vampire. Or she *was* a vampire. Until Ryder killed her."

Keys's foot slipped, causing the automobile to jerk around us. "Wh-*what*?"

"Take a breath, human. Your heart is beating far too fast for your mortal form." And I really didn't want him to crash.

I was about to compel him to calm down when he managed to harness control of his emotions all by himself, his inhales and exhales evening out within a minute of his initial freak-out.

"I'm going to assume news of Lilith's demise hasn't reached mortal circles yet," I murmured. "Perhaps the communication problems Michael claimed back at the compound were true."

Although, Ismerelda's mind told me she doubted it. When the situation had first occurred, she'd questioned Michael's veracity. Primarily because she'd noticed my laptop had never been connected to the internet, just the intranet. Meaning my computer only had access to internal files, not external ones.

Hmm, so you do know more about computers than you let on, I mused, entertained by this reveal in her thoughts. *You played me like a proper queen, mate. I approve.*

Even the way she'd tested me had been clever—claiming she'd cooked for me often while knowing the *real* Cam would be aware of the lie.

Apparently, she couldn't cook to save her life.

Thankfully, it hadn't come to that.

"I don't... I... the Goddess?" Keys sputtered

ineloquently. "The Goddess is—" A ringing sound interrupted whatever gibberish he'd been about to rattle off, his attention immediately shifting to the dashboard. "It's… it's Hazel Region Checkpoint."

"Answer it," I said calmly, anticipating this call. He'd warned the checkpoint that a vampire was coming, but hadn't elaborated on which vampire.

From what I'd read in the files, there were protocols in this new world regarding vampire travel and visitation to clans and regions. Whoever was calling would want my identity and to know which royal had approved this trip.

This vampire was about to be stunned.

Except as the screen appeared over the dashboard, it displayed a woman I didn't recognize. *Curly brown hair. Thin face. Gray eyes. Tan skin.* Definitely a unique appearance. Beautiful, too. Absolutely a vampire. But I didn't know her.

"How old are you?" I asked before she could speak, her gray irises flickering from my driver to the back seat.

Keys flicked a button that brought the image closer to me, the translucent screen reminding me of some of the technology I'd witnessed in Lilith's labs.

"Who are you?" she demanded, ignoring my question.

"Someone you shouldn't be questioning, young one," I answered flatly. "State your age."

She had to be newly turned. I could see it in the barely restrained fury glittering in her gaze—that brewing anger was too fresh to belong to an older vampire. She hadn't yet mastered her emotions.

And even with the training regimen Lilith had created for the mortals, being converted into a vampire would demolish all that hard-earned training.

"You're less than a century old. Maybe a decade or two at most?" I pressed.

Her jaw clenched. "I was turned twelve years ago by Sovereign Deirdre."

My eyebrow inched upward. "Black hair, pale complexion, penchant for fencing?" The flare of the woman's nostrils confirmed my description. "Call her and tell her Cam is on his way. She'll know what to do." I reached forward to flick off the screen, the method one Michael had taught me a few weeks ago.

It caused the image to dissolve and disappear, the hologram no longer hovering near me in the back seat.

"Her name is Abigail," Keys said after a beat. "She won the Immortal Cup when I was fifteen."

"Hmm," I hummed, recalling all the details I'd read about the Immortal Cup from Lilith's files. "Two mortals every year win immortality." It was a clever ruse to control the mortals—force them to compete against each other rather than work together. "Did you want to compete?"

"Of course I did," he replied. "We all do."

"So you want to be immortal?"

"It would beat being mortal."

"Vampire or lycan?" I wondered aloud. "Which would you choose?"

"What's the point in dreaming about something that can never happen now?"

"Well now, that's not a positive outlook," I told him. "You have the oldest of vampire kind in your back seat. You have no idea of the power that's lurking right behind you, Keys." I wouldn't turn him. At least, not right now. But I could.

Or maybe I'd recommend him to someone else.

"I can't compete in the Immortal Cup," he replied.

"Maybe you don't have to," I returned. "So answer my question—lycan or vampire?" Because he had to have thought about it. Especially if he'd wanted to compete for immortality.

All humans possessed dreams.

Hell, vampires and lycans did, too.

It was a part of life.

Unless Lilith's antics have completely demolished that side of humanity, I thought, my lips curling down as I glanced at my *Erosita. When was the last time you dreamed, little lioness?*

Her mind told me in a flash, the visuals of me warming my heart. Until those dreams melted into reality.

Her last dream had been particularly potent. She'd dreamt my memories had returned, only to discover that I was fucking her awake… and not at all who she'd just imagined me to be.

It'd nearly broken her then, her heart shattering into a thousand jagged pieces upon the realization that I was still a monster.

I swallowed, the burn in my chest rather unpleasant. I didn't like hearing her call me that. Oh, I was absolutely a beast. A predator in a sleek suit. But a monster? Not to her. *Never* to her. Only *for* her.

"A vampire," Keys said, drawing me away from Ismerelda's pain. "I would choose to be a vampire."

"Why?" I asked him, craving this distraction.

"Shifting into a wolf doesn't appeal to me. I'd prefer speed and agility on two legs instead of four." He shrugged. "Plus, vampire bites are kinder than wolf bites."

I snorted at that. "Truth. All of it." Although, if my inner animal could be released, he'd absolutely be a large, intimidating wolf.

Alas, I was all vampire. But my inner spirit was undeniably savage.

Keys said nothing more, his posture relaxed as he drove.

I checked the map, noting we still had another two hours to go before we reached the checkpoint, primarily because Keys was driving at a safe speed rather than a quick one.

Had it just been me, I would have demanded that he drive faster. But for Ismerelda, I was okay with this pace, especially since it seemed to be energy efficient as far as the battery was concerned.

There was no one else on the road. No signs of life. No security. Not even a hint of a maintenance crew, yet I knew one had to exist. These paved streets were too clean and well kempt to be completely abandoned.

Lilith had probably assigned the work to mortal teams.

Service workers.

Better than being dinner, I supposed.

Of course, that was the fate of all humans. *Including Vigils*.

Keys's commentary about not fearing the future was probably how he maintained his composure now—driving a predator through the middle of nowhere to another region.

He had to wonder if he was about to become dinner.

I parted my lips to comment on it, when the phone rang again.

Keys glanced at the screen. "I don't recognize the number."

"Answer it anyway," I said, expecting to see Deirdre or Abigail on the screen.

Except neither of them appeared when Keys hit the Accept button.

Instead, it was Hazel.

Her dark brown eyes instantly met mine, shock flashing across her porcelain features as Keys flicked his fingers to send the translucent screen back into the space in front of me.

"Jesus," Hazel breathed.

"Not a name I've ever answered to," I deadpanned. "But I'll accept *God* instead."

She released a delicate snort, then shook her head. "Where the fuck have you been?"

"Locked in a cell under the Vatican," I answered truthfully. There was no point in voicing riddles or wasting time. I needed to know if Hazel was an enemy or a potential ally.

And there was only one way to determine that over the phone—by testing her reactions to the truth.

"Or that's what I've gathered, anyway," I went on, referring to where the fuck I'd been. "Apparently, Lilith created a weapon that can render vampires mindless. She used it to hold me captive before destroying a thousand years' worth of my memories."

Hazel gaped at me, her lips parting soundlessly.

It was the reaction I'd hoped for because it confirmed she hadn't known about Lilith's antics. More than that, she wasn't amused by them—she was stunned. And not in a positive way.

Or maybe she's just a good actress.

Only one way to find out...

"The technology has something to do with the part of the mind where the *Erosita* bond exists," I went on. "Ryder recently experienced it for himself. I believe you know how that ended."

I was, of course, referring to Ryder randomly broadcasting a video of him holding Lilith's severed head for the entire alliance to see, shortly after Jace had decapitated Lajos.

"Those are some... heavy allegations..." The words

left her slowly, ending with her clearing her throat. "Do you have proof?"

"My sudden appearance and explanation are not enough for you?" I asked her.

"Through a phone?" she countered, scoffing at me. "No."

My lips curled. "Then an in-person meeting will have to do." Because once we met in person, she'd know the truth.

And, consequently, so would I.

"Indeed," she agreed. "I'll also be calling Ryder to corroborate your story."

I translated that to mean she intended to invite him to Hazel Region for a visit.

"I suggest asking Jace about it as well. He can be more eloquent than Ryder." And by that, I meant Jace understood vampire politics and respected his fellow royals. He would serve as an amenable intermediary. A translator for Ryder's bluntness.

Assuming Ryder even allowed that.

"I'll consider it," Hazel conceded. "Abigail will retrieve you from the checkpoint and take you to Deirdre City."

I stared at her. "Where?"

She blinked. "Former-day Bled."

"Oh." Right. The remaining functional cities in this new world had been renamed after royals and their sovereigns. I hadn't finished studying all of the hierarchy yet. "Keys will drive me there."

"Keys?" she echoed.

"My human escort. He's under my protection now. As is Ismerelda." I glanced down and back up just as Hazel followed my gaze to my *Erosita*. The royal vampire had been so caught up in my appearance that she hadn't noticed the female in my lap.

She swallowed, her brown eyes flickering with an emotion I couldn't quite define. Surprise, perhaps. Surprise and... *relief?*

"I look forward to seeing you both soon," Hazel said softly. "Abigail will still meet you at the checkpoint and serve as your guide. Your human escort—*Keys*—can follow."

Her words served as a formal invitation to her territory, one I was grateful for. "Thank you, Hazel."

"Don't thank me yet," she replied, ending the call.

My lips curled. It'd been a while since I'd spoken to the old vampire. However, she hadn't seemed to change much. Still formal—which reminded me of Jace—but with a hint of compassion.

It could be a ruse. She might be one of Lilith's former allies. But my instincts told me she wasn't.

She hadn't been noted in the files as a supporter of the cause. She'd been noted as neutral.

Then Mira had claimed Hazel was untrustworthy, her contention with Lilith well known.

So which is it? I wondered. *Is she neutral? Or is she against this new world?*

I would find out soon.

In the interim, I'd prepare myself for a mental battle. *And try to wake up Ismerelda.*

JACE

"Anything?" I asked as I stepped into the makeshift command center of my tower.

Damien glanced up from his monitors. "You're as bad as Ryder," he drawled. "Always checking in when you know full well I'll send you an update the moment I have something to report."

I snorted. "Maybe I just want a reason to see you."

"Careful now. You'll make that beautiful doctor of yours jealous."

"Hardly," said doctor replied from behind me. "You can have him." Calina uttered the words in her infamous deadpan, causing me to arch an eyebrow back at her.

Your mind says otherwise, little enchantress, I informed her. *As does that sweet scent blossoming between your thighs. Are you considering inviting Damien for a night of fun?*

Her blue-green eyes glittered as she met my gaze. *No. I rather like him alive. And we both know you'd kill him for touching me.*

I smiled. *So you have thought about it.*

You have access to my mind, she replied. *Have I thought about it?*

Hmm, I hummed, searching her thoughts and finding all of her sensual intrigue directed toward me. *And here I thought humans were susceptible to a vampire's* natural *prowess, thus making all of vampire kind irresistible and seductive by default.*

The words were a reference to a conversation my *Erosita* and I had engaged in shortly after we met, whereby she informed me her attraction to me was simply a response to my vampiric genetics.

"I'm being caressed by an apex predator with seductive properties meant to ensnare prey," she'd said. "Of course I'm aroused."

As we recently discovered, I'm not human, she reminded me now. *Therefore, I no longer fit the sample criteria.*

A laugh escaped me, causing Damien to sigh loudly. "If you're going to fuck around in your minds, then go do it somewhere else. I need to focus."

There were very few men who could get away with talking to me like that.

Fortunately for Damien, he was on that short list.

"What can we do to help?" I asked him. "Other than leave you alone." The latter part was added because I knew that would be his recommendation.

He sighed, the tattoo on his left arm stretching across his pale skin as his muscles flexed. "I've tried everything I can think of to break through their technology blackout. There have been a few blips of connectivity, telling me they're hitting the satellites intermittently for communication reasons, but otherwise, it's dark."

"A typical Lilith protocol." Calina tied her long blonde hair up into a ponytail while she spoke, her focus on the screens. "She used to shut down the bunker for drills, too. But never for this long."

I nodded because I'd gathered as much from Calina's thoughts. She hadn't been concerned when the bunker housing Cam—and now Ismerelda—had gone radio silent for a day. But after a week, she'd started to question the protocol.

And now that it'd been two weeks, she was concerned.

Damien drew his fingers through his thick, dark hair. "I've tried searching different channels and frequencies. I've also traced the various server networks, searching for other connections or potential avenues, but every single one comes up dead. There are satellites we—"

The ringing of my watch cut him off, all three of us glancing down at the mechanism around my wrist. I clicked a button to bring up a screen, my brow furrowing at the familiar name. "It's Hazel."

Damien blinked, then quickly pulled up something on his screen that appeared to be linked to my phone. We'd have a conversation later about how he'd done that so quickly. For now, I was too intrigued by the incoming call to question him.

"Answer it," he told me.

I nearly reminded him of who the superior in the room was but opted to do as he requested instead. Hazel's visage appeared before me on a see-through screen, her brown eyes round and focused before glancing to my left.

Calina instantly bowed her head, her confident facade falling behind a submissive mask—one she'd been working on perfecting over the last few weeks.

Hazel's nostrils flared in response. But I couldn't determine if that facial tell was in reply to Calina's initial boldness or the way she'd lowered her gaze.

Interesting, I thought. Hazel's allegiance had always been unknown, the blonde female tending to keep to herself and mind her own region rather than engage in Blood Alliance politics.

"Jace," she greeted.

"Hazel," I returned, my lips curling in false welcome. "To what do I owe the pleasure of your call?"

"Cam." The name from her lips wiped the smile right off my face. "Yeah, I thought you might react that way. He suggested I ring you to discuss a weapon that rendered him useless for over a century. Something about it being used on Ryder as well?"

I gaped at her. "You spoke to Cam?"

"You don't seem very surprised that he's alive," she replied, her blonde eyebrow inching upward. "That's interesting."

"I find it more interesting that you've seen him," I countered, not bothering to comment on my lack of surprise.

We'd reached the endgame in this political match.

No point in wasting time on feigning shock over something so trivial now.

Besides, it seemed Hazel wanted to get right to the heart of the conversation. I wasn't about to distract her from it. She clearly had worthwhile information to share.

"I saw a virtual version of him," she clarified. "I wasn't sure if he was real or not, but Deirdre just called to confirm that it's him. He and Ismerelda are now in Deirdre City. Which means his claims might be true, and as he suggested I reach out to you..." She trailed off.

"Cam asked you to call me?" *Why didn't he call me himself?*

"Yes, to confirm his comments regarding Lilith's weapon. He said you're more eloquent than Ryder."

Damien grunted at that, causing Hazel to glance around; searching for the sound.

"So you called me instead of Ryder." I voiced it not as a question but as a statement. Ryder would have mentioned Hazel reaching out to him.

Assuming he'd even answered the phone, anyway.

He probably would have sent her to Damien or ignored her entirely.

His little presentation of Lilith's severed head a few weeks ago had earned him a myriad of phone calls. Most of which he'd declined.

"Yes," Hazel said. "But I waited until someone I trusted verified Cam's existence. Now that I know he's really alive, I'd like some answers."

"Hmm." I looked beyond the screen to Damien. "Should I invite Ryder into this discussion?"

Damien's dimples flashed. "My maker certainly does have a flair for *eloquent* introductions; I'll give him that."

"Perhaps you, Ryder, and Damien should get on a plane instead," Hazel interjected, clearly having recognized Damien's Texan drawl.

Or perhaps his words gave him away since Ryder only had one progeny.

"I prefer in-person discussions over virtual communications. You never know who you're really talking to unless they're right in front of you," she went on.

A fair assessment.

But the invitation to visit had me on edge. *This could be a trap*, I told Calina.

It could also be an opportunity. Why would Cam choose to go there?

I don't know, I admitted, thinking through potential strategies that could involve Hazel. *I suppose it could be location based. Her region is close to the Vatican.*

When I considered the areas around Italy, Hazel would be the region I'd choose in Cam's situation, assuming I couldn't fly somewhere else.

"Chaos is on the horizon, Jace. I'm not interested in playing politics or engaging in games. Either join me in Deirdre City or don't. I'm giving Cam a day to recover—primarily for Ismerelda's sake—then I plan to meet with him."

"For Izzy's sake?" Damien echoed, his bored expression melting into brotherly concern. "What do you mean?"

"I mean she was unconscious and reeked of blood when Cam arrived. Or that's what I've been told, anyway. I don't know what happened, but it was clear they needed space for healing. So Deirdre supplied them with a suite and left Cam alone."

"How do we reach them?" Damien demanded. "I want to talk to my sister."

"Then get on a plane," Hazel returned, her gaze holding mine via the screen. "Your jet has clearance for a visit. Rooms will be prepared at Deirdre Tower. Use them or don't."

Damien moved forward just as Hazel cut the call, his expression furious. "Call her back. No. Fuck that. Call Deirdre."

He returned to his console while he spoke, his fingers flying over the keyboard to bring up my personal contact book on the screen.

"We need to have a conversation about you hacking into my electronics," I told him. "That's not why you're here."

"That's precisely why I'm here," he countered, the phone ringing already. "It was that or return to Ryder's compound, and you wanted everyone here. So I am making use of the connections I have to work with. And why the fuck isn't she answering the phone?"

"I'm going to assume Hazel instructed her not to," I replied, my hands slipping into the pockets of my slacks. *Can you go find Ryder for me, Calina? I suspect he's the only one who will be able to talk Damien off a ledge right now.*

Or he'll give him a gun and tell him to carry on, Calina murmured. *The latter seems more likely.*

Then perhaps you can talk with Darius about preparing the jet? I suggested.

She looked at me. *If you're worried for my safety, just say so. No need to task me with distractions to convince me to leave the room.*

Useful distractions, I rephrased for her. *Because we really do need Ryder and to prepare the jet.*

Am I coming with you? A hint of blue flashed in her eyes as she asked me that, her wolf side clearly at the forefront of her mind.

Yes, I decided after considering the options. We might be flying into a trap. Or this entire charade could be a distraction meant to leave my region vulnerable.

There were a lot of possible considerations as far as motives went.

However, one aspect of it all was very clear to me—I didn't want to go anywhere without Calina. Not with how potentially volatile everything was at the moment.

I imagine the others would feel similarly about their own mates right now, too.

We needed to stick together, not separate.

Calina must have heard the resolve in my mind because she nodded. *I'll let Darius know we need to prep the jet for a bigger party. Hazel said* rooms, *so she must be expecting a large arrival.*

I could warn her, but I suspect she won't answer the phone, I said, following Calina's train of thought. *She didn't define how many of us are invited, so I just assumed we are all welcome.*

Exactly.

I smiled. *Thank you for handling the preparations, sweet genius. In the interim, I'll handle Damien.*

She glanced at the still-simmering male. He was focused on the screens, pulling up code and typing furiously on his keyboard. *Good luck,* Calina murmured. *And be careful how you handle him. I'm just as possessive of you as you are of me.*

With that sensual warning, and a subtle sway of her hips, she left the room. *I have no intention of ever playing with anyone other than you, love.*

Her mind caressed mine as she verified the truth of my statement. Instead of replying, she allowed me to sense the echo of agreement in her thoughts.

Our relationship might be new, but our bond felt old. As though our souls had always been tied to one another, well before Calina was even born.

"When do we leave?" Damien asked, his emotions seemingly throttled by a mental fist of determination.

I'd always liked Damien, and this demonstration of restraint was precisely why. His twin sister had been injured by an unknown entity, and rather than futilely continue to search for a way to call her, he'd shifted focus to what he knew would work—even if it would take a bit longer to execute.

"If we work together, we can leave within the hour," I told him. "And if you can convince Kylan to come with us, perhaps he'll let us use his jet. It's faster." I hated admitting that, but this wasn't the time for arrogance. It was the time for practicality.

Damien smiled, but it didn't quite reach his eyes. "Leave Kylan to me. Ryder and I will convince him."

"Excellent." Then it appeared we were going on a journey.

To Deirdre City in Hazel Region.

To finally fucking find Cam.

CAM

"STUBBORN LIONESS," I WHISPERED AGAINST ISMERELDA'S ear as I held her in the bath.

We'd arrived in Deirdre City over an hour ago, Ismerelda having slept the entire time. I'd showered her off to remove all the blood and fluids from her sensual form, then I'd soaped up her skin and rinsed her thoroughly twice. All while sitting on the bench, holding her. Then I'd washed her hair.

When none of that had made her stir, I'd started a bath, my instinct to pamper her an intrinsic need deep inside me. One that said I had to apologize somehow. To show her that I cared. To be here for her. To *soothe* her.

"Hazel will be here soon," I told her now, passing on the information Deirdre had provided upon my arrival. Her progeny Abigail had guided us directly to Deirdre Lodge, which was a luxury resort built near Lake Bled.

I hadn't visited this area of the world in a very long time, making everything new to me. But I suspected the construction wasn't that old and had perhaps replaced whatever had been here before.

Lush views spanned the back windows of the room I'd been escorted to, the three-bedroom suite more than reasonable for me to share with Ismerelda and Keys.

I'd opted to keep the human with me instead of handing him over to Deirdre and Abigail. They'd said something about servant quarters, making me snort and reply, "He can take one of the rooms in my suite."

Keys hadn't reacted, but Abigail had. Her dark brows had inched upward in surprise, while Deirdre had simply said, "Enjoy your snack."

I hadn't bothered to correct her, instead showing Keys to a random room before telling him to order some food up to the suite. *Human* food, not blood.

Because I fully intended on feeding Ismerelda once she woke up.

"You need to eat, love," I informed her softly. "I'm not letting you starve." Although, I'd admittedly gotten a bit carried away with her before and forgotten how fragile mortality could be.

She needed more than one meal a day.

Obviously.

I'd just been too caught up in fucking her to consider her needs.

I wouldn't make that mistake—*or several others*—again.

"I'm not a perfect man, Ismerelda." I drew my fingers through her wet hair, combing the strands all the way down to the top of her breast. "But I'm going to do right by you."

And I wasn't talking about simply rectifying the last few weeks. I intended to fix *everything* I'd done wrong.

"I should never have left you," I whispered against her ear. "I was weak. Confused by my ties to humanity. Operating on a hero complex. But I'm not a hero, Ismerelda. I'm not a savior or a beacon of hope. Whoever that man was is dead. And good fucking riddance."

Because that man had been too caught up in his obsession with fixing the world to care about anything—*or anyone*—else.

"I'm not him," I vowed. "But, of course, you already know that."

She kept thinking about how I wasn't *her* Cam.

"We're just going to have to redefine what that means," I said. "I might not be the version you remember, but I'm still yours."

Assuming she'll still have me.

I pressed my nose to her throat and inhaled her sweet scent, my incisors aching for a taste.

But I refused to bite her.

I'd taken too much. Indulged in her to the point of pain—pain I could now feel as though it were my own as I relived the experiences through her memories.

What I'd seen as pleasure had actually been agony in her mind, her body betraying her wants and needs as she fell apart over and over again beneath my bite.

I swallowed, her torment piercing my heart.

This female had been mine to protect and cherish, and I'd hurt that trust. Betrayed her love. Damaged her *soul*.

I shook my head, confused by the onslaught of emotion that these realizations stirred within me.

This is the humanity you provoked from my spirit, I accused her. *The humanity that drove me to make insane decisions.*

Ones that had led to catastrophic events.

I bit down on my cheek and pulled my face away from

her neck. "We're going to figure this out, lioness. Together. As a mated pair." *As king and queen.*

Except… I wasn't sure I wanted to lead.

What point was there? This world wasn't my vision. And I couldn't say what my vision would be even if I were in charge.

I just want Ismerelda, I thought. *I have no need for immortal blood bags, not with an* Erosita. *I'm also more than fine maintaining this link between our souls.*

So what use did I have for a world of human slaves?

That outlook might change slightly if Ismerelda wanted to become a vampire, but we didn't need to rule for her to be my queen.

"What do you think, darling?" I asked her softly. "Do you want to run away from it all? Build a cabin high up in the mountains and hide from this fucked-up world?"

That was what I should have done over a century ago. Instead, my arrogant former self had tried to reason with Lilith.

Why? I wondered for the thousandth time.

Ismerelda's mind tried to repeat the reasoning, to show me links to my humanity. But I shoved it all away, irritated by that truth.

This had gone deeper than a need to protect humans.

Why me? I thought. *Why go alone?*

Because I was confident that would be enough. And yet, if that were true, I wouldn't have gone through the trouble of staging Ismerelda's death.

Not to mention whatever the fuck had happened at my supposed execution.

Had I been under the influence of the weapon then? Silently screaming for help while Lilith faked my death?

According to Ismerelda's mind, Darius had been there. He'd renounced me because I'd apparently told him to.

Had I confided in him more than in Ismerelda?

Hearing her memories, and knowing her the way I'd come to know her over these few short weeks, confused me. Because I had no idea why my former self would block her out.

To protect me, she whispered. *You always promised to protect me. Never hurt me. Never let anyone touch me. Yet you... you left me here... to die.*

I grasped her chin to pull her head back gently. Only, her eyes were still closed. She was talking to me as though we were in a dream.

I'm dead, I heard her marvel to herself. *He let me die. How cruel that the afterlife places me right back in his arms... Unless... Is he* my *Cam?*

My eyes narrowed. *We're both versions of* your *Cam, little lioness.* My version just happened to be the superior one. Because my version wouldn't abandon Ismerelda for an asinine cause like saving the old world.

Humans had tried to weaponize supernaturals. In what warped sense of reality had mortals expected to win that battle? They'd created a war and they'd lost. Just like they should have.

Lioness, Ismerelda repeated several times. *No, no. He calls me that. The evil Cam. The one without a heart.*

Her despair struck me right in the organ she claimed I lacked, leaving me momentarily breathless. *You think I'm evil?*

Left me to die, she started saying now, the broken sentence echoing in her mind with visions of vampires surrounding her. Forcing her to her knees. Shredding her clothes. Penetrating her—

Stop, I snarled, not wanting to see that memory again. Instead, I forced an image of their deaths into her mind, making her relive what came next from my point of view.

I let her feel my fury. My *agony*. Showed in slow motion how I'd ripped their heads off their bodies, killing them all instantly.

I should have made them suffer, I told her. *But I needed to prioritize you, to make sure you were okay.*

My throat worked as I tried to swallow, the pain of that moment intensified by her own torment and fear.

They'd bitten her. Played with her. *Hurt* her. All to drag out the moment, to taunt her with what they'd intended to do.

It didn't happen, I promised her. *I didn't let it happen. You're okay.* "You're alive," I added out loud, right against her ear.

She stirred in my arms, her naked body sleek and wet against mine.

"You're safe," I continued. "They didn't fuck you." Not in the way that would have ended our bond, anyway. "I killed them." That seemed to be worth repeating. "Everything is okay."

I heard her mind processing my words. *New Cam* floated along her thoughts. *Evil Cam* swiftly followed.

"Ismerelda, I—"

A scream rent the air before I could finish speaking.

A loud, angry, *soul-destroying* scream.

I flinched, my hands instinctively going to my ears.

Which was precisely the wrong thing to do.

Because the moment I released Ismerelda, she leapt up and out of the tub, slid across the slick tile floors, and collapsed onto her hands and knees.

The sob that followed caused me to freeze in the tub behind her. Mostly because I overheard the thought that had accompanied that sound.

I'm alive. God, I'm alive. *Why? Why do this to me? Why wouldn't you just let me die?*

IZZY

WHAT KIND OF FUCKED-UP PUNISHMENT IS THIS?

Cam sent me off to be raped just to save me?

Why? Why is he doing this to me?

So much darkness. So much pain. So much *anger*. A burning fire churned deep inside me, the tendrils resembling molten whips and sharp claws that scraped along my nerves.

I curled into a ball, my fingers in my wet hair, my mouth parted on a scream. It *hurt*. Everything *ached*.

Fuck! I just wanted it to end. Whatever game this was. Whatever experience I was meant to live. I just… *I'm done.*

Cam was dead. I accepted that. He was never coming back.

So why keep me around? Why torture me this way?

"Izzy."

I growled, the nickname spoken in that familiar voice resembled salt on an open wound. He'd left me to die the way I would have all those years ago. Only worse because he'd abandoned me to a horde of hungry vampires.

"Fitting," he'd called it. Or had that been Michael? I couldn't remember.

And it didn't matter.

This was hell. A reality where Cam existed. Only, he wasn't *my*—

"*Ismerelda.*" Rough hands grabbed the sides of my face, pulling my focus up to a face I used to love. Ocean-blue eyes I longed to get lost within. Chiseled cheekbones. Dark hair. Such a perfect fucking face.

All that strength and beauty.

That vampiric touch that made him slightly other. Stunning, even. Too damn alluring.

Cam had never been human. He'd been born a vampire. And it showed in the flawless symmetry of his eyes. His straight nose. Soft skin.

So dreamy.

And yet he was my walking nightmare.

A cruel version of my mate.

A monster—

"Izzy," he breathed, his palms cradling my jaw, the nickname sounding so foreign and wrong from that familiar mouth. "I'm not punishing you. And even if I were, I would *never* do something like this."

I snorted. *Liar.* He'd given me to Michael, told him what to do, had claimed it—

A visual of a conference room slammed into my thoughts, making me gasp as a memory I didn't possess unfolded in my mind.

Cam drumming his long fingers against a large wood table.

Boredom slowly shifting into concern.

A strange feeling in my—Cam's—*chest.*

The walls coming down between our minds. Cam's increasing worry. Devastation. Fury.

I swallowed, the emotions so intense that I could feel them as my own.

And it all melted into the violent scene Cam had shown me minutes ago—his rage as he ripped all those vampires apart.

But the recollection continued as he ran through the underground and up into Rome. Where he found a Vigil and a car.

All while learning history from my mind.

My head spun with all this unveiling of information, my reality turning upside down.

He took down the walls between us, I realized, my stomach turning. *I… I can hear Cam.*

Only, it still wasn't *my* Cam.

It was… it was *new* Cam.

And he really didn't like that distinction. I heard his growling response to it because our link was wide open.

No secrets. No lies. Merely truths.

Like the one rolling through me now. The one that promised he hadn't abandoned me. That it'd been a trick. A *hologram.*

I would never let anyone touch you, I heard him thinking. *You're mine.*

True. I was his. *But are you mine?* Because I didn't know this monster. Didn't understand him. Couldn't please him. Couldn't *love* him.

Not like my Cam.

Not like before.

This male was a stranger to me, his mind reminiscent of when we'd first met. I hadn't realized how little humanity he'd possessed back then. But I recognized it now.

Did I really change him that much? I marveled. *Did he change me?*

"Are you the same woman you were a thousand years ago?" Cam asked, his voice low and almost soothing. "Are you the same woman you were a century ago?"

I swallowed, his questions inspiring an immediate *no* inside my mind. Because I wasn't anything like the woman I'd been when Cam left, let alone who I'd been when we met.

But we'd grown together. Changed to suit each other.

And now... now I had no idea who or what we could be with one another.

"Powerful," he murmured. "Intense. Revered."

I blinked, his adjectives not making any sense.

He traced his thumb along my jaw, his other hand cradling the opposite side of my face. "I'm telling you who we could be together." His touch slowly dropped away. "But only when you're ready."

I stared at him, confused by his gentleness. By his *patience*. This wasn't the Cam I'd witnessed mere hours ago, the one obviously infuriated by me wandering the catacombs. This—

"I wasn't angry with you," he interjected, his brow furrowing. "I was angry with Michael."

My eyelashes fluttered as I blinked at him, the truth of his statement flickering through my mind.

This... I... I wasn't sure how to handle all of this. The deceptions. The pain. Waking up to a reality I couldn't trust...

Visions of those hungry vampires surrounding me assaulted my thoughts, causing me to wince and curl into a ball once more. It was too close to my past. To the night Cam and I had first met.

Fitting, he'd said.

Only, it wasn't Cam who'd said it.

Unless I'm dreaming again.

I shuddered, my shoulders hunching as I tried to disappear into the floor. To wake up. To escape my nightmares. Except that was my life now—a world of terror and blood. A place where I no longer knew my mate.

I'd promised not to give up on him. I'd promised to fight. But at some point, I'd lost my way. *Right around when I realized the futility of this situation.*

Yet now I could hear him. Connect to his thoughts. See the vacant space where our memories used to lie.

My throat ached with the need to swallow. I tried. I couldn't. Too dry. Resembling rocks.

I winced again, only to yelp as Cam scooped me up into a fluffy towel. He'd apparently put on a robe while I'd been cowering on the floor, the thick material loosely covering his broad chest.

"You need to eat," he told me. "Let's start there. Then we'll talk more."

The patience in his voice rendered me speechless, as did the careful way he handled me as he dried me off. It almost reminded me of the Cam I used to know, except his mind told a different story.

He didn't see me as fragile so much as hurt, and he was attempting to rectify the situation by comforting me. It wasn't about coddling or putting me on a pedestal, but about owning up to his mistakes and correcting them.

I wasn't sure how to respond to that. How to accept that. How to accept *him*.

I still couldn't even determine if this was really happening. *It feels real… but also dreamlike?*

My head felt foggy. Exceptionally tired. *Shattered*. I could still sense those icy fingers on my skin, the fangs against my neck… my thighs.

That vampire's cock against my—

Cam growled, the sound harsh against my ear and jolting me in his arms. His blue eyes captured and held mine, the intensity within them stealing my breath. Because that look came with a sharp thought. *If I could kill him again for you, I would.*

Visions of blood and headless corpses assaulted my thoughts as Cam wrapped me up in a robe.

I immediately shoved away from him, the sensation of fabric on my skin making me tremble.

Too much, I thought. *Too much sensation. Too much heat. Too much violence.*

God, their touch…

It's wrong.

I… I don't want this. Yet my thighs are already clenching.

Michael's fucking compulsion. He's going to make me want it. Make me enjoy *my death.*

I hate him. I want to kill him!

Fuck, I can't breathe, though. Their fangs. Their hands. Their clothes grazing my skin as they undress.

I flinched and hit a hard, masculine form. Powerful. Lethal in nature.

Arms banded around me.

My name whispered into my ear. "You're safe. I have you. They'll never touch you again."

I blinked, that sterile space melting away into a tiled bathroom decorated in warm tones. *I… I don't…*

I pressed my palms to my eyes as I tried to right myself. *I'm with Cam. Somewhere.*

I'm alive.

I... I can breathe.

But the sensation of heat had me spinning again, my palms shoving against the hard male holding me.

He didn't fight me, just let me go. I stumbled backward into a bedroom with lush curtains stretched across one wall. *Hiding windows?* I guessed.

"Yes," Cam confirmed aloud, causing me to whirl toward him. He stood just inside the room, his robe partially open as he held another out for me to wear.

Because I'm naked, I realized.

I'd pushed not just him away, but the fabric as well.

I swallowed, uncertain of how to proceed. I didn't want him to touch me, yet I craved his comfort at the same time.

His presence haunted me and soothed me.

Made me feel lost and safe.

This is what insanity feels like, I decided. *So conflicted and confused.*

"Let's start by eating something," he said, the words reminiscent of what he'd said in the bathroom.

His need to repeat himself almost made me angry. Mostly because I didn't appreciate feeling this weak.

I'm stronger than this. I don't crave death. I desire... my mate.

Except it was clear to me now that my Cam was gone. For good.

So now what?

"Now we find a way forward," he murmured, once again holding the robe out to me.

I didn't accept it.

But I didn't try to move away from him as he approached me either.

Instead, I simply froze while he secured me in the fluffy texture.

He studied me for a moment, his expression giving nothing away. However, I heard the analytical thoughts rolling through his mind.

After a beat, he picked me up and carried me through the opulent bedroom and into a hallway that led to a large living area framed by a glass wall.

The lake view outside had me momentarily distracted, my brain short-circuiting and firmly grounding me in the present.

Where are we? I wondered, confused by the scenery. Because this definitely wasn't Rome.

He'd shown me how he'd escaped, but not what had happened next.

Bled, he told me now. *Slovenia. Hazel Region. Whatever it's called.*

Deirdre City, I replied, aware of Hazel's sovereign and Deirdre's chosen location. I'd kept up with the rewriting of the world map, memorizing where all the most powerful of vampire and lycan kind had ended up across the globe.

"Why are we here?" I asked aloud.

"Because we needed to leave the compound and Hazel Region was our best option by car." His mind elaborated on how he'd come to that conclusion.

Cam had been going through my memories, gathering information from my psyche and filling in the gaps. Some might consider that invasive, but I welcomed his intrusion.

Because it meant the walls between us had finally disappeared. Except, with that breaking barrier came the confirmation of Cam's permanent condition.

There's no going back.

"I ordered one of everything because I didn't know

what you wanted," a deep voice said, snapping my attention away from Cam and toward a dark-skinned male sitting at a long wooden table. He had a plate of food in front of him, plus an array of platters spread out along the table.

His light brown eyes captured mine, his expression giving nothing away.

"Ismerelda, this is Keys. He drove us here. Keys, this is my *Erosita*. She needs to eat." Cam punctuated that last point by setting me in a chair across from the male. "If you need me, I'll be in the other room, arranging for some clothes to be brought up for us."

He gestured toward the adjoining living area and placed a kiss on my head.

Then he walked away, leaving me staring at his robe-clad back.

You're not eating? I asked him.

Keys ordered me some blood. I can smell it in the kitchen. I'll have that after I'm done issuing my request for our wardrobes.

He settled into a chair that faced another set of windows, his gaze on the view outside as a translucent screen appeared beside him. He spoke to the technology in hushed tones, but his mind confirmed his actions—he was placing an order for clothes. Not just for himself, but for me and Keys as well.

A human, I thought, looking at the male in question. *A Vigil Cam had taken from Rome.*

He arched a brown brow at me, probably because I was gaping at him. But instead of commenting on it, he scooped a bite of eggs into his mouth.

I studied his plate and noted all the plain foods. It was a typical balance of nutrients, one mandated for mortals in this version of the world.

Rather than follow suit, I went straight for the platter of Belgian waffles and slathered it in chocolate, then added a handful of berries and a dollop of whipped cream.

Keys watched, his nose crinkling in disgust before casting a furtive glance toward Cam.

"You think he's going to care about what I'm eating," I said conversationally, recognizing the fear. "He won't."

That much at least, I knew from the last few weeks. Cam liked watching me eat.

And his approving hum in my mind confirmed it.

He wasn't looking at me, though. He was still staring outside while conversing softly with whoever was pulled up on the screen.

I cut off a piece of my waffle and brought it to my mouth while Keys studied my food. After a minute, he took his own waffle and sniffed it.

When Cam didn't react at all, he stole a bite. "This doesn't seem very nutritional," Keys informed me after he finished swallowing.

"It's not supposed to be," I told him. "It tastes good. That's what matters." And it was what I needed right now —*comfort.*

Because I needed to feel more like myself. Stronger. Not broken. *Not dead.*

I wanted to feel alive, to remind myself why I'd survived this long.

Otherwise, I might…

No.

I couldn't afford to think like that. There could be no alternative. Not yet. Not right now. *Not until…*

My lips curled down. I wasn't even sure how to finish that thought.

Rather than try, I took another bite of my food, my

need to replace the taste in my mouth overriding my ability to truly enjoy the flavor.

It didn't matter that Cam had washed away the event. It didn't matter that he'd also apparently brushed my teeth —a memory I grasped from his mind that explained the minty kiss still lingering on my tongue.

And it didn't matter that Cam had killed them all before they'd been able to irrevocably change me. To *fuck* me. To sever my ties with immortality. To ensure I *enjoyed* it all because of Michael's compulsion.

No.

None of that mattered.

Because it had almost happened.

The beginnings of that threat would forever live in my mind. Along with the image of Cam walking away. Leaving me to my fate.

With those fucking words lingering in the hall.

I swallowed a particularly sour bite, my insides wincing as I fought the urge to throw it all back up.

The sound of ceramic hitting the table jolted me out of my memories, bringing me back to the present as Cam settled into the chair beside me.

"I added some brown sugar to make it less bitter," he told me, his focus shifting from me to the coffee mug he'd just set down.

He had another cup in his hand, the liquid masked by the opaque siding. But I guessed it was the blood he'd mentioned.

"Let me know if you need heavy cream, and I'll call for some," he added. "I didn't see any in the fridge, but I know you prefer it."

A subtle hint of all the details he'd been pulling from my brain. Or maybe it was meant to be a test to see how much I would mind.

He seemed to be seeking boundary lines, trying to determine how far he could push. I couldn't tell if he wanted that distinction as a personal reference point or because he wanted to make sure he didn't push me.

Regardless of the reason, it was different from what I was used to. Cam had usually kept our link open, always having free access to my thoughts. And he'd done that to constantly monitor my well-being, ensuring I was safe and alive.

This… wasn't that.

His concern now seemed to be more about my comfort than about my fragile state.

Because you're a lioness, not a swan, he whispered into my mind as he sipped his drink—which his superficial thoughts told me was blood-spiked coffee. But I wasn't focused on that information so much as the statement he'd just made.

Is that why you call me a lioness? To differentiate from my old nickname?

He hummed, his gaze grabbing mine. *I couldn't give two fucks about your former pet name. I call you my lioness because that's what you are.*

A stray memory lingering in his mind mentioned my eyes, how they were feline in nature—cunning and borderline predatory.

I frowned, his perception of me different from my own. Primarily because I'd always been the prey. Cam was the beast. The predator lurking beneath a handsome facade.

He didn't reply to my surprise, just sipped his drink and returned his focus to the lake. Because there were more windows here, the entire suite seeming to face the stunning view outside.

There was a balcony as well, one that appeared to frame the whole floor.

We had to be about five or six stories high, making me wonder if we were in a penthouse of sorts.

Or perhaps all the suites boasted balconies like this.

I'd never been to Deirdre City. Hell, I hadn't been much of anywhere since Cam's disappearance. I'd been hiding in Majestic Clan, waiting for him to return.

So while I knew what the world had become, I hadn't actually seen any of it.

Apart from what some of the others had shown me in photos.

I ate a few more bites, my stomach protesting each one. Mostly because I hadn't eaten much over the last... My lips curled down again. I wasn't sure how long it had been since my last meal. Hours? A day?

Cam's blood was probably the only reason I felt somewhat okay.

His blood had also been the reason I'd already healed from the *incident*. I'd imbibed some of his blood before Michael had dragged me away, which had turned into a curse of sorts because it had made me harder to hurt.

Fortunately, it seemed the vampires hadn't been given enough time to figure that out.

Or maybe they had.

I'd tuned them out the moment I'd realized I was about to die. Rather than remain in the present, I'd fled into my memories, choosing to remember the Cam I loved.

At some point, I'd become moderately aware that I was no longer in a state of pain.

But I hadn't realized what that had meant. I'd thought —*hoped*—I was dead.

Now, I wasn't sure about anything.

I massaged my temples, my head spinning through what I could remember.

Alas, it all came up blank.

The only memories I had of the last however many hours were from Cam.

I laid my forehead against the cool wood and inhaled slowly, my insides clenching as I again saw the bloody room. The ruined vampires. My unconscious form.

Instead of lingering, I pushed beyond that, speeding through what I already knew, and focused on our current location.

On Hazel.

And the meeting Cam apparently had to attend in a few hours.

We, he interjected into my thoughts. "We have a morning meeting," he reiterated aloud. "Hazel is making the arrangements. You and Keys will be attending with me."

I blinked.

And Keys coughed, choking on his food. "M-me?"

"I can't leave you here. They might try to relocate you to the service area again." Cam sounded irritated about that prospect.

Apparently, Deirdre had already tried to take Keys away. But Cam had decided he owned the human, and he now had no desire to give him up.

I arched a brow, curious about that development.

He's interesting, Cam explained. *I like him and would therefore prefer he stay alive.*

"We will all go to the meeting together," Cam reiterated. "And I strongly suspect Jace will be there, too. Maybe Ryder and Damien as well."

I started at that. "Damien's here?"

He lifted a shoulder. "I don't know. Hazel didn't say who else was coming, but I believe she called Ryder, or maybe Jace."

His reasoning for suspecting that became clear in his

thoughts. "You suggested it." And not only that, but he'd also told Hazel about Lilith's weapon.

Because he'd found all the details in my head.

"But you don't know for sure if she called them?" I went on, still sorting through his mind and what he'd just said.

"No. She didn't confirm it or mention who will be at the meeting."

"Oh." That could be solved with a phone call. *Maybe he doesn't want—*

"I don't know how to reach them," Cam informed me, cutting off my thought. "I've also been more concerned with waking you up."

"Oh," I repeated. "I… I could call Damien?" I phrased it as a question, as I wasn't sure if I was allowed to talk to my brother or not. Everything between Cam and me felt too tentative, too *insecure*, for me to push boundaries right now.

"You can do whatever you want, Izzy," he said softly, his use of my nickname sending a chill down my spine. It felt familiar yet foreign at the same time. Like it was wrong coming from his mouth. Except it was also oddly pacifying.

I'm not going to hold you back or tie you down, he added into my mind. *I'll do whatever I need to do to make this right. I'll kill anyone who so much as looks at you the wrong way. But I won't tell you what to do. I won't make decisions without you. And I won't disappear on you again.*

I swallowed, unsure of how to respond to all that. Primarily because it sounded a lot like a vow. One I wasn't sure I should accept. Yet I craved to do just that, to crawl into his lap and rekindle a millennium-old bond.

Rather than decide—or even consider my options—I focused on the task that had led to his declaration. *Calling Damien.*

Cam had said I could do whatever I wanted.

So I decided to test that theory.

And to also attempt to find a note of normalcy. Something to distract my mind. *To ground myself in the present.*

"I need a phone," I told Cam. "I want to talk to Damien."

RYDER

"STILL STALKING YOUR MATE?" KYLAN DRAWLED AS HE took over the executive-style chair beside me. "I'd have thought that would lessen with time, but you still watch her as though you're afraid you might lose her."

"Not all of us maintain mental connections with our mates," I reminded him. "Some of us rely on physical communication instead."

Kylan snorted. "All of us rely on physical communication. That's the best part of the bond."

"Hmm," I hummed, agreeing with him there. But Willow and I took our physical link to a different level. We were both viscerally aware of one another at all times.

Like now.

She could feel my eyes on her. Just as she could hear what I was saying from across the jet, her mixed lycan and vampire genetics providing her with unique senses.

Her eyes flicked to mine, a knowing smile lurking in her ice-blue depths.

I didn't respond to that look. But I didn't need to. Simply holding her gaze was enough.

She knew how I felt about her. How obsessed I was with having her near. She was my other half. A missing piece of my soul. *My heart.*

There hadn't even been a question in my mind as to whether or not she would come with me on this mission.

And given that she sat across from Rae now, it seemed Kylan had felt the same about his mate.

Kylan reached forward to pour us both a glass of blood wine, his focus on Rae rather than on his task. Yet he executed the task flawlessly, handing me a glass before taking his own.

"Darius and Jace seem to feel that we should be preparing our mates for this meeting," he murmured. "But I'm rather tired of watching Raelyn bow for others. I'm the only one who has earned that right."

The female in question glanced up at him with an arched eyebrow, her auburn strands flowing like fire against her pale features. She narrowed her eyes, the icy color reminding me of Willow's irises.

"I don't think she agrees with you," I mused.

"Oh, she agrees," he assured me. "I'll remind her why later." The sensual promise in those words had Raelyn—who preferred to be called *Rae*—blushing in response. "But it won't be at this meeting."

I hummed in agreement again, my eyes still on Willow. "Jace and Darius prefer to play the game. However, I've never been all that fond of rules—implied or otherwise."

Kylan smirked. "Hence Lilith's head in your freezer."

"I would have burned it," I admitted. "Show-and-tell is

already done. But Damien wants to turn it into some sort of wall mount. I'm not sure I want to see it that often."

"It may be useful to keep for whenever this Blood Alliance meeting happens," Kylan added. "Assuming it's rescheduled again."

"Who exactly is rescheduling it?" I asked, not for the first time. We all received a cryptic message a few hours ago stating that the rescheduled Blood Alliance meeting set for today had been canceled.

It'd originally been organized by Lilith.

Then she'd died.

However, we'd maintained appearances for a while, using Willow as a stand-in for Lilith, only capturing her blonde head from behind and leaking the photos to the masses.

Damien had also held on to Lilith's phone, using it to send sporadic messages and making it seem like she'd simply prolonged her stay in my region.

But then Jace had killed Lajos, and I'd been given permission to share Lilith's severed head with the world.

The meeting hadn't exactly been canceled, though. It'd more or less remained on the calendar until it was mysteriously moved a week ago.

And now mysteriously canceled.

So who's in charge? I wondered for the thousandth time. *With Lilith gone, who is pulling all the strings? And how does Cam fit into this?*

"Maybe Cam will tell us," Kylan replied, a sardonic twist to his words as he answered my query about who has been rescheduling the Blood Alliance meetings. "He's our intended savior, yes?"

I grunted at that. "So we've been told." Jace and Darius seemed to believe Cam had a master plan. That he would somehow set us all on the right path.

Cam might be the oldest of vampire kind, but he wasn't a god. He couldn't just snap his fingers and fix all of this.

"I look forward to learning more when we land." The deadpan quality of Kylan's statement rivaled my mental tones.

We were both skeptical of this plan.

And our current trajectory didn't help.

Hazel Region.

Fuck, I couldn't remember the last time I'd even seen the blonde-haired vampire. Two or three centuries ago? I had no idea who she was in this new world. Did she approve of Lilith's antics? Was she a loyal minion? Did she have no preference either way? *Is she more like Jace?*

None of the others seemed to have a good read on her either.

Hence the reason Jace and Darius were currently playing with the *Erositas* in the back cabin. Calina had a lot to learn about how to properly *behave* around other royals, and Jace was very much enjoying their current session.

Or that was what I gathered from the moans I could hear echoing from them now.

I'd conducted a similar training with my pet once on a jet. Only, it hadn't just been for her benefit, but for my own as well.

Damien had felt we'd needed to be more intimately acquainted to appropriately convince others that Willow was my toy.

I'd played along, mostly because it'd given me an excuse to touch her.

But I had no desire to put her in a box and make her conform.

Jace and Darius could play the political bullshit game.

I'd just be me. And Willow would simply be her—my perfect little disobedient pet. *Who likes to bite.*

She glanced back at me like she could hear my thoughts, a wicked promise flickering in her pretty eyes. She'd left a crescent-shaped indent in my shoulder mere hours ago. Alas, the wound had already healed.

Thus, she'd just have to do it again.

And again.

For all of etern—

"Ryder." Damien's unexpected voice had me blinking away from my mate and in the direction of the cockpit.

"Shouldn't you be busy flying the jet?" I asked him conversationally.

He gave me a look. "These things practically fly themselves."

So he says, I thought, glancing out a nearby window, my lips curling down. "If you somehow harm my mate with this recklessness, I'll—"

"Shoot me," he finished for me. "Yes. I know." His golden eyes rolled and he shook his head. "Izzy just called."

Well, I supposed that was somewhat worthy of him putting our lives in jeopardy. "What did she say?" I asked as I pushed away from my chair. "Tell me while you continue flying the plane."

He gave me a look before turning around and returning to the cockpit.

"He's right, you know," Kylan said as he joined me. "These jets truly do fly themselves. You really only need a pilot for takeoff and landing. It was that way when humans ruled, too."

"I seem to recall frequent reports about plane crashes back then." Perhaps *frequent* was an exaggeration, but my point remained—Damien needed to get back in his seat and fly the damn jet.

"Technology failures were more at fault than the humans who flew them," Kylan replied.

I ignored him. Mostly because Damien was obeying and settling behind his controls once more. "What did Izzy say?" I asked, driving straight to the point.

"I had no idea your maker possessed a fear of flying," Kylan murmured.

"He never feared anything until he found a mate," Damien muttered, both of them apparently ignoring my commentary and instead continuing the conversation about flight safety. "Now he's obsessed with keeping her safe."

Kylan glanced over his shoulder toward the couch our females were lounging on. "I suppose I can't fault him for that."

"Good. Can we focus on Izzy now?" I asked, done with their side conversation.

Damien sobered, his tattoos moving along his burly arm as he squeezed his hand into a fist. "She didn't say much, but something's not right. She didn't sound like herself. At all."

Kylan's relaxed demeanor shifted in an instant, his dark gaze suddenly sharper. "Do you think we're heading into a trap?"

"I don't know." Damien loosened his grip, only to fist his hand once more, his stiffness something I'd thought was just related to my commentary about flying the plane, but it seemed to run deeper than that. "I can't explain it. But my instincts are firing."

I'd known Damien for a very long time. If his instincts were afire about something, there was a reason. "It's too late to turn around and land elsewhere, isn't it." I didn't phrase it as a question because I already knew the answer.

However, Damien confirmed it anyway by saying, "Our options for landing would be limited now, yes."

Which made the timing of Izzy's call more than suspicious. Why reach out at the end of our journey and not earlier? Was she trying to find a way to warn us? To tell us to turn back?

Kylan studied the flight map on the monitor, his familiarity with this technology superior to my own. This was his jet, after all. "What are our options?" he asked, his tone all business.

"Helias Region, Sofia Region, or Robyn Region," Damien muttered, the last location making Kylan flinch. "We could also attempt to circle back up to Cormac Region, if you want to test his hospitality. I suspect he'll be the most agreeable of our choices."

He would be, yes. But that would entail running from our current fight.

And I wasn't the type to run.

"What's our weapon situation on board?" I asked.

Kylan and Damien had been in charge of preparing for this journey, so I knew there had to be at least a few guns. Maybe some explosives, too. Assuming Damien had been provided with enough time to secure them, anyway.

My trusty progeny immediately listed what we had on board, causing Kylan's eyebrows to lift. "Have you lost your damn mind? One wrong move and we could explode with all that shit below."

"Oh? Now you're concerned about him crashing?" I gave him a look of mock surprise. "How shocking."

Kylan growled. "I had no idea we were sitting on a fucking military arsenal."

"What did you think I had in all those bags? Clothes?"

The exasperated note in Damien's tone told me he'd had enough of the flying concerns. "Look, we have enough to defend ourselves if we need to. But we'll be neck-deep in foreign regions with Ernest Clan being our next known ally. If we lose the jet…"

He didn't finish his statement because it was clear where he was going with this—we'd be stranded.

"We need to prepare our backup team," I decided aloud, leaving the cockpit. "Jace! Stop fucking around! I need you to call Ivan!"

"I take it that means we're moving forward with the plan?" Kylan drawled, his tone only mildly irritated.

"Yep," I replied with a popping sound on the *p*.

Hazel might have an army waiting for us. Or maybe just a few vampires.

Regardless, I adored a good challenge.

And more than that, I loved killing shit.

"You don't think we should vote on what to do?" Kylan stressed, causing me to pause and look at him.

"What would be your vote?"

"To shoot them all," he answered immediately.

"Then what's the point of a vote? That's two against one, and we're both older than Jace." Darius's vote didn't count because he wasn't a royal. And even if it did count, I knew he'd approve of the plan. He might pretend to favor his books; however, a beast lurked beneath his fine suits.

"Who are we shooting?" Jace asked as he entered the cabin, his shirt only partially buttoned.

"Anyone related to the potential trap waiting for us in Hazel Region," Kylan explained before elaborating on what we'd been discussing with Damien.

"You know, a simple solution would be for me to call and confirm again with Hazel," Jace suggested. "We're close enough now that she might accept my call."

"What would be the fun in that?" I wondered aloud.

"What fun, indeed," Jace deadpanned, his English accent thicker than usual.

Rather than debate me, he pulled out his phone. "Hazel, darling," he murmured a second later. "Kylan and Ryder seem to be under the impression that you have an army waiting for us on the ground. Given how volatile Ryder can be, I wouldn't recommend proceeding with that plan, assuming they're right."

A gentle snort followed. "Cam was right to include you, Jace. However, I had no idea you were bringing so many guests to my region."

"I would have called you to warn you, but I suspect you wouldn't have answered the phone had I tried."

"I guess we'll never know, will we?" she returned, her voice more amused than annoyed. "Who exactly is with you other than Ryder and Kylan?"

"Our *Erositas* and mates," Jace answered honestly, making me roll my eyes. "Darius and Damien, too."

Way to ruin the element of surprise, I told him with a look.

He ignored me, his focus on Hazel.

"I see." She seemed to consider him for a moment, then shrugged. "Hold on and I'll show you who is waiting for your arrival."

Kylan and I wandered over to peer at the screen, the only sound the subtle clicking of heels over cement. Hazel had pointed the visual away from her, giving us a view of the hangar and the two jets tucked inside.

"Ryder and Kylan think we mean to attack them upon arrival," she said to a shadow lurking near one of the jets.

My lips curled down as the shadow stepped out into the light, the hood-wearing royal unmistakable. Primarily because he *always* wore that or a formal headdress.

"Khalid?" Jace inquired, voicing the obvious.

The male on the screen pulled his hood down to allow us a glimpse of his gleaming gaze, the black marbles flickering with touches of turquoise. A very unique appearance, one that seemed to be enhanced on-screen.

"Was Ryder hoping to spar?" Khalid mused. "Because I might enjoy that."

"Assuming you like the concept of death, then yes, you probably would," I replied.

The other man grinned, taking control of the video. "I'll consider that a formal acceptance of a future date, old friend. But in the interim, we have no army. Just me and one of my sovereigns, as well as our mates."

That information had Jace lifting his head. "Mates? And which sovereign?"

"Land and find out," he replied. "Or hide and miss out."

The call went dead.

Amusement taunted the edges of my mouth. "Oh, we're definitely going to land now." Because he'd just issued a formal invitation to play my kind of game.

One involving guns.

And knives.

And *blood*.

"Willow," I called. "Follow me. It's time to find some toys."

IZZY

Talking with Damien hadn't distracted me like I'd hoped it would. Instead, it'd just left me feeling wary.

Everyone was coming.

Jace. Darius. Kylan. Ryder. All of their respective mates. And my brother.

Normally, I would be excited to see them. But not right now. Not like this.

Swallowing, I opened the garment bag Cam had ordered for me. I expected to find a translucent dress, the attire common for a vampire's *Erosita* in this current world.

However, what I found waiting for me wasn't translucent at all. It wasn't even a dress.

"Jeans and a sweater?" I asked, unable to hide my surprise.

Cam glanced up from his own garment bag—a black

suit lying inside—and arched a brow. "I read in your mind that this is your preferred attire. Did I get it wrong?"

"I... no. You didn't get it wrong." My voice was soft, bordering on uncertain.

I wasn't sure how to handle this version of Cam.

Hell, I wasn't sure how to handle any of this.

"The other *Erositas* won't be dressed like this. They'll probably be in see-through evening gowns." Maybe he just wasn't aware of the current protocols. While I didn't really care for them, it seemed wise to warn him of them.

He snorted in response. "I am not putting you on display for others to admire. You're mine until you tell me otherwise."

I stared at him, stunned once again. Only this time, it was by his words and not what was in the garment bag.

Mine until you tell me otherwise...

"What do you mean by that?" Maybe it was a stupid question, but I couldn't determine the answer.

For the better part of the last two weeks, he'd essentially intended to use me until he found a suitable replacement.

A new immortal blood bag.

An obedient human pet.

But that wasn't what his words implied now.

"I mean the choice of how we proceed is yours, Ismerelda. I'll respect your decision, even if I don't like it." His mind echoed that proclamation, causing my stomach to tighten with nerves.

This... this was all so different from the last few weeks.

How had so much changed so quickly?

Or had it been gradual and I just hadn't noticed it? Maybe I'd been too lost in Cam's cruelty to see it.

Too confused by this version versus the old version.

Who is this Cam? I wondered, hating that I even had to

ask. It would be so much easier if his memories returned, if *he* returned. But he wouldn't. *He's gone.*

"It's true. I don't think I'll ever be that man again," he agreed. "But my former self was weak. That version of me chose a mission over you. Put the world's fate before your own. I'm not that man anymore. I'm not altruistic. I'm selfish. Arrogant. *Possessive.* I'm the type to put you first, and that includes putting you before my own needs or desires."

He held my gaze for a long moment, allowing those words to sink in. Then he pulled the suit out of his bag and went into the bathroom to change.

He must have sensed my inability to reply. Because I had no idea what to say to that. How to react. How to *feel.*

Cam had essentially insinuated that if this version of him had been in charge of his decisions over a century ago, he would never have left me.

Because he would have thought about my needs first. *Our* needs. He wouldn't have abandoned me.

What would we be today if he'd stayed? I wondered as I set my sweater on the bed. *Would we even be alive?*

Yes, he whispered back. *But you would likely be a vampire, not a human.*

I'd been in the process of grabbing the jeans when he said that, the fabric slipping through my fingers in surprise. *A vampire?*

You're strong, Izzy. You would be formidable as a vampire. I'm not sure why I never turned you, but it's another mistake made by my past version.

I blinked at the garments on the bed. *You would lose your immortal blood source.*

Yes, but I would gain a queen. That's worth far more to me than blood.

The sincerity underlining his statements hit me right in the chest, making it difficult to breathe.

He meant every word.

And he showed me with his mind that he'd been thinking about this for the last week, not just today.

He'd been trying to figure out why he'd never turned me, because I was clearly made to be a vampire. Made to be his queen. His equal.

Cam had intended to talk to me about it, too. He'd been planning to lower the barrier between our minds.

Then I'd crashed through that barrier when Michael had left me to die. *Under orders from Cam.*

But it hadn't been Cam at all.

My head spun while I dressed, my heart pounding in my chest.

Can I trust this Cam? Can I... love him?

He wanted to turn me. But only if I desired it. I heard that in his mind. He felt I was more than worthy of being a vampire, that I should have become one centuries ago.

My brain started down a trek of what our lives might have looked like today had Cam sired me.

But I quickly derailed that train of thought because there was no point in musing over the potential of something that had never happened.

I needed to focus on the future and where we should go from here.

Except I had no idea what path to take.

Cam walked out just as I finished pulling the sweater over my head, his blue eyes trailing over the creamy fabric and down to my fitted jeans. Appreciation brewed in his gaze, an appreciation I shared as I took in his all-black suit.

He wandered over to my garment bag to take out a pair of thin socks and a set of flats.

No heels.

Because he'd searched my mind to learn how much I hated them.

Silently, he knelt before me and gently gripped one ankle to lift my foot into the air. My heart skipped a beat as he slid the sock over my toes and up my heel. Then he repeated the action on my other foot before slipping on my shoes.

It was such a small action, yet so incredibly reverent in nature that it took my breath away.

By the time he stood again, I felt lightheaded from a lack of oxygen.

He brushed his knuckles along my jaw, his gaze intense. "I might not be your preferred version, Ismerelda, but I'm the *right* version. Because you're not who you used to be either. You're not a swan anymore, darling. You're a lioness. A queen. And if you let me, I'll be your king."

His thumb traced my bottom lip, his eyes following the motion.

"The choice is yours," he concluded softly, then leaned in to press a kiss to my cheek. "But don't rush, my queen. Take your time. I'll wait for you to decide. And I'll honor whatever decision you make."

With those words lingering in the air, he turned and left the room.

I swallowed, my lungs burning with the need to *breathe.* When I finally inhaled, it was a cloud of Cam's scent.

Peppermint. Woodsy. Masculine. *Virile in nature.*

I closed my eyes and allowed his cologne to overwhelm my senses, momentarily lost to his familiarity.

So much had happened over the last few weeks. Hell, so much had happened over the last twelve decades.

The world had completely collapsed.

Humans had become slaves.

Vampires and lycans had created a new government.

I'd been locked away for safekeeping while my mate had been brainwashed. Changed irrevocably. *Reborn.*

Mere hours ago, I'd almost been raped to death.

And now… now the man I loved was a complete stranger to me.

Yet he was exuding a patience I very much admired. A patience I *needed*.

My fingers curled into fists at my sides as I concentrated on my breathing. *In, one, two, three. Out, one, two, three, four, five.*

Cam wanted me to attend this meeting.

No, not just me. Keys, too. The human he'd apparently adopted in the last twelve hours.

My lips almost tilted upward, only because it was a very *my* Cam thing to do. He had always been the type to instantly decide if he liked or disliked someone. Most people fell into the latter category. When that happened, he simply dismissed them.

But when his instincts latched on to someone he admired or someone who intrigued him in a unique way, he gave them his full attention.

And it seemed Keys had piqued Cam's interest enough for him to preserve his life.

I shook my head. This juxtaposition between old Cam and new Cam was making my head spin.

Focus, Izzy, I told myself. *You can navigate this. Just take it one step at a time.*

Damien and Ryder would be at the meeting. Jace and Darius, too. I'd relayed all that information to Cam already, primarily through my mind. He hadn't reacted one way or another. No excitement. No fear, either. Only calm acceptance.

I wished I could be that calm.

Damien's concern had been palpable over the phone.

He'd known something was wrong even though I'd kept saying otherwise. This wasn't his business. He didn't need to know my struggles with Cam or what exactly had happened under the Vatican.

Cam's permanent memory loss was the only aspect of our situation that I intended to share with Damien and the others. And only because that particular point impacted everyone, not just me.

However, all the other details were between me and Cam. No one else.

Including the almost-raped-to-death event.

And everything Cam had done to me before that, too. Like fucking me while I slept. Using me for his pleasure while forcing orgasms out of me via his bite.

I shivered, my eyes still closed as a jolt skittered up my spine.

My body seemed to be recalling those moments favorably.

My heart, however, released a pang I felt in my very soul.

It left me conflicted. Exhausted. *Overwhelmed.*

I stole another deep breath, my nails digging into my palms.

Cam could hear every single one of my thoughts, yet his mind remained carefully blank. He appeared to be accepting my pain, and responding to it with another wave of patience.

Move, Izzy, I told myself. *Standing here accomplishes nothing.*

Besides, a meeting might just be the distraction I needed right now.

Assuming Damien and Ryder didn't drown me beneath their brotherly protection.

Gritting my teeth, I forced my eyes open and left the room.

IZZY

Keys and Cam both stood in the foyer off of the living area, the two of them dressed in matching suits.

You made him your twin, I see, I thought at Cam.

I dressed him as an equal so the others won't treat him as a servant. His eyes ran over me with interest. *And I dressed you as my queen.*

"I'm wearing jeans and a sweater," I replied out loud. "That's not very queenly."

"Queens don't need dresses or formalwear to reign," he returned. "They simply rule by existing."

"And kings?" I asked, deciding to engage in this distraction from my thoughts.

His lips curled, his irises glittering like a moon hovering over a midnight ocean. "Kings dress to impress their queens."

My cheeks warmed at the obvious insinuation in his tone. He knew I liked how he looked in his fitted suit. And he was suggesting he'd worn it for me, no one else.

Cam had never referred to me as royalty or a queen before. At least, not before today. It was... an interesting change.

You're not a swan anymore, darling. You're a lioness. A queen.

His words from moments ago rolled over me, my spine straightening in response. Cam saw me as strong, not fragile and delicate. He saw me as a potential equal. Worthy of being a vampire.

Worthy of reigning alongside him.

Whatever that actually meant.

A partner he could make decisions *with* rather than *for*.

All that information lingered in his head, the words mine to absorb and respond to in whatever way I desired.

But I still had no idea what to say, how to react, how to *comprehend* everything that had happened.

So I chose not to try. Not yet.

I have time to figure this out. Just take it one step at a time, I repeated to myself.

Cam held out his hand, but not in an offering to take mine. Instead, he was gesturing toward the door. No words accompanied his motion, just a knowing glance.

He was waiting for me to follow my own advice—*to take a step*.

Straightening my spine once more, I did just that, and led us to the door. Once in the hallway, I looked to him to lead, our surroundings foreign to me.

Rather than step in front of me, Cam pressed his palm to my lower back and guided me to the elevator bay. His mind provided me with the details of the building as we went, the codes and exits ones he'd already memorized and was now passing on to me for safekeeping.

Keys moved along behind us, his presence feeling oddly protective, like he'd instinctually taken on a bodyguard type of role. Which was odd since he was human and far more vulnerable than me or Cam. But perhaps that was what came naturally to him as a Vigil.

He took up a position in front of the elevator after we stepped in, his back to us as he faced the doors.

Cam kept his palm against my lower spine, his touch gentle but not exactly tentative. His fingertips resembled a possessive brand through my sweater, his protective instincts a loud growl in his mind.

Yet it was again different from the Cam I knew. Because these protective instincts weren't a result of him seeing me as breakable or easily hurt. Instead, his actions felt more feral in nature, like he was ready to kill anyone and everyone in our path for simply breathing the wrong way.

He saw me as his.

And he wasn't going to tolerate anyone trying to interfere with that claim.

Nor would he tolerate anyone's attempt to harm us.

In his mind, we'd already been through hell. He refused to let us go back there.

Only forward.

Together.

As a team.

It was such a startling contrast to the Cam who'd only wanted to fuck me mere days ago.

However, as I observed those memories from his point of view, I discovered that it had been more than pleasure to him.

It'd been a rekindling of his spirit. A connection he hadn't realized he'd been missing.

He leaned in to press a kiss to my throat, his touch both

soothing and terrifying. Because I knew what that mouth of his could do, the bliss it could evoke. The pain, too.

Yet I found myself craving him. His tongue. His comfort. His *bite*.

I shivered, my thighs clenching at the thought of everything he'd done to me and everything he could still do.

Alas, he merely straightened and gave my back a little nudge as the doors opened to reveal an opulent lobby. The three-story room was decorated with windows, allowing the moon to bathe the red-and-black interior in warm rays of subtle light.

Candles flickered everywhere, adding to the romantic ambience.

And only a trio of vampires seemed to be working the floor. They greeted us as we entered, their positions behind a long desk suggesting they were receptionists.

One stepped forward to bow her head slightly at Cam. "Your party is waiting for you in the Lake View Conference Room. Allow me to escort you."

Cam said nothing, just waited for the redhead to move.

Once she did, we followed with Keys trailing in the rear again.

The conference room in question was just off of the reception area, the large space looking more appropriate for a gala rather than a small meeting.

However, it seemed *our party* consisted of over a dozen people. Some of them I knew. Others I'd only heard about through Luka.

Damien reacted to our entry first, his golden irises finding mine as he moved across the room to yank me away from Cam.

My mate growled internally but remained stoic on the outside.

It's fine, I told him as I returned my twin's hug. He made me feel small with his over-six-foot height and strong arms, his genetics favoring our father rather than our mother.

Looking at us, no one would even guess we were related.

His hair was dark, whereas mine resembled sunshine. My eyes were green; his were gold. I was shorter and slender, while he possessed the body of a professional athlete with his large biceps and thick thighs.

He and Ryder would be a better match in terms of relation, the two of them rivaling one another in size and hair.

Except Ryder's eyes glittered like obsidian diamonds— especially right now as he prowled toward us.

I learned long ago that a silent Ryder was never a good sign.

However, Cam stood his ground as Ryder moved into his personal space, my mate merely arching a brow.

"Are you all right?" Damien asked me.

"I'm fine." I wasn't, actually. But he didn't need to know that.

Unfortunately, he seemed to sense the truth anyway because his eyes narrowed before he shifted his attention to Cam. "What the fuck were you thinking?" he demanded.

"Damien. I'm fine," I repeated.

But he ignored me, instead asking, "Are you happy with how all this turned out?"

"He doesn't look very happy," Ryder inserted conversationally. "Still looks smug as fuck, though."

"Seriously. I'm fine. Leave him alone."

But, of course, Damien continued to ignore me. Ryder, too, as they started bantering about Cam and his arrogant decisions.

They were pissed that Cam had abandoned me, and felt a need to make that known.

I was the sister they needed to protect. And while they'd both provided me with ample lessons on how to physically defend myself, they'd never actually allowed me to try.

Forever my protectors.

But right now, I didn't need them to protect me from Cam. I needed them to *listen.*

"*Stop,*" I commanded, stepping in front of Cam and capturing their focus. "Stop acting like I'm not here. Stop insinuating that I can't protect myself. *And stop treating me like a porcelain doll.*"

Ryder froze.

As did Damien.

Meanwhile, Cam grasped my hips, a content purr seeming to rumble from his mind to mine. *My alluring lioness,* he praised. *You roar so beautifully.*

I ignored him and the heat simmering along my cheeks in response to his remark.

"I'm over a thousand years old," I said, focusing on Damien and Ryder. "If I was going to shatter, I would have by now. And the only one with a right to be mad at Cam for abandoning me is me."

I looked between Damien and Ryder, then took in the other faces in the room, as well as the solitary table situated beneath a chandelier.

Definitely meant to be a ballroom, I decided, noting the velvet drapes covering what I assumed were more windows that likely overlooked the lake. Hence the name—Lake View Conference Room.

Clearing my throat, I glanced at Jace next. "Can we start with some introductions? I'd love to officially meet your *Erosita,* as well as the others." I focused on Hazel next, then Khalid and the three people standing near him.

I only recognized one of them—Cedric. An old vampire who I thought resided in Silvano Region. Or, *Ryder Region*, as it was now called.

I had no idea why they were here, but I hoped someone would explain. And soon.

"Well?" I prompted when no one spoke. "Introductions?" It seemed like a good place to start and a way to calm the mounting tension in the room.

"You heard my queen," Cam said, his voice ringing with authority. "She wants names. Provide them. Preferably now."

Not the most eloquent way to begin a meeting, but it seemed to get the point across because Jace cleared his throat.

"Izzy, Cam, this is my *Erosita*, Calina." He gave the blonde female beside him an indulgent smile. "Calina, meet Izzy and Cam."

Ryder grunted. "This is going to take forever." He stepped back to stand beside another blonde woman, this one with slightly unique eyes. I assumed this was his mate, Willow.

From what I knew about her, she was a rare vampire-lycan hybrid. Which explained the glimmer of yellow I caught in her otherwise ice-blue eyes.

"Willow, meet Damien's twin, Izzy," Ryder drawled. "And that asshole beside her is her vampire mate, Cam. He's the one who is apparently going to fix all this shit. But so far, I'm highly unimpressed."

Kylan snorted. "Same."

Hazel cleared her throat. "Perhaps we should all sit down?" she suggested.

"Oh? Is that supposed to facilitate this magic trick?"

Ryder asked. "Okay." He made a show of taking over a chair and pulling another out for Willow. "Come sit, pet."

The female narrowed her gaze, some sort of silent conversation flowing between them. Whatever it was, it seemed to amuse Ryder.

He kissed her on the cheek as she sat beside him, the show of affection uncharacteristic for the notorious loner. The only fondness I'd ever seen Ryder exude was toward his guns and knives.

And that fondness had tended to be underlined in lethal intent.

"I forgot how fun you can be," Khalid murmured, his attention on Ryder. "Emine, you should take notes. See how beautifully Willow obeys her master?"

The female beside him smiled as she gazed up at him. But it wasn't a kind grin. It was one that said he'd better hide. "I'd rather die, My Prince."

"I believe we've already been through that," Khalid replied, his gaze going to Cedric. "Fond memories, hmm?"

Emine rolled her eyes.

Cedric said nothing.

And Ryder, well, he was staring at Emine with fascination. "Now *that* impressed me." He returned his gaze to Cam. "Your turn. Tell us all how you plan to fix this shit show."

"Yes, Cam," Kylan echoed as he sat beside Ryder and pulled a redhead into his lap. "We're all very eager to learn how finding you is the solution to all our problems."

So much for introductions. But at least the focus was no longer on me.

Unfortunately, it was on Cam now. Because everyone wanted an explanation for his actions.

Which was going to be rather difficult for him to provide without his memories...

CAM

"WHAT PROBLEMS?" I ASKED, EYEING KYLAN'S EXPENSIVE suit and the pretty female vampire seated on his lap. "You appear to be doing just fine."

I shifted focus to Ryder, my mind automatically cataloging all the potential weapons hidden within his casual attire. I'd known him for a very long time. Even without all my memories intact, I knew he was the biggest threat in the room. The others might rival him in power, speed, and agility, but they usually put formalities first.

Ryder, however, didn't care for rules. He cared about survival.

And he clearly cared about Ismerelda.

If he thought I'd wronged her in some way—which appeared to be the case for him and Damien—then that made Ryder the one I needed to keep an eye on.

Although, Khalid was a close second on my watch list.

Primarily because he was a master of mysteries and secrets. He'd never been an ally.

Which made his presence here surprising, if a little intriguing.

"Hazel," I said, ignoring whatever witty retort Kylan had just tossed my way. Because he'd said something in response to my observations regarding his comfort. But I hadn't been interested enough to listen to it.

Assessing the room had been more important.

As was regaining order.

"You called this meeting," I went on, my words for Hazel. "Perhaps you'd like to lead it?"

Her brown eyes held mine for a beat, her expression carefully blank. "I'm not one for formalities, Cam. Let's call this a discussion rather than a meeting. And I'd actually love for you to begin by telling us where the fuck you've been for the last century or so."

"Well, that's going to be a very short story," I informed her. "I woke up a few weeks ago with only a handful of memories from the last millennium. It seems my brain was fried by some kind of weapon."

"Lilith had him watching video logs that suggested he was responsible for this world," Ismerelda added. "And Michael played a role in ensuring it was all carried out effectively."

"Michael?" Jace repeated, his dark brow inching upward.

"He's alive," Ismerelda muttered, her distaste for the vampire echoing inside her mind.

I agreed with her sentiment. *We'll track him down, and I'll watch you kill him,* I promised her. *I just ask that you make it painful.* Because he deserved to suffer for what he'd done.

She stiffened in my arms, then glanced back at me,

shock registering in her pretty green eyes. *You'll let me kill him?*

My brow furrowed. *I won't let you do anything. Your choices are your own, Ismerelda. I just assumed you'd want to be the one to rip off his head or set him on fire.* Both options would ensure he never woke up again.

She blinked at me. *Oh.*

I studied her, not understanding her confusion at first. Then I realized the cause—she was comparing me to old Cam again.

He would never have let me kill someone, she was thinking.

I believe we've already established that my former version was a fool, I replied to her. *I'll happily watch you destroy Michael. Fuck, I'll even hold him down for you. Hand you the blade or the match. Whatever you desire, my queen.*

Her eyelashes fluttered again, her surprise palpable.

I don't see you as a fragile doll, I reminded her. *You're my lioness. And lionesses like to hunt and kill their prey. I won't stand in your way, love. I'll only help.*

Someone cleared their throat, drawing Ismerelda and me out of our mental conversation and back to the party watching us.

"Michael's demise was Lilith's trigger," Jace said, his focus on Darius before returning to Ismerelda and then me. "Do you know how he survived?"

Ismerelda remained silent, allowing me to answer instead, as she didn't know.

Unfortunately, I didn't know either. "He claims I sired him, but I've been questioning that for weeks." Primarily because he didn't seem worthy of my time and energy. I also didn't feel connected to him in any way. "That said, recent events made it evident that he's not my progeny."

And by "recent events," I meant what he'd done to Ismerelda.

But I didn't feel it was necessary to elaborate on that. She didn't seem all that keen to share the details with the group, either.

"Perhaps it would be prudent to start with what you remember and go from there," Hazel suggested. "Not necessarily memories from a thousand years ago, but the most recent ones? From after you... woke up?" She phrased that last part as a question, likely because she wasn't sure what exactly had happened.

To be fair, I wasn't sure either.

However, her suggestion seemed appropriate.

But I wasn't going to relay the entire story while standing just inside the doorway of this oversized space. It was clearly meant to be a ballroom, the random table in the center dwarfed by the open area around it.

While it was a decently sized round table, it clearly didn't belong in here. Hazel or Deirdre had probably pulled it together at the last minute, needing a place to house all of us for an impromptu *discussion*.

The couches off the lobby would have been more comfortable, but less private.

Although, who knew what kind of listening devices and cameras lurked in this large room?

Rather than openly agree to Hazel's request, I stepped up beside Ismerelda and slid one of my palms to her lower back, then guided her to one of the chairs.

I could feel everyone's eyes on us, observing our behavior as though we were an experiment of some kind. It was an unnerving sensation, one that irked my *Erosita* as well.

However, she took her seat with the elegance of a queen while I settled beside her, my arm loosely draped over the top of her chair. Then I waved at the table with my opposite hand, silently inviting everyone who was still standing to join us for story time.

It seemed a bit juvenile, if slightly redundant, but I indulged Hazel's request to share everything I knew, starting with how I'd been told I'd simply been asleep these last one hundred and eighteen or so years.

I provided a summary of Lilith's logs, how they'd informed me of what had transpired while I'd been unconscious. I didn't elaborate much, as I imagined they already knew their own history. But I did supply more details when I told them about Lilith's experimentations and her quest to create immortal blood bags.

None of them commented while I spoke, although a few of them flinched when I mentioned Lilith using the Blessed Ones.

Jace and Darius had already known about the lycan labs, as well as some of the *Erosita* testing, and they'd seen a video of the Blessed Ones—something I knew because I'd witnessed their reactions to it while observing them via a security feed—but they hadn't been aware of the full extent of Lilith's research.

My final commentary was about Michael again, how he'd led me to believe I was in charge, but my connection to Ismerelda had made me realize it was all a lie. "At least most of it, anyway," I concluded.

Silence lingered in the air, the others seemingly stunned by everything I'd just shared.

I ran my thumb up and down Ismerelda's shoulder, the light touch grounding me beside her as I studied the expressions at the table. Darius and Jace seemed to be deep in thought. Khalid and Ryder appeared bored. Cedric wasn't giving anything away at all. Kylan's focus was on his mate. Ismerelda seemed to be the focal point of Damien's attention.

And Hazel… was staring over my shoulder.

At Keys.

He'd chosen to stand behind me even though the chair beside me was open. I probably should have told him he could sit, but I'd thought it was implied.

I glanced back at him. "You can sit."

"I'm okay, thank you," he replied.

"They're not going to bite you," I promised him. "You're under my protection."

"I prefer to stand," he returned.

I shrugged. "All right." I wasn't going to force him to take a seat if he didn't want to.

When the silence continued, I said, "Look, I'm not sure what the point of this little *discussion* is, or what plan you wish to develop, but my only interest right now is in finding Michael so Ismerelda can kill him."

Jace and Darius gaped at me while Ryder cocked his head to the side, his gaze flicking between me and my mate. "You want Ismerelda to kill him?"

"It's not about what I want." And I wasn't elaborating further on the topic. "When Ismerelda is ready, and if she so desires it, we'll hunt down Michael. That's our part in this. The rest is up to your discretion." Because I didn't care how it all turned out.

The concept of immortal blood bags made sense to me, especially if the numbers Lilith had given me were accurate.

That said, the method of achieving that goal could use some work. But I wasn't going to be the one to refine the research or make suggestions on how to move forward.

I had put humanity first twelve decades ago.

I wouldn't be doing that again now.

"We needed a safe place to rest and consider our options," I continued, my comment for Hazel. "I appreciate your hospitality and for allowing us to stay here. I've provided you with what I know. If there's nothing else…?" I trailed off, allowing the sentence to complete itself.

Because if all they wanted was my story, then we were done here. If Ismerelda wanted to stick around for a reunion or to catch up with her brother, I'd understand. But thus far, this conversation hadn't proved to be worth the time and effort I'd put into attending it.

Fortunately, Hazel's accommodations were adequate enough for me to overlook the slight against my personal resources.

However, if someone didn't start saying something important soon, I would be leaving.

They're in shock, Ismerelda murmured. *Give them a minute.*

I've given them several minutes, I returned. *They seem to be under the misconception that I have a plan. I don't.*

Because you seemed to have one the day you disappeared, she informed me, her memories reminding me of the moment I'd blocked her from my mind. *You told Darius to continue what you started.*

Her mind showcased a moment between her and Darius, one that took place after my disappearance.

"Why didn't you tell me what he was going to do?" she'd demanded.

"I assumed you knew, Ismerelda," he'd replied. "He…" My progeny had sighed, his dark head hanging as he shook it ruefully. Then he'd swallowed and shared some of my comments with her.

"They're calling it a harmonious future, saying it's the only way for lycans and vampires to live in peace—by enslaving humankind," I had apparently said to him. "But it's a classist system meant to benefit the royals and alpha packs. It's a game of power and blood and death. We are the superior race; of that I harbor no doubts. But that doesn't mean we must be cruel and torture our food."

That sounded enough like me that I could hear myself saying it.

"Play the game, my son," I'd apparently also told him. "Move all the pieces into place and strike from within. You know the chessboard better than anyone, including me. Use it. Embrace it. Own it."

If that's all true, then surely he knows what plan I'd supposedly concocted? I thought, not just to myself but to Ismerelda as well.

From what he's said, your decision to sacrifice yourself seemed sudden.

"I'm sorry to lay this burden on you, Darius, but it's the only way," I'd supposedly said to him the last time he'd seen me. "You must continue what I started, or all of this will be for naught. My death will mean nothing. My sacrifice will be in vain. Do you understand? You're humanity's protector now. You're the future's only hope."

So I expected to die...? My lips curled down. *That doesn't seem right.*

You wanted to reason with Lilith and had probably thought she wouldn't really kill you, but were perhaps preparing for the chance that she would, Ismerelda replied, a bitter note to her mental voice.

Which was entirely fucking warranted.

Because if I'd known I might die, it meant I'd been willing to sacrifice not just my own life but hers as well.

And this is the version of me you miss? I asked her. *The one who put the fate of the entire world above your own?* I'd said something similar to her earlier, but it was worth repeating. *I will never be that man again, Ismerelda. Not even for you.*

I'd rather burn the fucking world down than sacrifice her life for it.

The hero you loved is dead. Consider me your villain instead, I added, furious at my former self for jeopardizing our souls in such a way.

Ismerelda squirmed a little beside me but didn't reply, her mind whirring with everything I'd said and all her recollections from the past.

She'd been furious with my choices on more than one occasion. However, she'd told herself that what I'd done was right, that she was wrong for feeling upset.

Now it seemed that she was conflicted about all those instances and second-guessing her mental chastisement.

You have every right to be angry, I told her. *What I did was wrong. I should have at least provided you with a voice in the decision.*

Yet I hadn't even done that.

I'd just run off and played my hand without a single care for what mattered most to me—*my heart.*

How did I miss that before? I wondered, studying her profile now. *How was I so blind when you first woke up in the underground?*

Hell, how had I missed this connection with her when she'd arrived in Rome?

I'd been too caught up in Lilith's bullshit to realize what Ismerelda had meant to me.

Fortunately, my lioness had been ruthless and cunning when it came to reminding me of her place by my side.

I just hoped my behavior hadn't ruined us entirely.

"They're going to love learning that," Ryder drawled, his words returning me to the table and our present company.

Apparently, they'd chosen to speak while I'd been distracted with Ismerelda.

"It'll sway them to our side," Jace pointed out.

Sway who? I repeated, unsure of what they were discussing since I hadn't been paying them any attention.

The lycans, Ismerelda whispered back to me. *They were talking about Lilith's experiments, specifically the ones involving the shifters.*

I see. I drew my thumb along her arm again. *Thank you.*

"And what side would that be?" Ryder asked him. "What is it you think we're going to do here? Your king is broken." He gestured toward me with the words, causing my eyebrow to cock upward. "And your entire plan hinged on him telling us what to do."

"Our plan involved Cam reclaiming his throne," Jace returned, a note of irritation lurking in his tone, thus deepening his English accent. "He's the oldest of vampire kind, and Lilith lied about his death. The Blood Alliance isn't going to take kindly to that, especially when they learn what she was doing with him."

"Yes, the weapon is going to sway several of the royals away from Lilith's reign," Darius added.

"Which means what exactly?" Kylan interjected. "Lilith is dead. There's no reign for them to follow."

"There's Cam's reign," Jace stressed. "He's the eldest. It's his rightful position. And when he tells them what Lilith was up to, no one will want to openly support her former rule. They'll be more amenable to change."

"You're assuming I want to lead." Something I would have claimed as my right yesterday, but a lot had happened since then. "This isn't my mess to clean up or to magically fix. So what if I prefer to tell you all to fuck off instead?"

Ismerelda stiffened beside me, her surprise rippling through our bond. She hadn't expected me to say that.

And it seemed that sentiment was shared among several others in the room.

"You were right, Jace. This was absolutely worth waiting for," Kylan deadpanned, his hand gesturing toward me. "He's a political genius. We're saved."

"What is it you expected me to do?" I demanded. "Pull a magic wand out of my ass and rewrite history?"

"That would be an entertaining trick," Ryder mused. "But no. I think they expected you to have some sort of revolutionary plan on how to lead the alliance into a future where humans have a few more rights."

When Jace and Darius remained quiet, I assumed Ryder's summary was an accurate one.

"I see," I said slowly. "Well, if I did have a plan, it's gone now. And I won't be getting my memories back. So how shall we proceed?" Because I wasn't going to sit here and brainstorm ideas I knew nothing about.

Lilith's files had prepared me to lead her version of the world, and I happened to agree with a few of her points. Perhaps not all of them, but enough to understand what she'd been trying to accomplish.

Vampires needed blood to survive. Lycans needed fertile females to procreate and carry on their packs.

Thus, without humans, we would all eventually die.

And the mortals of this world were slowly going extinct.

Creating immortal blood sources was practical.

But we wouldn't even be in this situation had lycans and vampires been a little more conscientious of their human supply. They'd become greedy. Insatiable. Borderline wasteful.

Therefore leading the Blood Alliance to their current dilemma—one Lilith's files had suggested many of the alliance members weren't even aware of.

"Where would you recommend we start in cleaning up this disaster?" I asked, genuinely curious as to whether or not anyone had considered a strategy outside of the one I'd supposedly concocted twelve decades ago. "Moreover, what precisely do you want us to do?"

"Exactly what was done a hundred and eighteen years ago," Khalid responded, his interjection unexpected, considering my questions had been geared toward Jace and Darius. "Rewrite society and implement a new way of life," he clarified.

The rest of the room stared at him.

Well, everyone except Hazel, anyway. She was too busy grinning. "I think it's time to show them, Khalid."

"I think you might be right," he murmured, removing his hood—the one he'd been hiding behind since I'd entered the room. The candlelight flickered in his gaze as he stood. "Come with me, Emine. It's time for a game of show-and-tell."

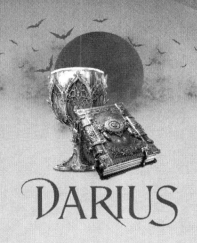

DARIUS

ARROGANT.

Cold.

Utterly lacking in humanity.

Not the Cam we lost.

Except the way he looked at Ismerelda said otherwise. That possessive glimmer in his gaze was one I recognized. I'd witnessed it countless times over their millennium together.

Yet everything else about his behavior reminded me of a former life. A time when he'd been a bit more removed from mortal kind. He'd seen humans as a means for pleasure and food.

But Ismerelda had changed that.

I just hadn't realized how much until now.

His memories are gone, I marveled. *How does that even work?*

Because clearly, he could recall some things. Otherwise, he wouldn't be speaking with such a subdued English accent. He'd be using older terms, be completely inept in this technology-driven world, and lost to the mannerisms of the past.

However, he presented himself as someone who understood his current reality, even if he didn't know how we'd arrived here.

It was confounding and borderline unnerving.

Although, Khalid seemed to be trying to compete with Cam for king of the *confounding* category. He'd pulled up a screen from a device that resembled a small disk, the size of it rivaling my thumb. It wasn't a technology I'd ever seen before, but I refrained from asking questions.

Observing had always been my specialty.

So that was what I did now, studying both Khalid and Cam while feigning disinterest.

Emine reminds me a bit of Rae, my *Erosita*, Juliet, mentally whispered to me as the female beside Khalid glared daggers at him. *Only, she seems to truly hate Khalid, whereas Rae obviously loves Kylan.*

I hummed in response, the sound one only she could hear.

My intrigue was also piqued in regard to whatever dynamic existed between Khalid and Emine. I couldn't tell if it was a facade or if their antagonistic relationship was real.

Regardless, it fascinated me. Mostly because Khalid had been such an unknown in this new world, his likes and dislikes unclear.

Did he favor the new world? Hate it? Not care either way?

Or were his feelings decidedly other?

It seemed we were about to find out. However, I suspected based on his behavior that his desires better compared to mine rather than Lilith's.

It appeared Hazel felt similarly to me, too.

Because neither of them had forced the humans in the room to bow.

And Khalid was more than tolerating Emine's disrespect.

Would that be different if she were human? I wondered. She was a vampire, based on her scent and behavior. Although, I couldn't quite predict her age. Nor was I familiar with her.

Of course, I'd mostly kept to myself up until about a year and a half ago. Perhaps Emine had been made at some point during my recluse era.

Or maybe I'd just never met her.

There were ample lycans and vampires in this world that I didn't know. But I was usually at least somewhat acquainted with those involved in the political hierarchy. As Emine was here with Khalid, it suggested I should recognize her.

Yet I didn't.

And I'd gathered from the others that they didn't know her either.

However, we all knew Cedric. Which made his arrival a surprise, particularly as he'd brought along an *Erosita,* one none of us had known even existed.

This trip is certainly not what I expected, I thought at Juliet.

For one, I'd anticipated Cam wanting to meet her. Except he'd barely said a single word to any of us upon arrival, his focus entirely on Ismerelda. Even when he'd demanded introductions, they hadn't been for himself but for his *Erosita.*

Then, when Ryder had derailed those introductions by more or less demanding that Cam explain himself, my maker hadn't even attempted to pull us back on course. He'd simply suggested that Hazel lead.

It was baffling. After a millennium of telling me how

wonderful the *Erosita* bond was, I'd assumed he'd be thrilled that I'd taken a mate.

Alas, he hadn't seemed all that interested in me or Juliet.

Instead, he appeared to be bored. Like he didn't even want to be here.

Without his memories, he clearly had no interest in a revolution.

So where does that leave us? I wondered.

In addition to his strange behavior, though, was that of everyone in this room.

Jace and I had expected this meeting to be like every other we'd attended in this new era—a pompous demonstration of immortal superiority.

Yet none of that existed here.

Oh, Ryder and Kylan had postured a bit with Khalid upon arrival, but it'd been more playful in nature. Less formal.

And the posturing had been directed at each other rather than at the humans in our entourage.

Juliet had been prepared to bow and supplicate, as most of my kind would require, yet she'd been able to sit beside me with her head up from mere moments after we'd arrived.

It was refreshing.

Calming.

Right.

Oh, I was more than happy to make her submit in the bedroom. But here? With everyone else? I wanted her to be my equal, not a toy. Or a *fuck doll,* as my grand-progeny, Trevor, enjoyed calling her.

Granted, now that he had a *fuck doll* of his own—one he shared with his maker and my progeny, Ivan—he'd stopped calling Juliet that.

"Well?" Khalid asked, his intense focus on the female beside him.

She gave him a look that was borderline hostile. "You already know the information."

"Yes. But they don't. Hence the game of show-and-tell, darling mirage." He waved at all of us seated at the table. "Share what you know."

Her jaw clenched, her blue-gray eyes sparking with barely contained violence.

Most royals in Khalid's shoes would quickly put a lower-ranking vampire in place for such behavior, mostly to assert dominance and reinforce his royal position. However, Khalid merely chuckled at her show of blatant defiance.

"Shall I tell them how we met then, habibi?" he asked her, his knuckles brushing over her cheek. "How I turned you into my pretty little dragoness?"

"You're going to do whatever you want to do, My Prince. You always do."

"Yes, that's true," he agreed, smiling. "Would you all believe that Emine should have attended the most recent Blood Day? That a little over six months ago, she was still human?" He glanced at Jace first, then Ryder, both of them observing Khalid with polite intrigue. "Of course, she was no ordinary human, were you, little mirage?"

She simply stared at him.

As did Cedric and Hazel. The former appeared bored while the latter had subtly arched her brow. I wasn't sure if she disapproved of what Khalid intended to reveal or if she didn't know.

Either way, my interest was piqued.

"Go on then, habibi," Khalid encouraged. "Show them what you can do." With that, he focused on the screen and started pulling up what appeared to be a statistical graph.

Emine sighed before looking at the room, her attention first going to Cedric and his *Erosita*, Lily. The female resembled a delicate flower, thus making her name rather appropriate. However, she held Emine's gaze for a long moment, the two of them having some sort of silent conversation.

It reminded me a bit of how Rae, Willow, and Silas communicated sometimes. Like they'd known each other for a while and had grown accustomed to furtive discussions that didn't require speaking aloud.

I used to do something similar with Cam. As my maker and oldest friend, he'd known me better than anyone.

However, he'd barely glanced my way since he'd arrived.

I tried to catch his eye now, to see what he thought of all this. But he was too busy studying Ismerelda's profile to notice.

That wouldn't be strange on a normal day—he'd always been quite taken by his *Erosita*—but nothing about today could be described as normal.

Emine cleared her throat, drawing my gaze back to her.

"Jace, son of Johan and Livia," she said, causing Jace's eyebrow to arch. Likely because she'd named his mother, which very few vampires ever did.

The Blessed Ones were well known. Their mates were not.

"Mated to Calina," she went on before looking at the female in question. "Calina, daughter of Mira and Michael." Her head canted a bit. "And Milania, a deceased golden-blood mortal. Hmm, former *Erosita*, too. A surrogacy, I believe. Mixed bloodlines. Very unique."

Khalid glanced away from his screen, his dark eyebrow arching in a manner that matched my own. "You didn't tell me that," he said, surprise evident in his tone.

"No, I didn't," Emine replied, a hint of amusement touching her lips before they flattened and she moved to me. "Darius, son of Armand and Junia. Mated to Juliet, daughter of Human Male Breeder Number Twenty-Seven and Blood Virgin Number Sixty-Five."

I… My parents? Juliet's soft mental voice pierced my heart, her wonder mingled with a hint of sadness and overwhelmed by uncharacteristic shock. *She knows who… who created me?*

I didn't get a second to reply, Emine's focus having returned to me. "Darius was made by Cam." Her attention shifted to my maker. "Cam, son of Cronus and Cava. Mated to—"

"How did you know my surrogate's name?" Calina interjected before Emine could continue with her *show-and-tell.*

"You know my… my parents?" Juliet echoed aloud, her typically subdued demeanor having disappeared in the face of Emine's blunt commentary regarding Juliet's origins.

I again glanced at Cam, expecting some sort of reaction. Yet he was still admiring his *Erosita*, his disinterest in this conversation palpable.

Emine had mentioned Cava—Cam's *mother*—and he hadn't even flinched.

What the hell is happening here?

Cava was a sore spot for him. He'd never liked talking about his mother, let alone hearing someone else mention her name.

And how did Emine know all these things?

Juliet's mother was noted in her records, but not her father. The breeding camps made it difficult to tell whose sperm went where. There were usually a dozen or more men assigned to over a hundred women, their sole jobs to fuck the females until they became pregnant.

And the males were often replaced after their services were complete.

From what I could tell, their records barely existed.

Yet Emine knows the name of Juliet's sperm donor...?

Not to mention what she'd just said about Jace's *Erosita.* We'd only recently learned about Calina's ancestry through some of Lilith's informational logs.

And none of those logs had included the name of Calina's surrogate.

How could this baby vampire know such a thing?

"It's fascinating, yes?" Khalid asked, his lips twitching. "Imagine my surprise when she addressed me as *My Prince* after I'd been wandering the Blood University grounds for days without anyone recognizing me."

My brow furrowed. I supposed if anyone could move around without being recognized, it was Khalid. He usually masked his features with a headdress or a low-hanging hood. But I would know him even without those items, his features rather remarkable in nature.

His images in my political preparation courses depicted him with black eyes, long hair, and a thick beard, Juliet informed me, her mental tone lacking her previous shock.

She'd recovered quickly, a habit that had been trained into her during her formative years. She was still surprised by the information Emine had shared, but she was forcing that surprise to subside.

Humans were taught to suppress emotions in this world.

And Juliet was a master of that suppression.

He looks nothing like the photos I've seen, she added. *The trimmed beard and shorter hair, I understand. But his eyes?*

His eyes are naturally turquoise. They only turn black when he feeds, I told her, aware of Khalid's tells because of Cam.

Cam had taught me everything I knew about the vampire royals. About politics. About what the world could be like if humans and supernaturals worked together.

Yet he still sat there now with an air of disinterest hovering around him.

"Aside from Cedric, the Blood University staff were all too young to realize who I was, particularly as I chose to go without my usual robes," Khalid went on. "But Emine saw right through me. Directly into my bloodline."

He gazed at her fondly.

She stared back at him, her expression bored.

"My Emine has a rare talent, one I thought was killed off by our kind several centuries ago. She's rarer than a golden blood. She's a dragon blood." His eyes gleamed with the words. "She's resistant to compulsion and other vampire tricks. And she naturally senses bloodlines."

My eyes instantly went to Cam, the familiar description sending a chill down my spine.

I'd met a dragon blood once.

A human with sun-kissed skin, dark brown eyes, and long black hair.

Alluring.

And fucking deadly.

She'd tried to kill Cane, her naturally enhanced senses allowing her to see the predator lurking beneath his skin. However, he hadn't recognized her true nature at first, his vampire side falling almost instantly in love with her.

She'd used him for months, gathering intelligence on known vampire nests and assassinating creatures of the night while playing the part of his lover.

He'd been considering turning her, only because he couldn't make her his *Erosita* since she hadn't been a virgin.

Except she'd tried to kill him instead.

Cam ended up having to rip her throat out—right after she'd driven a blade through his brother's heart.

He'd saved Cane with mere minutes to spare as the female's next move would have been to cut off his brother's head.

Because she'd known how to slay vampires. And her unique genetic makeup had given her the strength and abilities to do so.

A human? Juliet asked, her mind connecting to mine as she absorbed the information from my past.

Not just any human, I told her.

"A slayer?" Jace asked, his eyebrows rising as he used the term I'd been about to share with Juliet.

Khalid shrugged. "I believe the term varies by royal."

A slayer? Juliet repeated.

A human with unnatural strengths and abilities. They're not immortal, but they're not necessarily mortal either. I've only ever met one. The majority of them were supposedly assassinated before my time.

Cam had been the one to teach me about their existence, as well as demonstrate the need to kill them on sight.

However, he remained perfectly at ease now. Like the presence of a lethal human didn't bother him in the slightest.

Does he not remember what happened? I wondered. *Is that one of his misplaced memories?*

The incident with Cane had happened after Cam had met Ismerelda. The whole experience was what had led to his brother choosing eternal sleep.

Cane had wanted to kill any and all mortals that he'd thought might be a threat, which had unfortunately led him to distrust and loathe most of humankind.

"We should enslave them all. Make them worship at our feet. Ensure bitches like that can never exist again," his brother had said a few months after the slayer incident.

Cane had been enraged that a beautiful woman had duped him so spectacularly that he'd almost died as a result of his innate attraction to her.

When he'd started talking about mortal connections being a weakness—and claiming Cam's link to Ismerelda was a curse, not a gift—Cam had convinced his brother to rest.

"He's losing touch with his humanity," Cam had told me. "It's the downside of living for eternity—we often lose sight of why we exist in the first place."

Why are they called slayers? Juliet asked me now, drawing me back to the present.

Because they can naturally sense vampires, I replied. *And they used their talents to hunt and slay my kind.*

She glanced at me. *Humans? Killing vampires?*

I dipped my chin in confirmation, then refocused on the conversation flowing around us.

Ryder had just called Emine an assassin in Arabic, something that made Khalid grin. "That, too," he agreed.

"So you turned her, thus creating a lethal pet," Ryder translated, sounding amused by the prospect.

However, he seemed to be the only one at the table who was entertained by this development.

Cedric wasn't surprised, confirming he already knew. Although, Hazel's eyes radiated astonishment, suggesting Khalid hadn't shared all of this with her. Which was interesting, considering everything else she appeared to know.

And Cam maintained an air of indifference. He hadn't once glanced my way, which was decidedly unlike him.

It's like I don't even know him, I thought, befuddled by his behavior. *What the hell did Lilith do to you?*

It had to go deeper than mere memory loss.

Although, I suppose our past is what defines us. Without our history to guide us, we lose ourselves.

But he can regain some of those memories from Izzy, right? Juliet asked. *At least the ones they share?*

Yes, I thought back to her. *Perhaps that's what has allowed them to remain connected.*

And why he was maintaining such a protective position beside her now despite being in a room of allies.

He might be exuding an aura of disinterest, but the way he watched Ismerelda betrayed a very different emotion where she was concerned.

If I were in his shoes, I'd be protective, too. Not just because of her being his *Erosita*, but also because she was his only link to the last millennium.

"I wasn't going to risk losing my dragoness to the Blood Day shenanigans," Khalid murmured, his reply capturing my focus once more.

He seemed to be responding to some question about interfering with Blood Day. Or maybe about why he'd turned Emine—something that was a direct violation of the Blood Alliance rules.

I wasn't sure who had asked the question or what exactly it was about—I'd been distracted by the slayer reveal—but Khalid's answer intrigued me.

"As it is," he continued, "I have a much better use for her in my region."

"Doing what exactly?" Jace asked, his voice calm despite the fact that he was sitting closest to the supposed vampire slayer.

Of course, Emine seemed far more interested in killing Khalid than engaging with anyone else in the room.

Does she even know how to use her natural gifts? I wondered. *Does she still have them now that she's a vampire?*

The latter answer seemed to be a *yes* since she'd been able to sense bloodlines at the table. But how far did those talents extend?

"She's leading the revised Vigil training in my territory," Khalid replied as he turned toward the translucent screen. "Although, we don't call them Vigils in Khalid Region. We call them Slayers. And their sole purpose is to protect the mortals within my borders from vampires and lycans."

IZZY

Silence blanketed the room.

Trained slayers protecting humans from vampires and lycans.

But they weren't *real* slayers. Not like the ones I knew of —the supernatural humans with abilities to track and kill vampires.

They didn't normally pursue shifters, but they could. That was what Cam had once told me, anyway.

Except they'd all supposedly been hunted down and killed by vampire kind. At least according to Lilith's logs. They were so rare to begin with that there hadn't been many to exterminate when lycans and vampires had taken over the world.

Cam had only known of a handful over his long lifetime, too.

Yet he didn't seem to remember his most recent

encounter with one. While I hadn't been part of the incident between him and Cane, I knew enough about it to share the information with him now.

His mind brushed mine as he absorbed the memories.

Cam coming home covered in blood.

"Aurelia tried to kill Cane. She's a slayer. Or she was, anyway. She's dead now."

The finality with which he'd delivered that last line had haunted me, primarily because I'd considered Aurelia to be a friend at the time.

She'd fooled us all.

But it was Cane she'd impacted the most.

"He needs to sleep," Cam had said. "It'll help calm his mind, bring back his humanity, and put him on the right course."

Which had led to us helping him fall into an immortal sleep.

Except he's no longer in his coffin, I remembered, frowning as I realized I hadn't yet told Cam what I'd discovered in his family crypt.

He heard me now, though, his psyche prodding mine for every detail I'd observed.

When Cam finished following my memory trail—learning everything from what I'd seen all the way through Michael arriving and manhandling me back into the underground lab—he growled, his instincts firing.

Yet outwardly he remained stoic. Calm, even.

Just like he had during Emine's display of power. He'd been uncomfortable with her knowledge and had internally questioned if she'd been coached by Khalid.

But it wasn't until Khalid had announced what she was that Cam labeled her as a threat.

Most vampires were familiar with the Blessed Ones, knew their names and where they rested. However, their mates—the mothers of the royal vampires—were not as well known. Because they'd all lived normal human lives, dying young.

Therefore, they weren't as notable to vampire kind, their names whispered memories carried by their children and the Blessed Ones they'd left behind.

For Emine to be aware of their names, to know what she did about Calina, proved she was unique.

There's something not quite right about her and Khalid, Cam had thought a few minutes ago. *Something that suggests this animosity between them is all a charade.*

Do you think they're mated? I'd asked him.

Possibly, he'd returned.

Then Khalid had dropped his bomb about Emine being a slayer and her purpose in his region.

And Cam's mind had fallen silent with the rest of the room.

At least until I informed him about Cane's disappearance.

Now his mind was running through a myriad of scenarios.

Did Lilith make me wake him?

Is he stuck in a lab somewhere?

Does Michael know where he is?

Is Cane still alive?

That last self-asked question had Cam internally wincing. He regretted not exploring more of the underground, for taking Michael at his word rather than questioning every detail of the operation.

Did I just leave my brother to a fate worse than death? Are his memories fried like mine?

His mind continued to whir with questions, yet outwardly he remained calm, even while Khalid started talking everyone through the graphic he'd pulled up on his screen.

"While I have you all silenced," he began, "we'll review some important numbers."

Those numbers turned out to be a projected trend line for mortal life and when he predicted humans would officially go extinct.

"This was my statistical projection from a year into lycan and vampire reign," he said after he finished explaining the drastic downward trend. "This is our actual trend line." He pulled up another graphic that had me wincing.

However, Cam wasn't shocked, his mind telling me that Lilith had projected similar timelines.

The other vampires in the room also didn't seem to be reacting, something Khalid noted with a smile as he said, "But you all already know this. At least according to Cedric."

"Damien has charted similar trends," Cedric replied, his near-black eyes going to my twin. "Your graphs are more legible than Khalid's."

Damien arched a brow at Cedric. "You've seen them?"

"I've seen them," Cedric echoed, causing my brother's gaze to narrow.

"When?"

"Here and there," Cedric answered vaguely. "Your security is impressive, by the way. A proper challenge. Thanks for that."

Khalid grinned. "Yes, Cedric was very impressed, if a little irritated by it all. Fortunately, Kylan removed the primary obstacle in his path—Silvano's head—thus creating an easier entry for Cedric when Ryder took over Silvano Region."

"There are a lot of back doors in Silvano's

programming. Perhaps I'll elaborate in the future," Cedric added cryptically.

My brother studied him, a hint of respect brewing in his golden irises. While I didn't know much about Cedric, I knew the two of them were familiar with one another. They weren't exactly friends so much as allies who occasionally worked together.

It seemed Cedric had been spying on Damien, though. Which suggested he might be privy to a lot of important information—information Damien had thought he was safeguarding for Ryder, Jace, and the others.

"I tasked him with keeping an eye on your little rebellion for me," Khalid added. "I needed to know when it would be appropriate to reach out. However, Cam's appearance escalated my timetable slightly." He looked at Ryder. "As did your work with Lilith." His focus went to Jace. "And yours with Lajos."

"While we appreciate the compliments, I would much prefer to learn why you were spying on us and what your intentions are with your *slayers*," Jace replied, a hint of steel underlining his tone.

Jace rarely expressed anger or demands, his easygoing nature one of his popular traits.

But he was all business now, his icy irises brimming with barely restrained power.

Approval radiated from Cam's mind, his thoughts mirroring his cousin's. Outwardly, however, he didn't show any reaction. He merely observed while keeping his arm loose along the back of my chair, his thumb gently tracing my shoulder and upper tricep.

Khalid nodded. "Yes, I'm getting there." He pulled up an aerial perspective of a city, the graphs disappearing completely. "This is Dubai, or Khalid City, as it's known today. But within my region, we call it Blood City. And this is a live feed."

He tapped on the screen to zoom in, the streets coming into view from what I assumed were building security cameras. Or perhaps he had another type of technology that none of us knew about. It was hard to say because everything on the screen looked unreal.

Primarily because the streets were bustling.

During daylight.

"It's only eight in the morning," Khalid murmured. "But as you know, that's usually when vampires retire." He clicked on a set of building doors across the street, the camera moving along with him to enter.

"What kind of technology is this?" Damien asked.

"Hmm," Khalid hummed. "Play nice with Cedric and maybe he'll explain it later." He moved the cursor up a set of stairs and into a lobby, then toward what appeared to be a restaurant. "Late-morning snacks," he said. "But perhaps not the kind you're used to?"

He paused on a table of vampires and humans, all of them chatting quietly while eating a meal. Though the humans appeared more subdued than the vampires beside them, they weren't dressed in revealing clothes or being forced to kneel. Instead, they were eating right alongside the immortals.

The only difference in their meals appeared to be the drinks on the table. Blood wine for the vampires and various other beverages for the humans.

"In Blood City, we've imposed a strict blood donation program," Khalid informed everyone. "All mortals in my territory are required to give blood every eight weeks. They're also required to find gainful employment or attend schools, unless they've recently had a child, in which case we provide all care until the offspring reaches two years of age. Then one of the parents is required to return to work while the other stays home."

"You have children in your region?" Jace asked.

Khalid grinned. "Yes. Many. And their parents bred willingly, not forcefully."

He panned over to another screen that had my lips parting.

Because it appeared to be a daycare.

The technology automatically hid all the children's faces, too, surprising me more.

"This can't be real," Ryder said, his tone and expression indicating his distrust. He wasn't one who could be easily convinced by some fancy camerawork. And neither was my brother.

Neither am I, Cam murmured. *This could all very easily be a lie.*

Yes, I agreed. *But what would be the purpose of it?*

To provide a distraction of some kind? he suggested.

"It's real," Hazel insisted. "I've seen it."

"Me, too," Cedric echoed. "I didn't believe it at first either. But…" He trailed off, his shoulders shrugging. "You'll have to see it to understand."

"Let's say I believe you," Jace said slowly, his tone suggesting he didn't actually believe any of this but was playing along for now. "How have you hidden this from Lilith? From the other royals?"

"By being known for my inhospitable nature, of course," Khalid drawled.

Jace's responding expression conveyed his need for Khalid to elaborate. It was all in his eyes, the way they narrowed just enough to display his annoyance without him actually voicing it.

"When a royal visits—which is rare—I host them in one of the sovereign cities. Never in Blood City," Khalid went on. "My sovereign cities are all scarcely populated, but they maintain an appearance that rivals our current world order."

"And Lilith accepted that?" Jace pressed.

"I never gave her an option to decline," Khalid returned. "Nor did I entertain her often. She relied on her satellite surveillance, just like she did for monitoring everyone else. However, as we all know, video feeds can be easily manipulated and contrived."

"Which is why I still call bullshit on everything," Ryder drawled. "All that fancy tech you just showed? Humans dining with vampires? It's a beautiful notion, Khalid. But it's too much of a fantasy for me to believe it."

Khalid grinned. "I was really hoping you would say that, old friend. That's why I already have a jet prepped and ready to go, should you choose to accept my offer of a visit. Or, I suppose, more accurately worded, should you choose to accept my *challenge*."

The room fell silent once more.

Ryder's gaze narrowed.

Jace and Darius shared a glance.

Cam merely observed like he'd done this entire time, his mind already rejecting the idea of traveling to Khalid Region. He didn't want to relocate until we discussed all our options.

And he wasn't thinking *we*, as in everyone at the table, but *we*, as in *he and I*.

"You're inviting all of us to Blood City?" Kylan asked, incredulity coloring his tone.

"No. Just Ryder. It would be too conspicuous to host everyone." He shifted his gaze to Damien. "But I'd allow you to accompany your maker. Then you both can report back with your findings." He looked around the room. "I imagine you all would believe them over me, Hazel, and Cedric, yes?"

More silence.

Ryder and Damien were both studying each other now, their ancient friendship allowing them to communicate without words. But then Ryder's attention went to Willow, his gaze softening.

After a beat, he smiled. "My mate accepts. My progeny accepts. So I guess I accept, too. But I have a condition."

Khalid merely arched a brow, seeming to wait for that condition.

"You leave Emine here and escort us personally. If something happens to me, Damien, or my mate, your pet dies."

All signs of Khalid's amusement fled. "No."

"Then I decline your *challenge*," Ryder returned.

Khalid studied Ryder for a long moment, his turquoise irises glittering in the candlelight. "I have a counteroffer."

Ryder leaned back in his chair, a lazy grin tugging at his lips. "I'm listening."

"I'll remain here with Emine while Cedric and Lily give you and Damien a tour of Blood City." His gaze bounced around the table. "We'll spend a few days reviewing everything you know and develop an approach for the next Blood Alliance meeting."

"What kind of an approach?" Jace asked. "What do you intend to achieve?"

"Change," he answered without hesitation. "Which should be relatively easy to accomplish once we show the alphas the experiments Lilith was running on the lycans. I also doubt many of our brethren will be thrilled by the experiments involving the Blessed Ones."

A few grunts of agreement sounded at the table.

"But to share all of that, we'll need proof of her

antics." His gaze landed on Cam. "Which is why you'll need to provide details and schematics of Lilith's underground. I have information on several of her former bunkers, but nothing from the labs beneath the former Vatican."

Cam stared back at him, saying nothing.

But I heard him calculating a response in his mind.

If Cane's locked up somewhere, it could be beneficial to have powerful royals on our side.

A darker part of him whispered, *It'll also be interesting to see how this game between Ryder and Khalid ends. Maybe Khalid will kill Ryder. Or vice versa.*

That would be a waste of royal blood, his practical side replied dryly. *We might need them to help us find Cane.*

A low growl followed that thought, his annoyance mounting over the possibility of what might be happening to his brother.

What the fuck did Lilith do? She was his progeny. What the hell was she thinking? he demanded, the words meant for himself and not for me.

But I responded anyway. *She was a selfish bitch who wanted to destroy humanity. She wasn't thinking about anything other than her endgame.*

Which had unfortunately been robust and thorough, as evidenced by what she'd done to Cam. And how her work was still being carried out, despite her death.

"Willow comes with me," Ryder said, his negotiation with Khalid ongoing.

"Fine. Your pet can tag along with you and Damien," Khalid agreed. "Do we—"

"My *mate*," Ryder interjected. "I may call her 'pet' lovingly, but you will refer to her as my *mate*."

Khalid considered him for a beat. "Then you will refer to Emine as my dragoness."

"Fine."

"Fine," Khalid echoed. "Do we have a deal?"

"Yes. When do we leave?" Ryder asked, his tone still holding an edge to it.

"Whenever you'd like," Khalid told him. "The jet's ready for you."

"Then we'll go now and report back our findings in two days." Ryder focused on Kylan as he spoke.

The other royal nodded in understanding.

Clearly, Ryder meant that if he wasn't in touch by then, Kylan should respond accordingly. Presumably by killing or harming Khalid.

But given how Khalid grinned at the exchange, I doubted he would go down easily.

Damien cleared his throat. "Apparently, I'm going to Dubai."

"You like palm trees and sand," Ryder reminded him. "Think of it like a holiday."

"Maybe I don't want a holiday right now," my brother returned. "Maybe I should stay here with my sister."

Ryder opened his mouth, then closed it as he switched his focus to me. "I didn't consider that."

My brother's eyebrows shot upward. "No shit."

I rolled my eyes. "Since when do you ever make plans around me?" I demanded of them both. "I've been living on my own for a millennium. I'll be fine."

Damien gave me a look that suggested he felt otherwise. Which only made me glower at him. Because I didn't need his pity or his concern right now. I needed his support. And the best way to do that was to report back on Blood City.

Because if what Khalid had just shown us was real... I wanted more details.

Perhaps it was dangerous to put faith in such a dream.

But I'd spent the last twelve decades living in a cloud of constant hope, only to have that hope crushed at every turn.

It would be nice for something positive to bloom in this nightmare.

And if it happened to be in the form of a city where vampires and humans had figured out how to live cohesively among one another, then I'd take it.

Because maybe then all this pain and suffering would have accomplished something.

Anything.

A way forward.

A potentially improved life.

Not really for me, but for others. Which had been the entire point of all this sacrifice, right? To find a way for immortals and mortals to build a future together, one where both sides benefited from the other.

That'd been Cam's supposed goal.

Maybe Khalid would be the one to help us achieve it.

CAM

Damien wrapped his arms around Ismerelda, his lips at her ear. "Are you sure you're okay?"

"Yes," she whispered. "Now go see if Blood City is real."

His golden eyes lifted to mine, a warning lurking in his gaze. Or maybe it was a threat.

Either way, I ignored him.

Ismerelda could handle herself. She didn't need a brother to coddle her or do the work for her.

Of course, Ryder sent a similar look my way, one that was absolutely a promise to kill me later. I merely held his gaze, welcoming the challenge.

He might be old and strong, but I was older and stronger. Perhaps he and Damien could work together to kill me. Perhaps I'd kill them. Regardless, the dance would be lethal.

And Ismerelda would be upset.

Which wasn't acceptable.

"Try not to get yourself killed," Kylan said, momentarily distracting Ryder from our staring contest.

He glanced over his shoulder at the other man, his dark brow arching. "Worried about me?"

"Not really," Kylan drawled. "But you seem to be the only one here with common sense, and I'd hate to lose a powerful ally." He clapped Ryder on the back and walked away before his *ally* could respond.

"I think he likes you," Damien murmured. "Maybe you should bring him instead."

Ryder rolled his eyes. "We've already established that you're coming with me. Consider it your due for London all those years ago."

"You mean over a century ago," Damien clarified. "And you can't seriously be bringing that shit up now."

"I can and I am," Ryder informed him. "Now go pack a fucking bag."

"It's already fucking packed," Damien returned. "I haven't had a chance to *unpack*."

"Then I don't see why you're complaining. You used to love Dubai."

Damien's nostrils flared. "I *hate* Dubai and you know it. Fucking humidity."

"We live in Texas, Damien," Ryder stressed. "*Texas has humidity.*"

"It's not the same," Damien argued.

Ryder scoffed at that. "It's exactly the same."

"Fine."

"Fine."

The two males squared off, causing Ismerelda to release a tiny giggle that went straight to my heart. "Good to know you two haven't changed at all in this new era."

"Kind of hard to change when one of us hid through most of it," Damien muttered.

"I offered to let you join me," Ryder reminded him. "You chose to assimilate."

"Because one of us had to." Damien folded his arms, his thick muscles flexing with the movement. "Don't act like I didn't do us both a favor by *assimilating*."

"Let me know when you two are done with whatever the fuck this is," Cedric interjected, his tone flat. "Lily and I will be waiting outside." He gave me a slight nod as he passed, his display of respect not lost on me or the other two men.

"I always did like Cedric," I noted aloud, purposely goading Ryder and Damien—both of whom had definitely *not* shown me an ounce of respect since I'd entered the room.

Ryder grunted. "Bows have to be earned. And after what you did to Izzy, it's going to take a long time for you to earn any respect from me."

"Same," Damien echoed, the two males deciding to gang up on me rather than fight with each other.

I mimicked Damien's stance by folding my arms and said nothing.

Ismerelda sighed as she stepped between us. "Just go to Blood City and report back. I want to know if what Khalid has shown us is real."

"It's not," Ryder replied. "This is some sort of game. But I'm looking forward to playing. Besides, your brother could use some shooting practice. His aim isn't what it used to be."

Damien made a noise in the back of his throat. "My aim is perfectly fine, jackass."

"Prove it," Ryder dared him.

"By shooting you right here, right now?" Damien

asked, a gun seeming to magically appear in his hand. It wasn't that he possessed a supernatural gift; he was just quick. "Okay."

Ryder chuckled. "You're right. You are packed and ready to go." He gestured to the door. "Well, we shouldn't keep Cedric waiting any longer."

Damien shook his head, a low growl escaping him. "I'm going to end up leaving you in *Blood City*."

Ryder lifted a shoulder. "That's fine. You can take over Ryder Region in my absence. I know how much you love politics." With a chuckle, he moved toward Ismerelda and pressed a kiss to her cheek. "Give him hell, Iz," he murmured, his eyes meeting mine as he said it. "We'll be back in a few days to kill him for you."

Ismerelda sighed again. "Just be safe."

"Never," Ryder replied with a wink, then he focused on Willow, his dark orbs glittering. "Ready for an adventure, pet?"

"Am I allowed to have a hammer?"

"No. But you can have Damien's gun." He took the weapon from Damien's grasp, checked the safety, and handed it to her without so much as blinking. "Consider it a treat for good behavior."

The female's blue eyes iced over. "Brave words for a man who just handed me a gun."

"Foreplay, mate," he purred back at her. "It's all foreplay." He wrapped his arm around her and pulled her alongside him as he whispered, "You're perfect, pet. So fucking perfect."

Willow shivered in response, her body seeming to melt into Ryder's as he guided her out the door.

Damien ignored them, his focus on his twin again. "You're sure you're all right?"

"If you ask me that one more time, I'm going to go get

that gun from Willow and shoot you myself," Ismerelda returned.

Her brother heaved a long breath. "I'm allowed to worry about you, Izzy."

"And I'm allowed to tell you I'm fine," she replied. "Besides, I'm the one who should be worried about you." Her expression softened a bit as she said that last part. "Do you really think it's a trap of some kind?"

Damien considered her for a moment, his gaze flicking across the room to where Khalid stood with his slayer. They seemed to be engaged in some sort of conversation, yet neither of them was moving their lips.

Definitely mated, I thought. *Or something else entirely.*

Khalid glanced up at me, his eyes telegraphing a story that piqued my interest. I couldn't say what that story was, but I could tell it would be interesting to hear.

We'd known each other for a very long time. He'd always been a quietly intimidating royal, his origin murkier than others. Primarily because his mother was rumored to have had a unique blood type. She'd died a mortal death, just like all of ours had, but she'd lived slightly longer than the rest.

Or so I'd been told.

In truth, Khalid's history was vastly unknown. His father, Erinas, was a Blessed One. But beyond that, he'd kept his background to himself.

And it seemed he still harbored a great many secrets.

As well as a city full of intrigue.

Perhaps he truly had found a way for humans and vampires to live in peace.

The concept of it had sparked interest in my mate. She wasn't sure she believed Khalid's presentation, but it had kindled a hint of hope in her thoughts, one that had warmed our bond.

Ismerelda wanted to believe change was possible, that all of this pain had been worth something.

I wasn't sure how to respond to that yet.

It seemed she needed all of this to result in some sort of positive conclusion; otherwise, everything she'd sacrificed would have been for naught.

What does that mean for us? I wondered. *What does she need from me to aid in these desires?*

They were questions she heard but didn't answer. She wasn't ignoring me, though. She simply didn't know how to respond yet.

It was a conversation we needed to have, among many others.

However, this was neither the time nor the place for it. Especially as my progeny and cousin were approaching me now, and she was still discussing risks with her twin. He felt Blood City might be a trap, but finding out the truth outweighed the potential for danger.

"There's also an interesting connection between Lily and Willow," Damien went on. "We found out when we landed that they've met before."

"They have?" Ismerelda sounded surprised. I supposed that made sense with how regulated human life had become in this world. There wasn't a lot of opportunity for socializing, even within the universities.

"At the breeding farm," Damien explained. "The same one I met Cedric at last year after he asked me for a favor."

Her eyebrows shot upward. "He took Lily from the lycans?"

"Yep. And I helped him. So he owes me a favor. We've also allied in the past. I suspect that's actually why Khalid offered him and Lily up as a counter when Ryder rejected the original plan."

"So you're saying you trust Cedric?" Ismerelda asked

slowly, her thoughts hopeful. She wouldn't let her brother see it, but deep down, she was concerned about his safety. And this new detail helped ebb some of her worries.

It also made the prospect of Blood City that much more real. Because, in her mind, if Cedric truly was an ally, then he might want a future similar to what the others desire.

And she'd already witnessed firsthand how Majestic Clan had treated humans differently from other territories.

Damien shrugged. "Trust is fickle. But Ryder and I have been taking care of ourselves for a long time now. We'll be fine."

Her eyes narrowed. "I just said something similar to you a bit ago. Perhaps you should consider taking your own advice."

Damien gave her an indulgent look, his expression saying their situations were very different. Fortunately, though, he didn't voice that aloud. Instead, he just gave her another hug. "We'll be back soon. Then you and I need to catch up. It's been too long, Iz."

"Yes," she agreed, a hint of emotion trickling through our bond. "I've missed you."

"I've missed you, too," he whispered back to her, his lips ghosting across her cheek. He gave her another squeeze, then looked at me. "Be good to my sister, or I'm going to play target practice with your head."

I simply arched a brow, daring him to try.

"Go before Ryder leaves without you," Ismerelda told him, her hands appearing much smaller up against the other man's chest.

It was like her brother had taken all the muscle and height from the womb they'd shared, leaving her slender yet curved in all the right places.

My palms itched to touch her, but I held myself back.

After everything we'd been through, I needed to take this slow. Let her come to me. *Allow her a choice in the matter.*

I'd taken that choice away from her before, not realizing what it meant. She was mine. I'd thought she wanted to be with me.

Now that I'd relived some of those memories from her point of view, I wasn't so sure.

I needed to reestablish trust. Rebuild us from the ground up. Create a new connection, one founded in the present and not the past.

Explore who we could be together now, as a king courting his queen, not as a superior predator romancing a delicate swan.

Her pretty eyes met mine, her mind in tune with my thoughts.

Alas, before she could comment, Darius and Jace stepped forward, their expressions all business. "We need to talk," Jace said to me.

I repressed the urge to sigh. The only one I wanted to talk to right now was Ismerelda, but given how Jace and I had left things during our last conversation, I wasn't surprised he wanted to discuss more now.

When we'd spoken a few weeks ago, I'd been under the impression that Jace and Darius were trying to undo my hard work.

Now I knew the truth—we were all on the same side.

Well, in theory, we were, anyway.

I didn't agree with some of Lilith's antics, and I wanted to know what she and Michael had done to my brother. But I wasn't going to stand against the current regime as a competing monarch.

Ismerelda was my priority now.

Along with finding Cane, I decided. *And helping my lioness hunt and kill Michael.*

Jace cleared his throat. "Cam."

"Jace," I countered. "I'm listening."

He gave me a look.

I returned it with an eyebrow arch.

"Perhaps we would all be more comfortable upstairs," Darius suggested. "Hazel gifted us a case of blood wine when we landed. She mentioned that humans are not a common menu item in this tower, as Deirdre City is rather short-staffed."

"Deirdre failed to mention that upon my arrival," I replied, looking for Hazel and finding her standing near Khalid. Both of them were observing me with interest. "Is that why Deirdre tried to take Keys?"

Hazel glanced from me to the silent human behind me. He'd been shadowing me and Ismerelda since we'd entered the room, his natural instinct to protect one that might become useful at some point.

Hazel cleared her throat. "She likely wanted to ensure he had appropriate accommodations."

"Or she planned to turn him into wine," I returned. "If your staffing issues are a result of gluttony, then consider that your problem to fix. Not mine. And certainly not Keys's, either. He stays with me unless he chooses otherwise."

Khalid and Hazel shared a look.

Then Hazel shrugged. "You're among friends here, Cam. Or, if you prefer, allies. We want similar things. A world where we respect our origins rather than exploit them. I have no interest in harming anyone here, including the humans under your protection."

"I echo that sentiment," Khalid murmured. "But feel free to talk amongst yourselves. The technology Damien gave you will check the rooms for listening devices.

However, I recommend you use this scanner to help remove that tracker in your neck."

He held up a small item in his hand while he spoke that last line and moved across the room to hand it to me.

"You'll just need a blade. Maybe your *Erosita* would like to do the honors?" he suggested. "I know Emine enjoys cutting me."

His dragoness scoffed from across the room, but her blue-gray eyes glittered with the prospect of making Khalid bleed.

They definitely have an interesting dynamic, Ismerelda said.

Would you like to have a similar one? I asked her. *Because I can find you a knife.* It would only be fair after how much I'd made her bleed for me over the last two weeks.

She hummed, considering it. *We'll see. But maybe not right now. Your neck is a bit risky for our first time.*

Worried you might slit my throat?

Yes, she admitted.

I would probably deserve that. I'd killed her upon our reunion. She should probably return the favor.

That won't fix anything, she whispered to me. *Besides, I need you alive right now.*

Do you?

Yes. There are too many unknowns. And you're my link to immortality.

A practical assessment, I murmured back to her as I took the item from Khalid. "How do you know I have a tracker in my neck?" I asked him.

He glanced at my hand. "I scanned each of you with this earlier. It's a useful toy. Feel free to keep it." With that, he returned to Hazel and his dragoness. "Shall we take a walk? I think there's a lot we should discuss."

"Yes," Hazel agreed, leading him to the exit, only to pause on the threshold. "Oh, if any of you need anything, feel free to work with Vincient in reception. He'll see to all your needs. Otherwise, we'll plan to meet again tomorrow. After you've had some time to discuss things."

The three of them disappeared through the doorway, leaving me with Jace and Darius.

As well as their mates.

Kylan and Rae.

And my *Erosita*.

Well, this should be interesting, I thought. "Who wants to help me remove the tracker?" I asked out loud.

Jace immediately smiled. "An opportunity to cut you? The pleasure will be all mine."

IZZY

I studied the back of Cam's neck, noting the smooth skin. An hour ago, he'd bled. But his immortality had healed him almost instantly.

It'd been quick—a slice of the knife, pliers to remove the tiny disc, the washing of hands and instruments, and the destruction of the tracking device.

Then Jace had used Khalid's scanner to ensure Cam didn't have any other trackers embedded beneath his skin.

His ocean-blue eyes had held mine the entire time, memories of Cam scanning my naked body flooding both of our minds.

He'd been aroused and furious by the recollection at the same time. Aroused because he'd enjoyed caressing my skin. Furious that Michael had set it all up.

I can't wait to watch you rip him apart, Cam had growled

into my mind. *Just say the word, and I'll turn you. Then you can shred him with your vampire teeth.*

His comment had been so unexpected that I'd nearly gasped aloud.

And I hadn't been able to stop thinking about it since.

Because he'd meant it. If I wanted to become a vampire, he'd turn me.

No discussion needed.

No concern regarding him losing his immortal blood supply.

Not even a thought about the waning human race or how it might be difficult for him to maintain a food source without me.

He'd turn me. And we'd go from there.

It would ensure my independence while also making me stronger, something he saw as a benefit.

I have no idea why I didn't offer you immortality before, he'd thought at me. *But it seems obvious to me now that you shouldn't have to rely on my immortality to survive.*

I really wanted to discuss it more, but Jace, Darius, and Kylan were all drilling him right now about everything that had happened. They were also filling in a lot of gaps, telling him what Lilith's logs hadn't reported on.

Such as Cam faking my death and how Lilith had forced all known allies to denounce him.

"Your name has been a forbidden topic since she presented your ashes to the alliance," Jace was saying now. "She made an example of your rebellion, saying anyone who defied the alliance would meet a similar fate."

"She claimed you were insane," Kylan added with a snort. "Tried to do the same with me recently. Didn't work in her favor."

He was lounging on a couch with Rae tucked up

against him. I'd officially met her on our way up to the suite Hazel had given Cam.

Juliet had led the introduction, then she'd pulled me aside to ask if I was all right.

That seemed to be the theme.

Everyone kept wondering how I was doing, and I was starting to hate answering the question. Because I didn't know if I was okay or not.

A lot had happened.

I needed time to process it, yet I'd more or less been expected to perform since the moment I'd woken up in that tub.

Well, perhaps not immediately. Cam had been patient. But having my brother and all the others show up so soon after rousing from my unconscious state…

I swallowed, a shiver traversing my spine.

I just need a few minutes of quiet to think through what to do next, I thought.

Shall I make them leave? Cam immediately answered. Although his focus appeared to be on Jace, he was clearly listening to my mind ramble to itself.

No. They've been hunting for you for over a century. They need this. And I wasn't going to take it away from them. Not after everything we all had been through.

I don't care what they need, Ismerelda. I care about what you need.

I'm trying to figure that out, I whispered back to him. *Right now, I need you to listen to them.*

Because we had to find a way forward.

Cam's missing memories had muddled the plan. No one knew what to do now.

Pair that with Lilith's death, and everything felt uncertain.

Who was leading the Blood Alliance? Michael? Mira? Someone else?

What was their plan? To finish Lilith's experiments and present the alliance with immortal blood bags?

That might win over the vampires, but it certainly wouldn't attract the lycans. Especially since their kind had been used as lab rats in the pursuit of perfecting vampire food sources.

"What's the end goal here?" Cam asked, cutting off something Jace had been saying regarding Cam's disappearance. "My memories are not going to be triggered by this conversation. I can't elaborate on any plan I might have had. So how do you want to move forward? What do you need from me?"

His direct questions were underlined with a hint of impatience. He wanted to get to a point, not belabor the past.

Jace cleared his throat. "You're right. We need to focus on our next move, which I think involves bringing in our lycan allies. Lilith's experiments are the key to persuading the alliance in our favor. We need the wolves to help with suggestions on how to disseminate the information."

"Not just how, but who," Darius clarified. "Jolene will know who best to engage with on the topic. Just as we have a reasonable idea of which vampires to share it with."

"Except we entirely misjudged Khalid," Kylan pointed out. "If he indeed has a city where mortals are treated better than food, then how many others have we mistaken as pro-Lilith?"

"A fair point," Jace agreed. "What did Lilith's logs say about Khalid?"

"She called him content. There was nothing in her files that suggested otherwise. So if Blood City is real, it wasn't on her radar," Cam replied. "Assuming I was given access to all her files, anyway."

"Do you have reason to believe that you weren't?" Jace asked.

"Yes." Cam cleared his throat, then told them about what I'd discovered in his family crypt. "I have no idea where my brother is, and there was no mention of him in Lilith's reports. Michael also never mentioned him."

"Suggesting they were keeping things from you," Jace summarized.

"They also limited his laptop access," I added, recalling his inability to leave the internal network. "I had to go in through the admin mode to see certain things as well, such as the security feeds. But even that had limits in place."

Cam glanced at me from his seat beside Jace. I'd chosen to sit across from them in a chair while Darius and Juliet shared a similar one beside me.

Keys was the only one not in the living area. He'd excused himself upon arrival, grabbing some food and taking it back to what I assumed was a bedroom.

The rest of us were all seated in the ample living space, watching the sun rise outside the windows.

The light would eventually bother the vampires in the room. It wouldn't harm them, just irritate their enhanced senses.

From what I'd seen, there were blackout curtains lurking along the edges of the windows, suggesting a remote somewhere would draw them across the glass when needed. Or perhaps it would be automatic.

Regardless, only a few rays of orange and red had appeared thus far, painting the room in an eerie twilight rather than morning sunlight.

"Do you think Lilith left behind notes for Michael and

Mira to follow?" Jace asked, his focus on Calina, not the others. "Or is there a silent partner we've yet to uncover?"

"Similar to Lajos?" she suggested, her brow creasing. "It's definitely possible. We know she has other allies."

"Jasmine and Ayaz," Jace murmured. "Helias and Sofia, too."

"Maybe Robyn," Kylan added. "I know she punished her after everything that happened with Raelyn, but we haven't seen it enforced yet."

Jace nodded. "Yes, true. We also have so many unknowns, like Khalid and Hazel. It's hard to say what side they truly fall on. We've all mastered this game of charades."

"So hold a meeting and see how everyone reacts to the news about Lilith's experiments," I suggested, thinking aloud. "That'll tell you what side everyone is on. But you'll need several strategies in place to handle their reactions."

"You also need a goal," Cam stressed. "One that doesn't involve me leading."

Everyone, including me, stared at him.

Rather than meet their gazes, he focused on me. "I will not repeat the mistakes of my past, and that includes choosing humanity over my *Erosita*." He finally looked at Darius and then Jace. "I am not that man. Therefore, I am not your king."

I blinked at him, his declaration not matching the one in his thoughts. He kept calling me his queen, saying we were equals in this life.

But now he proclaimed himself not to be a king, even though it was his birthright as the eldest vampire.

I'm not their king, he whispered into my mind. *I'm your king, Ismerelda. I won't serve them. I'll only serve you.*

"I think we've said enough for today," Cam concluded out loud. "Ismerelda and I have things we need to discuss.

Things that don't involve all of you. So make your calls. Invite your lycan allies. And we'll meet again after dusk."

With that, he stood and left the room.

I'm going to cool off in the shower, he informed me softly. *You're invited to join. Or you can stay and talk with the others. But I need a break.*

His mind was rioting with conflicting statements, his frustration at his memory loss palpable. Yet he seemed to be angrier at his former self for putting him—*us*—in this position.

I stared after him, the hallway he'd walked down vacant. However, his scent lingered. His presence did, too.

Do I want to follow him? I wondered. *Or do I want to wait?*

Jace cleared his throat. "I suppose we should… leave."

"That's what I gathered from that, yes," Kylan drawled, his dark eyes taking in the sunrise. "I suppose it's time to retire on this side of the world. Besides, we probably won't hear from Ryder for at least a few more hours."

"I'll talk to him," I said, referring not to Ryder but to Cam. "He just needs some time…" I trailed off. Because it wasn't just Cam who needed time, but me as well. "I…" I cleared my throat. "We'll figure this out."

I hope, I added to myself. *Maybe.*

Did I want to figure this out?

Did I want to fight for us?

Was what we have worth saving when only one of us remembers the last millennium?

It would be like starting over. *Do I even want to start over?* It would be with this version of Cam, not the old one. *Do I want this version?*

I couldn't answer any of those questions because I didn't know what I wanted. Everything was too fresh, too confusing… I just… I swallowed. I just wanted to talk to

Cam. Determine who he might be now. Who we might become together.

Then I could decide.

But I couldn't do any of that with an audience.

Which I still had because everyone was staring at me.

"We'll meet after dusk," I said, echoing Cam's final words. "But if you hear from Ryder before then, please let me know. I would like to know if he and Damien are safe."

"Of course," Jace replied softly.

I nodded and stood, my throat working as I fought the emotions clawing at my insides.

"Izzy," he called after me.

I paused but didn't face him.

"We're here if you need us," he said after a beat.

I nodded again. *I know,* I thought at him, the words suddenly too heavy for me to speak. He wouldn't be able to hear me, but hopefully he understood.

Rather than wait to find out, I followed in Cam's footsteps.

I needed a break as well.

To breathe.

To think.

To simply exist.

And maybe even to forget. Just for a little while. *Until dusk.*

Then we could start all of this again.

Because it seemed Deirdre City had just become the official base camp for the rebel party. *And so it begins…*

CAM

I PRESSED MY FOREARM AGAINST THE TILED WALL AND LET the water pour down my back.

It was hot. Scalding, almost. And exactly what I needed.

But when I heard Ismerelda's resolve to join me, I reached over to cool it down. I didn't want to burn her or chase her away. She'd been standing in the bedroom for the last five minutes, debating what to do.

I'd said nothing, waiting for her to choose on her own —which ended up being to *escape*.

She wanted to forget for a moment. To relax. To be free and exist only in the present.

I turned as she entered, my gaze automatically memorizing her sensual form.

Beautiful, I thought. *So fucking beautiful.*

"I don't understand why I never turned you," I

marveled aloud, the comment one I'd already made to her —at least in our minds—but it was worth repeating. "You would make a stunning vampire."

"But what would you eat?" she asked, taking a tentative step toward me. "I'm your immortal blood source."

I narrowed my gaze. "You are so much more than blood, Ismerelda." I wrapped my palm around the back of her neck to pull her closer to me. "You're fierce. Cunning. Stubborn. Brave."

I leaned down a little more with each word until my lips hovered over hers.

"Alluring," I breathed against her mouth. "A lioness cloaked beneath a fragile facade." I nipped her lower lip, not hard enough to break the skin, just playful enough to tease her. "I should have offered you immortality long ago. Blood can be easily replaced. A queen cannot."

She shuddered, her mind telling me I'd overwhelmed her with my comments. She was also battling memories of our showers last week, how I'd fucked her senseless and without remorse. Ismerelda was struggling to reconcile the differences, her mental voice vacillating between hope and fear.

And underneath it all was a layer of sadness.

Sadness for what she'd lost.

Sadness for what may never be.

Sadness for her inability to trust the mate she'd known for over a thousand years.

Hearing her conflict sent a pang through my heart and calmed any instinct I possessed to claim her.

She needed time. Comfort. *Worship.*

A chance to embrace me as her mate. To see what we could be.

"I'm not him," I said, something I'd already confirmed before. "But he was a fool."

I used my grip on her nape to guide us beneath the water.

Others might say that what I did was heroic or an act of selflessness, but it wasn't, I thought at her. *What could I have possibly hoped to achieve by going to Lilith alone? It was an arrogant decision. The wrong choice. I won't make it again.*

"Is that why you told Jace you're not their king?" she asked, her voice soft beneath the flow of water.

"Yes." I released her neck to run my fingers through her dampening hair. "I have no intention of leading this revolution."

Rather than elaborate out loud, I merely mentally voiced my thoughts to her.

I don't understand the purpose. Humanity's already mostly dead. Vampires killed their food source. Lycans... I blew out a breath and shook my head. *I know they want me to lead, but it's not about them.*

It was about *us*—me and Ismerelda.

I'd left her out of my decisions twelve decades ago. I wouldn't do that again.

"I should have turned you," I said yet again, irritated with my former self for decisions I couldn't understand today. "Maybe I wanted to keep you in this fragile state, leave you on your pedestal. But that was a selfish choice. I should have given you the power to strengthen you, not coddle you."

She shivered as I drew my hand down her spine, her eyes falling closed while she absorbed my words and my touch.

Her mind told me she wasn't sure how to reply. She'd never really considered becoming a vampire before, her purpose always having been to feed my hunger. To be my mate.

Turning her would destroy our mating bond.

Or so she'd always thought.

But it seems Rae and Kylan have made it work, she was thinking now. *Maybe Cam and I could do the same. Assuming I can be with him... after everything.*

I didn't reply, instead leaving her to the puzzles of her mind. She could hear my intentions now, knew I intended to make this right.

But oftentimes, actions were worth more than words.

So I opted to demonstrate that now by dropping my hands to her hips and gently turning her toward the wall.

She instantly stiffened, no doubt expecting me to bend her over and fuck her. While I couldn't deny that part of me—a very *hard* part of me—longed to do just that, I chose to ignore it and instead focused on Ismerelda and her needs.

Goose bumps pebbled down her arms when I reached around her to grab a bottle of shampoo. The move placed my cock right against her plump ass, my arousal impossible to hide.

She was naked and wet.

Of course I wanted her.

But I was more than capable of taming my hunger, something I proved now by lathering the shampoo into her hair.

She didn't immediately relax, her memories holding her hostage as she recalled similar behaviors from just the other day. Moments where I'd taken care of her just to brutally fuck her again.

I listened to her recounting of the events, my mind sifting through her thoughts and finding soft admissions of longing deep inside.

Yes, I'd hurt her. But she'd enjoyed it, too.

What had been missing from it all was trust. An open connection. Our bond.

We had that now.

The next time I took her would be different because she'd hear my intentions just as well as I would hear her needs.

With our minds wide open to one another, we would be cataclysmic together. Combustible. Fucking otherworldly.

However, she wasn't ready for that yet.

We needed to continue rebuilding trust, and that would take time.

I conveyed that knowledge to her via my touch as I rinsed her hair and replaced the shampoo with conditioner. Letting that sit, I started massaging her body with a floral-scented soap, one that created suds all over her skin as we engaged in a sensual dance in the shower.

I didn't rush our movements, instead taking care with every inch of her. She stared down at me when I knelt before her to tenderly massage her ankles and calves, then she put her hands on my shoulders for balance when I went to her feet.

By the time I finished, her gaze was hooded with a combination of exhaustion and desire.

She hadn't eaten much today, but I could hear in her thoughts that she wasn't hungry. She'd nibbled on some things during our impromptu meeting in the suite. And now she was ready to sleep.

I stood and nudged her beneath the rainfall, then grabbed one of the other showerheads—there were three —and proceeded to rinse her off again.

Slowly.

Thoroughly.

Tenderly.

She resembled liquid in the end, her body so relaxed she was nearly asleep already.

I moved behind her and pressed my palm to her lower

back to keep her standing, then bent to kiss her throat. "I'm going to worship you for eternity," I vowed. "If you let me."

More goose bumps responded to my words, her body going limp against mine. *I don't even care about what you might do to me now. I'm too relaxed to feel it.*

My chuckle wasn't quite one of amusement, but not completely self-deprecating either.

"The only things I'm going to do to you are dry you off and carry you to bed—to sleep." I kissed her throat again and reached around her to grasp the knob, only her hand caught mine before I could turn off the water.

I waited to see what she would do, her thoughts providing a myriad of possibilities.

She drew her nail along the top of my hand and rotated toward me, her soft green eyes meeting mine. I studied her beautiful face, my heart aching from all the memories I'd lost.

All those moments I'd never remember for myself.

The feelings I'd acquired over a thousand years.

Every sensation she'd ever awoken within me.

None of it would be mine again.

But I could make new experiences with her. Create everything all over again, only do it better this time.

By not repeating my mistakes.

By not abandoning her. Abandoning us.

She reached up to palm my cheek, her gaze still holding mine. "If you don't lead them, then all this loss will have been for nothing, Cam." Her words were whisper soft. "I'm not sure if I can live with that. Live with knowing we gave up so much... for nothing."

Those weren't the words I'd expected her to say. However, I'd heard a variant of them mingled within her other thoughts.

She lifted onto her toes to press her lips to mine. It was a tender kiss, one filled with conflicting emotions.

Longing.
Fear.
A chance at a new beginning.
A potential goodbye.
Hope.
Desolation.

I felt each one of those sensations as though they were my own.

But it was the resolve in her mind that spoke the loudest, the mental voice saying, *I need all of this to have purpose. We have to see this through, or the last century of pain will have had no meaning at all. And I would have survived all of this... for nothing.*

"You're asking me to be their king," I translated.

No, she wasn't asking. She was *begging.* Saying she needed this to help her heal. To give our sacrifice a purpose.

It wasn't about whether or not we would succeed; it was about trying to create a positive result from all of this pain.

I'd set us down this path with my choices. And now she wanted—*needed*—me to finish it.

I swallowed, the concept of leading this revolution making my insides tighten with unease. Primarily because we had no strategy, no *plan.*

Because I'd selfishly never shared it with anyone, just provided a few vague notions and fucked off to handle Lilith on my own.

And look how well that turned out, I chastised myself.

Alas, I could ridicule myself all day and night, and it wouldn't fix a damn thing.

Ismerelda wanted me to lead, to soothe the agony of our past, and guide all of us into a new future.

I had no idea how to do that.

But for her, I would try.

"This will be for you," I echoed out loud. "If I become their king, it'll be because you're my queen, and you asked me for this. No other reason. No point of pride. No sense of entitlement. It'll all be because you desired it. Do you understand?"

I needed her to know this would be different from a hundred and eighteen years ago. If I led the revolution now, it wouldn't be out of some misplaced need to save humanity or a selfish choice disguised as a selfless act.

It would be because Ismerelda asked me to lead.

And she would dictate if I ever stepped down, too.

"Every decision will be ours, not mine," I went on. "I won't sacrifice your safety again." I cupped her cheek. "And if you want me to turn you, I will. Just say the words, Ismerelda, and I'll stop whatever I'm doing to fulfill your wishes. Because while I may become their king, I will always serve you first, not them."

Her light-colored eyelashes fluttered, her cheeks pink from the heat of the shower. Or perhaps she was blushing from my words.

Regardless, they appeared to be the right ones to voice because she kissed me again, this time with a little more pressure.

I waited a beat before deepening our embrace, my desire to feel her tongue against mine a stark need I couldn't ignore. Not with her breasts pressing into my chest and the hints of need floating through her thoughts.

Her lips instantly parted for me, her nails finding my shoulders as she pulled me closer.

I palmed her lower back, closing the final gaps between us, and fisted her hair with my opposite hand.

Our embrace felt desperate. Overwhelmed. *Intentional.* Like we were meeting for the first time, yet saying goodbye to one another as well.

It was twisted and dark and utterly intoxicating.

I wanted more. *So much more.*

But my connection to Ismerelda's thoughts grounded my instincts. She needed this kiss, this subtle promise of a new beginning.

And I fully intended to deliver.

I pressed her up against the tiled wall, my throbbing cock nestled against her belly as I devoured her with my mouth. It served as a promise of what we could be, how my dominance would always exist between us, but she was the one truly in charge of our fate.

One word from her and I'd stop. One thought and I'd back off.

She was mine to fuck, but also mine to cherish. And I could do both. *Would* do both.

I'd bow to her every need, including the one where she'd asked me to lead. I'd do whatever it took to earn her love, to rekindle this fire between our souls, to be a man she could spend eternity with.

She'd experienced a thousand years with someone who'd treated her as fragile, making every decision for her, and inevitably leaving her to fend for herself during the darkest time of her life.

That man hadn't prepared her to survive. He'd prepared her to rely on others.

But the swan he'd left behind had been reborn into a lioness. A queen. *My intended mate.*

And I'd evolved into the man she needed to stand beside her, not in front of her.

I would never mistake her for a breakable toy. I'd always see her as my equal. Intelligent. Strong-willed. Tenacious.

This woman was my ideal everything.

Just as I would prove to her I was her perfect match as well.

Starting with this kiss.

I engraved every promise, every intention, into her mouth with my tongue. Mastering her with my prowess while softening to her will.

She moaned, her supple form pressing into mine as her nails dug into my skin.

I let her cling to me as I devoured her.

Then I sliced my own tongue and fed her my blood, the offering meant to be a sealing of my vows to her. An example of who I would be by her side.

I would bleed for her, not the other way around.

She accepted my essence with a tentative swallow, her thoughts instantly on guard as she suspected I was emboldening her so I could ravage her.

But that wasn't my intent at all.

I just wanted her to be comfortable. Alive. *Strong*.

My grip gentled in her hair as I softened our kiss, my tongue less vigorous, my mouth not as demanding.

It turned sensual. Seductive. *Worshipping*.

She shivered in response, her body melting into mine as the power of my blood heightened her senses. I didn't take advantage of that reaction, simply kissed her until we were both panting with the need to breathe.

Then I reached over to turn off the water.

She blinked startled eyes up at me, her mind still anticipating a brutal fucking.

It didn't matter that my thoughts telegraphed

otherwise. She'd more or less come to expect it during our short time together. And a darker part of her craved it.

However, this wasn't the time.

I needed to restore her faith in me before I released my beast again.

With one last brush of my lips against hers, I guided her to the shower exit and grabbed a towel. She quivered as I wrapped her up in the cotton, freshly warmed from the towel rack.

Then I took another for myself before lifting her into the air and carrying her to the bed.

She didn't protest as I laid her down, her mind and body too exhausted from the day to even care that her hair was wet against the pillows.

While my blood invigorated her soul, it couldn't cure her of being tired.

I leaned down to kiss her cheek, my lips lingering against her ear. "Sleep, my queen. Tonight, we'll tell the others that they have a king. And together, we'll chase away the pain. Define our future, and give purpose to our past."

KYLAN

"Mmm," I hummed, my hips pressing Raelyn's into the mattress beneath us. "I really do like you in this position."

Ice-blue eyes glared up at me. "Good evening to you, too."

I chuckled and brushed my nose against hers. "It's not good yet, little lamb. But it's about to be *great*." I caught her lower lip between my teeth before she could comment, my cock sliding through her slick heat.

She arched into me, her body responding to mine the way it always did, her pussy ready to be fucked. Pleasured. *Owned*.

I drove inside her, eliciting a delicious scream from her mouth. She'd been asleep when this game had started, my lips caressing her neck while my hands had fondled her tits.

I'd been pressed up behind her, my body hard against her soft curves.

And when she'd moaned, I'd moved her to her back.

Then I'd woken her with my dick right against her clit.

Sleepy foreplay had become a favorite between us, her body coming alive for me in ways that made me want to make her mine over and over again.

I would never tire of this female.

My Raelyn.

My vampire mate.

"*More*," she whispered. "Please, Kylan. I need—"

The sound of a door opening in our suite had me rolling off of her and to my feet in an instant, my hand automatically going for the knife in my nightstand.

"If we're going to share this room with you all, I'm going to need you to not fuck my best friend for a few days," a deep voice announced from just outside our bedroom door.

My brow furrowed as I glanced down at a scrambling Rae, her cheeks pink.

"You realize he's going to demand the same of you, yes?" another male voice drawled back at him. "Were you planning to spend those days on the couch by yourself? Because I'm not agreeing to a no-sex policy. And I suspect Luna won't either."

"Silas," Raelyn whispered, her expression brightening as she began to dress.

"I don't recall giving you permission to put on clothes," I told her.

"I don't recall *asking*," she returned, her jeans already half up her legs.

I had half a mind to grab her, pin her, and fuck her just to make a point. But a buzzing from the nightstand interrupted my yearning.

"The whole world is full of assholes," I muttered, grabbing my discarded watch.

Raelyn giggled and walked around the bed as she pulled on her sweater. It was the complete opposite of what I wanted, but at least she went without a bra. "I'll make it up to you in the shower," she whispered before kissing my jaw.

I fisted her hair before she could walk away and caught her mouth with my own, ignoring the secondary buzz coming from my other hand. She melted into me, allowing my tongue to master hers as she wrapped her arms around my waist.

You're going to do a lot more than make it up to me, I said into her mind. *And this mouth of yours is going to prove its worth.*

It's a good thing I'm well trained, she returned, her teeth sinking into my bottom lip, just as mine had done to hers moments ago. *But if I'm going to kneel for you, I expect you to return the favor.*

Oh, I will, I promised her. *We're going to chase that* best friend *of yours right out of this suite with your screams.*

The item in my hand vibrated a third time.

I ignored it.

If that mutt thinks he can tell me what to do, he's going to be wildly surprised by how I react, I went on. *Warn him before I demonstrate.*

She grinned against my mouth. *No fighting with the wolves, yet. They just arrived.*

Your best friend *started it.*

She nipped my lip again. "You're my best friend, Kylan. I'll make sure he knows that."

I narrowed my gaze at her playful tone. "Be sure that you do. *Mate.*"

Her icy gaze glittered in response. "I love you, too," she deadpanned.

I tightened my grasp in her hair. "I believe I love you more."

"We'll see."

"Yes, we will," I agreed, releasing her. "Now go play with your *friend*. Tell him to behave like a good little wolf. He still owes me from when I saved his life."

She shook her head at me, but the upward tilt of her lips told me she was amused. "You should answer that," she said as it hummed for a fourth time.

Sighing, I glanced at it. "It's not a call. They're text messages." And they appeared to be from Ryder.

I sat on the edge of the bed, still naked, and pulled up a translucent screen so I could flip through the short statements.

It's true, was the first message.

All of it, was the second one.

And there's so much more.

We'll talk soon.

I narrowed my gaze at the screen. *How do I even know this is Ryder?* I typed back. *You should probably call to confirm.*

Visual tech is just as manipulatable as texts, Ryder replied within seconds. *Besides, I hate phone calls. All that talk, talk, talk, when it could all be wrapped up in a few sentences. Such as the above.*

That was a lot of words for someone who claims to dislike talking, I returned.

Because you keep replying.

Because I don't believe it's you. Which was sort of a lie. I could practically hear his snark coming off each word.

I stared at the screen expectantly, half anticipating Ryder's face to appear. Rather than leave the room, Raelyn joined me on the bed. The wolves were murmuring amongst themselves in the suite, clearly choosing one of the bedrooms for themselves.

443

There were three total, all of them masters in their own way.

Raelyn and I had chosen this one for the lakefront terrace. I suspected the shifters would want the woodsy option since we were on the ground floor and they might want to go for a run in wolf form.

Willow wants to know if Rae remembers how they used to try to best Silas on exams, prior to them all becoming friends.

The message scrolled across the screen, causing Raelyn to laugh, her mind unleashing a variety of memories of the two of them trying to sabotage Silas's efforts on exams. When those exams turned sexual in nature, however, I growled.

Raelyn cleared her throat. "Tell her I remember pointing out how she and Silas were the same person."

I fought the urge to grin, immediately understanding why she'd chosen that reply as I typed it back to Ryder.

His response came a few seconds later. *Yeah, except Silas and Rae were the similar ones, and Willow was the one who said it out loud. Which led to their friendship.*

Raelyn nodded. "At least you know you're talking to Ryder now. No one else would ever care about those details or know about them."

"I care," I argued.

"You know what I mean."

I did, but it'd been worth saying to her.

When will you be back? I sent to Ryder, driving us back to the point of the conversation.

In twenty-four hours, he returned immediately.

Don't die, I told him.

I really am starting to think you like me, Kylan. As more than just an ally.

Return and find out, I taunted him.

That sounds suspiciously like a threat, as well as a date, he mused.

I only date Raelyn.

I only date Willow, he immediately sent back.

Why are we still talking? I demanded.

Because you keep fucking replying.

I shut off the screen with a growl and found Raelyn smiling at me, her humor warming our bond. My eyes narrowed at her now instead of Ryder. "Keep looking at me like that, little lamb, and I'm going to eat you."

"Promise?" she asked before leaping out of reach and running for the door.

I phased after her, but she was already out of the room and down the hall, her vampire talents rivaling my own. *I'm going to make you pay for that later.*

I look forward to it, My Prince.

My lips curled at the title, mostly because I knew what it meant. Raelyn used *My Prince* when she agreed to my terms. It was her way of saying she approved and consented to whatever I was doing, something that proved to be particularly helpful in sexual situations. *Your Highness* was her safe word, the one she uttered when she was uneasy.

Thus, *My Prince* was an invitation to play.

And play we would.

After we met with the wolves and brought them up to speed.

Because apparently we were now sharing space with Edon, Silas, and Luna. The mated triad from Clemente Clan.

Sighing, I went to find a suit.

It was going to be a long fucking night of meetings.

But at least I had a playdate to look forward to...

445

CAM

THE LYCANS PACED, THEIR AGITATION ADDING AN undercurrent of tension to the air.

An undercurrent I didn't appreciate.

We'd been in this space for far too fucking long. Yesterday, I'd thought this ballroom was too big for a meeting of this size. Today, it felt too damn small.

After hours of discussion, I was more than ready for a break.

But I held still and remained patient for Ismerelda. She sat beside me, her focus on two of the pacing lycans. I'd been reintroduced to both of them even though I'd met them before.

One was Jolene, an older alpha from Clemente Clan. The other was Luka, the lycan I'd entrusted with Ismerelda's safety. He'd given my *Erosita* a hug the moment he'd seen her earlier, his concern for her well-being notable. Primarily as it'd been his mate who had betrayed everyone and taken Ismerelda to me.

Ismerelda had whispered her forgiveness, telling him it wasn't his fault.

And now he was in full debate mode with Jolene.

Jace and Darius inserted comments every now and then. Khalid and Hazel did as well.

Kylan seemed bored, his focus more on his redheaded mate than on the prowling lycans.

And I just wanted this to end.

I'd agreed to be their leader—something I hadn't actually mentioned out loud yet. But until someone gave me a goal, I had nothing to do. Mainly because all of my knowledge was either outdated or manipulated.

About the only thing that had interested me thus far was Luka's need for vengeance against his mate, Mira.

"When we find her, she's mine to deal with," he'd snarled an hour ago. "No exceptions."

I hadn't argued his desire to kill the treacherous bitch. I'd merely added, "And Michael is Ismerelda's to deal with."

Which had drawn a few curious looks, but no one had countered my claim.

It seemed the overall consensus was that we needed to infiltrate the compound beneath the catacombs, kill everyone, and capture proof of Lilith's work.

Then we would call an alliance meeting to present everything to the royals and alphas.

But Jolene felt we needed a few more lycan allies to ensure our raid was successful, which had led to the conversation about whom to call in.

Fortunately, they seemed to have come to an agreement on their list.

"Fantastic. We have a plan. Do you want them here

before we discuss the underground schematics, or can we begin that conversation now?" Jace asked.

"I need a break before we do that," Kylan interjected, his commentary rivaling my own thought. "We should also wait for Ryder and Damien to be part of that conversation. They're skilled at infiltration and assaults."

"As is Cedric," Khalid murmured. "I agree that we should wait and focus on bringing in the lycan allies for now."

Several nods appeared around the table, and Hazel stood first. "More blood wine will be delivered to your rooms. Food can be ordered as well. Otherwise, my hospitality remains at your disposal."

She opened her hands and bowed her head slightly, then left the room.

Khalid and Emine soon followed, leaving most of the revolutionary unit lingering behind.

"We'll start making calls right away," Jolene said, his focus going to Edon, the new Alpha of Clemente Clan. "Your room or mine?"

"Yours," Kylan answered for him. "Raelyn and I have plans."

Silas grunted.

Edon smirked.

Do you want to go on a walk with me? I asked Ismerelda, ignoring the others. *Watch the sunrise over the lake?*

I'd caught her wistfully staring outside on more than one occasion. From what I'd gathered, she'd never been here. I had once, a very long time ago. Well before resorts existed.

Before I'd met her.

She glanced at me. *Yes, I would like that.*

I stood and reached for her hand, only then realizing the room had fallen silent and everyone was staring at us.

"Did I miss a question?" I asked, eyebrow arched.

Jace cleared his throat. "No."

"Good." I closed my fingers around Ismerelda's and pulled her up to my side. "We're going to explore. See you all tomorrow." I started toward the door, then paused to look back at my cousin. "Oh, I've decided I'll lead. Not for you, but for my queen. Anything you want me to do, she has to approve."

With that, I tugged my mate into the hallway and started toward the exit.

"We'll meet you back in the room, Keys," I told our dark shadow.

He'd definitely taken on the role of bodyguard, but we didn't need one right now. I wanted to be alone with my mate. Without an audience. And without interference.

"Feel free to order yourself dinner. Whatever you'd like," I added.

"Thank you," he replied, pausing in our wake.

I felt that pause more than saw it, my focus on the exit and my mate.

Chilly air kissed my senses in the next few steps as one of the glass doors automatically opened, revealing the stunning scenery outside.

It wasn't exactly strolling weather, the snowy mountains in the distance providing a cooler atmosphere.

I actually had no idea what month it was, not that it would matter much. From what I understood, the climate expectations had changed drastically over the last millennium. Couple that with human destruction, then human desertion, and everything had changed.

Ismerelda threaded her fingers through mine, her attention on a path ahead that led straight to the lake.

I let her lead, my thumb brushing her skin to test her temperature. It seemed the sweater and jeans she was wearing were providing enough warmth for now. She also had on thick socks and boots, and a winter hat—something she'd referred to earlier as a *beanie* before donning it for the meeting.

After living in former-day Canada for the last twelve decades or so, she seemed quite content with the weather here.

We wandered without speaking, her mind lost to the scenery while I observed her enjoyment.

Maybe that humanlike innocence is why I never turned her, I mused to myself. *It certainly is charming.*

But it would be a selfish reason to keep her mortal.

She said nothing, her thoughts quiet as we walked.

After over a half hour of wandering, she stopped and looked at me. "We used to do this when we first met."

I arched a brow. "We did?" I hadn't heard any memories in her mind about this, but I caught them now as she started remembering certain walks.

One in particular caught my interest because it'd ended with me fucking her up against a tree.

Her already pink cheeks darkened a shade at the thought, aware I'd overhead that particular gem.

Alas, she cleared her throat and looked away. "We should head back. But I'd like to do this again before the meeting tomorrow. Sitting all day is exhausting."

"Listening to them debate is exhausting," I countered.

She gave me a look. "They're trying to shift the alliance, Cam. That takes strategy and conversation."

"Is that how Lilith did it?" I asked.

"Yes," a deep voice replied, drawing my focus to my approaching cousin. Calina was with him, her gaze filled with awe as she stared at the lake like she'd never seen water before. "She made alliances, hence the name, and coaxed the royals and alphas into following her lead."

"Hmm," I hummed. "More like intimidated them into it. That was the point of my public death, yes?"

"True. Is that what you propose we do, then? Throw Lilith's head on the table alongside Michael's remains?"

"It would paint a lovely picture," I admitted.

"So that's the kind of leader you want to be?" Jace pressed.

"If it is?" I countered.

His gaze narrowed. "Then I think we need to discuss it more."

I shrugged. "Sure. We'll do that tomorrow." I wrapped my arm around Ismerelda's shoulders and led her away, intent on avoiding further discussion.

It worked.

For a day.

Then Jace brought it up again. And again. And again.

By the fifth day of meetings, I was ready to kill everyone and walk away. But Ismerelda was engaged with the plan, her hope deepening with each conversation.

I observed her as she offered suggestions, told them what she'd seen on the cameras, and reviewed what little intelligence Damien and Cedric had on the underground compound.

It seemed both of them had been trying to hack into the network, their work not nearly as successful as they'd hoped. Primarily because there didn't appear to be cameras everywhere in the bunker.

Which confirmed there were sections, perhaps even full floors, that I hadn't seen while under Vatican City.

Ismerelda stood in front of me now, her focus on the schematics the team had crafted over the last few days since Ryder and Damien's return.

The ballroom had more or less turned into a war room over the last few days, curtained walls now covered in images. Some of them were potential royal allies. Another section held known Lilith supporters.

Then across from it were notes drawn up by the lycans, their lists mostly revolving around those they still needed to convince of Lilith's lab work.

Without proof, it was difficult to bring a lot of them to the table.

Which led to the urgency of attacking the compound and the strategies strewn across the meeting table.

I waited, observing as Ismerelda leaned over to study one of the items intently. It was an image of the interior Coventus, one Juliet had drafted based on her time there.

Ismerelda was mentally pairing it to the video feeds she'd observed from my laptop.

She seemed to feel something was missing, like perhaps the feeds she'd seen had been of another area.

It was something she'd need to ask Juliet about tomorrow, as we were the only two left in the room, everyone else having gone back to their rooms for morning dinner.

I'd expected to go on another walk, as that'd been our routine since our first one the other day.

The walk usually led to dinner, which ended in a shower. Whereby I worshipped her with my hands—in a chaste manner—then tucked her into bed.

However, watching her bend over this table right now had me wanting to do something else entirely tonight.

It wasn't just her sensual position, but also the thoughts rolling through her intelligent mind. My cunning lioness was a little strategic genius.

Yet the others didn't seem to call upon her much. They listened when she spoke up, but they kept looking to me for answers—and that was despite Jace's obvious dissatisfaction with my leadership plans.

Not that I truly had plans. I simply liked the idea of delivering Lilith's and Michael's remains to the alliance.

Ismerelda hummed, the sound a sweet benediction to my ears. It drew me closer to her, my need to touch her mounting with each passing second.

I wanted to grab her hand. Tug her from the room. Distract her with the view. Then disrobe and bathe her. Just like I'd done all week.

Yet she bent over again, derailing that desire and inspiring a dark hunger. One that involved stripping her here. Devouring her. Making her scream on that very table. And leaving the scent of my queen's pleasure behind.

A marking.

A claim.

A *mating*.

My beast growled inside, approving of this craving.

But I fisted my hands at my sides, determined to temper the urge. To respect my *Erosita*. To win her trust. *To wait*.

At least, that was my intention.

Until her thoughts started responding to mine.

Visions of me between her legs, staring up at her while I licked her to completion. Her body subtly tensed with the recollection, her thighs seeming to quiver.

But then her memory evolved into a more recent encounter, one where I bit her and left her to suffer.

Another when I'd pushed her too far, causing her to pass out.

And finally, to all the times I'd fed from her there without remorse. Taking. Forcing. *Hurting*.

I grabbed her hips from behind, burying my face in her hair as I accepted her agony. Rather than comment, I shared the experience from my point of view, showed her how I'd thought she was enjoying it. How I'd wanted to pleasure her. Yes, it'd been for me. But I'd wanted it for her as well.

And I still did.

I longed to feel her come against my tongue. To do it properly without a bite. To make her beg for more, not because she was overstimulated or drugged from my vampiric kiss, but because she truly needed it.

Because she *wanted* it.

I won't push you, I promised her. *But when you're ready, I will consume you. I'll make you fly. I'll show you what kings are meant to do to their queens.*

It went deeper than worship. It was about making my mate feel like a goddess. To introduce her to an ecstasy she'd never experienced before.

I won't go easy on you. I'll treat you like an equal, prove that you're not breakable, and unleash every ounce of adoration I feel for you. You'll feel what I feel, our minds connected, our hearts beating as one, our bodies in sync. It'll be intense. But it will only hurt in the best way.

There would be no biting. Not unless she asked for it.

I'd only memorize her body with my mouth. Caress her. Protect her. Push her limits while ensuring she felt safe.

Love her.

She was mine.

I would do anything to prove that to her. To help rebuild this trust between us. But she had to let me try. She had to let me in.

And I could hear in her mind that she still wasn't ready.

Which meant I needed to give her space. Give her time. Let her come to me rather than force it.

I wrapped my arms around her, my chest against her back as I dropped my lips to her ear.

"I'm not giving up, Izzy. I'm here. I'm yours. And I'll

wait as long as it takes for you to let me in." I pressed my mouth to her neck, her pulse throbbing under my touch. "The future is ours if you want it."

She swallowed, saying nothing.

But she didn't have to speak.

I already heard her thoughts, her desire to think.

She wanted to be alone. Not for a while, just a few minutes. And it was a gift I could give her.

"I'll go order our dinner and meet you back at our suite," I told her softly. "The choice on how we proceed here is yours, my queen. I won't push you. And I don't expect an answer tonight. So take your time. Heal. Just know that I'm here if you need me, all right?"

She nodded slowly, her mind thanking me while her words seemed to fail her.

With another kiss against her pulse, I left her in the makeshift war room.

Keys stood just outside the door, his stance protective. I hadn't excused him back to our suite, not because I'd wanted him to stay, but because I'd forgotten he was still here.

I briefly considered telling him to come with me, but it seemed wise to leave him with Ismerelda. Just in case. One could never be too cautious.

"Escort her back when she's ready," I told him.

His brown eyes glittered with pleasure, the assignment clearly one he desired. "Consider it done."

I gave him a nod and headed toward the elevators. I'd order him some food as well.

Then hopefully Ismerelda would let me bathe her again.

Or, if her heated thoughts were to be believed, maybe she would let me do a little more.

Maybe she would let me play.

It seemed something I'd said had been right.

Because she was picturing it now, and struggling not to chase after me.

My lips curled. *You can hunt me any day, sweet lioness. I'll always be easy prey. For you. And only you.*

IZZY

Cam's words hummed through my mind, stirring heat across my being.

His promises had been so sensual. So alluring. *So perfect.*

Why am I fighting this? I marveled. *Cam's mine. I want him. He wants me. We're mated…*

He might not be the man I remembered, the man I'd fallen in love with, but maybe he was right. Maybe we could be something new. Something even more powerful.

If I can trust him again.

Can I…? I wondered. *Can I trust him again?*

It had only been a few days since our link had been restored, but Cam was notably a different person. Not the same as his previous version, yet also not the same as the one I'd met mere weeks ago.

He was… unapologetically dominant. Thoughtful.

Caring. *Protective*. And he treated me as his equal, not as a pawn or a toy. Not a delicate swan or a breakable doll. But a woman. *A queen*.

My heart fluttered, his words warming my skin once more.

When you're ready, I will consume you. I'll make you fly. I'll show you what kings are meant to do to their queens.

He'd been direct. Straight to the point. Honest. And respectful.

The choice on how we proceed here is yours, my queen.

He hadn't pushed me. Hadn't bitten me. Hadn't attempted to use me in any way. He'd simply been there for me, feeding me, bathing me, holding me while I slept, whispering all the right statements into my mind.

They weren't lies. They were truths. He wanted to make this work, to move into the future and be stronger than our past.

While he might not be the old Cam, he was still *my* Cam. Just a revised version of him.

Maybe even a better version, I thought, my lips curling as I recalled Cam's certainty that he was the superior version of himself.

I hadn't agreed at the time.

But now I found myself wondering if he was right.

Neither of us was who we used to be. I'd changed, too. Grown in a way I hadn't fully appreciated until Cam had started calling me his queen. His *lioness*.

I used to be the soft one of the group, always listening rather than speaking up.

But this week, I'd voiced my part. Provided my input. Made suggestions. Served as a leader in a way I could never have anticipated.

And I'd done that with Cam by my side, his silent presence a supportive force that no one could deny. He'd deferred to me, asked for my thoughts instead of voicing his own, and made it clear to everyone that we were a team.

It'd been… surreal. Beautiful. *Empowering.*

I stared at the maps on the table, not really seeing them. Because all I could envision was Cam hoisting me up onto the messy space, spreading my legs, and pleasuring me. Just like he'd considered doing mere moments ago.

Yet I let him walk away.

Why did I do that?

Why am I not chasing him?

He was my mate. My vampire. *My Cam.*

I stepped away from the table, his voice suddenly in my head as he whispered, *You can hunt me any day, sweet lioness. I'll always be easy prey. For you. And only you.*

His deep tones sent a tremble down my spine, my thighs clenching at the insinuation in his words.

Why am I still standing here? I asked myself. *Go hunt him.*

It was the only way I could determine if we had a path forward. Either he upheld his words and intentions, or he hurt me. But I wouldn't know which way this would go unless I attempted to trust him again.

Standing here and wallowing in the past would never move us into the future.

Cam knew that.

And it was time I knew that, too.

Straightening my spine, I headed toward the door. *I'm prowling your way,* I told Cam, purposely using a verb that seemed lioness-like.

His resulting amusement warmed my mind. *I'll be waiting for you to pounce, my queen.*

Goose bumps pebbled down my arms at the notion of *pouncing* on Cam. Maybe I'd straddle his face again. Only this time, I'd ask him not to bite me. I wasn't ready for that yet.

I... I just wanted to experience this version of him. But without the underlying threat of violence.

Or maybe with just a hint of it.

His inner predator enthralled me. That beast tempted me to want things I shouldn't.

I just needed to be able to trust him not to harm me in the process.

There's only one way to know for sure, I decided as I reached the hallway. *I have to try. It's the only way to forgive...* My brow furrowed, my thoughts trailing off. "Keys?"

He was sitting against the wall, his head canted at a strange angle.

Frowning, I moved toward him, my brain struggling to process what I was seeing. *His shirt is wet.* The candlelight seemed to be reflecting off the black fabric.

And his tie was... askew.

His jacket torn.

One shoe was missing.

But his neck was what held my focus. His dark skin was damp there, too.

No, not damp. Bloody.

Ismerelda, Cam said into my mind. *Go back into the room and lock the door. Now.*

The urgency in his voice had me freezing midstep, my mind processing his command in slow motion. I understood him. It was just the... the scene in front of me... I...

Ismerelda!

I blinked, my feet moving backward in a frantic motion until I hit the wall.

Wait, no... not a wall. It was too soft. Too pliant.

I'm coming, Cam vowed. *I'm almost there!*

I…

Pain shot through my skull, darkening my vision. Blurring Keys's lifeless form. Dimming the candlelight.

Silencing Cam's roar…

Cam? I whispered. *I can't see. I can't…*

Vibrations shook my limbs as the world spun around me. So fast. Too fast.

Then the only thing I could feel was nothing at all.

Everything had gone silent.

Cold.

Deathly still.

Cam…?

Nothing.

Not even the sound of my beating heart.

I'm dying, I realized. *Just like before…*

Only this time, it wasn't Cam who'd killed me. It was someone else entirely.

But who? I wondered, my mind fading. *Who has betrayed us now…?*

CAM

"FUCK!"

I phased down the hall, Ismerelda's blood a beacon to my beast. Except the moment I stepped outside, the sweet essence dwindled.

I chased it to a nearby parking lot, where it disappeared entirely.

Less than ninety seconds was all it had taken for someone to abduct Ismerelda.

I punched a nearby wall, a roar ripping from my throat. I had to figure out who had her. What car the culprit had taken. *Anything.*

I also needed her to talk to me. To tell me she was all right.

I shouldn't have left you in that room, I told her, furious with myself. *I should have just stayed in the hallway with Keys.*

Thinking of the human made me wince.

I'd left a mortal in charge of her safety.

What a fucking mistake that had clearly been.

But I hadn't thought... *"Fuck."* That was precisely the problem. I hadn't thought at all. I'd blindly trusted.

I'd made assumptions.

And now...

Now Ismerelda is gone.

With a snarl, I phased back into the hallway, my nostrils flaring as I hunted for any familiar scents. But all I could smell was Ismerelda's blood.

And Keys's blood, too.

I knelt beside him, his pulse nearly nonexistent. Whoever had bitten him had done so haphazardly, the wound more lycan-like than vampire-like. Yet the two pinpricks at his vein were definitely the latter.

An inexperienced vampire, I deduced. *Young. Unpracticed. Impatient.*

There was a certain finesse when it came to killing a human. And whoever had done this to Keys had lacked the art of a clean bite.

I sank my fangs into my wrist and held it to his mouth. *"Drink,"* I demanded, that single word underlined in compulsion. It was necessary, his mind and body too far gone to willingly follow my command.

I grabbed a fistful of his dark hair and pulled his head back, his lips against my bleeding wound. He didn't suckle or try to pull my essence into his mouth, but this angle would allow a few drops to fall over his tongue.

With my age and power, that was all he'd need.

His throat eventually worked, my compulsion forcing him to swallow. Unfortunately, though, it would take a while for him to recover. And I didn't have time to waste.

I glanced around the hall, searching for any signs of cameras or security surveillance. Keys may or may not be able to tell me who had tried to kill him when he woke up. Hopefully, he could. But in the interim, I needed to pursue other avenues for information.

On his fifth swallow, I cut off the persuasion and slowly lowered him to the ground. He'd eventually wake up with a headache, but he'd be alive.

Leaving him to heal, I phased to the reception area. "Are there security cameras in the ballroom area?" I demanded, not bothering with formalities.

Three vampires gaped back at me, none of them speaking.

"Do not make me repeat myself," I warned them. "I am not known for my patience."

"What's going on, Cam?" The female voice came from overhead, drawing my gaze upward to a speaker.

One of these vampires must have hit a button of some kind to notify Hazel of my appearance.

I would be irritated if it hadn't been so efficient. Because if anyone could get me what I needed, it was the royal of this region.

"Ismerelda has been taken," I gritted out. "I want all the video surveillance you have available of Deirdre City, and I want it right fucking now."

Silence fell across the room, the lack of immediate movement grating on my nerves.

"I'm coming down," Hazel announced into the quiet, her words momentarily placating me.

I paced the tiled reception area floors as I waited, my mind desperately trying to connect to Ismerelda's thoughts. But her psyche remained mute, her unconscious state creating an eerie stillness I didn't like.

Is this how you felt for over a hundred years? I wondered. *Lost and alone in this disconnected abyss?*

Just thinking about it made me that much angrier at my former self.

But I was equally furious with my current self for letting her down.

Where are you? I thought at her. *Who took you?*

"What happened?" Hazel asked the moment her elevator opened. Then she stiffened, her gaze going to the ballroom hallway.

And she vanished.

Frowning, I phased after her and found her crouching over Keys, her wrist pressed against his mouth. "I already did that," I told her. "He'll be fine."

Her brown eyes blazed with furious power as she looked up at me. "Who did this?"

"I'm hoping he'll wake up and tell us that," I returned, slightly taken aback by her fury. If anyone had a right to be angry here, it was me. "I assume whoever bit him also took Ismerelda."

Hazel took in the state of his neck, the wound already having begun to close as my vampiric essence worked magic through his veins. "A youngling. Someone who has never fed before."

"Yes," I agreed. "Or someone with very little experience."

She released a sound that was part growl and part hum, her wrist still at Keys's mouth. His throat seemed to be working much more vigorously now, his healing well on its way. But it clearly wasn't good enough for Hazel.

She lifted him into her arms with the kind of care I would only bestow upon Ismerelda and carried him into a nearby lounge. The dark room boasted blackout curtains along the back wall and had a stage on the opposite end.

I didn't ask what this space was used for, as it didn't matter. "I need the security feeds," I reiterated.

"I know. Cedric is on his way down with them." She laid Keys on a couch and situated his head on a pillow before kneeling beside him. "You're safe," she told him softly. "You're going to be all right."

I was starting to question whom this human belonged to—me or Hazel.

"What the fuck happened?" a deep voice demanded, the accusation underscoring that tone the kind only a brother could deliver. "Why the hell was she even alone?" Damien walked right up into my space, his golden irises glittering like twin flames. "Not even three weeks in your care and—"

"I have the feeds," Cedric interjected from behind Damien, a small disk in his hand that he pointed at the stage.

Light bloomed beyond it as a giant screen flickered to life. An array of small images soon followed, essentially creating a makeshift security console. Only, rather than being in a handful of computers—the way I'd seen in the compound—this took up an entire wall.

Cedric climbed onto the stage and grabbed images with his hands to move them, the screen apparently manipulatable.

"There," he said, bringing up the feed of me leaving Keys.

I left Damien to simmer in the entryway and weaved my way through the various couches and luxury chairs to follow Cedric.

By the time I reached the stairs leading to the stage, a hooded figure had appeared on the screen. He or she seemed to have come in from outside, their coat a typical accessory, which explained Keys not immediately identifying the person as a threat.

He bowed, though. So he'd clearly determined the culprit was a vampire.

Probably because he could see his or her face from his angle. However, the vampire kept tilting away from the camera, suggesting he or she knew about the surveillance feeds in the hallway.

I winced as the hooded being went for Keys's neck, the brutal strike an unappealing visual.

Keys threw up his hands in a defensive maneuver, taking the culprit by surprise as he nearly toppled the offender. But he wasn't fast enough to stop the vampire from attacking again, a gloved hand going over his mouth before he could scream.

They tussled, but he went down quickly and silently.

While it was fast, it certainly wasn't painless.

The culprit lowered Keys to the floor, leaving him sprawled at an awkward angle as the being propped him up against the wall.

Keys grasped his neck, his mouth parting on a gasp—or maybe he was still trying to yell, perhaps to warn Ismerelda—but he soon lost consciousness due to the blood loss.

Then the figure moved farther down the hall to wait in a doorway.

"Given the stature, I'd say it was a woman." Khalid's voice came from behind me. "She was much smaller than Keys."

Considering the human was taller than my six-foot-two height, it was rather easy for most people to be shorter than Keys.

But I agreed with Khalid's assessment, primarily because the cloaked figure hadn't seemed to reach Keys's chin. She also appeared rather petite beneath the coat.

Still, I wouldn't rule anyone out.

Ismerelda appeared next, her face taking my breath away. Because she was smiling. Determined. So fucking beautiful.

Only to turn concerned at the sight of Keys on the floor. She moved forward as though entranced, all the while giving the villain the opportunity to creep up behind her.

It was fast, yet felt drawn out in slow motion.

Ismerelda's understanding of the situation. Her mounting fear. Her stumbling backward into the cloaked figure.

The vampire slamming the butt of a pistol against my Erosita's *head.*

My fingers curled into fists at the sight, my fury burning even hotter. "Whoever that is came here with a very specific purpose," I growled, fully aware that there was only one reason to even have a gun—to slow down fellow immortals.

The hooded culprit caught Ismerelda before she hit the ground, but the movements were not gentle. They were efficient and executed without care.

And all completed without once revealing the face beneath the hood.

My teeth gritted as the vampire ran out of view. The next movement caught by the camera was my arrival.

Cedric cut the feed and pulled up another from outside, his hands somehow rewinding the footage to show the cloaked culprit running—not phasing—down the path toward the car park.

Where the hooded woman disappeared from view again.

More video footage appeared, but there was no sign of the vampire or Ismerelda.

"She must have parked somewhere outside of the

surveillance area," Cedric said after several long minutes of searching. He rewound the feed to display her entry to the building and shook his head. "This is useless. She knew where all the cameras were and hid her face from them."

"Not necessarily useless," Khalid murmured. "It has to be someone familiar with the security setup or the building. Surely that narrows down the list."

"It does," Hazel replied. "I've already paged Deirdre. She'll be here soon."

How soon? I wanted to demand, but instead I focused on the screens, searching for any angle that might reveal the culprit's face.

All the while, I remained connected to Ismerelda's silent mind, waiting for her to wake.

I could *feel* her, which was the only reason I knew she was alive. But not hearing her was a debilitating experience. It felt as though I'd been disconnected from part of my brain, missing a huge piece of my soul.

Living without a heart.

If there was any doubt in my mind that Ismerelda was my sole link to humanity, it was gone now. Because without her psyche balancing mine, I didn't give two fucks about anyone or anything else.

The plan.

This place.

These people.

All that mattered was survival. *And Ismerelda.*

I hadn't saved Keys because I liked him or cared about him. I'd saved him because he might have useful information. Just like I tolerated everyone else in this room because they might be helpful.

Maybe that made me cold. Ancient. *Unfeeling.* But without my link to Ismerelda, my focus shifted to survival mode. Eat. Fuck. Live. That was all that mattered to my inner beast—fulfilling his sensual and physical appetites.

Ismerelda, however, gave me *heart*. She made me see the world in a way I otherwise wouldn't.

I'd woken from my sleep without any true goals in mind. The video logs from Lilith had convinced me to be a king, to finish what I'd started. Yet I hadn't been all that passionate about the project.

Creating immortal blood bags would satiate my vampiric tastes. It made logical sense to see that through to the end.

But I hadn't been married to the concept.

Leading was a natural inclination for one in my position, my ancient blood marking me as king. That didn't mean I wanted to be a monarch; I simply was one.

Ismerelda had changed everything.

She was my queen. My reason for seeking the throne. My purpose for ruling all the others.

Because she wanted me to.

Except she hadn't wanted me to disappear all those years ago. So why the hell had I done that? Had I misinterpreted her desires?

Or was it something else entirely?

I'm missing a key detail, I decided. *Did my link to her humanity give me a hero complex? Did it shift my mindset over the centuries into a desire to find peace between immortals and mortals? Why would I choose to lead in that way?*

Because I had absolutely no yearning for it now, even with my rekindled link to Ismerelda. If anything, I desired the opposite. I just wanted to find her and shelter us both from the madness of the world. Hide and exist in our own quiet peace, and fuck everyone and everything else.

"Here's a list of all the cars registered in the lot,"

Cedric was saying to Damien, their conversation pulling me from my thoughts.

"They're all still there," Damien replied, his focus on the screen—one of which he was now manipulating like Cedric had. The two of them appeared to be scanning through ample datasets and video feeds, their knack for technology showing.

It almost made me smile. Mostly because Ismerelda had pretended not to understand laptops mere weeks ago, and that had very much been a lie.

She possessed skills similar to her brother's. Perhaps she would even be better than him if properly trained.

"Here." Damien enlarged a black sedan with tinted windows. "It passed through checkpoint seven's camera feed but didn't reach checkpoint eight. The parking lot is between those."

Cedric pulled the image away from him, then fast-forwarded to show the same sedan going back through the feed.

"That's thirteen minutes later," he said. "It stopped somewhere between the two, then backtracked." He made a motion that flung the detail back to Damien while he pulled up another screen. "I'll track it while you review that feed to see if there's a clear indicator somewhere on there. A vehicle identification number. A shot of the driver. Anything."

Damien was already zooming through the footage before Cedric even finished speaking, the rest of us watching.

The rest of us being Ryder, Darius, Jace, and several others, I thought, glancing around the room. I had no idea when they all had arrived, but they were here now and had clearly been brought up to speed.

I scanned the group, searching for anyone noticeably

missing. Because that lycan or vampire might be our culprit, or perhaps related to the incident.

The lycans were all huddled together, talking quietly amongst themselves about the hallway scents. Nothing apparently stood out to them, just like none of them particularly stood out to me, either. They all appeared to be accounted for, with Jolene and Luka leading the discussions.

Darius and Jace spoke in hushed tones with Kylan and Khalid, the four of them reviewing next steps, most of which included hunting Ismerelda down.

But there was also a hint of strategy lurking in their conversation, their need to push forward and find a way into the underground an import—

A buzzing in my mind instantly stilled all my thoughts, my psyche searching for the source.

No. Not a buzzing, I thought, frowning. *An... engine?*

I glanced around, seeing if anyone else could hear it.

No one seemed to be reacting to anything in particular, their stances and discussions remaining unchanged. Cedric and Damien were also still focused on the screens, their words clipped as they passed things back and forth.

Meanwhile, the rumbling grew louder in my mind, the sound reminiscent of a growl. *What is that?* I marveled. It was too impactful to be a car engine. Too much like an explosion, except controlled.

It roared through my senses, making me wince.

Then a soft, sweet voice groggily whispered, *Plane...*

Ismerelda? I straightened. *Are you awake?*

I... I don't... Her words trailed off, that roaring sound disappearing.

"What is it?" The demand came from directly in front of me, causing me to blink as I realized Ryder was right in my face.

"Back off," I snarled, needing to concentrate on my mate. *Ismerelda?*

But she was quiet again, lost to her unconsciousness once more.

A vibration met my chest, my irritation over her silence and Ryder's intrusion causing me to glower at the male before me. "I lost her."

"I'm aware of that," he drawled, though his tone lacked his usual humor and was instead underlined with a sense of violence that appeared to be directed toward me.

"No, I mean, she was talking to me, and now she's gone," I said through my teeth. "You distracted me."

His eyebrows shot up. "If my presence distracts you that much, then that doesn't speak highly of your connection to Ismerelda, does it?"

My fists itched to meet his arrogant face.

Instead, I ignored him and searched for the rumbling sound.

Plane, Ismerelda had said, causing my lips to curl down. *Are you on a plane?* I asked her now, starting to follow.

No reply.

My forearms flexed, my irritation mounting. *Talk to me, my queen. Tell me where you are. Tell me how to find you.*

Silence.

Another growl reverberated inside me, one Ryder matched with his own, thus forcing me to return my focus to him.

Only, he wasn't standing in front of me now, but in front of the screens. "Abigail," I recognized aloud. "Why…?" I trailed off as Damien pulled up a shot from inside the car he'd been tracking, the woman's curly brown hair identifiable.

"She used her access card to enter the city an hour ago," Deirdre said from beside Hazel. Apparently, she'd slipped into the room without my noticing as well. "I thought she was coming to see me."

"You clearly thought wrong," Ryder replied, his attention still on the screen. "Which way is she headed?"

"Already searching," Damien told him.

"I'm going to need your fastest car," Ryder went on, causing my eyebrows to lift.

"*We* are going to need your fastest car," I corrected him.

I also considered telling him he would not be coming with me, but opted against it, as Ryder's penchant for killing first and asking questions later might be useful.

He ignored me, which was fine. I'd either join him in the car or take it from him.

I suspected it would be the former, as he would come to a similar conclusion regarding my usefulness. I was, after all, the only one mentally connected to Ismerelda, thus making me the biggest asset in this situation.

"I'm already arranging it," Deirdre said, one of those translucent screens hovering in front of her.

Wha...? The gentle hum of Ismerelda's voice whispered through my mind again, followed by more of that rumbling. *Where...?*

Ismerelda. Can you hear me?

C-cam? she replied. *Wh-where...? I don't...*

Shh, take a minute to gather your strength, I told her. *Try not to move. Just... focus on steady breathing. And then tell me everything you hear.*

If she could feign unconsciousness for a few moments longer, she might be able to provide me with enough details to track her down. And it would hopefully prevent her from being knocked out again.

I... She trailed off again.

It's okay. Take your time, love. I'm here. Maybe not physically, but I would forever be there mentally.

More of that growling came through our bond, her mind trying to decipher the sound. *Plane*, echoed through her thoughts once more.

I waited and listened to her reasoning with her surroundings.

Am I on a plane? She seemed to be becoming more lucid. *I think... a jet. It's loud. But what's beneath me? It's... soft. A bed? A couch? And what's that smell?*

My nails bit into my palms, my hands still clenched into fists. I needed more information. A location. A landmark. *Anything* to help me find her.

It's... metallic? she went on, the scent making her head spin. *Blood...*

I stiffened. *Your blood? From the head wound?*

What head wound? she asked.

I frowned. *Does your head hurt?*

No.

Maybe my blood cured you, then? I'd given her some every day with each meal, my need to strengthen her a compulsion I couldn't ignore. *Abigail hit you with the butt of a gun.*

Abigail? she repeated, her voice holding a note of confusion. *Who is Abigail?*

But she followed in the next second as she pulled the information from my mind.

Only then she was even more confused because she didn't understand why Abigail would hit her or why everything around her was rumbling.

I... She paused, shock ripping through our bond. *Cane?*

I frowned. *Cane?*

No response.

But none was needed.

Because I could hear her mind processing what she was seeing.

My brother in an all-black suit.

Sitting across from her.

On a jet.

IZZY

I BLINKED, MY BRAIN FAILING TO FULLY PROCESS THE SIGHT before me. It was sideways, primarily because I appeared to be lying down.

But the askew view wasn't what had me confused. It was the scene that had my mind struggling to focus—to *comprehend*—what I was seeing.

Cane. I recognized him. I just... I just couldn't believe he was here.

And sitting next to Michael.

In two opulent executive-style chairs.

While sipping what appeared to be blood wine.

"Delicious," Cane praised, his gaze dancing over me as he finished his drink.

A naked woman appeared not half a beat later with a

477

knife poised at her wrist. I flinched as she cut herself and began refilling his glass.

She stared blankly at the liquid pooling in the crystal stemware, her ashen skin the only indication of her body's reaction to her actions.

Either he's compelling her, or she's trained not to feel, I thought, my stomach clenching.

Ismerelda, Cam whispered into my mind. *I—*

"That's enough," Cane stated flatly, his gaze on me. However, the words appeared to be for the human. "Now kneel and serve your purpose."

"Yes, my liege," she replied robotically, her shaking limbs bending as she adhered to his request.

"Are you sure, my liege?" Michael drawled. "She seems rather... ghostly."

Cane finally looked at the brown-haired woman. Then he shrugged. "Seems capable enough to me."

I swallowed, a sense of dread churning inside me. Not because of the act unraveling before me, but because of that *voice.* I recognized it.

I'd heard it over and over again in my head for what felt like years. Except it'd only been days.

"Seems fitting enough to me..."

"If she fails, perhaps I'll taste my brother's whore, find out why he fancies her so," Cane continued.

Michael grinned. "I've been dying to determine that for myself, my liege. Unfortunately, I missed my opportunity."

"Yes, you did," Cane replied, his green eyes—one of the few physical differences between him and Cam—meeting mine.

Cane... Cane's the one who sent me to be... I couldn't finish the thought. But I didn't have to.

Cam had already followed the concept to completion,

his resulting snarl sharp and loud in my mind. *It wasn't a hologram. It was my fucking brother.*

I trembled, unable to handle his anger and Cane's scrutiny. They were both so intense, so overwhelming, but in entirely different ways.

Pull yourself together, I told myself. *This is Cane. You know Cane. He's Cam's brother. He would never hurt...*

I nearly frowned, that last thought a blatant lie. Because Cane had tried to hurt me. He'd impersonated Cam and left me with Michael, his malicious intentions clear.

Maybe this isn't really Cane...? That stray consideration was too close to the one I'd initially conceptualized about Cam.

And Cam had turned out to be very real.

Cane's green irises glittered as he held my gaze, the female's palms grazing his thighs as she went to unfasten his belt. From my prone position, I had a perfect view of her pulling out his cock.

Which I very much did *not* want to see.

I pushed upward, my stomach rolling with the motion.

"You should be bowing," Michael remarked, his expression hard.

"And you should be dead," I grated out, the retort one I couldn't swallow. Because *fuck* him and *fuck* this. "Why am I here?"

To be reminded of what our world has become? I thought darkly. *To watch a human service a vampire in the most degrading of ways?*

Cane said nothing, his body completely relaxed while he sipped his wine. He didn't seem all that interested in the female bobbing up and down between his sprawled thighs.

Michael stood, malevolent energy pouring off of him as he stepped forward. "*Bow.*"

"It's fine," Cane drawled. "Let her misbehave. I'll enjoy punishing her for it later."

Cam growled in my head, obviously having heard me absorb that comment into my thoughts, because I'd immediately wondered, *How?*

Michael took another step forward, his hand disappearing beneath his jacket.

"Sit. Down." The order from Cane's mouth had Michael freezing right in front of me.

While that command might have stopped Michael's forward progression, it didn't erase his lethal expression or the promise of death lurking in his gaze.

Only it wasn't Cane's death he was promising with that look, but mine.

His square jaw clenched as he heeded his master's command, causing my brow to furrow. Michael had bowed to his command like one would a Sire. *Or a king,* I supposed. *But what if...? What if Cane actually sired Michael?*

That would explain my lack of a connection to him, Cam replied immediately, his mind clearly in tune with mine. *It would also suggest Lilith has been working with my brother all along. Or rather, for my brother.*

But why would he do this? I wondered, confused as to what would prompt Cane to desire this life.

He never slept, Cam whispered back to me. *Or Lilith had me wake him. Regardless, it's his humanity. He has none.*

I swallowed, Cam's thoughts unraveling through our bond as he essentially showed me how he knew that—because he understood it.

He, too, lacked humanity to an extent. Mortals were food. Pets. Beings who provided pleasure and sustenance. They weren't equals; they were inferiors.

Like how humans used to see cattle, I translated. *Except we don't fuck animals. We also don't need them to survive.*

Yes, Cam agreed. *But if there was a species beneath your own that you could use in that manner, your kind would have considered enslaving them. History proves that.*

His mind told me he wasn't referring to any recent events, but situations he'd witnessed throughout the thousands of years he'd been alive. Events from well before my time.

I shivered, his visions of the past painting a horrific future before my eyes.

Because he was right.

Humankind would do that. They *had* done that.

And vampires technically came from those roots. They were merely following in the same trajectory a mortal would if handed superior abilities and supernatural powers.

Just because I understand it doesn't mean I desire it, Cam whispered into my mind.

But a part of you does, I replied.

A part of me agrees with the concept of an immortal blood source, he admitted. *However, the part of me linked to you wishes for it to be humane.*

And without me?

Without you... He trailed off. *I'm honestly not sure, Ismerelda. I'm not a hero, and I won't pretend to be one. But I would not be opposed to a peaceful coexistence, so long as vampires were provided with what they needed to survive.*

What about lycans? I asked him.

I believe my brethren would say, "We're not lycans. The wolves can fend for themselves."

"What's my brother saying?" Cane asked, reminding me of his presence. "Is he telling you to remain calm? That he'll save you?"

I blinked at him. "No," I answered honestly. "He's telling me how he understands your decision."

He arched a brow. "My decision?"

"Your decision to lead this new era," I clarified, testing our theory aloud. "He's telling me why vampires need an immortal blood source and how humans would do the same to a lesser being, if provided the means and opportunity to do so."

Cane studied me for a moment. "Interesting. And here I assumed he intended to renew his quest against my reign."

I relayed that reply to Cam, the words seeming to confirm our understanding of the situation.

My mate remained quiet as he evaluated how to play this, his strategic mindset flaring to life. *Tell my brother that I have no desire to lead,* he finally said. *Then ask what he wants from me.*

"Cam has no desire to lead," I told Cane, allowing that statement to settle first.

"Oh?" Cane set his glass aside, his palm going to the back of the woman's head as he fisted her hair. "I find that hard to believe." He started guiding the female's movements, his jaw clenching a bit while she moved.

It was a very clear depiction of this current world, his actions speaking much louder than words ever could. Because he was showing me with his hand how he controlled the human race. How mortals *bowed* and *served.*

Worse, that glimmer in his gaze suggested he was imagining me being the one to service him.

And just thinking about that had my insides churning in discomfort.

Because no. *Hell* no.

I would never kneel for him or anyone else.

Ismerelda, Cam murmured into my mind. *Ask him what he wants from me.*

My throat worked as I forced the bile back down, my

stomach rioting at the act unfolding before me. Mostly because the human was clearly struggling to breathe, her body tense and quivering and depleted of energy as Cane fucked her mouth like she was just some doll.

Some being to be used.

Just like Cam had done to me the other day, I thought, my heart skipping a beat. Except unlike Cam, I suspected Cane wouldn't feed this woman his blood to help revive her afterward.

If she died, she would remain that way.

A discarded doll.

Not a life.

I hated it. Hated this. Hated them.

We might be physically inferior, but our minds… our spirits… are equals.

Cam didn't reply to me, but I heard him processing my words and debating their merit.

"What do you want from Cam?" I forced myself to ask, needing to refocus on this conversation and not Cane's crude actions. "Cam is asking, not me," I clarified. I wanted to know the answer as well, but I suspected Cane would respond better if I pretended to be a translator rather than an interested party.

"Mmm," Cane hummed. "Tell my brother that I'm going to personally ensure your bond is broken—just like it should have been the other day."

His words sent a chill down my spine, my brain automatically parroting his sentence to Cam.

"Unless…" Cane went on. "Unless he meets me at the compound."

He relaxed more into his chair, his grip seeming to tighten on the female as he worked her over his cock, his gaze never leaving mine.

I focused on repeating his comment to Cam rather than on the *view*.

"He has three hours," Cane continued. "I suggest he borrow Kylan's jet. Tell him Damien can fly it. But no one else is allowed to join them."

My jaw clenched as I reiterated all of that to Cam.

He means it, I added. *I can see it in his eyes, Cam. He...* I trailed off, the words unnecessary. Because Cam could no doubt hear the fear blossoming in my mind.

I couldn't help picturing it.

Cane issuing commands meant to seal my fate. Commands about my purpose and the way I should have died a thousand years ago.

Only, as Michael drags me to the room now, it's Cane waiting inside. His smile sadistic. His eyes cold. His hands ripping and tearing. His cock in my throat, not that girl's on the floor.

"Now that's a good little blood whore, relaying everything to my brother just like I told you to," Cane mused, his accented tones sending another chill down my spine. "What's he saying? Is he agreeing to my demand?"

"He hasn't replied yet," I admitted, my voice raspy. Which I hated. I needed to be stronger than this. But watching Cane fuck that poor woman... hearing his cruel words... it was difficult to maintain my composure.

It wouldn't take much for Cane to destroy my link to Cam.

Rape me.

Kill me.

Only this time, I wouldn't wake up. My ties to Cam's immortality would be forever fractured. *I'll die. For good.*

I'm not going to let that happen, Cam promised me. *Tell my brother I'm on my way, but if my link to you becomes severed at any point, I will strongly reconsider my leadership role in this world and take his throne.*

You're... you're going to the compound? It was a stupid

question to ask, but I couldn't stop myself from thinking it. Primarily because the repercussions of that choice were starting to settle into my brain, our precarious position becoming clear.

Cane had taken me as a bargaining chip. A pawn. A way to lure Cam back to the catacombs… and what? Imprison him again?

Did Cane imprison him the first time? I wondered. *Is he really behind all of this? Was Lilith working for him? Or did she wake him in a fashion similar to how she woke Cam? Fuck with his mind?*

Ismerelda, Cam said, trying to grab my attention.

But now that my brain was deciphering our situation, I couldn't stop thinking. I merely started talking to Cam instead of myself.

What if Cane uses Lilith's weapon against you? I asked him, another thought immediately following. *What if…? God, what if it wasn't Lilith's weapon at all, but his all along? If she was working for him… then… then he's the mastermind. Right? Cam, what if—*

Tell him what I said, Ismerelda, he interjected, his sharp tone making me flinch.

But—

That weapon already fried my brain. It likely won't even work again. The assuredness of his tone told me he'd already considered that possibility and had decided it was worth the risk.

Except that wasn't enough. *This is too much of a risk, Cam. You can't go to the compound. If Cane's been in charge this whole time, or even if he's just brainwashed, it's too dangerous. They could wipe your memory again. And then what?*

Tell him what I said, Ismerelda, he repeated, making my hands curl into fists.

Are we not even going to discuss this? I demanded.

What is there to discuss, Ismerelda? He has you. He's given me his terms. I accept his invitation for a meeting, but only if he guarantees he won't break our bond.

Okay, you're agreeing to his meeting, but at what expense? I snapped. *The last time you met with someone, you disappeared for nearly twelve decades!*

Yes, but this time, I'm not attempting to be humanity's hero. I'm doing this because it's the practical recourse. My brother wants a meeting. So I'll give him a meeting.

My jaw tightened.

"Ismerelda?" Cane prompted. "What has my brother said?"

Tell him, Cam reiterated. *Tell him I accept his terms, but only if your mind remains open to mine.*

I gritted my teeth. Cam's mind told me he wouldn't be changing his decision. Primarily because he saw no other way to let this play out.

And while I hated this choice, I couldn't think of an alternative.

Other than to let Cane rape and kill me, I thought, wincing.

That's not an option, Cam growled at me.

Technically, it was. But it wasn't one I wanted to entertain.

Izzy, Cam breathed. *This isn't like last time. My mind is open to yours. You can see why I've arrived at this decision. And I'm not leaving you behind; I'm coming to you instead. It's a different situation.*

It's still an unknown.

I agree. That's why I want this meeting—to determine my brother's role in this. Perhaps Lilith fucked over his mind as badly as mine. Or maybe he's been lucid all along. I won't know until I see him for myself.

My nails bit into my palms, my frustration mounting. Mainly because he was right. We had no other choice.

And this was different from last time.

Very different.

Come on, lioness. Play his game, Cam whispered to me. *Just remember your position in this match, my queen. It's the most powerful one of all. And together, we'll make them all bow.*

His words helped thaw some of my frigid thoughts, his confidence melting the ice coating my spine and allowing me to straighten once more.

Cam was right—we had to play the game.

Vampires were all about strategic moves and political negotiations. They didn't react impulsively. And they loved operating in riddles.

Cane had clearly plotted his most recent initiative— kidnapping me—carefully. He wouldn't spoil that by killing me outright.

He wanted Cam for something.

I wasn't sure what.

But we would be finding out soon.

By indulging Cane in this dangerous match.

I boldly met his stare and reiterated what Cam had said.

His lips curled. "I accept that term." With that, he groaned, his eyes falling closed as his grasp tightened in the woman's hair, causing her to writhe in pain.

Or perhaps she was convulsing due to a lack of air.

I couldn't tell, and Cane clearly didn't care. He merely growled, his ecstasy reverberating throughout the jet as the woman lost consciousness between his legs.

There was no consideration given to her dying state.

No glance.

Not even a wince.

Just the jerking of his hips as he emptied himself inside her slackened mouth, literally drowning her in his seed.

Michael chuckled as he watched, his amusement seeming to be a result of my expression more than the act itself. Probably because I couldn't hide my disgust. "That'll be you soon, little whore," Michael informed me.

I inhaled slowly, a vision of me staking him replacing the one his words threatened to evoke.

"You can't touch her yet," Cane murmured, his eyes still closed. "But I'll let you have her in front of Cam later if that's your wish."

"I just want to kill her," Michael returned.

"Hmm," Cane hummed, the sound reminding me of Cam.

Tell my brother I'll see him soon, Cam whispered, distracting me momentarily.

I repeated his words, my voice devoid of emotion.

Cane's lips curled, his eyes finally opening as he released the woman's hair, her body crumpling into a dead heap on the floor. "I look forward to it."

SILAS

CHAOS.

Complete and utter fucking chaos.

I stood in the corner of the club—or what I assumed was a club, anyway. The couches and the stage were similar to those of a lounge, but the darkened walls reminded me of the ritzy nightclub featured in a movie Rae had made me watch last month. It'd been from a time I didn't know, one she'd been learning more about from Kylan.

All the atmosphere needed was some soft red lighting, and it would match perfectly.

Alas, the only red here seemed to be in some of the lycans' faces, their anger a virile scent that called to my inner wolf.

"Do you think he's been brainwashed?" Jace was asking nearby. "Similar to what Lilith attempted to do with you?"

"I don't know," Cam replied. "And the only way I'm going to find out is by getting on that jet with Damien."

Darius put a hand on Cam's shoulder, holding the man back before he could finish his step away from the group. "You're missing history, something I think you need before you face him."

"I can hear all of Ismerelda's memories, Darius. I'm up to date."

"With all due respect, you're not. You have *her* point of view, not mine. And I suspect I know a great deal more about the real Cane than she does."

Silence fell, the two vampires locked in some sort of silent conversation. From what I'd learned, Cam was Darius's Sire, making him the dominant of the pair.

But they both exuded alpha energy, enough so that the hairs along my arms danced in warning.

"This is insane," Rae breathed as she joined me in the corner.

"Madness," Willow echoed, the two of them having wandered over to me together.

It said a lot that no one even looked our way, those two comments lost to the ongoing debates around the room.

"Do you even remember Aurelia?" Darius demanded. "Or what she did to your brother?"

"I don't remember her, but Ismerelda filled in the gaps," Cam replied. "The incident with Aurelia led to Cane's immortal sleep."

Darius smiled, but it lacked humor. "Aurelia was far more than an inciting incident, Cam. Her betrayal changed your brother. Rid him of his humanity. Made him want to enslave the human race, just like Lilith has done."

"I can't believe we didn't consider him," Jace said, pacing. "He's her bloody maker."

"Who was supposed to be asleep," Darius pointed out. "He wasn't even on our radar. And we all assumed some rest would cure his humanity problem."

"Yes, I find a nap often cures me of my hatred for others," Ryder deadpanned. "Honestly, how did any of you expect to lead with notions like this guiding your principles?"

Rae and Willow shared a look, only to be distracted by a growl coming from the lycan circle. They appeared to be posturing with one another, something that was leaving my mates—who were taking part in that conversation —uncomfortable.

"It's an ancient custom that has been used for millennia by the Blessed Ones," Jace countered, grabbing my attention once more. "It has been shown to help their sense of humanity thrive."

Kylan snorted. "It's a glorified excuse to avoid *living*."

"Exactly," Ryder echoed. "It accomplishes nothing."

Kylan nodded. "My maker, or I suppose you would call him my *father*, chose eternal rest shortly after my immortal rebirth or whatever the fuck you want to call it when we stopped aging. Regardless of the term, Kratos escaped reality and left me to fend for myself for centuries before waking once more. And you know what happened next?"

"I could guess," Ryder drawled, his dry sarcasm underlining those three words.

"He woke up with the same memories and feelings that followed him into eternal sleep," Kylan informed them all. "And promptly chose indefinite rest. I'll never disturb him again. He's dead to me now."

"So you mean he didn't magically regain his sense of humanity?" Ryder asked. "Love life all over again? Feel like a brand-new man?"

"Nope," Kylan replied, his voice flippant.

Ryder feigned shock, his palm covering his heart. "That's so utterly surprising."

Kylan smirked, but it lacked his usual carefree undertone, his eyes too intense to complete the look.

Ryder's mock surprise melted into a severe expression as he refocused on the others. "If Cane went to sleep without his humanity, he woke up without it, too. The whole concept of eternal rest is simply to pass the time and potentially wake up to something new. That's it. Our motives and desires remain unchanged."

"Meaning if Cane went to sleep with a yearning to enslave humankind, he woke up with that same yearning," Damien translated.

Sounds right, I agreed.

What does? Edon asked, his mental voice tense from the lycan discussions.

I summarized what the vampires were discussing, my role in the corner being to observe and listen while he and Luna engaged with our fellow lycans.

The tension among the group had left the three of us feeling uneasy for days.

"Unless he never slept at all," Darius said, his words seeming to silence the vampire group as he met Cam's gaze. "He never wanted to rest. That was entirely your idea. What if he only went along with it to placate you? Maybe he had a contingency plan to ensure he didn't actually sleep."

Cam stared back at him for a long moment before replying, "That may be the case, but it doesn't fix the present issue. Cane has Ismerelda and wants me to meet him beneath Vatican City in just under three hours. Which means Damien and I need to leave. Now."

"How kind of Cane to recommend my jet," Kylan deadpanned.

Cam faced him. "He has my *Erosita.* If he had your Raelyn, what would you do?"

Kylan stiffened, his nostrils flaring. "Kill him."

"Then you understand why I need your jet," Cam returned.

The two royals stared each other down in a fashion similar to that of the lycans on the other side of the room.

We're definitely missing something, Edon told me, his attention still on the arguing lycans. *I just can't figure out what it is, and Jolene isn't sharing.*

The three of us had suspected something was off—beyond the tension—for days. But we couldn't define it, and Edon's grandfather Jolene wasn't helping. Neither was Luna's brother, Logan.

It was as though we'd been left on the outside, all of us serving as a third party in the room.

That sensation worsened as the lycans and vampires focused solely on themselves, all of them completely disregarding the future of humankind.

It was all about taking down Lilith's former operation. *Or perhaps it's Cane's operation,* I thought, glancing at the vampires again.

They wanted to convince the alliance to enter a new phase, to deviate away from their prior course. Yet no one had defined what that would look like, other than potentially following the Blood City model.

But that model didn't satisfy the lycans, especially after everything they'd learned. They wanted blood. *Vampire* blood.

It left the two kinds divided, something Jace had been trying to resolve with Edon and Luka.

However, the efforts had felt stilted at best. While the lycans seemed to respect the royals present here, they hadn't promised to be respectful of the entire alliance.

In fact, some of the lycans appeared to be meeting in

private, their discussions taking place away from Deirdre Tower.

We only knew that because we'd stumbled upon one during a run.

The alphas had gone silent upon our approach, their tense forms betraying their serious conversation. Yet they'd played it off as though they'd just been catching up.

Edon had smelled the lie, but he'd let it go.

Yet all three of us had decided then and there that something was going on. Something big. We just had no idea what.

And the bomb Cam had just dropped on everyone— the information about his brother's potential involvement —was not helping matters.

The wolves were already struggling to trust Cam, his lack of memories and aloof demeanor marking him as ineligible for leadership.

"Why should we follow him?" I'd heard one of them ask in a whisper.

"We shouldn't," another had replied.

But the vampires had been too busy debating amongst themselves to hear it.

Just like the lycans were too consumed with their own conversations now to even notice Cam and Damien leaving with Ryder and Kylan right behind them.

Rae cleared her throat beside me. "Kylan says we should follow." The comment was clearly for Willow, not me.

"No," Willow replied. "Everything is too tense. Too…" Her lips curled down. "All they're talking about is themselves, who might oppose them, and the potential for revenge. I don't see how this is a plan for the future. It's so fucked in the present."

"It is," a cultured voice agreed. *Khalid*. He ran his turquoise gaze over Willow. "I see why Ryder chose you."

Emine made a sound that had him wrapping his arm around her athletic yet lean shoulders.

"Don't worry, darling mirage. I'm not looking to switch, just appreciating Ryder's taste."

The slayer—a title that had absolutely fascinated me when I'd learned about it the other day—leveled him with a glare. "Feel free to switch, My Prince. I could use a break from your company."

The vampire royal chuckled. "You say that now, habibi. But I'll remind you later why you don't actually mean it."

He leaned in to kiss her throat, causing the woman to stiffen.

I couldn't quite figure out their relationship. *Antagonistic yet clearly enamored*. Because I could smell their interest in one another.

Stop playing with vampires and join me, Luna whispered into my mind. *These alphas are giving me a headache.*

I met her honey-brown gaze from across the room, my heart instantly skipping a beat. *All right, little moon.* I could never say no to her, my mate the owner of my heart and soul.

You never obey me like that, Edon muttered.

Because you enjoy my defiance, Alpha, I replied before nodding to Willow and Rae, the action meant to signify my exit.

They didn't reply, but that was mostly because their two vampire royals had just reentered the room. And they didn't appear pleased with having to come back for their *Erositas*.

I enjoy making you kneel, Enforcer, Edon returned.

I ignored his sensual taunt and moved to stand behind

him and Luna. *The vampires have left the room*, I told them. *Presumably to go to the airfield.*

Although, Cam had said only he and Damien were allowed to fly to the compound. So I wasn't quite sure why all of them had left. Perhaps they were working on a contingency plan.

Or maybe Darius was continuing his discussion with Cam about Cane.

Even Khalid had left. Hazel, too. And the human who had been harmed—*Keys*—was nowhere to be seen.

Yet the wolves remained oblivious, their debate seeming to be about who should lead the inevitable raid.

When it became clear a consensus wasn't going to be reached, they finally realized the vampires were gone.

Luka and Jolene instantly growled.

"Typical," Finn muttered, the seven-foot-tall Alpha of Ström Clan among the most intimidating in the group. I'd seen him briefly at Blood Day and knew of him from my studies. But none of that had prepared me for his physical presence.

"I believe they left to prepare Kylan's jet," Edon told them. "They were discussing Cane as they went."

"Nice of them to notify us," Polka drawled, his black eyes flickering with his barely restrained wolf. He was the Alpha of Apinya Clan, and nearly half a foot shorter than Finn.

Several of the wolves grunted in annoyance.

Jace did say something as he was leaving, but the alphas were too consumed with each other to hear him, Luna muttered via our mental connection. *It's like they tuned the vampires out entirely.*

Yes, this divide is… a problem, Edon replied.

It is, I agreed. *And I have no idea how to fix it.* Because it seemed to be an old wound rather than a new one, the lycan animosity too robust and ancient to be inspired by this week's events.

Of course, this week hadn't helped cure that wound. If anything, it had worsened it. And now the lycans were done playing nice. Done partnering with vampires. Done putting supernaturals as a whole above everything else.

Because most of it benefited vampires, not lycans.

That much I'd gathered from the few conversations I'd overheard.

Something big was coming. Something world-altering. And it seemed to go deeper than simply swaying the alliance.

Because the lycans appeared to be planning something.

I just didn't know what that something was, and neither did Luna or Edon.

But we were going to figure it out.

Then we would decide how to proceed.

However, our triad would always come first. Because as long as we had each other, we would survive.

To the moon and back, Luna whispered to us, her way of expressing her love.

To the moon and back, I echoed.

For eternity, Edon vowed.

For eternity, Luna and I agreed.

IZZY

DAMIEN AND I ARE ON OUR WAY, Cam informed me, his mental tone lacking emotion.

I attempted to replicate that tone as I replied, *We're descending now.*

Or it felt that way, anyway.

No one had confirmed it. But that wasn't surprising, given my hostage status on this jet.

Cane had fallen silent for the last several minutes, his focus on finishing his glass of blood wine while the human who'd provided it lay dead at his feet.

His choice to keep her there felt purposeful, like he'd wanted me to watch her die. Rather than focus on her dead body, I studied him.

Noting his green eyes. His sharp features. The cruel

angle of his jaw. His thick, dark hair. The same aristocratic nose as his brother.

Cam and Cane could almost pass as twins.

It was no wonder I'd fallen for that act the other day. But I should have noticed the accent. Or at least realized that soft lilt had meant something.

Only, I'd been too caught up in Cam's behavior that I'd accepted my fate. I'd believed the charade. Because everything he'd done had suggested he would replace me with a new toy and leave me to die.

Had you been inside my mind, you would know how untrue that is, Cam whispered softly. *I would apologize for not taking the wall down sooner, but I didn't know. I thought it existed as a way to keep you out of my thoughts. And I'm starting to wonder if that had been true, just for reasons I'd originally misinterpreted.*

My lips threatened to curl down, but I forced them to remain flat. The last thing I wanted to do was betray my emotions to Cane.

What do you mean? I asked Cam.

I originally assumed I locked you out as a result of a superiority complex. But now it seems I did it to protect you, and I strongly suspect the incident with Lilith wasn't the first time.

Confusion tugged at my mouth, the instinct to frown hitting me again and forcing me to look out the tinted window beside me. Cane likely saw it, defeating the purpose of trying to hide it, but I couldn't help my reaction.

I'd been so focused on Cane that I hadn't been as tuned in with Cam's thoughts. That changed in an instant, his mind immediately providing me with what I'd missed— Cam had been searching my memories for what I knew about Cane's behavior and comments after Aurelia's betrayal.

The conclusion he'd recently come to was that either I didn't have the full story, or Darius was lying to him.

Cam very much suspected the former.

I think my previous self blocked certain things from you, Cam muttered. *Likely in my effort to coddle you and preserve your fragile state.* That last sentence was uttered with a sardonic twist, one that said the very concept of it irked him.

If you did, I wasn't aware of it. I swallowed. *Do you think it happened often?*

Because that would be... troubling.

Cam and I were already walking an emotional tightrope. If he thought for a second that his old version didn't truly trust me or love me, it might change our entire dynamic.

Further, the very concept of Cam keeping secrets from me went against everything I'd thought existed between us.

My guess is I didn't block things long-term, so much as short-term, he replied. *I likely assumed that if you didn't know the memory was there, you wouldn't go looking.*

Which I wouldn't have done anyway because I would have trusted you to tell me everything, I admitted. Perhaps that made me naïve, but Cam had owned my mind, body, and soul. I had never possessed a reason to question him.

Something I clearly took advantage of in this situation. That note of irritation lingered in his tone again. *Your memories of Cane paint him as brokenhearted and angered by Aurelia's betrayal. I warned that his already waning humanity was hanging on by a thread due to Aurelia's attempt on his life.*

Yes. That was what I recalled from the situation. *I never really saw him after it happened. You said he wanted to be alone. And he was already resting in his coffin when we arrived for the sleeping ritual. He never even opened his eyes.*

Hmm, well it seems I lied. According to Darius, my brother had been obsessed with the concept of vampires and lycans ruling the world. Apparently, it started with him wanting to guarantee the extermination of all slayers, but the concept grew into a desire to enslave the human race.

I stared out the window and focused on my breathing while trying to calm my heart. It wasn't working. I knew Cane could hear me. But I refused to glance his way and simply let him guess at my mounting anxiety.

Because what Cam was saying now implied—or perhaps even *confirmed*—that his brother was indeed behind all of this. And Lilith had merely been the face of his operation.

Darius says I told my brother the idea was flawed because the lycans would never agree to it. Many of the wolf clans had found ways to quietly coexist with humans. They had no reason to provoke change.

I swallowed again. *That's true. Many of them had working arrangements in small human settlements. They provided protection in exchange for secrecy.*

That was essentially how Majestic Clan still operated today, except the humans residing there had been assigned to the territory rather than born there.

Overall, the lycans had still been very much an unknown in the world, as they'd chosen their human settlements carefully.

But that had all changed when the wrong humans discovered their existence. All because a lycan had stolen a mortal woman.

And then the human governments had tried to find a way to weaponize the shifter race.

Which had led to the revolution and our world today.

I wonder if that inciting incident was planned—the one that led to the lycan discovery, Cam murmured thoughtfully. *It's what I would have done.*

This time, I couldn't control my urge to shiver. Because Cam's mind... the strategy he revealed... it was chilling.

Primarily because he was likely correct.

And also because I could hear his internal appreciation for his brother's due diligence.

Cam didn't fault his brother for his methods or his goals. He understood them and almost admired his work.

Except he recalled all the charts in the next moment, the careless use of resources and the waning blood supply, and sighed. *That's where he made his error.*

You think that's his only error? I asked. *What about removing the human right to choose?*

Humans would never choose to be food, Ismerelda. Just as cows and pigs would never ask to be slaughtered.

But Blood City demonstrates a way for humans to donate their blood willingly, while also living decently.

True, he agreed. *However, even that system has flaws. Vampires and lycans like to hunt. We're predators who desire prey. Not a blood bank.*

The same could be said about humans today being willing blood slaves. Where's the hunt? Humans are simply stripped and forced to lie down on tables like glorified food, I demanded. *Does that excite your predatory instincts?*

A fair point, my queen, he replied. *I'm not saying Blood City doesn't have its merits or that today's society is perfect. They both have their advantages and disadvantages.*

But you only see the blood supply as important in that evaluation, not the humanity aspect, I muttered. *I—*

"What's my brother saying?" Cane interjected, his voice reminding me of his presence and instantly sending a chill down my spine.

I'd almost completely forgotten he was here despite him being a primary topic in my mental conversation.

"Is he promising to save you?" Cane continued, sounding amused. "To make me pay for what I've done?"

I blinked away from the window and forced myself to meet Cane's gaze. "No. He's evaluating your work and saying what he would have done differently."

Cane's dark brow inched upward. "Is he now?" He cocked his head to the side. "In what way?"

Tell him, Cam whispered into my mind. *I want confirmation that this has all been him, that he's the one who did this to us.*

I followed Cam's line of thought, noting that he also wanted to learn more about Cane's motives and plans, thus providing even more reason for me to be forthcoming.

He wanted to make his brother talk.

And he suspected this might be the way to do that.

I cleared my throat and told Cane what Cam had said about the lycans, how Cane had obviously found a way to convince the wolves to help vampires lead. "Or he assumes that was you, anyway, as it's what he would have done," I added before going into Cane's failure to find a stable blood source.

I didn't mention Blood City, as I didn't want to reveal Khalid's version of utopia. If Cane knew about the city, I'd let him reveal it.

"And now Cam's thinking about how he would fix the blood shortage," I concluded. "Beyond the potential for immortal blood bags, I mean."

Cane stared at me for a long moment. "Interesting." He shared a glance with Michael. "What do you think?"

"I think your experiment might have been more successful than we originally thought. Assuming she's telling the truth, anyway," Michael replied.

"Indeed," Cane murmured in agreement.

"Of course, you should probably still kill her to

guarantee your outcome," Michael added. "Or turn her, like you did for Lilith."

Cane nodded. "Yes, that did work well. The traumatic aspect of your mortal demise assisted in my plight as well."

Michael's lips curled. "A brilliant maneuver, my liege."

"Exceedingly, yes." Cane smiled, his gaze returning to mine. "Lilith wasn't entirely divested of her pesky humanity, so I orchestrated an informative event to show her what mortals were capable of when left to their own devices. The results were rather immediate."

I blinked at both of them. "You arranged for Michael... to be killed?" I translated.

"Hmm, I more so created a situation that led to his brutal demise. One where the mortals could have left him alone but chose to follow herd mentality instead." He lifted a shoulder. "Mortals have always been easily manipulatable, their minds... fragile."

Meaning he compelled the humans, I realized.

Or perhaps only compelled one human, thus provoking the others around him or her to follow suit, Cam replied. *Ask him what happened next. Tell him I want to know.*

Clearing my throat again, I repeated Cam's request.

Which resulted in Cane's gaze practically glittering in triumph.

"Michael was Lilith's *Erosita*. Hence, he survived the violent assault. But Lilith felt his death. And, more importantly, she saw how he died. What those humans did. Then, right as her compassion toward mortals was beginning to fracture, I had Cam sire Michael, thus severing Lilith's ties to her humanity entirely."

Swallowing, I repeated the explanation to Cam. Not that it seemed to be needed; he was so in tune with my mind right now that it was almost as though he sat beside me on this couch.

I wouldn't be surprised if he could sense everything I did, including the rumbling of the jet as we made our final approach.

It was loud. Fast. Overwhelming. *Concerning.*

Because I could see the calculative glint forming in Cane's gaze, his urge to repeat his actions on me. To kill me. Force Cam to feel it. *Then turn me.*

Or leave me for dead.

"Cam says not to do anything rash," I told Cane, the lie rolling easily off my tongue. "He's already pissed that you lied to him, that you made him believe he was the Liege. Taking this choice away from him would infuriate him."

Hmm, Cam hummed.

I ignored him, my focus on Cane as he drawled, "Or free him."

I shook my head. "No. You took his memories away, Cane. Now I'm his only link to the past. And he's not done using me yet."

Cam grunted but didn't otherwise comment, mostly because he was too busy following my frantic thoughts to their inevitable conclusion.

A conclusion I knew Cane would appreciate.

"I'm a means to an end for him now," I informed him flatly. "Our bond was broken the second the weapon zapped that part of his brain, but I'm his only connection to his past right now. If you remove me before he's done with me, he'll be even angrier than he already is."

Cam fell silent, my words repeating throughout his thoughts as a dark part of him wondered if what I'd just said might be true.

He had been using my mind to discover information from his past, his psyche constantly caressing mine for answers and experiences as needed.

But he swiftly disregarded it in the next instant. *It's simply one of the many benefits of having a mate,* he told himself. *And that's definitely not why I've kept Ismerelda for as long as I have.*

"Cam isn't Lilith," I said as the jet's wheels hit the tarmac, my entire body jolting backward into the couch at the impact. "What worked for her won't work for him. Especially after everything you've already done to him."

Cane had yet to officially confirm he was the one behind Cam's imprisonment and treatment. But the flare of his nostrils as I delivered that last line confirmed it all.

He was concerned.

As he should be, Cam murmured into my mind. *I'm starting to wonder if it wasn't Lilith I intended to meet with that fated day, but my brother. And I failed to tell anyone else about it, my arrogance making me assume I could handle it on my own.*

If you were hiding other things from me about Cane, that could explain you blocking me out entirely. The words sounded like grating rocks to my ears, my irritation mounting.

Because Cam should have trusted me with the truth.

He should have said something. *Anything.*

Yet he'd left me behind. Worried. Hurting. *Alone.*

Yes, he agreed. *I won't be making that mistake again, Ismerelda.*

And he proved it by keeping his mind wide open now, his analytical side playing through a dozen scenarios at once.

Tell him I want to learn more, that I'm willing to hear him out. But only if he allows me to choose your fate.

My teeth ground together in response, my instinct to tell him only *I* would pick my future a very real retort in my thoughts. However, I swallowed the urge and instead allowed my mounting agitation to color my tone as I delivered Cam's message to his brother.

Cane considered me for a long moment. "I already said

your link would remain intact, so long as my brother arrives in peace. I'll uphold my end of the agreement, assuming he does as well."

I will, Cam said before I could relay the comment. "He agrees."

"Then it's settled." Cane smiled. "How about a little tour of the compound while we wait, hmm? I'd love to show you what I've really accomplished these last few decades. Perhaps it'll assuage some of my brother's concerns regarding our global blood shortage."

He ran his palm over his tie as he stood, then he stepped over the dead human and held his hand out for me.

"Shall we, darling?"

Play his game, Cam told me.

Not that I needed his coaching.

I was already accepting Cane's hand because I had no other choice.

He pulled me to my feet and started leading me toward the jet's exit, only to pause and glance back at Michael. "Oh, put my little toy back in her cage. Once she wakes up, she can join the others in the playroom."

My brow furrowed. *Little toy?*

I followed his gaze to where Michael was picking up the dead woman.

"Shouldn't be too long now," Cane went on. "I can already hear her heart trying to beat again."

Michael smirked. "She seems to regenerate faster every time you kill her."

Cane's lips curled upward. "Depends on the method of death."

"True," Michael agreed, his focus going to me. "Depends on how hard she's fucked, too."

Ice pierced my abdomen, my veins freezing over in response. *He... Cane... he has an...* Erosita....?

No, Cam replied, his mind having processed the scene in an entirely different manner.

One that I couldn't even fathom, but was almost immediate in his thoughts.

She's an immortal blood slave, Cam said, his mental tone holding a touch of curiosity—a curiosity that had my insides churning.

Cane chuckled beside me. "My brother's intrigued, isn't he?"

Cam said nothing.

But he didn't have to.

He'd been trying to create an immortal blood bag for weeks.

And it seemed his brother had already accomplished it.

Cane ran his knuckles down my cheek to my neck. "She's an immortal toy. One who bleeds. Screams. Dies. And regenerates."

Cam still said nothing.

However, he was clearly listening, something his brother seemed to be keenly aware of.

"Tell my brother I have dozens of them," Cane murmured. "Perfect consorts. Perhaps he'll *choose* one of those to replace you with and free himself of his humanity. Reign by my side or over me. I don't care. I just want him to join me, once and for all."

CAM

ISMERELDA'S REVULSION SOURED OUR BOND, HER DISTASTE growing harsher with each passing minute.

My brother had essentially turned my *Erosita* into a living, breathing communication device. Every detail he provided to her on their way to the compound was meant for me, as was each word he spoke while leading Ismerelda into a building located at the ground level. It wasn't the Coventus, but near it.

Ismerelda remained quiet, simply replying with whatever I told her to say, her dutiful behavior seeming to appease my brother.

Yet I heard her simmering inside. Felt her anger. Her disbelief. Her *distrust*.

I couldn't hide my curiosity, my brother's accomplishment something I wanted to know more about.

But that didn't mean I approved of what he'd done, just that I desired more details.

That said, I was beginning to understand how and why my former self had compartmentalized and concealed certain details from Ismerelda.

It had nothing to do with wanting to lie to her and everything to do with protecting her.

Right now, her emotions and reactions needed to be believable. Keeping my mind open to her could impact that, as all it would take was a few moments in my head to know I didn't condone what my brother was doing. And that would be enough to provide relief, something Ismerelda couldn't afford to show.

Thus, my instincts told me to hide my feelings from her, and I knew exactly how to do it—something that proved I'd done it often before. Likely out of a need to safeguard Ismerelda's mind.

But I refused to do that now.

I couldn't block her out. It would be counterproductive to us being equals.

I'd meant what I'd said—Ismerelda was my queen.

And right now, I was trusting her to act as such. To manage her external reactions while knowing the truth about me deep down.

Our link was wide open, my thoughts and desires hers to decipher.

"We'll be on the ground in three minutes," Damien announced from the cockpit.

I nodded, not that he could see me, and passed the information on to Ismerelda.

She parroted my statement to my brother in a bored tone as he led her into a bedroom. Her mental voice told me it was similar to the one we'd shared in the underground, only this one appeared to be above ground, as it had tinted windows that overlooked a sunny courtyard.

Because it's morning now, I grumbled to myself, irritated by my brother's choice of timing for this kidnapping and forced meeting.

But I supposed it was what I would have done in his situation.

Those twilight hours around dawn were the most vulnerable hours for a vampire, mostly because it was when we all tucked ourselves in to avoid the brightness of the day.

While the sun's rays didn't harm me, they certainly irritated me.

How surprising, Ismerelda muttered, drawing my attention back to her evaluation of the room. *No surveillance cameras in here. At least not in the same place, anyway.*

Cane must have followed her gaze or noted her scrutiny because he remarked on her observation, saying something about having enjoyed watching me fuck Ismerelda nearly to death.

"If only he'd succeeded," he concluded, his words echoing in Ismerelda's mind.

Tell him it's a good thing I didn't and remind him that you're my only link to my memories. Because he erased them all with that fucking weapon.

My brother hadn't actually confirmed that yet, but his lack of a denial seemed to be proof enough.

"I did what needed to be done to fix you," he said before following up with a command to repeat that via our bond.

He didn't seem to understand that I could already essentially hear him through Ismerelda's thoughts. Of course, his voice was her interpretation of it as she absorbed the words in her mind. But the general concept of his statements translated just fine.

Hmm, we'll discuss that more very soon, I thought at Ismerelda, my words for my brother. She repeated them aloud just as the jet touched down, a roaring sound ripping around me.

Only for silence to fall in the next instant, the abruptness of it leaving me dizzy.

While I'd likely flown before, this was my first remembered experience. Although, from what Damien had said, Kylan's jet was unlike anything I would have ever known.

However, I had nothing to compare any of it to, as I had no recollection of flying before.

Thanks to Cane.

His little game has taken a thousand years of memories from me. And I wanted to know why.

What had he hoped to accomplish? Was it all a way to break my ties with Ismerelda?

If that was the case, he should have just killed her. It would have been faster and more efficient.

Not that I wanted her to die. Quite the contrary, I was prepared to do whatever I had to do to keep her alive.

But something about my brother's motives wasn't adding up.

"It seems Helias, Ayaz, and Robyn are here," Damien said. However, his words didn't appear to be for me because he didn't utter them over the sound system. "Yeah, there's a fourth jet as well. But there isn't a decal on it. Maybe that's the one Cane used?"

I unbuckled myself and met him in the cockpit, his gaze on the tarmac as he took in the airfield. He hummed in agreement to whatever he was hearing via his earpiece, the frequency of it too low for me to pick up the words.

"Looking forward to it," he drawled, his lips curling as he touched the device with his thumb. "Ryder wants to play." That statement appeared to be for me.

"He's going to have to wait."

Damien snorted as he shifted his attention to me. "I realize you've had the last thousand years zapped from your head, so perhaps you're not aware, but Ryder isn't a patient man. He doesn't *wait*."

"Well, then you'd better hope I can reach your sister before your maker's impatience gets Ismerelda killed," I told him.

His gaze narrowed. "You mean when *we* reach Izzy."

"No, I meant *I*." I leveled him with a look. "You need to stay here and ensure no one fucks with the jet. We're likely going to need it, and soon." Because I fully intended to grab Ismerelda and take her to Damien. Then I would determine how best to deal with my brother.

But I wouldn't make the mistake of trying to handle him on my own.

Jace and Darius were perfectly capable of assisting me.

As were Damien and Ryder.

However, my first priority was protecting Ismerelda.

If she were a vampire, none of this would be an issue, I thought, once again furious with my former self for never turning her.

Was she a divine treat? Yes.

Did a dark part of me enjoy her fragility? Also yes.

But my Ismerelda was meant to be a vampire queen. Not a docile doll designed for display only.

"What do you plan on doing?" Damien asked, his hard expression matching his tone.

"Whatever is necessary to guarantee Ismerelda's safety." I turned to leave, only to find my upper arm caught in his strong hand.

"The last time you went off on your own, my sister ended up paying a price for your arrogance." He shoved me back into the cabin and stalked around me. "You're wearing a comm."

"A what?"

"An earpiece," he grated out, pointing to the device in his ear. "It'll let us communicate while you're off doing whatever the fuck it is you plan to do."

I folded my arms but didn't argue as he found what he needed in a bag he'd brought with us for the trip.

Cane was very likely going to make me remove it. Or maybe he wouldn't care.

If he truly wanted me to partner with him in this venture, then he needed to let me make my own decisions.

Of course, he'd been clearly trying to make all my choices for me, so that likely wasn't going to change.

Which leads me right back to his true intentions, I muttered to myself as I accepted the earpiece from Damien. I put it in, clicked a button—per his demand—and arched a brow. "May I go save your sister now?"

He rolled his eyes and thumbed the button of my shirt.

Frowning, I glanced down, trying to figure out what the fuck that gesture meant.

"It's your microphone," he said, making me blink.

"Where?"

"There." He pointed at my button. "It's thin and filmy like a translucent sticker. Kind of amazing, actually. Just like your earpiece."

"Cane's very likely going to make me remove it."

"Assuming he detects it."

"He seems to be familiar with your technology," I reminded him, thinking of his hacking attempts.

Damien bent to retrieve something else from his bag of

tricks. "Then it's a good thing it's not my tech." He held up a mirror to show me my ear. "It's Khalid's tech."

My eyebrows lifted. "Fascinating." I couldn't see any evidence of the comm unit at all.

"Like I said, amazing," he murmured. "The sound frequency is also low, making it so only you should be able to hear me."

I eyed the piece in his ear. It was clearly a different sort of communication unit since I could see it. However, I hadn't been able to hear anything from it mere moments ago, so perhaps they were related technologies.

Or maybe he had left his visible for some reason.

"I don't know if this tech has been tested around lycans, so a wolf might detect the earpiece," Damien went on as he clicked something that opened the jet door. "Right, then. You'd better fucking keep my sister alive, or I'll kill you myself."

I grunted. There was nothing useful or relevant to say in response to that.

Thus, I said nothing.

And simply phased off of the plane, not bothering to wait for the stairs—which were apparently being wheeled up to the door I'd just leapt out of.

Ignoring it all, I teleported out of the airfield, only to pause as Ismerelda said, *Cane says to tell you that there's a car waiting for you at the hangar.*

I see. I probably should have expected that.

With a low growl, I phased back to the tarmac where the stairs were now being affixed to the jet. "Great work so far," Damien deadpanned, his voice an unwelcome sound in my ear.

Disregarding him, I walked over to a vampire standing sentry by a black car. He immediately opened the back door for me, his gaze downcast.

Ask my brother if the compound staffing reports were a lie, I told Ismerelda. There hadn't been enough vampires to provide adequate security, yet here was one playing chaperone. Seemed a bit conflicting, given what I'd been told by Mira.

Not a lie, Ismerelda replied after a beat. *He says this vampire belongs to Robyn.*

Robyn? That was unexpected.

But as my brother began explaining himself to Ismerelda, I started to understand. "Cane has recruited reinforcements from his royal allies," I told Damien. "There are several more vampires in the city now."

The driver met my gaze in the mirror and cleared his throat. "Uh, yes," he said, apparently believing I'd been speaking to him.

Which I supposed made sense, as he couldn't see my microphone or earpiece. In his mind, who else would I be talking to?

"Five of us came with Robyn," he went on, the information thankfully useful. "I'm not sure how many came with Ayaz, Helias, and Jasmine."

"Jasmine?" Damien repeated, a frown in his tone. "Maybe that's the fourth jet..."

If the vampire in the front seat heard the other man—which, according to Damien, he shouldn't have been able to—he didn't show it.

Instead, he cleared his throat again and started to drive.

Unlike Keys, this male obviously knew who he had in his back seat. Because he was sweating—a rare physical reaction for a vampire.

But this one appeared to be young.

Similar to Abigail. I frowned. *Where is Abigail? Was she on the plane with you and Cane?*

Not that I saw, Ismerelda replied. *Should I ask your brother?*

No. I'll ask him when I arrive. Which would be soon, as the airport wasn't far from the compound—something Lilith had apparently done while renovating Rome. Apparently, the human-made airfield had been too far away for her liking.

"There's, uh, also a few lycans," the driver added, causing my brow to rise. "They came with the Thida and Tómasson Clan Alphas."

My brother is working with lycans? I asked, my shock making it sound like I was demanding that Ismerelda explain it to me.

Fortunately, she understood what I'd actually meant and instead voiced it as a question to Cane.

His response was loud in her mind. *"Where do you think our test subjects came from, brother?"* The question possessed an irritating mix of derision and superiority.

Fuck, I thought.

"Or… or is it Winter Clan?" the vampire rambled. "I… I often get confused by what it's called. I think the alpha, uh, Jenkins, refers to it as Tómasson Clan now."

"Your driver appears to be a useful idiot," Ryder deadpanned into my ear, his unexpected voice nearly causing my eyebrow to jump.

"It's Tómasson Clan, but a lot of vampires still refer to it as Winter Clan," Damien clarified. "If you want to educate the *useful idiot.*"

I didn't.

I was too busy processing this new information.

"It's amazing what lycans are willing to provide for just a little bit of promised favor," my brother was saying to Ismerelda now. *"Of course, Lilith helped me identify the most willing of alphas. Ones who craved power over love."*

My *Erosita* fought a grimace in response to my brother's

chilling smile, her mind berating him for essentially turning the wolves into pawns.

"Alas, I will say, breaking the lycans of their penchant for familial bonds has proved to be quite cumbersome," he continued. *"My brother once told me that would be my biggest hurdle in convincing the wolves to join my plight. In addition to turning them against humanity, I mean. Overall, He was right. But degrading the clan matriarchs—the alpha females—has somewhat helped."*

I wonder how Mira feels about that, Ismerelda muttered to herself.

She likely doesn't consider herself among the alpha female ranks, I replied. *She's an immortal lycan. One of a kind. Therefore, she's superior to all of the others.*

Ismerelda fell silent as she considered my response.

"We're looking for Luka and Jolene now to bring them up to speed on this latest development," Darius said into my ear.

Apparently, Damien had connected me to everyone he could think of.

I'd have to thank him later for the warning.

"It's a good thing I made Cam wear a comm," Damien added, causing me to nearly grunt. Because he didn't *make me* do anything.

"Yes, good on you for not letting him run off on his own again," Ryder drawled.

Your brother and his maker are giving me a fucking headache, I groused to Ismerelda.

When she didn't reply, I poked a little more at her psyche, curious as to what my brother was saying to her now.

Nothing, I thought, allowing myself to frown. *Ismerelda?*
Silence.

Not a single flicker of emotion or feeling coming through the bond.

No link. No memories. *No Erosita.*

"Stop the car," I demanded.

But it was already too late.

We were within the old Vatican City walls.

And my brother was waiting for me near a set of entry doors.

With my dead mate at his feet.

CAM

"Did I not make myself clear, Cane?" I demanded as I nearly ripped the car door off its hinges. "Sever our link and I'll take your throne."

Cane frowned, glancing down at Ismerelda and then up at me as I phased to stand before him. "I haven't severed anything. I simply snapped her neck."

"Which means I can't *hear* her," I said through my teeth. "Thus, *severing* our link."

"Hmm." He glanced down again. "Well, I assumed that your arrival meant her consciousness was no longer required. I didn't realize she needed to be aware for you to use her." He paused for a beat, then shrugged. "She'll wake soon. In the interim, we can talk."

With that, he turned toward the door, leaving my dead *Erosita* on the cold ground.

I growled and scooped her up into my arms, causing

my brother to turn around with a knowing glimmer in his green eyes. "So you do still care for her?"

A test, I realized, irritated as hell by my brother's antics.

I allowed some of that irritation to show in my tone as I replied, "I care about what's in her head, brother. Such as the memories you and Lilith stole from me."

Obviously, that wasn't the full truth. But it was the truth that mattered most to him.

Cane studied me for a moment, perhaps evaluating the veracity of my words. Or maybe he was attempting to discern how angry he'd made me with his actions.

Whatever it was, I didn't allow him to see it. I simply stared at him with an arched brow.

"She didn't feel it," he finally informed me. "I asked her to come with me to meet you outside and snapped her neck the moment she moved through the door. Then I let her fall to the ground. Her head will be fine when she wakes up."

I made a show of checking her hair, pretending as though I were searching for any potential wounds that might have damaged the part of her I needed most.

The action afforded me the precious seconds I required to rein in my temper.

Because all I wanted to do was punch my asshole of a brother in the fucking face.

But doing that would guarantee retaliation.

Alas, I couldn't afford that at the moment. Not with Ismerelda unconscious. And not without some answers.

Oh, I could phase her away and make a run for the airport. However, my brother was nearly as powerful as me. He also apparently owned this compound. Who knew what surprises he had waiting for me if I chose to attack him?

Another weapon?

Lycans and vampires?

Fellow royals?

Some other kind of immortal pet?

Whatever it was, I intended to find out. "I need a safe place to set her down," I told him. "Then we can talk."

He nodded. "Of course. Follow me."

Michael stood waiting inside, his head bowed. *It would look much better on the floor and removed from his neck*, I thought darkly, envisioning the scene. *Once my lioness wakes up, I'll ensure that image comes to life in a very vivid way.*

Followed perhaps by my brother's head, too.

"I simply snapped her neck," he'd said.

How about I simply snap your *neck, hmm?*

It took serious effort to maintain a bored expression as I followed him down the hallway to a doorway that led to the room I'd seen in Ismerelda's mind.

"This is part of my personal compound here," my brother explained to me. "If it meets your approval, you can make this suite yours until you pick your own building within the city walls."

"An upgrade from the quarters you keep your lab experiments in?" I asked, referring to my old suite underground.

His lips curled. "This is the building I had renovated for my allies. Ten suites, all equipped with every luxury imaginable." He gestured down the corridor to a set of ornate stairs. "Plus there's direct access to the immortal toys below. Perhaps we'll take a tour after you dispose of your baggage."

I hummed noncommittally and entered the suite instead. "There are answers I'd like to hear before I agree to a tour."

"Such as why I fried your memories?"

"That would be a good start," I replied as I laid

Ismerelda on the bed. I took great care with her head, mostly because I wanted to ensure her neck was aligned for the best possible healing position.

Then I faced my brother and arched a brow, telling him without words to start talking.

Because this wasn't a fucking reunion or a happy family moment.

This was a test of my own, a way of determining if I could allow my brother to continue existing or not.

Oh, I might not kill him outright. I might just bury him alive for a century and see if that fixed his humanity problem or made it worse.

And then I might end him.

Or I might find another creative way to punish him. Maybe I'd even use that bloody weapon on him, see how he likes it.

Maybe zapping his memories will fix his humanity problem, I mused.

Some would probably tell me not to stoop to his level.

But I was well beneath his level. I was at the bottom of the underworld where light didn't exist.

Ismerelda was the one who could pull me from my inky depths.

And my brother had snapped her fucking neck.

Thus cascading us all into the pitch black of night.

Not even the blazing sun could save my brother from my darkness now.

"It was an accident," my brother began as he walked over to the en-suite bar to pour us both an amber-colored drink.

Michael must have taken that as a cue to leave because he simply closed the door, sealing me inside with just my brother and Ismerelda.

"I suppose I should start at the beginning," my brother

clarified as he handed me one of the crystal tumblers. "As you've likely ascertained, I never slept. It turns out you have to be a willing participant for the ritual to work. But you knocked me out prior to performing it, and, well, I woke up."

I took over one of the chairs in the seating area, my focus on my brother while I monitored my mental link to Ismerelda.

Still nothing.

Which I supposed was to be expected, given that she'd died only minutes ago. But that knowledge didn't placate my nerves. Being cut off from her like this was even worse than when she'd fallen into her catatonic state.

And to think I'd killed her mere weeks ago.

If I'd been connected to her when that had happened... *Fuck.*

"Do you know why you knocked me out?" my brother asked when I didn't comment.

"No. I'm only aware of what I've seen in Ismerelda's mind, as well as the brief summary Darius provided me with about Aurelia and your waning humanity."

Cane's jaw clenched, his gaze narrowing. "I'm sure that summary was missing a few key elements."

I relaxed into the chair and brought my ankle up to rest over my opposite knee. "From what he told me, your contempt for the world strengthened after the slayer seduced you and attempted to kill you. However, I warned you the lycans would never agree. Which it seems I was wrong about."

"Oh, no, you were right. But I found a way to convince them."

"Yes, you outed lycan kind, thus prompting the humans to respond in their usual manner—a manner grounded in insecurities and underlined in violent tendencies," I summarized.

"Not quite." He finally sat down on the couch across from me. "I uttered a few suggestions, or I suppose we'll call them *compulsions*, that led to humans attempting to militarize the lycans. I figured that would anger the wolves and force them into action. Then vampires would be credited with helping the shifters fight back."

I took a sip of my drink and hummed, approving of his methods.

Well, not exactly *approving* of them, but appreciating them nonetheless. It was a clever ploy to sway the wolves to his side and essentially allow them to do all the work for him.

And frankly, it'd worked.

"However, it wasn't just the lycans we discussed that fateful day, brother, but *Erositas* as well."

I took another sip, then swirled the contents in the glass. "What about them?"

"I told you having one is dangerous, that it secures your link to humanity and initiates false instincts. When I recommended that you kill Ismerelda, you knocked me out. And the next thing I knew, I woke up in our family crypt just as you were closing my coffin."

"I see."

"Of course, I suspected that might be your next move," he went on, ignoring my reply. "I had contingency plans in place, including a vial of my blood and Lilith's promise to do whatever was needed to revive me. But testing the strength of the ceremony wasn't necessary at all. It simply didn't work."

"And you went on to live in secret?" I guessed.

"I went on to perfect my plans. Then I reached out to you to offer you the throne as the oldest royal. Well, technically, Lilith reached out to you. But you weren't at all surprised to see me that day. Deep down, you knew I was responsible."

Yes, I'd begun suspecting that.

But my arrogant self had thought I could handle my brother on my own.

Clearly, that went well, I muttered to myself.

"You rejected my offer," Cane went on. "Actually, you threatened to lock me up, tell everyone the truth, and fix my mess before I destroyed the world."

He chuckled and finished his drink, setting the glass down on the wooden coffee table between us. Then he leaned back and spread his arms out across the back of the couch.

"You were under the impression that I needed to be rehabilitated. But it was you, dear brother, who needed to be freed from your bond. Which I tried and failed to do."

I glanced at Ismerelda's prone form before refocusing on Cane. "Was that the point of the weapon you used to subdue me? To free me from my bond?"

"What you refer to as a weapon, I call a tool. It's meant to block the part of our minds susceptible to the *Erosita* link. But it's not perfect. And the older the link, the harder it is to destroy. Unfortunately for you, it ended up removing your memories instead. Which, as I said, was an accident."

Hmm. Understanding what had been done to me evoked a new thought, one I voiced aloud. "Shouldn't I just be able to heal that part of my mind, then?"

I could regenerate every other part of me. Why not this part?

Cane's lips twisted. "One would think so, yes. But the *Erosita* link isn't exactly tangible. Whatever magic allows us to exist also allows the bond to be created. And that enchantment works in ways we don't fully understand. Hence the reason it's so fucking dangerous."

"Well, right now that dangerous link is the only connection I have to the last thousand years. So I need her alive, Cane."

He studied me, his gaze astute and direct. "Is that the only reason you want her alive?"

I considered the question and looked at Ismerelda again, my mind processing through the responses I knew my brother would want to hear. "It's the primary reason," I said slowly. "But her blood and pussy are also excellent reasons."

It was a crass statement, but the upward tilt of my brother's lips told me it was the right one to make.

"Perhaps my tool worked better than I'd realized," he mused. "When you abruptly took off with Ismerelda last week—on the day I'd decided to reveal myself to you, of all days—I thought I'd failed. But maybe I haven't. Maybe you're cured after all."

I snorted. Mostly because there wasn't anything in me that required a *cure*.

But I shifted that derision into a scoff as I replied, "Ismerelda somehow managed to dismantle the barrier between our minds. When that happened, her memories were suddenly mine to explore. I'd been enthralled and then pissed to realize my access to the past was about to come to an abrupt end. I reacted accordingly."

He nodded. "Understandable. I hadn't considered what she might offer you beyond the obvious. I'd only brought her here to test your humanity. Had I realized she could assist with the memory problem, I would have encouraged that much earlier on."

"You weren't concerned her memories might trigger my humanity?" I asked him.

His shoulder lifted and fell. "It was always a possibility. I have plans in place should that happen."

"And do those plans involve killing her?" I guessed, my tone carefully devoid of emotion.

"Yes." An emphatic answer that didn't require elaboration, which explained why he didn't continue after uttering it.

In his mind, removing Ismerelda from the equation would immediately rid me of my ties to humanity. He might be right. What he failed to realize was what I would do to him if he removed my heart.

Because Ismerelda was so much more than a link to humankind.

She was *mine*.

And I would not take kindly to him harming her in any way.

Still, I needed to play this just right. Learn what safety measures he might have in place. Discover exactly what he'd accomplished and what he intended to do.

Then I would strike. *With my queen by my side.*

Which meant I had to keep indulging him in this game.

"I can't say if your experiment worked or not," I told him. "I can't remember who I was a century or so ago. But I know who I am today. And the only part of this that truly angers me is how you led me to believe I was the Liege when I originally woke up."

His dark eyebrow inched upward. "What about your missing memories and what the tool did to you over the last twelve decades?"

"I don't remember any of it. If I did, I might feel differently. But what I do recall is waking up to a bunch of information that turned out to be lies. I don't take kindly to being manipulated, Cane."

"They weren't lies. Lilith's logs were originally meant

for me, but I had them altered for you to give you purpose. If you want the throne, it's yours. I don't want to lead. That's not my skill. I work much better behind the scenes, which is why Lilith was the face while I focused on curing you."

There was that word again—*curing*.

My brother truly believed he'd been helping me.

"I'm going to need some time to process this," I told him honestly. "The sun is also giving me a fucking headache."

That last part wasn't necessarily true, but I wanted some time with Ismerelda. I could feel her beginning to stir, our mental link humming with life as her body started to heal.

"I know we still have a lot to discuss, and I'm very interested in how you created your immortal toys. But it's been a long fucking night. I want blood. Maybe a good fuck to work out some of this aggression. And a nap."

He nodded. "I've already started showing you how I created them—by using the Blessed Ones. I'd set it all up for you to replicate the process, but you left before I finished the demonstration."

He stood before I could reply, not that I knew what to say.

"What I haven't determined yet is how to prolong lycan life. But that part hasn't been my priority. I've put Mira in charge of that since that's her desire more than mine." He ran his hands over his suit jacket. "However, we can review everything in depth in a few hours."

I joined him in standing, mostly because I could feel Ismerelda starting to breathe again. It made me want to be closer to her, to hold her as she regained consciousness.

Although, it would be tricky.

Because I had no doubt there were cameras in this

room. They might not be in the same place as they were in my previous quarters, but there was no way my brother trusted me to behave.

All of this was another glorified experiment.

The only difference now was I knew about it.

Play the game, I told myself, the words similar to what I'd said to Ismerelda a few hours ago. *We're both going to have to play the game together.*

Which meant her waking wouldn't be very enjoyable. For her, anyway.

"I'll leave you to feed and fuck," my brother murmured. "If you'd like a different flavor, just use the staircase I pointed to earlier. You'll find an entire room full of treats below. Maybe they'll appeal to you more than the blood virgins did."

He gave me a knowing look as he issued that last line—telling me he'd absolutely observed my time with the blood virgins and knew I hadn't really touched any of them.

"Enjoy your day, brother," he added.

He left when I didn't respond, a smirk teasing the edges of his mouth.

I locked the door behind him. Not that it would make much of a difference.

Growling under my breath, I prowled around the room, noting the contents of the fridge, checking the bathroom, which contained the basic necessities, and eventually found myself standing next to the bed, my focus on Ismerelda.

"Wake up," I demanded, the anger in my tone meant for my brother, not for Ismerelda. But he wouldn't know that. He'd read it as impatience.

Because that was the purpose of this—to provide Cane with proof that his little experiment had worked. That I no longer possessed my humanity.

That Ismerelda meant nothing to me.

Oh, I could flee with her.

But he would just find a way to bring us back. Or worse, he'd hunt Ismerelda down and try to kill her.

No. The solution was to stay here and indulge him. To gather information and form a plan. To work with Ismerelda to resolve this situation, not run from it.

I'd tried to handle my brother on my own once before. I'd failed. Now it was time to trust my mate to help me see this through.

And in the interim, I'd give Cane what he wanted—a demonstration of who I'd become.

All the while, I'd try like hell to keep Ismerelda calm.

I need you to be my queen, I whispered to her as I removed my suit jacket. *Not a breakable doll.*

She'd be aware soon.

Then the show would begin.

KHALID

"Abigail is dead." Hazel's flat tone preceded her entry into my suite, her irritation palpable. "Deirdre found her near the border. Head sliced clean off. A too-easy death."

"I see," I murmured, my neck currently experiencing a similar threat from Emine's blade.

Her blue-gray eyes glittered with triumph.

At least until I phased out from beneath her and pinned her to the floor with my hips, her wrists caught in one of my hands over her head.

"Drop it," I told her, giving her wrists a little squeeze.

She growled in response, causing my lips to curl.

"Oh, I do love the way you fight me, habibi."

Her teeth clamped down on my bottom lip in the next instant, her fangs immediately drawing blood.

It wasn't a love bite either, but a harsh one.

Yet that didn't deter my hard cock in the slightest. If anything, it just made me want her more.

I licked my wound, then kissed her, forcing her to swallow her minor victory.

She hummed in contentment, my blood an addiction for her slayer senses.

My darling dragoness was the first of her kind—a slayer turned vampire. It made her that much more lethal. And oh so fun to play with.

I ended up on my back in the next second, her thighs straddling mine.

My lips curled, my body all too eager for what was coming next. I phased right as her blade would have sliced through my throat, this time placing myself on the opposite side of the room and on my feet.

She snarled in frustration but didn't lunge as she joined me in a standing position. Instead, she sheathed her dagger, her defiant gaze telling me the whole time that she was proud of herself for standing up to my command.

That made two of us.

Emine was quite possibly the most alluring jewel in my collection of rare objects.

Her expression darkened as she glared at me, her eyes telling me how she felt about my obvious admiration.

You're mine, habibi, I whispered into her mind, this gift between us one that had existed from very early on in our acquaintance.

Fuck you, My Prince, she returned.

Later, darling mirage. Definitely later. I winked at her before giving Hazel my full focus.

Cam's human, Keys, stood just behind her, his all-black suit crisp and clean, his stature healthy.

"You healed nicely," I told him.

"Thank you, My Prince," he answered dutifully.

Hazel rolled her eyes. "You can call him Khalid."

I chuckled. "Trying to divest the poor human of his training?"

"Yes." Her emphatic answer highlighted her annoyance. "We need to talk about Cane."

Hmm, yes, I suppose we do. "We heard everything he said to Cam. Cedric recorded it as well." We'd also turned off the microphone on our end once we'd realized there might be lycans present.

My advanced communication technology had been tested around vampires, not shifters. So while I knew my brethren couldn't overhear chatter from the earpieces, I wasn't sure about the wolves.

It was easier to just turn it off entirely and go into listening mode.

"Yes, I'm aware," Hazel replied, her words in response to my comments about the recording.

She collapsed onto the couch closest to Emine, not at all fearful of having my deadly dragoness at her back.

"We need to find out what Cane knows about Blood City," Hazel said bluntly.

"Well, Abigail wasn't privy to any of our conversations, and Deirdre turned off all the surveillance in the room. So she shouldn't have been able to tell him much, if anything, about Blood City." I walked over to the fridge to grab a water bottle for Emine while I spoke.

My darling mirage continued to narrow her eyes at me as she accepted the offering, her inner voice conveying gratitude while her face displayed unveiled hatred.

I kissed her cheek, the gesture a taunt. She growled in response, her hand going for a blade as I phased over to sit in a chair across from Hazel.

Emine simply stared at me.

Then popped the lid off her bottle and guzzled the contents.

Now you're just teasing me, habibi.

You're entertained by asinine behaviors, Khalid.

Such as watching you swallow? I suggested. *I find that very entertaining indeed.*

She nearly choked in response.

Careful, darling. I have plans for that throat later.

Keep dreaming.

Keep fighting, I returned.

She rolled her eyes and went to grab another bottle, her unique genetics making hydration a requirement. She needed more than blood to survive.

But that was a secret we didn't share with anyone.

"While true, we don't know what Cane has discovered via his own surveillance," Hazel told me, drawing my attention back to her. "He obviously knew Kylan was here since he recommended that Cam take Kylan's jet. Which means he also knows you're here."

"Likely," I agreed. "I imagine he thinks the revolutionaries are trying to woo me to their side."

"And given how long you've been here, he probably thinks they've been successful," Hazel concluded.

I shrugged. "He can think whatever he wants."

"You're not concerned?"

"If I were, then it would be an indicator that I haven't planned well enough for this inevitability," I drawled as Emine sauntered toward me. Rather than take the chair beside me, she settled into my lap.

Right on my hard cock.

Temptress, I accused.

She leaned back, her neck exposed as I wrapped my arm around her stomach. *You need blood.*

I'll drink from your cunt later.

She scoffed at that, but her body remained relaxed against mine.

I kissed her pulse just as Cedric and Lily entered the room, their flushed faces leaving no doubt as to what they'd been doing while Emine and I had sparred.

When they took the chair beside me, it left poor Keys as the only one standing.

"You should sit beside Hazel," I told him. "She helped save your life, after all."

"He's free to make his own choices," Hazel informed me before he could reply. "So if you're not concerned about Cane discovering Blood City, what does concern you?"

Clever minx, I thought, my lips nearly twitching again.

I'm starting to see why she's your friend, Emine said, her mental tone holding an edge to it. *She reads you well.*

Jealous, little mirage?

She shifted on my lap, her delectable curves caressing my arousal. *Hardly.*

I smiled. *I do love how much you've matured, Emine.*

She snorted. *Clearly not enough, My Prince.*

I hummed, pressing another kiss to her neck. *I told you, love. I won't fuck you properly until you beg me.*

And I told you that will never happen.

Hence, here we are, I murmured back to her.

She said nothing, but I sensed her irritation. I couldn't quite read her mind, our connection more telepathic than anything else.

However, I'd been around her long enough now to pick up on her feelings.

"Khalid," Hazel prompted. "I know something is concerning you. That's why you're awake, despite the noon sun beating down upon us. If you felt safe or at ease, you'd be asleep right now."

"Maybe I wanted to play with my dragoness," I suggested.

Hazel gave me a look. "I've known you for thousands of years. Your playful sidestepping doesn't work with me."

"Well, that's not true," I murmured. "We verbally dance all the time."

"*Khalid.*"

I sighed. Hazel was one of the few beings on earth I'd accept that admonishing tone from. Emine would be on that short list, too.

"I'm concerned about the lycans, Hazel," I told her quietly. "They're up to something."

"Can you blame them?" Cedric asked, his imperious eyebrow arching. "They've been pawns for over a century. And hearing that Cane orchestrated their fallout with humankind can't have helped matters."

"I'm sure it didn't," I admitted. "Which is why I'm concerned. I'm waiting to see what they will do."

"You think they might breach the compound without us?" Hazel asked.

"Yes." Because it was what I would do in their position. "While we may not be at fault here, our brethren are. They're within their rights to retaliate, and I wouldn't blame them if they didn't trust us to be part of that retaliation."

Which was precisely my concern.

Lycans were prone to emotional reactions. They were animals at heart, their feelings passionate and aggressive.

And Cane had hit them right in the fucking heart.

He'd orchestrated all this madness, ensured lycans were discovered by humans, all but facilitated their temporary enslavement in the mortal armies, and had been experimenting on them for well over a century.

The fact that the lycans in Deirdre Tower didn't seem

all that keen on discussing any of this with us only made matters worse.

"I would offer to surveil them, but I suspect that would worsen the problem," Hazel said.

"Yes, it very much would," I agreed. "At this point, all we can do is wait for them to come to us and hope they include us in their plans."

"We could try to talk to them," Cedric offered. "Reinforce our supportive stance."

"They already know we're not like Cane," I replied. "But the fact of the matter is, all we've done is look out for ourselves. Blood City is proof of that." At least in terms of what the lycans here knew.

Oh, I had a few wolves in my territory. But they were all lone wolves who would have no interest in coming forward to discuss their current living situations. As far as the lycans in this tower were concerned, I'd built my city for vampires only.

Just as Jace and the others had really only ever focused on a revolution with vampires in mind. Blood rations. Protecting their food source. Never any true discussions about lycans and their needs.

It wasn't that they wanted to exclude the wolves; it was just natural to do so.

And that sort of divide was coming to a head now.

It had been for days.

Ever since the vampires arrived first, just to invite the wolves along later. Almost as though they were an afterthought, not a primary partner in this initiative.

I had no idea if Jace had run the revolutionary side like this all along or not, as I hadn't paid much attention to their movements. While I'd been aware of some of it via Cedric's spying, I hadn't been privy to all of it.

"What happens if they move on the compound without us?" Lily asked softly, her gaze on Cedric while she spoke.

"They'll probably kill every vampire inside," Emine answered, her blue-gray eyes meeting mine. "Right?"

I nodded. "Yes. And that will very likely initiate a war between vampire and lycan kind."

"Or end it before it can even begin," Cedric murmured, drawing my focus to him. "I think we need to discuss a secondary plan, one that factors on the very real possibility of a lycan-led attack, and how we need to respond to it."

I cocked my head to the side. "It sounds like you already have a suggestion."

"I do," he replied, making me grin.

When Cedric had proved to be bored with the current world regime, I'd offered him a place in Blood City.

Well, that wasn't quite true. I'd demanded he join me in Blood City. As a royal and his superior, I could do that. But there'd been a reason for my heavy-handed behavior, and it hadn't just been because he was a skilled spy.

It'd been because he often presented reasonable ideas with fair outcomes, his practical mindset ancient and strategic.

Thus, I looked at him now, curious as to what he would recommend. "Let's hear it, Cedric," I murmured. "What should we do?"

He replied, his answer a simple solution that proved to be eternally wise.

"That just might work," I admitted, catching Hazel's gaze. "We need to phone Jace and the others."

She nodded, her focus shifting to the screen she'd just pulled up from her watch. "I'm already sending out a notice to meet us downstairs in an hour."

"Send it to the wolves as well," I told her. Although, I fully expected them to not show up.

We were at odds now.

Fighting for our own species.

Seeking revenge for entirely different reasons.

We were vampires. They were lycans.

The humans were collateral.

And the Blood Alliance... was a means to an end.

IZZY

WATER TRICKLED DOWN MY NECK, THE SENSATION WARM and confusing against my skin.

How....? I thought groggily, lightheaded from the unexpected caress.

Shh, someone hushed into my mind. *It's just me. You're safe, Ismerelda.*

Hmm? I hummed back, lost to the heat flooding my veins. *What is that?*

A bath.

My brow furrowed, my limbs tensing in response.

Only for me to jolt as something hard pressed against my ass.

A harsh band of muscle locked around my stomach as I attempted to leap upward. The air left my lungs on a whoosh, my head immediately swimming with dizzying thoughts as a sharp pang echoed down my spine.

I yelped and squirmed, my instinct to flee nearly suffocating me.

Yet I couldn't move.

I was drowning.

Trapped against a wall of simmering steel.

Locked in a male's embrace.

"Ismerelda," he growled against my ear. "*It's me.*"

Who? I wanted to demand, my brain failing to supply me with an identity or any semblance of a reality. *Where am I? Who am I? Why…?*

Fangs bit into my neck, the stinging prick sending a familiar shiver through my being. My yelp morphed into a moan, my body instantly relaxing into my masculine cage.

Cam, my soul seemed to whisper.

Yes, he replied, his blazing form a brand against my back. *Cane snapped your neck. You've been out for a few hours.*

My brow furrowed, his words slowly processing through the befuddled mess of my mind.

He's given me the day—which is really just an afternoon now—to process everything he's told me. But I suspect there are cameras in here, so I need you to play your part.

M-my part? I repeated, still muddling through everything he'd said.

Yes, love. Your part as my queen. His lips caressed my pulse, reminding me of the fangs in my neck from moments ago.

You bit me, I marveled. *You… you haven't bitten me in…* I frowned harder, memories weaving together behind my eyes.

Cam killing me.

Me waking up in his underground lair.

My quest to make him remember me.

Our bond nearly shattering.

His emotions and intentions slamming into me. His goal to make me his queen. His comments about old Cam not being worthy of me.

Me being taken.

Cane…

My eyes opened, the tiled wall foreign and cold. However, the body beneath me was the complete opposite —familiar and *hot.*

I shivered, the juxtaposition of our situation slamming into me and stealing the air from my lungs.

Cam's mouth moved against my neck, his muscular arms still resembling bands around my stomach. "It's been a long fucking night, Ismerelda. And I'm about to turn it into an even longer day."

Cam's mind elaborated on what he meant, his dark intentions glittering to life via our bond.

This was the new version of Cam. The one who didn't hold back. The unrepentant predator.

A shudder worked through me as I realized what this would entail.

He's going to use me again.

Fuck me.

Bleed me dry.

Because we were on camera.

And likely being spied on by his brother right this very moment.

That realization sent a chill down my spine, Cane's earlier taunts echoing in my mind. He'd watched Cam fuck me. Had said how much he'd enjoyed the show. How he'd liked observing me on the brink of death.

He'd expect a similar demonstration now.

And Cam was ready to oblige him.

I originally wanted to take you back to the jet, Cam whispered to me, his thoughts confirming the veracity of his words. *Back to your brother, where you'd be safe. But it would only be*

543

temporary, Izzy. If Cane thinks he can't cure *me of my humanity, he'll kill you. And I can't let that happen.*

His mind revealed how he'd come to this conclusion, his conversation with his brother replaying for me to hear. It was an abridged version that touched on all the important bits and quickly brought me up to speed.

Based on what I'd recently observed of Cane, I wholeheartedly agreed with Cam's assessment.

I'm going to fuck you, he continued. *I'm going to drink from you. It's probably going to hurt. I would apologize, but it wouldn't mean much.*

I swallowed, aware of why he'd said that last bit. These were all things he wanted to do.

I could sense his hunger.

His desire to rip me apart. To feed until his inner predator was fully satiated.

If he gave in, he'd kill me.

His beast would take far too much.

And he was letting that part of him play right now, putting on a show for the cameras while holding on tight to his control inside.

I trembled in response, my heart skipping a beat.

This wasn't my old Cam—the safe version.

This was the new Cam—the one who treated me as an equal. Who didn't think of me as fragile, but powerful. The man who handled me like I could take anything he wanted to give me and more. Only, before, he'd done so without regard for my feelings and emotions.

Now... *now* was different.

I could *hear* him. *Feel* him. *Understand* him.

This was my new Cam. The male I was bonded to for eternity. I either accepted him or rejected him.

But first, I wanted to experience him. Experience *us*. And embrace what we could be together.

I tilted my head, pulling my throat away from Cam's mouth as I forced myself to look over my shoulder at him.

His blue irises radiated sensual violence, his beast lying in wait.

The old version of Cam had never looked at me like this. He'd hidden this side of himself from me, never truly fulfilling his cravings.

And perhaps never truly indulging my cravings, either.

I could see it now. All the gentle touches. Restrained movements. Careful considerations.

He'd never even given me a chance to meet his inner beast.

Yet I was staring right at him now.

Cam's chest rumbled against me, his growl a promising vibration that had my lips parting in response. Those dark blue eyes of his glanced down, then up, his hand snaking up my side.

I gasped as he fisted my damp hair in his strong fingers, my neck protesting as he repositioned the angle of my head to better suit his needs.

Then he kissed me.

Hard.

His tongue wasted no time in demanding entrance, the taste of his blood instantly hitting my senses and causing me to moan in response.

Drink, Ismerelda, he commanded into my mind. *You're going to need it.*

There was no asking. No concern. No second-guessing my willingness to participate.

This was simply Cam taking charge and declaring his intentions with his tongue.

He understood that he'd hurt me before, that he might very well do it again. But he couldn't change this part of him. He refused to treat me like a doll.

And frankly, I didn't want him to, either.

I needed this—needed *him*. It was the only way I'd know if I could accept this version of Cam. If I could *handle* him.

He growled again, approval radiating through our bond as he sensed my acceptance. And not only that, but also my willingness to move forward. To see if this could work. To indulge in his darkness.

Maybe I could even forgive him.

This place seemed appropriate for that. A way to heal my wounds. Relive our previous experiences and create new layers.

Meaningful ones.

Impactful ones.

"Mmm, this is much better than the last time you died," he mused against my mouth. "When you accused me of being someone else."

You are someone else. However, you're still mine, I replied into his mind, uncertain if there were any microphones in here. There hadn't been any in his old quarters, but who knew what Cane had done to this space?

Am I? he returned via our link, his lips briefly curling against mine before he unleashed another growl.

I winced as his grasp tightened, his beast threatening to take control.

"You won't deny me this time, though, will you?" Cam went on out loud, clearly putting on a show for his brother's benefit. "Hmm, but I may try to make you fight me, just so I can admire your struggle."

His words elicited a shiver from deep within.

He'd said we needed to play our parts, and I knew exactly how to play mine.

"Whatever pleases you, my liege," I answered dutifully, my voice holding a slight rasp to it.

His growl almost turned into a purr, only it was too deep and vicious to be so content.

"Biting you pleases me," he told me darkly. "I want to feast on your pussy. Make you come until you pass out, then fuck you back into awareness."

I swallowed.

Because none of that had been for show.

Cam had meant every word.

And while the prospect of all of that would have been devastating a week ago, I... I rather liked the potential for it now.

Why? I marveled. *What's changed?*

Trust, Cam whispered back to me. *You trust me to take care of you now because you know I care. You know you're mine. And, perhaps more importantly, you know I'm yours.* Your *Cam. Maybe not the previous man you once loved, but an improved version who is willing to do whatever it takes to be the* right *man for you.*

His grip tightened even more, his teeth dragging along my bottom lip.

"Beg me, lioness," he murmured, speaking aloud again. "Beg me to make you come."

My lips parted on a sharp exhale as he bit down, the sensation instantly traveling to all my nerve endings and causing my thighs to clench.

"Cam..."

"Mmm," he hummed, tsking under his breath. "That's not good enough, lioness. *Beg.*"

His fangs pierced my lower lip again, making me jolt as the pain melted into ecstasy, stealing my ability to speak.

Vampiric kisses were addictive, especially ones delivered by this man. And he knew it, too.

He was playing with me.

Escalating my need.

Ensuring I would enjoy what he was about to do to me.

His blood had served as both a healing agent and an aphrodisiac. I felt nothing but pleasure now, memories of my neck snapping nonexistent. And not just because I couldn't remember Cane killing me, but because the ache I'd awoken with was long gone.

All I could focus on was *Cam*.

"You're not very good at begging," he admonished, his deep voice commanding as he tugged on my hair. "Do I need to take my brother up on his offer to find a replacement downstairs?"

Those words were uttered for Cane, not for me, something Cam told me with his mind. But that didn't mean I *liked* his question.

My gaze narrowed, my spine straightening despite my strange position on his lap.

He arched a brow, his impatience lighting a flame within me.

Because fuck that. And fuck this. This man was mine. He would *not* be replacing me with an immortal fuck doll. How dare he even fucking say that!

I dug my nails into the arm he had wrapped around my abdomen and ignored the sloshing water as I forced him to let me turn around. To truly face him. *Straddle* him. Look him dead in the eye. "You will not replace me."

"Oh?" He canted his head to the side, his cock throbbing against my slick center. "And what makes you think that, hmm?"

"I don't *think* anything," I told him. "I *know* you won't."

Such a good fucking queen, he replied into my mind. *Are you going to help me show my brother why I'll never replace you?*

He fisted my hair again, his torso flexing as he pressed his hard chest into mine.

Demonstrate why none of those blood virgins ever appealed to me? Not even when I didn't remember you? he went on.

He nipped my lower lip, the skin already healed despite his recent bite.

Prove once and for all why you're my mate? My equal? He punctuated those final questions by sliding his tongue into my mouth, his eyes holding mine while he devoured me.

I bit down, angry that he'd even uttered that question about replacing me out loud. It didn't matter that it'd been for his brother to hear. *I* hadn't wanted to hear it.

And I wouldn't even fucking entertain it.

Not after everything I'd overheard between him and Mira. Their conversation about him playing with blood virgins. The insinuation that he'd been with other women before I'd arrived.

Nothing happened, Cam promised me now, his memories confirming his truth. *I bit one of them and barely drank from her. It was a complete waste.*

How would you feel if I did the same to another man?

His chest rumbled, his muscular arm banding around my back. *I'd kill the man.*

Then you know how I feel about the blood virgins. Plural. Right? Because Mira had definitely implied that Cam had tasted *several* blood virgins.

I was offered a few, yes. I only bit one, he reiterated. *If you want her dead, I'll give her to you to kill.*

It was an enticing offer, even if it was wrong to consider it. The blood virgin was innocent. Just as it hadn't exactly been Cam's fault that he'd been tempted to bite her.

It says everything that I didn't want any of them, Izzy, he whispered into my mind. *My body rejected them because my soul belongs to you. As it always will. Even if you no longer want me, I'm still yours.*

His eyes fell closed with the statements, his kiss turning

gentle rather than hungry, the words a vow in my mind as he tried to heal the wound he'd reopened with his hurtful question.

And it was precisely the wrong response.

I wanted to fight him.

To let out some of the rage he'd awakened over the last few weeks.

To make him understand my place by his side, to *earn* that position and test whether or not I could truly accept it.

I needed wicked Cam. The beast. The predator lurking beneath his skin. *The vampire.*

I conveyed that by biting down again, this time drawing blood from his tongue and causing him to wince. *Consider that a marking,* I growled into his mind. *You. Are. Mine.*

Then I get to return the favor, my queen, he mused right back at me. *Only, I'm going to mark you right between your thighs.*

I shook my head. "Get out."

He pulled back, his eyebrows shooting upward. "Excuse me?"

"Get. Out." I didn't mean for him to get out of the bathroom, just the tub. "You want to see why you won't be *replacing me?*" I told him. "Sit right there"—I pointed at the edge—"and I'll fucking show you."

He stared at me for a beat, his mind quickly catching up to mine as his lips curled slightly upward. "As you wish. But I'm going to fucking drown you in my seed. Then I'm going to drink my fill while you beg me for mercy."

CAM

ISMERELDA'S FELINE GAZE TRACKED MY MOVEMENTS AS I settled onto the marbled edge of the tub.

She looked ready to eat me.

Or maybe kill me.

Either way, I anticipated her ferocity.

I had no idea what kind of recording equipment my brother had set up in here, and I no longer cared. If he wanted to see my queen devour me, I'd let him. Maybe then he'd understand why I had to end him.

Because he'd hurt my queen. My mate. *My Ismerelda.*

No one fucked with my lioness.

No one except me, anyway.

Her eyes narrowed as she knelt between my splayed thighs, that look of hers radiating violent intent.

I welcomed it. Knew I deserved it. And more, I *craved* it.

She needed this experience to rekindle our relationship. To trust me. To have faith in our future together.

It was fucked up. Yet it was right. This place. This room. These circumstances. They set the boundaries for who we would be with each other. How much we could accomplish together, no matter the situation.

And most importantly, it would introduce us to the passion our souls had been meant to experience long ago.

There would be no hiding.

No limits.

No holding back.

Just us.

Her nostrils flared, her green irises glittering as she echoed the sentiment back at me while lowering her head.

My dick pulsed in anticipation, precum already pooling for her on the tip.

She didn't seek permission or ask me how to proceed. She merely licked the offering from my cock while holding my gaze.

I fought back the urge to grab her hair and force her to do more. *Take* more.

I would follow through on that instinct if she kept taunting me. But I'd let her try to lead first.

This was about trust. And I trusted her to know what we both needed as she parted her lips around my cock.

She hummed, the vibrations taunting my shaft as her feline irises conveyed her every thought.

Anger. Lust. Determination. *Possession.*

Her teeth skimmed my sensitive skin, her threat clear. I'd promised to mark her between her thighs, and she was vowing to do the same in a very different manner.

Fuck, but that felt good. Her velvet tongue against my skin. Her incisors threatening to bite. Her fucking throat around the bulbous head, swallowing and massaging my dick in a way that made me want to explode.

Gods, Ismerelda, I thought at her, my hand going to her hair—not to guide her but to touch her. To anchor myself. To fucking indulge in the heaven she was creating with her damn mouth.

"You're owning me," I groaned out loud. "*Fuck.*"

She'd just started and I was ready to come.

I fisted her strands, holding her in place while I regained control.

Her teeth clamped down around my cock in response, her bite eliciting a growl from my inner beast. He wanted me to yank her out of the water and sink my fangs into her neck. Her breasts. Her *pussy*. To fucking own her. Claim her. Ensure she understood he was just as possessive of her as she was of him. Perhaps even more so.

Instead, I leaned back into the tiled wall behind me and absorbed the pain.

Her tongue traced the indents in the next breath, her hot mouth instantly providing me with relief and amping up my need that much more.

It'd been a long night. An even longer fucking week. All I wanted was to lose myself in this female, let her suck me dry, then fuck her all over again as soon as I finished recovering.

She was my mate.

My fucking queen.

My *goddess*.

I wanted to worship at her altar and pray between her thighs.

Yet she was kneeling for me now, which made this all the more powerful.

I drew my thumb down her pretty neck, noting her

throbbing pulse. *You're so fucking perfect,* I whispered to her. *You slay me, my queen. Fucking slay me.*

The phrasing wasn't lost on me. But I would happily die for this female. Especially like this, with my cock deep in her throat, her nails dragging up my thighs, and her eyes holding mine.

So fucking beautiful, I told her. *Gods, I'm addicted to your mouth.*

The way she moved up and down. Hollowing her cheeks. Massaging my tip with her tongue only to deep-throat me again.

My fingers flexed in her hair, my thighs straining beneath her sensual assault.

Centuries of need built inside me, threatening to drown her, just like I'd promised to do.

Her mind readily accepted the challenge, her eyes daring me to try.

"You'd better swallow all of it," I told her, my hand re-fisting her tangled strands as I held her to me. "Every drop belongs inside you."

Marking her.

Claiming her as mine.

In every fucking way.

She hummed around me, the vibration going straight to my balls and drawing a curse from my mouth. Then the little vixen bit down, the sharp sting at odds with the sensual torment yet heightening it at the same time.

Replace me, she hissed into my mind. *I dare you.*

I nearly laughed, but that instinct melted into a growl as she sucked me so damn deep that I couldn't focus on anything other than fucking her mouth.

She took each thrust, her eyes watering from the impact while her throat remained open for me.

It was harsh. Amazing. Fucking incredible. And so damn powerful.

My hand locked in her hair, my body forcing her to take it. To swallow. To accept me. My brutality. My strength. My desire. My *seed*.

And fucking Ismerelda did exactly that. She took it all, her watery eyes staring up at me with such alluring determination the whole time.

By the time I finished, she was dying for a breath, her cheeks turning a pale color that was too close to death.

I released her, then reveled in the sound of her panting. Not just because it signified that she was alive, but because it represented her ability to truly take me. To accept this. To embrace *us*.

I couldn't be the old version of myself who'd handled her with care. That would be a disservice to us both. Hell, it had been a disservice to us already.

This was our path forward.

And she'd just shown me that she could accept it.

Using my grip on her hair, I yanked her up to me, my lips needing hers. She yelped in response, then moaned as I pulled her close, my tongue already bleeding and ready to revitalize her for the next round.

Because we weren't fucking done.

I still had a prayer to bestow upon her.

One I intended to deliver against her clit.

She gasped as I spun us, my vampiric speed causing water to spill all over the damn bathroom as I set her on the ledge I'd just been sitting on.

Then I knelt for her, the way a king should for his queen.

Her breasts rose and fell with her pants, her body not yet recovered from her exertions. Rather than force her to continue, I granted her a moment of peace and focused my attention on her tits.

My tongue traced her nipple, the little rosebud puckering beautifully in response. Then I moved to the other, my eyes on her face as I went.

Her cheeks were pink again, her lips swollen and parted.

You're stunning, my queen, I murmured via our bond. *I'll never tire of seeing you like this.*

And I proved it by showing her my previous memories —the ones I possessed from the last few weeks. Each one displayed my thoughts, my continued analysis of why I'd kept her for a thousand years.

So many alluring traits.

So much to love and cherish.

The perfect mate in every way imaginable.

She tested me. She strengthened me. She accepted me.

I don't deserve you, I acknowledged. *But I'll spend eternity worshipping you.*

I didn't elaborate on what I meant, instead kissing a path downward to her hot center. She froze as my lips found her intimate flesh, her mind instantly anticipating my bite.

But this was about her and her pleasure.

Not mine.

Not yet.

I licked her from opening to clit, my gaze finding and holding hers. I fully intended to make her come on my tongue before indulging in her sensual blood.

She shivered, her pupils dilating as I wrapped my mouth around her sensitive bud.

While she could hear my intentions, she still expected me to bite.

I toyed with that expectation by gently nibbling her in response, then I chased away the sensation with my tongue.

She moaned, her fingers threading through my hair as she held me to her.

You taste so fucking good, Izzy, I breathed to her. *I could feast on you for days and never get enough.*

Cam…

Shh, I hushed her. *Let me worship you, my queen. Let me make you feel good.*

Her legs trembled around me, her palm gripping the ledge of the tub to hold herself upright while her opposite hand remained in my hair.

Every lick seemed to heal her concerns, her mind slowly succumbing to the cloud of lust building inside her. *More,* she whispered. Not as a demand, just her body begging me to keep going. To never stop. To give her what she needed.

I slid a finger inside her, curling it in a way I knew she'd like. When that didn't seem to be enough, I added a second. She clamped down around me, causing my dick to swell once more with interest, eager to be inside her. Eager to fuck her.

We wouldn't be sleeping much today, if at all.

This desire was too thick, too intense, for us to rest.

We needed this. It served as a vow between our bodies to match the one our souls had made a millennium ago.

My tongue whispered promises against her flesh. Promises to adore her. Promises to protect her. Promises to be her equal, not her superior. Promises to kill anyone who ever touched her—including my brother. Promises to never leave her in the dark again.

She was mine in all ways.

And I was hers.

One day, I'd turn her. But it would be on her terms, not mine.

Then she would be my vampire queen. Immortal. Unbreakable. Fierce. A goddess destined to be revered.

Everyone would bow to her, including me.

Like I was now.

Pleasuring her.

On my knees.

My mate…

Her legs quivered, her hand tightening its hold in my hair as her lips parted on a gasp. She was close, her pussy pulsing against my fingers, making my dick throb with the desire to be inside her.

Not yet, I told myself. *Oh, but soon. Very… very… soon.*

But I needed her to come first. Hard. For a prolonged period of time. Over and over again. Until she lost her damn mind.

Then, and only then, would I fuck her.

"Cam," she breathed.

"Mmm," I hummed back. "I want you to come for me, darling lioness. Give me what I crave. Sweeten your blood. Invite me to bite you. Right. *Here.*"

I sucked her pulsating nub deep into my mouth, the impact almost immediate, her scream echoing throughout the room. Fuck, it could probably be heard everywhere in the damn building.

And it was *my* name she shouted, making my lips curl in triumph.

That's it, my queen. Let them all know that your king is kneeling for you. Pleasuring you. Making you scream…

Her responding tremble instantly tipped her into a prolonged climax, my little lioness liking my words.

But she was about to like my bite so much more.

I waited until she was almost finished, her orgasm

tumbling into aftershocks as her limbs slowly unlocked from their quivering state.

Then I bit down, my vampire venom penetrating her clit and forcing her into another heated spiral of intensity. I could feel her ecstasy as though it were my own, our link wide open as she cried out from the impact.

Her moans were music to my ears as I finally allowed myself to drink. To suck. To *bite*.

My inner predator growled in approval while Ismerelda writhed, her mind blanking from the euphoric assault on her senses.

She started to thrash, her body wanting to reject the overwhelming nature of her climax. But I coaxed her through it, my tongue replacing my fangs as I soothed her throbbing clit.

Only to bite her again and drive her off the cliff once more.

Her voice became husky from her harsh screams, her fingers tugging on my hair. Her nails digging into my shoulder. My name a plea inside her mind.

Yet she wasn't asking me to stop.

She was accepting her pleasure and battling through it, my lioness proving herself to be my equal in every way. Maybe because she could hear how much I loved doing this to her. Or maybe because she actually enjoyed it. Probably a combination of both.

You're fucking gorgeous, I praised her. *Taking my assault like this. Embracing it. Letting me devour you.*

I bit her again, earning me a silent scream, her voice so hoarse that she seemed incapable of sound.

Keep flying, Ismerelda. Fly until you can no longer breathe. Then I'll fuck you back to life.

Her thighs squeezed around me, her mind openly accepting my challenge.

I drank from her sweet cunt while she clenched around my fingers, her chest heaving, her grip nearly lethal.

Until slowly she started to fade, the pleasure lulling her into a submissive state. One where she floated, her mind losing consciousness and taking her to somewhere safe. Somewhere warm. Somewhere no one but me could hear her.

I gave her one last lick as my hands grabbed her hips, her body going limp in the next beat. I held her steady as I healed the wound I'd created, then I straightened my spine and pressed my lips to hers.

She didn't kiss me back, too lost in her rapturous state to process my movements. I grinned, pleased by her satisfaction. "I can't wait to fuck your back to awareness," I said against her mouth.

No reply.

But I didn't need one.

I'd heard the acceptance in her mind earlier when I'd told her my intentions. She knew what I wanted. And she was more than willing to oblige.

Standing, I picked her up and grabbed a towel, while she remained limp against me, her weight supported by one of my arms.

I haphazardly dried us off, my body too eager for me to be thorough.

It didn't matter.

All I wanted was Ismerelda's hot cunt wrapped around my cock.

CAM

Ismerelda didn't move as I settled us into the bed with her back to my front.

"Mmm," I murmured against her ear as I drew my palm up and down her side. "Your nipples are hard, my queen. I bet your pussy is still wet, too."

I allowed my touch to slide onto her flat stomach and up to her breast. She felt so damn perfect in my palm. So full and firm.

Her little rosebud tightened even more in response to my touch, her breathing seeming to hitch as well.

I feel you coming down from your high, I whispered into her mind. *Try not to move when you wake up. I want you to remain still. Quiet. Presumably asleep.*

There was something forbidden about it. Something dark.

And knowing my brother was watching made it that much more appropriate.

He wanted me to be a beast. To not care about humankind. To disregard my *Erosita's* wants and needs. So I'd pretend to do just that, all the while knowing my mate not only liked it but desired it, too.

As evidenced by the goose bumps pebbling down her arms now.

No moving, love, I repeated into her mind. *Just focus on breathing.* I circled one stiff peak with my finger. *In and out, my queen. Yes, just like that.*

Her body threatened to tense against mine, her instincts rioting inside. Yet she remained steady. Still. My perfect fucking queen.

"You're magnificent," I said against her neck. "I just want to drink from you all day while I fuck you over and over again."

I bit down to draw blood while I palmed her perfect tit.

She jolted slightly, a wave of molten arousal assaulting her nerve endings.

Don't make a sound, I warned her. *We're putting on a show, remember?*

She didn't reply. At least not with her mental voice. But I heard her moaning inside, her mind right on the precipice of consciousness.

It was intoxicating to listen to her processing the sensations burning through her body. She understood my words, could feel what I was doing to her, but wasn't fully aware yet. Her reactions were instinctive. And soon, she'd be struggling to hold them in check. That was when the real fun would begin.

I took another pull from her vein, my palm drifting toward her belly and down to the heat between her thighs.

"So fucking wet for me," I told her, exceptionally

pleased. "Tight, too," I added as I slid a finger inside her. "Gods, I love how you feel after you come, Ismerelda. It's like foreplay for sex."

Not only because I could *feel* her pleasure, but because of what it did to her pussy.

"I promised to fuck you back to awareness, didn't I?" My palm slid from her wet heat to her hip and along her thigh. "I'm going to do just that."

And you're going to be silent for me, I added into her mind as I guided her leg back over mine. *No screaming or moving until I give you permission.*

Because something about that made it even hotter.

I pulled my hips back a little to rearrange where our bodies connected. Instead of pressing my cock into her ass, I moved to align the head with her weeping entrance.

Don't move, I told her again as I slid into her from behind. *Pretend to sleep for me.*

It was reminiscent of what we'd done a few times last week. Only it was different now because she could feel my need. Hear my intentions. Understand that this wasn't just about me. This was about us. Our mutual pleasure. Our enjoyment.

It had always been that way, even when I'd tried to see her as a fuck doll. Yet I hadn't been able to perform when I'd sensed her fear. It hadn't felt right.

But now... now I could feel her arousal. Smell her need. Hear her internal intrigue.

She wanted this. Me. *Us.*

And I gave it to her with a thrust.

God, she breathed. *I... I don't... I can't...*

Shh, I hushed. *You're doing so good for me, Ismerelda. Stay still. Let me fuck you. Let me use you.*

I said that last part on purpose. Because she'd thought

that was what I'd desired. That all I'd cared about was getting her off for my own gratification.

She hadn't been wrong.

But she hadn't been right either.

I loved making her come because it meant I'd pleased her. And there was no bigger turn-on than knowing I'd done my job.

Which her pussy confirmed now as she clamped down around me, her slick walls tight and hot and fucking exquisite.

I growled against her neck, my hips slamming into her as I drove myself home, my palm holding her hip.

Cam...

Not yet, I told her. *Stay still.*

Her body tensed down below, sweat populating her brow as she fought the urge to press back into me.

My fangs slid into her neck again, making it that much harder for her to control her reactions.

A scream sounded in her mind, her climax rolling through her and leaving her gasping against me. But she didn't otherwise move, her body tense and perfect and fucking incredible.

You're so good, Ismerelda. You feel amazing, too. Keep coming for me, love. I moved my hand to thumb her clit. *Mmm, yes. Just like that.*

I... I... Oh... I can't... Cam!

You can, I promised her. But rather than force her to take more, I used my tongue to close the wound on her neck and granted her a temporary reprieve from my bite.

But I didn't stop massaging her or fucking her.

Her tight sheath pulsed around me, choking my dick as I drove myself into her.

Again and again.

"You're taking me well," I whispered against her ear. "So fucking good, my queen. So damn good."

She shuddered in response, still trying to feign unconsciousness for me.

I kissed her temple and pulled out of her. Then flipped her to her back and slid right back into her.

A startled gasp left her, her eyes fluttering open and then closed.

I smiled. "I saw that." My lips captured hers. "Kiss me back, Ismerelda. Give me your tongue and wrap your legs around me."

Our game was done. She'd played her part beautifully. Now I wanted her fully aware and engaged.

And her quick response to my demand confirmed she wanted that, too.

Her long, athletic legs encircled my hips, her hands clutching my shoulders as her tongue slipped into my mouth.

It was aggressive. Hot. *Angry*.

All of it underlined in passion, which I happily returned.

Her lips bruised mine, her tongue seeking dominion and coaxing my beast out to play. I grabbed her hips and slammed into her, my inner vampire reminding her who was in charge here. Only for the little vixen to bite my tongue in response.

I growled.

She moaned.

And our passionate dance turned feral.

Blood. Sweat. Tears. *Sex*.

It was so damn intoxicating that I nearly lost my fucking mind.

Her nails bit into my skin, clawing at my back, encouraging me to go harder. Faster. Deeper.

I devoured her mouth while I destroyed her pussy, my hands bruising her hips. But she didn't care. She took it and demanded more.

My queen.

My mate.

My Ismerelda.

My Cam, she whispered back. *Knock me out again. Make me see the stars.*

My inner beast rumbled in approval, the sound vibrating my torso and hers.

And then there was no stopping us, my ferocity taking over as my predator turned absolutely savage.

She bled.

I bled.

Our essences mingling in our mouths.

Her hips arching into each of my thrusts. Her tits pillowing my chest. Her little claws marking my skin. My palms branding hers.

Until both of us tumbled over the edge into an intense darkness, the overwhelming heat knocking us off-kilter and causing a strange ringing sound in our heads.

I growled, lost to the sensations—both hers and mine —because I could feel everything, as could she.

It was amazing.

Stunning.

Absolute insanity.

And so incredibly loud, I thought, delirious from the orgasm wrecking my being.

My hips continued assaulting her, my dick hell-bent on coating every inch of her insides with my cum.

All the while, that blaring sound itched at my senses.

It… it didn't feel right. It felt *unnerving*.

Ismerelda hummed, her mortal sensibilities lulling her into a drunk-like state, while my beast roared in triumph.

No. Not triumph. *Alarm.*

My eyes flashed open, the darkness immediately dissipating as reality crashed down around me.

Alarm, I repeated to myself. *There's a fucking alarm sounding.*

It was one I recognized from the logs.

One of the compound protocols had been triggered.

And it wasn't one of Lilith's protocols because she hadn't been the mastermind behind this operation.

My brother had always been in charge.

Which meant this protocol could have been triggered by anything.

Including me and Ismerelda.

Or something else entirely.

I grabbed my queen's throat, noted her sleepy expression, and immediately kissed her. My blood poured into her mouth, my mind compelling her to swallow.

Because I needed her awake. Aware. *And ready to fight.*

EDON

FUCKING KYLAN, SILAS GROUSED VIA OUR MENTAL BOND. *I should have taken Luna up on her offer to switch places.*

If I hadn't been in wolf form, my lips would have twitched. *Is he staking his claim again?* I asked, amused.

Kylan had made quite a show of ensuring Silas knew just who Rae belonged to over the last few days. He seemed to enjoy making his mate scream *his* name, likely because it'd been Silas's name she'd moaned while at the university a year ago.

Not that Silas and Rae had ever fancied each other in that way. They'd just been paired in class and knew how to fake their affections—something that seemed to agitate the royal vampire.

Again and again, Silas muttered. *I'm about to go find a new room to sleep in.*

We'll make it up to you when we get back, Luna replied, her sweet voice causing my wolf to nearly purr with delight. We were about half a mile away from one another, hunting for the other lycans in our animal forms. But hearing her in my mind almost distracted my beast from his task.

Almost being the operative term.

Alas, while fucking would be a far more enjoyable endeavor, we needed to figure out what was going on with the other lycans.

They'd all but disappeared hours ago, leaving the three of us as the only shifters near the tower.

The assholes kept hosting meetings out here in private, and my mates and I were done being left out of these secret conversations.

My wolf lowered his snout to the earth again, seeking familiar scents and finding a mixture of them traveling in competing directions.

It was as though the lycans had gone out on a hunt, scattering throughout the wooded area beyond the lake. *A diversion*, I growled to myself. *A way to confuse our senses.*

Because they didn't want to be found. Not by us or by the vampires we'd left behind at the tower.

Something is definitely going on, I thought, my mind open to both Luna and Silas. *Something big.*

Want me to do a tower sweep again? Silas asked, his irritation fleeing in favor of our businesslike discussion.

No. They haven't come back. I was sure of it. Because, otherwise, Luna or I would have caught one of them. It was as though they were going farther and farther away from the tower.

Toward a meeting place, or...

My wolf lifted his head. *Which way is the airfield?* I asked, searching our surroundings. *East? West?*

Southeast, Luna answered, her mind telling me she'd followed my thoughts and was sniffing in that direction as well. *You don't think...*

She trailed off.

Primarily because I *did* think exactly what she'd been about to ask.

Both of us took off toward the airfield in the next second, leaving Silas growling in our heads. *Don't say anything to Kylan yet,* I told him. *We need to know for sure.*

No shit, he muttered back at me.

Careful, Enforcer, I warned him.

Bite me, Alpha, he returned.

I will, I promised. *Right on your ass before I fuck it.*

I swear to God all you two ever think about is sex, Luna inserted. *We're trying to find a bunch of lycans who may or may not have gone rogue, and you two are fucking flirting.*

Jealous, little mate? I asked her. *Would you prefer we flirt with you instead?*

I'd prefer you both to focus on the task at hand, she replied.

Liar, I murmured to her. *You want us to talk about your sweet pussy and what we plan—*

My wolf froze, a familiar cypress-like scent wrapping around us and forcing our attention to the left.

Gramps, I thought, meeting my grandfather's dark eyes through a low-hanging tree branch. His silver fur glittered in the sun, the color similar to his hair in human form.

But I could immediately sense the wrongness pouring off of him as he stepped forward, his severe expression one he rarely bestowed upon me.

Keep going to the airfield, I told Luna, aware of her current hesitation. She'd slowed the moment she'd realized I'd found my grandfather. *I suspect he's here to distract me.*

I'm coming, Silas said, the words for Luna.

I can handle myself, she told him.

I know. I just want to watch, little moon. Even I could hear the lie in Silas's words. Oh, he wanted to watch, but he also wanted to guard her.

Luna simply sighed, aware there was nothing she could

do to thwart Silas's protective instincts. It was why I called him our enforcer.

Well, one of the many reasons why, anyway.

My grandfather began to shift, causing me to follow suit. My limbs easily transformed, my wolf bowing to my command to heel.

"Edon," my grandfather said, his back straightening as he stood to his full six-foot height.

I matched his position, only I had a few inches on him. A good twenty or thirty pounds more in muscle, too. However, while I physically bested him, he mentally beat me. At almost seven hundred years old, my grandfather possessed a wealth of knowledge.

And I'd been taught from a young age—by him—to respect my elders.

"Grandfather," I replied, my head tilting downward in the requisite show of courtesy. I might be the Clemente Clan Alpha, but I'd only achieved that position through this man's help. I would forever bow to him.

He studied me for a long moment, his dark eyes—the same color as mine—radiating an intensity I felt to my very soul. *Something has already happened*, I told Silas and Luna. *Or it's in progress.*

I'm still at least five miles away from the airfield, Luna said, her mental voice holding a note of exhaustion to it.

Wolves were fast.

But sprinting took a lot of energy.

And we couldn't maintain a top speed for too long.

Be careful, I murmured to her.

I'm fine, she bit back.

I know you're fine, little mate. That doesn't mean I can't worry about you.

Between you and Silas, it's a wonder I'm even allowed to take myself on a walk, she grumbled back at me.

I'll catch her, Silas told me. *Nothing will happen to her on my watch.*

I heard that, she snarled at him.

I know you did, little moon. His voice softened for her, his adoration clear.

I would have smiled, but my grandfather's stern expression grounded me in the present, seizing my full focus. "What's going on?" I asked him. "And don't tell me 'nothing.' I'm young, not naïve."

He nodded, his lips pursing as he took my measure. "You have a decision to make, son. One I know won't be easy for you and your triad. But I hope you'll take the right path. The only one, in my opinion."

My eyebrow inched forward. "You're going to have to explain it to me a bit more before I can agree one way or the other."

He blew out a breath, his chin dipping into another nod. "I know." He glanced around the forest, his attention going to a space between the trees that revealed a stream of sunlight. "Come on."

I frowned but followed him.

That frown deepened when we entered a small clearing.

My grandfather bent to pick up a black duffel bag that he must have carried here. Whether that had been in human form or wolf form, I wasn't sure. But whatever path he'd taken, my animal hadn't sensed him until he'd made his presence known.

As a former clan alpha, he was powerful. Perhaps even more so than he let on.

"Here," he said, tossing me a pair of jeans. The label showed they were my size, confirming that my grandfather had arranged this little meeting.

He pulled on some pants as well, the bag falling to the

ground to reveal additional clothes inside. I couldn't tell if they were for him or for my mates. I suspected it might be the latter, but I didn't ask.

Because it didn't matter.

He was clearly trying to divert my attention. But he was going to do it in a manner that provided me with information, too. That was my grandfather's way—distract with purpose.

"I've taught you the olden ways," he began. "How packs used to be about family. Love. *Loyalty*."

"Yes. Alpha pairs were revered. Mates worshipped instead of frowned upon. Triads openly accepted." Very much not the way of the world now, but I was determined to help our clan return to the heart of being a wolf. To embrace our emotions. To be a true pack again.

"Exactly." He sat on the ground, his lithe movements confirming his health. Most wolves his age would be geriatric by now. But not my gramps. He was as spry as a century-old shifter.

I joined him on the ground, my mind partially tuned in to Luna's thoughts. She was within a mile of the airfield now. Silas wasn't far behind her, his athletic form much faster now than when he'd first turned.

"Vampires don't value family. They're not programmed in that way. There is no pack psyche. No ability to conceive children. Just a single desire to drink blood and survive."

I wasn't quite sure where he was going with this, but I felt compelled to point out, "Some have mates."

"Yes. And the few who do are quite possessive of their human halves. But that possession—that *care*—doesn't extend beyond their *Erositas*. Hell, even Sire-progeny bonds lack true kinship."

"Why are you telling me this?" I asked, not needing a

breakdown of vampire kind. I was fully aware of their penchant for emotional detachments.

"Because I need you to understand that lycans and vampires have always possessed different goals. Different relationships. Different manners of life. At least until about twelve decades ago when humans became a common enemy between us. Everything changed after that."

His expression darkened, his gaze seeming to focus on a tree across from us.

"Lycans felt obligated to conform. To run away from our humanity. To be more like our vampire relatives. To no longer care." He finally looked at me again. "Family was seen as a weakness. Family was why we lost so many lycans during the revolution."

My brow furrowed. "What do you mean?"

"Our emotions dictated our actions. We thought about our packs and loved ones, not ourselves. And the humans took advantage of that. They killed our children. Our females. Leaving us heartless and broken. Incapable of fighting properly because we were too ravaged to think clearly. Then the vampires stepped in and ended it all with flawless efficiency."

I swallowed, the picture he painted vivid in my mind.

"This is why so many of our kind have assimilated to vampire rule, choosing to follow their lead and take to their preferences rather than embrace who we used to be. It's easier to survive when all you care about is yourself. No pain. No heartache. No potential weakness."

I frowned at that. "I disagree. I've survived this long because of you. Because of Luna and Silas. They're not weaknesses. *You're* not a weakness. All of you give me strength."

"Yes. And that's the heart of a lycan. But now imagine losing us. Who would you be without your heart?"

"I would kill everyone who touched what was mine," I replied immediately. "I'd *destroy* them."

"Which was exactly what many of our kind did. But the humans were ready for them. The lycans were so blinded by rage that they didn't think strategically. And many of them lost their lives as a result."

"How?" I demanded. "Mortals are not nearly as strong or as fast as our kind."

"No, but their weapons were deadly. And they knew exactly how to use them." His jaw clenched with the words, his gaze narrowing. "It was almost as though someone told them how to kill us."

Edon, Luna whispered into my mind. *The jets… they're all gone. There's no one here. No one at all.*

"We couldn't prove it," my grandfather went on, my heart skipping a beat as my mind processed everything he was saying along with what Luna had just revealed. "But now we know Cane is the one who outed lycan kind. He's the one who suggested that mortals try to weaponize us. And he very likely told them how to disable us, too."

Even Jace's jet is missing, Luna said. *It's not in any of the hangars either.*

We'd taken the royal's jet here because the Clemente Clan one was too slow.

"Once we acquire proof of what he's done, who his allies are, and everything else involved, we can finally fix our broken packs," my grandfather continued. "We can be who we are supposed to be. We can lead how we want to lead. And we can stop residing in the shadows of vampires."

"The other alphas have gone to get Cane," I realized aloud. "To gather their own proof."

"Yes. They've gone to kill him and his allies."

"And what about Cam? Ismerelda? The vampires who

have been leading this revolution?" The majority of them were still at the tower right now, all working on a plan to breach the compound and save their loved ones.

Or the vampire equivalent of "loved ones," anyway.

"Cam's their leader," I stressed. "They're not going to react well if he dies from this lycan attack."

"I know. Which is why you have a decision to make, son. Either you join us or you join them. Because regardless of how this plays out, it won't end well."

"Why not just ask them for help? To work with you? There doesn't have to be two sides here. I think they've proved that." They'd included us every step of the way these last few months. Why go against them now?

"The only thing they've proved is how different they are," he replied. "They don't care about coexisting with humankind. They care about their blood supply. They care about treating their food somewhat humanely. But it's all about their needs. They're immortal. As such, they need their food to thrive. That's it."

I just found two dead vampires, Silas informed me. *Not permanently dead, just shot in the heart and regenerating.*

Fuck, I muttered, not only in response to Silas but also in response to what my grandfather was saying.

"They've spent the last twelve decades perfecting their food source at the expense of lycan lives. And they won't be ridiculed for that; they'll be praised. Even our supposed allies can see the importance of what Cane has accomplished. They're intrigued, Edon. And they're not hiding it."

My teeth ground together. Because he wasn't wrong.

"I don't blame them for it, either," my grandfather added. "But again, our goals are not aligned. Lycans used to live among humans in peace. Cane changed all of that. *Vampires* changed everything. We can't just let that go."

"What about Blood City?" I asked him. "Khalid's vision has humans and vampires living together in peace."

"Yes, with a few lone wolves woven into his society," he returned, his tone underlined with derision. "He didn't build that city for lycans. He built it for vampires because he is a vampire himself. What use do we have for a blood tax?"

"What use do we have for humans in general?" I countered.

Mortals were treated as toys for the moon chase. Potential breeding dolls for procreation. Nothing more.

"Wolves can mate with each other," I added. "In fact, they should. Our children are born wolves." And they didn't have to go through the painful turning process.

Unlike Silas, who'd had to be bitten and forced to shift.

It'd been painful for him. So painful that he was lucky he'd survived.

"Exactly the point."

I blinked, surprised by his reply. "What?"

"We don't need humans. We never have. We once lived with them in harmony, primarily because they left us to our own devices. But that all changed when Cane—a *vampire*—revealed our presence to the world. The mortals became violent and hurt us. We wanted revenge. However, that desire has long since passed."

I stared at him. "Which leaves us where, exactly?"

"In a stage of rebirth. In a place where lycans can thrive again as packs. But we need the vampires to stop trying to control us first. We also need assurances in place that humans won't be able to harm us again."

"And what do those assurances look like?" I wondered aloud. "How would the lycans handle humankind?"

"That's the debate, isn't it?" he murmured, his gaze flicking up to the sun before returning to the earth. "We might not need humans now, but if our kind fails to procreate, mortals would serve a purpose. Therefore, exterminating them isn't an option. However, regulating them is a must. They can't be allowed to obtain or own weapons again."

I stared at him. "And what about the vampires?"

He released a long breath, his head moving back and forth. "That's complicated."

"No shit."

His dark eyes glittered sideways at me, his look one of disapproval.

But fuck that.

He'd essentially just told me the lycans wanted to rebel against the vampires and start a war. At the very least, he could tell me the plan.

"Why tell me all of this now?" I added. "Why not before? Why not include me in these discussions?"

"Because you weren't ready," he replied. "And one of your mates is best friends with a vampire and a hybrid, both of whom are mated to royals. Not to mention your own ties to the hybrid. Your allegiances are unstable."

My eyebrows rose. "My allegiances have been guided by you from the day I was born."

"And now they're influenced by your mates," he returned. "Silas and Luna will always come first. I respect that. But it complicates matters, Edon. That's why the lycans voted to keep you in the dark."

"I'm your grandson."

"Which is precisely why I'm here right now, talking to you, instead of helping the others."

My eyes narrowed. "Helping them do what, exactly? Attack the compound? Start a war with vampire kind?"

"It's inevitable," he fired back.

I scoffed at that, ready to point out that some of our allies might feel differently.

But my grandfather wasn't done speaking.

"We're living in a world run by vampires, Edon. They've given us a few scraps to keep us content over the last hundred or so years. Scraps that included human toys and bloody hunts. But it was never going to be enough. And frankly, it was never meant to be enough."

Meaning my grandfather felt this fate had been unavoidable from the beginning. "So why work with Jace and the others? Why pretend to be their allies?"

"We weren't pretending, son. We were working with them while it suited our purposes, just as their kind has done to us. However, now that we know where to find proof of their manipulations, our purposes are no longer aligned."

Kylan just showed up, Silas said into my mind. *Apparently, he followed me here.* His irritation was palpable, yet he didn't seem all that surprised. He'd left in a hurry, wanting to protect Luna and not bothering to be stealthy about it.

Kylan had probably assumed something had happened.

And, well, he wasn't wrong.

This is going to be a shit show, Luna whispered, her words the ones I would have uttered aloud if they were here.

"It's too late to warn them, son," my grandfather informed me softly, obviously aware that I was mentally speaking with my mates. "The lycans touched down outside of Rome an hour ago. The war has already begun. I only remained here to give you a choice—our side or theirs. The decision is up to you."

RYDER

"ALL RIGHT, WILLOW. IT'S JUST LIKE WE PRACTICED," I said against her ear. "Look through the scope and tell me what you see."

She blew out a steady breath, one eye pressed against the scope. She didn't immediately respond, my pet patient and thorough as she studied the scene before us.

We were about three stories up and just outside of the former Vatican City walls. I'd volunteered us for reconnaissance, while Khalid and his dragoness had opted for the underground. And Cedric had chosen to locate Damien.

Any minute now, I'd hear my progeny's angry tones in my ear. I couldn't wait.

Of course, Jace and Kylan would likely be angrier. But I needed their royal asses alive in case this mission failed.

Not that it would.

After all, Khalid had involved me in his fun and games.

An intelligent move on his part. It also saved me from a world of boredom.

Meeting after meeting.

A fucking waste of time.

The impromptu one Hazel had called earlier had been focused on a future alliance gathering, plus a detailed discussion on the notable shifter absences. Edon, Silas, and Luna had been the only lycans in attendance.

They'd been tasked with finding the others.

Meanwhile, Khalid and Cedric had other plans.

"You still want to play?" Khalid had asked me shortly after the dull conversation with the others.

I'd arched my brow. "Depends on what you have in mind."

"A surveillance mission. Or maybe an opportunity to stop a war." He'd shrugged. "That remains to be seen."

"Stop a war?" I'd repeated, arching a brow. "Doesn't sound like something I'd do."

"It'll likely involve killing some vampires and lycans," he'd hedged, his turquoise gaze glittering with dark knowledge.

"Now that's a bit more appealing. Keep talking," I'd said as he'd led me and Willow to a waiting car.

An hour later, we'd boarded his private jet.

Khalid had strongly suspected the lycans were headed this way.

And he'd been right.

Roughly thirty minutes after our arrival, the lycans landed at an old airport outside of Rome—something we knew because of Khalid's fancy technology. He'd placed a tracker on each jet back in the Deirdre City airfield, then he'd monitored the devices on his scanner.

We'd watched them all take off and follow our flight

path. Only, we'd landed on an abandoned road just outside of the city rather than at the old airport.

Then we'd phased through the Vigil security line and separated into our teams, our primary focus on avoiding lycan detection since we knew Thida and Jenkins had some wolves on the ground.

Meanwhile, Lily, Hazel, and Keys had all remained on the jet, their presence concealed by some sort of protective shield.

Khalid's penchant for advanced technology was beginning to impress me.

Including this pretty little toy he'd allowed me to borrow for Willow.

Much better than Lilith's artificial intelligence shit and voice impersonators.

"I don't see anything or anyone," Willow whispered, her voice barely audible.

As a hybrid, she knew how to modulate her tones for supernatural hearing. We were high enough up and away from wind streams to avoid our scents being detected. But we needed to be careful with sound, too.

"It's like they're all underground…" She trailed off, her brow furrowing a little. "I understand the vampires because the sun is still up. But where are Thida's and Jenkins's lycans? Underground, too?"

I hummed against her ear, my body lying alongside hers as she stared through the scope. She felt strong and sensual beneath me, my leg casually draped over one of hers.

It really was too bad that we had to work. Fucking her up here would be quite enjoyable.

"Ryder…"

"Willow…"

"I can feel you," she told me. "You're supposed to be teaching me how to scout."

"I am training you, pet," I murmured, purposely changing the verb in my sentence. "I've been training you since the moment we met."

She huffed, her gaze shifting away from the scope to glare at me. "Luka and the lycans should be here by now."

"They're likely drawing up a plan of attack. Or you're not scouting hard enough."

She gave me a look.

I gave her one right back. "For example, you're staring at me, not at the city. That's not a very good way to scout, mate."

She growled, the sound going straight to my balls.

"If you would prefer to play in other ways, I'll happily grant that request since we seem to have some time to spare," I told her.

"I hope the sun gives you a sunburn," she countered, drawing a soft chuckle from my chest.

"We're hiding under an alcove, little warrior. But your concern for my skin is noted."

She rolled her eyes and went back to the scope while I playfully nipped at her neck. Maybe I could test her ability to focus while I—

"Where the hell are you?" a voice suddenly demanded in my ear.

And there goes my fun, I thought with a sigh.

"On a rooftop with my mate," I murmured. "I'm teaching her how to scout with a sniper rifle. Or I'm trying to, anyway. And I'm hoping to show her how to shoot with it as well. But the wind—"

"A warning would have been fucking appreciated," Damien interjected. "I almost killed Cedric."

A snort sounded in response to that. "Like you, I'm not easily killed."

"We almost tested that theory today," Damien bit back.

Cedric snorted again. "You're good, Damien. But I'm better."

"Care to wager on that?"

"Sure." The confidence in Cedric's single-word acceptance reminded me a bit of myself.

"Name your target," Damien demanded.

"Cane."

"That's everyone's target," Damien retorted. "Give me something else."

"Are you two done flirting?" I interrupted.

"Jealous?" Damien asked.

"Of your and Cedric's little bromance over there? No. Some of us are simply busy trying to work," I reminded him.

Willow grunted at that.

I nipped at her throat again in response.

To which she pushed her hip sideways into my groin, making me growl. *Maybe I would have some fun after all,* I thought, my incisors taunting her pulse.

Only, the whimper she released in response wasn't one of arousal. It resembled pain instead, causing me to pull back and stare at her profile.

Her eyes were closed.

Her forehead scrunched.

"Willow?" I asked, my palm going to her nape. "What is it? What's happening?"

She groaned rather than answered, her face turning white as ripples of agony seemed to tremble through her being.

"*Willow.*"

I was only vaguely aware of Damien talking in my ear,

my entire focus—my fucking *world*—revolving around my writhing mate. She curled into me, her cries breaking my damn heart.

"Talk to me," I begged her, my palm still curled around her nape. "Fucking speak, Willow."

"R-ring... ing..." she managed to get out, her hands going to her ears. "H-hurts..."

My gaze narrowed. "Another weapon." It had to be. Only, this one appeared to be designed differently from the one Lilith had once used on me.

Or perhaps it was the same one. However, the frequency currently being used was hurting Willow instead of me.

Except, last time, she'd heard the hum before I had, the subtle buzz having irritated her lycan senses. She'd felt Lilith's weapon as she'd been configuring it to be used on me, yet I hadn't sensed it at all until it had knocked me on my ass.

Is that what she's sensing now? I wondered with a frown. *Is Cane unveiling an even worse weapon? Something meant to knock out an entire fucking city?*

"Damien, we need to move," I told him. "Send a warning to the others. Tell them what's happening here. And try to get in touch with Cam." Communication with Cam had been cut off earlier this morning around the time it'd become clear that he intended to fuck Izzy back into consciousness. None of us had wanted to hear that.

If anything, it had just made me want to kill the bastard even more.

But that was a task for another day.

Right now, I needed to get my mate off this rooftop and somewhere safe.

She'd curled herself even tighter into a ball, her skin

turning an odd shade of blue, like she'd forgotten how to breathe.

Forcing her to her back, I took in her expression, noting the wild panic in her eyes. My mouth immediately sealed over hers, my air becoming her air as I forced her to inhale.

Her chest moved, but only through my insistent push.

What the fuck? This hadn't happened to me when Lilith had knocked me down. I'd still been able to breathe. But her voice had controlled everything in my mind, rendering me utterly paralyzed while she'd spoken to me.

Lifting Willow into my arms, I jumped off the building, not caring at all about the three-story drop, and landed on my feet. Then I phased us away from the old Vatican walls.

Seconds felt like minutes, which resembled hours.

But the moment I heard my mate gasp, I paused, my eyes instantly searching for hers. She remained curled against my chest, shuddering as she caught her breath.

Only then did I feel the pain in my ankles, telling me that three-story drop had been a bit much. Fortunately, my age and experience allowed me to heal quickly.

And fuck if I was going to let a few bruises hold me back from saving my mate.

"*Ryder,*" Damien growled into my ear.

I hushed him, my attention still on Willow.

"I can't reach Khalid," Cedric said, his voice more distant, like he was talking to Damien in the background rather than into his communication unit. "The last I heard from him, he was entering the underground."

"What about his tracking beacon? Anything?" Damien asked.

A beat passed before Cedric replied, "Nothing. Hazel said the tracker disappeared around the same time we lost audio."

"Shit," Damien muttered.

Willow coughed, her hands going to her ears again as she violently shook her head.

I didn't think; I moved, phasing another three miles away from the compound. We were somewhere deep in the heart of former-day Rome, the buildings all deteriorating from lack of use and repair. Wildlife had returned to the city in the form of animals and greenery, giving the town a distinctly dystopian feel, just like most of the world.

No Vigils here, I thought, glancing around. They had various blockades set up around the city, along with a few architectural changes that made driving impossible without going through a checkpoint. But it didn't exactly deter vampires from teleporting in and out.

Humans, however, would probably struggle with the obstacles, which was entirely the point—this city had been restructured to keep *mortals* inside of it. Vampires and lycans were free to come and go as they pleased in any way they desired.

If I were building a fortress for my dynasty, I would have made it so *no one* could enter at will. But Lilith hadn't thought like that. Neither had Cane.

That arrogance had been Lilith's downfall, and soon, it would be the cause of Cane's demise as well.

Just as soon as my mate resurfaced and told me what the fuck was going on.

She was breathing again, thankfully, but she'd passed out against me, the pain seeming to have caused her to lose consciousness.

I phased another handful of miles, just to be safe, then found a soft patch of grass to sit on with her in my lap.

Running my fingers through her hair, I said, "Come on, pet. We have blood to spill, and I need you on your feet."

Alas, my stubborn mate didn't listen to me, making me growl in irritation.

"I don't know what did this to you, but I'm going to destroy it and whoever used it." Preferably with my bare hands. But if Willow wouldn't wake up, I'd settle on a gun because then I could keep one palm on her while I used the other to *kill*.

"Damn it, Ryder," Damien growled into my ear. "I just received an earful from Kylan and Jace. Every fucking word was meant for you."

I grunted. "Tell them to schedule a meeting to discuss it. They seem to like those." Well, Jace did, anyway. Kylan... Kylan just wanted to play with Rae.

A preference I understood, as I felt similarly about Willow. Except I also had Damien to think about, as well as Izzy.

Which, naturally, had made coming here the wise choice, as I wanted to ensure their safety. And maybe kill a few things along the way. Willow could also use the target practice.

But I needed her to wake the fuck up for that to happen.

"Fucking weapon," I muttered.

"What weapon?" Damien asked.

"Whatever knocked Willow out." Something I hadn't exactly explained to him yet, my actions consumed by making my mate breathe again. "Seems to be similar to the device Lilith used on me, only it impacted Willow this time. Can you or Cedric hear anything?"

"No." He didn't elaborate, just fell silent.

I waited a few seconds before saying, "Damien?"

"He's talking to Jace again," Cedric replied. "Well, no, he's *listening*. Seems the rebel king isn't a fan of our surveillance mission."

"Then tell him it's a killing mission and see if he prefers that," I suggested, done with this conversation and everything else. "Time to wake up, mate," I told Willow before biting my wrist and holding it against her mouth.

Her vampiric side took over in the next second, causing her lips to part and allowing me to feed her.

"Good pet," I praised her. "Take what you—"

The hairs along the back of my neck lifted, my instincts firing.

I didn't waste a second in looking, just phased out of the grassy area to the side of a building.

Only for Willow to scream as a deadly crack rent the air.

And my world went black.

CAM

An Hour Earlier

THAT FUCKING ALARM IS GIVING ME A HEADACHE, I THOUGHT as I finished buttoning up my dress shirt. It was a clean one that had appeared in my room while I'd been in the bath with Ismerelda, my old one nowhere in sight.

I probably should have been more careful with it, but had I attempted to hide it somewhere, my brother would have grown suspicious. So I'd discarded it in a closet laundry bin like I normally would, stripped Izzy in a similar fashion, and carried her into the bathroom.

Which was where I'd lost the earpiece. I'd put it in one of the cabinets while searching for bath supplies. And now I needed to find a way to subtly retrieve it.

While Damien wouldn't be able to hear me, it might be useful to hear him.

"I'll go find you a brush," I told Ismerelda as she finished putting on the silky, barely there dress that had been left for her in the closet. Or maybe it was one that had already been there.

Regardless, it was the only thing for her to wear, as her clothes had also vanished. Same with her shoes, leaving her with just a pair of stiletto heels for her dainty feet.

I started toward the bathroom but paused as the door to the suite opened. Michael stood in the doorway, his blond hair tied back at the nape.

"My liege," he greeted. "Prince Cane has requested that I lead you to the underground where all the other royals on the property are gathering."

"Prince Cane?" I repeated, arching a brow. "And you dare refer to me as *liege* after everything that's been revealed?"

Michael blinked, his innocent expression one I didn't believe for a second. "Prince Cane made his desires clear, my liege. You are his chosen leader, and mine as well. Therefore, I will address you as such."

"Hmm," I hummed, tempted to tell him to refer to Ismerelda as my queen, then. Because if he wanted to play by the logic that I was his king, then he could see my mate as his queen, too.

But that would defeat the point of whatever game my brother had in store for us.

So instead, I simply conceded by not voicing anything at all and looked at Ismerelda. "Go in the bathroom and find a brush." *I also need you to try to locate the earbud in the cabinet,* I added mentally as I showed her where I'd unceremoniously deposited it. *Put it in your ear while I distract Michael.*

There might be cameras in there, she said as she started

toward the bathroom, her head bowed in an obedient manner for the benefit of our guest.

Try to use the cabinet to mask your movements like I did earlier, I told her. It wouldn't be as easy since she had to actually set the device inside her ear, but I had faith in her to manage it.

"What protocol has been engaged?" I asked Michael, opting to acquire some information as a form of distraction. "I assume that's why all the royals are meeting underground, as you said. But to what end?"

"The rebels are coming. Prince Cane needs everyone to join him in the bunker before he deploys our security response."

My eyebrow arched. "The rebels? As in Jace and the others?"

"No. Ryder and Khalid, as well as the lycans."

Earpiece in place, Ismerelda whispered to me. *It's silent.*

Let me know if that changes, I replied while I absorbed Michael's comment regarding the rebels. *It seems Ryder couldn't sit this one out.*

Are you really surprised? Ismerelda asked as she reentered the room, her blonde hair brushed and framing her pretty face. My only complaint was the way she lowered her gaze. She was doing it for Michael's benefit rather than mine.

As she approached, I grasped her chin and pulled her in for a kiss. One meant to brand. To own. *To claim. That* was my version of *bowing* to Michael.

Was she supposed to be my plaything? Yes. But that still made her *mine*, something I needed my *progeny* to understand.

Ismerelda melted into me, her heart racing through the thin fabric of her dress. I bent to sink my fangs into her neck, openly marking her and taking a long pull from her vein. *I'm not going to heal you,* I warned her. *I want everyone to know you're mine.*

The blood you've given me this afternoon is going to heal me quickly anyway, she replied.

Then I'll just bite you again, I told her.

She shivered in response, causing me to nearly grin against her neck. But I couldn't afford to let Michael see me react in such a way.

Thus, I simply pulled away and met his gaze. "Touch her and I'll kill you. She's my toy, not yours. Now lead the way."

Michael cleared his throat and bowed his head. "Of course, my liege."

He stepped through the threshold while Ismerelda imagined all the ways she'd like to kill him. It made for an entertaining journey downstairs. *I had no idea you were so creative, my queen.*

Neither did I, she returned as we entered an elevator at the end of the hall. *But I really want him to die.*

Me, too, love. Me, too.

I needed to determine if the same could be said about my brother. He'd hurt Ismerelda, which had to be addressed. The problem was that I couldn't determine how to ensure it didn't happen again.

Other than to kill him.

Which a dark part of me longed to do.

However, he was my brother. My only kin. If I could find an alternative, I'd take it. I just feared there wasn't one.

Sleep obviously hadn't worked.

Nor would it work—a point Ryder and Kylan had readily made earlier this week.

So what alternative is there? I wondered as we reached a floor deep underground. I hadn't recognized the code

Michael had used to bring us here, confirming we were in a different part of the compound.

That fact became even more evident when the doors opened to resemble a crimson hallway lit by gothic-looking candles.

Wow. Talk about stereotypical vampire, Ismerelda said.

Stereotypical? I echoed, not following her logic. Only, her memories of a more modern era—one I didn't recognize or remember—helped fill in the gaps. *I see.*

It didn't feel *stereotypical* to me so much as dark and deadly. The crimson color reminded me of blood.

Which was a theme that continued as we entered a large room decorated with red and black fixtures.

Instead of a table, there were leather couches adorned with gold accents. Coffee tables made of glass and stone. Candles flickering with low flames. Scantily clad humans in every corner.

And a group of ancient vampires and lycans lounging about, some with females in their laps, others with men on their knees.

All the royals donned suits and dresses, while the lycans wore jeans and sweaters.

"King Cam," Michael announced to the room, causing me to glance at him as he bowed.

My brother stood, tossing a human to the floor, her head landing with a thud that suggested she was either already dead or close to it.

The gash on her breast told me why, as did the blood on my brother's lips. He licked them clean and excused Michael with a flick of his wrist. "Go help Mira."

"As you wish, My Prince," he uttered reverently, leaving the room while Cane wandered to a naked man holding a tray of champagne flutes and a bloody knife.

Michael called him "my liege" on the plane, Ismerelda

informed me. *I know he explained it back in the suite, but it still feels sudden to me.*

Yes, I agreed, taking in the room once more. *Either they're playing with me, or my brother believes I've already accepted my role as king.*

No one seemed all that intrigued by our appearance. Hell, most of them hadn't even noticed my arrival, too lost in their feeding frenzies to care.

If I am their king, they're not very respectful, I remarked to Ismerelda as Cane started back toward us with two glasses in his hands.

From what Luka told me, the royals and alphas all consider themselves to be equals. So their ignoring you doesn't confirm anything.

Hmm.

"Brother," Cane greeted, handing me one of his crystal glasses. The liquid inside appeared to be fresh blood from the human waiter's wrist—something I gathered because the male now appeared ashen and ready to pass out. Yet he remained standing as though compelled to do so. "Sorry for the alarm. It appears we're expecting company."

"So I heard," I murmured, my grip tightening around Ismerelda's hand while my other hand held the flute. "Lycans?"

He nodded. "Yes, my source says they're gathering. There are a few rebellious royals on their way, too." His tone suggested excitement rather than dread, something that didn't bode well for the situation. "I've been waiting for a chance to test our defense system, and it seems that chance has finally arrived."

"I don't recall seeing any logs on this *defense system,*" I told him.

"No, we didn't reach that point in the learning process. I had you focused on immortal blood bags instead, hoping to re-create the joy I'd experienced upon perfecting the solution." He glanced at the mortals on display throughout the room, his pride evident.

Ismerelda didn't comment beside me, but her mind was whirring with discomfort. Primarily because of my taunt just hours ago, as well as the comments I'd once exchanged with Mira.

I'm not replacing you.

I know, she replied instantly. *I won't let you.*

I released her hand to palm her lower back, the move drawing her closer to me.

My brother eyed the movement with interest.

"I assume we're all here to receive a tutorial on this defense system," I said, drawing Cane's focus back to the topic at hand.

"No, just you," he murmured. "The others are simply enjoying the playroom. Only you and I will review the city's security, as it's ours, not theirs."

"I see." My thumb traced a circle against Ismerelda's spine as I took in the room once more, noting all the pleased royals and alphas. "Is the alarm an indicator that it's unsafe above ground?"

I was trying to determine the reason he'd invited them all to his *playroom.* If it wasn't for a schematics demonstration, then he had another motive. Perhaps one that involved me and my *Erosita.* Or just me.

A show of force, as it were. A way of saying, *These are my allies, so you had better behave.*

"The alarm only sounded in your suite; everyone else was already underground. They prefer to be secure while they play, primarily because they don't want to be interrupted. But I invited them here to see you."

My eyebrows lifted. "They don't appear to be all that interested in my arrival."

He shrugged. "They're otherwise engaged, but as they

finish, I expect them to say hello. They've been waiting for this opportunity for a long time."

"Opportunity?" I repeated.

"To observe the results of my experiment." When I just stared at him, he added, "In curing you, I mean."

Ismerelda made a noise via our mental bond, one that sounded a lot like a derisive snort. Yet she remained outwardly submissive, her eyes downcast in a way she knew Cane would appreciate.

Unfortunately, *I* didn't appreciate it.

Fuck, I didn't appreciate any of this.

But we had our roles to maintain.

Roles we couldn't ignore. Especially now. *Lycans and royal vampires are coming. Cane has a source. Who?*

The communication unit is still silent, Ismerelda replied. *Either I didn't put it in right, or they've cut off our transmission.*

I suspected it was off because Damien and the others had figured out that I'd lost the microphone.

Or Cane was running interference somehow.

Perhaps his security demonstration would explain it.

My brother cleared his throat. "I can ask them to leave," he offered, obviously interpreting my silence as irritation. Only, my irritation wasn't directed at our audience so much as this situation.

"As long as they don't interfere with our business, they can stay and play," I told him. "But I want a thorough tour of your defense system."

"Of course," he agreed. "I'll provide one shortly. We just need the pieces in place first."

I frowned, not sure what he meant by that.

"In the interim, can I interest you in tasting one of my immortal toys?" he gestured to the array of flesh on display throughout the room.

"I have what I need at the moment, but perhaps I'll

take you up on that after the security demonstration," I replied, eliciting another mental snort from Ismerelda. "Maybe you can tell me more about this source of yours while we wait for your *pieces* to fall into place."

"All in due time, I promise," he murmured, grinning. "Go find a seat first. Relax a bit. It's going to be at least twenty minutes before we can begin, so feel free to drink your blood champagne, have a snack, observe. Whatever you desire, brother. All of this is yours."

He took a sip of his own champagne then and wandered out of the room, leaving me and Ismerelda in the middle of a sexually charged feeding frenzy.

Your brother is a lunatic, Ismerelda thought at me as I flexed my palm against her lower back. *A raving mad lunatic.*

He's immortal, I returned while surveying the room for a place to sit. *And very, very old.*

So are you, yet you're not throwing a fucking orgy while preparing for… for whatever the hell it is he's planning to do.

When you're our age, you process time and threats differently. He sees this as entertaining, I replied as I began guiding her toward a leather couch near the back of the room. *He's obviously been very bored.*

Not that I considered boredom to be an acceptable excuse—I merely meant to offer an explanation. Or, at least, the only reason I could fathom for his behavior.

He'd been betrayed, yes. But this went far beyond revenge or a need to ensure the safety of our kind.

Time to play, my queen, I murmured into her mind as my palm left her spine.

She paused as I took over the center of the couch.

"Straddle me," I said aloud, my voice underlined with authority.

We had a show to put on.

And fortunately, my mate more than understood her role.

She slipped onto my lap, her dress parting up both legs almost to her hips as she settled on my thighs.

I fisted her hair with one hand, then used my other to place the glass at my lips. Holding her gaze, I took a sip and allowed her—and everyone else—to see the disgust in my features.

"Definitely not what I'm craving," I muttered, setting it on the end table before sinking my fangs into her neck.

She clung to my shoulders, her thighs squeezing mine as I took several deep pulls from her vein.

"*Much* better," I told her, wincing as the taste of the other human's blood lingered in my mouth. I'd only taken a sip to pacify my brother. And now I was making a statement—*nothing and no one can replace my* Erosita. *So don't fucking touch her.*

Ismerelda arched into me, her pleasure cascading around us as I imbibed her essence. It provided the perfect cover for me to observe the room, to glance at the other royals as I devoured my mate.

The others would see my move as a detached one—just a vampire enjoying his meal while taking in the scene.

In reality, I meant it as a proprietary move. A way of publicly claiming my *Erosita*.

It also allowed me to evaluate each and every attendee.

Helias.

Robyn.

Ayaz.

Jenkins.

No sign of Thida or Jasmine.

Perhaps they were in their private rooms, wherever those were in this part of the underground. I'd never been in this area before, leaving me slightly uncertain as to what exactly my brother had in store.

He'd said the royals had all wanted to see me.

Definitely a lie, I decided, taking in their sensual antics.

Robyn was playing with two males, her long, manicured fingers wrapped around one of the men's throats as he fucked the other human beneath him.

Helias was a bit tamer, his eyes closed as a female knelt between his thighs.

Ayaz, well, he'd always been a sadistic fuck, and it seemed time had only worsened his penchants.

I'm glad I'm facing you, Ismerelda whispered via our bond.

Me, too, I admitted as I pulled my lips away from her neck. The mark I'd left earlier was once again fresh, denoting her as mine.

"Kiss me," I told her out loud. "I want to feed from your tongue."

A lie.

I intended to make her feed from mine.

Because I fully expected her to soon need every bit of immortal strength I could give her.

Ismerelda leaned into me, her mouth sealing over mine as she accepted my tongue. My kiss. My *brutality.* Because I didn't go easy on her. I tightened my hold in her hair and fucking devoured her.

Drink, I commanded in her mind. *Something is about to happen, and I need you to be as strong as possible. Fuck, if I could, I would turn you right here and now.*

But that wasn't possible. We needed time, blood, and a grave to make that happen.

I would agree, too, she responded, nearly causing me to break our kiss. Mostly because I hadn't expected her to say that.

You would?

Yes. And not just because of this situation. I... I'm tired of being weaker *in every situation. But it's more than that. It just... The idea feels right.*

I could hear her processing the pros and cons, this debate one she'd been considering since I'd first mentioned turning her.

There was definitely still some hesitation, primarily where our bond was concerned and how we would drink blood, but she seemed to favor the idea of being my vampire queen. Of being my true equal.

You're already my equal, I told her.

Not physically, she replied. *Not—*

Cane collapsed onto the couch beside me, interrupting my moment with Ismerelda. "It seems our rebels have arrived sooner than expected," he informed me.

He pulled up a translucent screen from a small disk in his hand, the device reminding me a bit of Khalid's technology.

Could he be the source? I wondered.

That... that wouldn't make sense. Damien went to Blood City. He saw the humans living peacefully among the vampires, Ismerelda replied. *Why would Khalid build such a place while allying with your brother?*

I don't know, but I intend to find out. I ran my fingers through her hair, thus releasing her silky strands from my fist. Then I placed a final kiss on her mouth and looked at Cane.

"You have my attention," I told him.

"Excellent." He grinned, his screen multiplying until nearly a dozen of them swirled around us, all of them depicting various surveillance feeds. "Welcome to my version of the future, brother. Let's proceed..."

IZZY

Cane might be a lunatic, but he was a brilliant lunatic. That much became clear after his ten-minute tutorial on the city surveillance and all the security mechanisms he had in place.

"You can see here," he was saying, gesturing at an image of an exterior door that I assumed led to the underground. "We have cameras embedded in the cement siding. But they do more than watch. They detect movement and…"

He trailed off as another screen appeared with a blazing red film over it.

"Ah, perfect timing. Here. You can see an actual demonstration." He selected the crimson image and brought it to the front of the others, causing the color to vanish. "This is what happens when the city's security protocols are engaged. The detectors come alive and react to movement, sound, and body heat."

He started showing his brother the logistics, explaining how the detector was programmed, all while I watched from beside Cam.

Cane didn't seem to notice me. Or maybe he just didn't care that I was watching. Because he hadn't looked at me once, not even when I'd moved off of Cam's lap.

"See these heat signatures?" Cane said, pointing at an infrared image showing five reddish-colored shadows. "Those are some of the incoming rebels. Although, it seems they're separating…"

Three more screens populated the air before us, Cane's hands immediately reacting to bring them into view.

"The system automatically scans the intruders, detecting their origin and even their name, if they're a known entity in the system." He drew one of the feeds into the center, leaving the others at the back, and touched one of the red blurs. "Identify."

"Vampire," a feminine voice said. "Name: Khalid. Age: over four thousand. Allegiance: uncertain. Please update system preferences regarding lethal force."

"No lethal force allowed," Cane replied before placing his finger against the other figure on the display. "Identify."

The screen blinked. "Female vampire. Age: unknown. Blood type: unknown. Origin: unknown. Name: unknown."

Emine, I guessed.

Cane's nostrils flared. "Fucking slayer bitch."

I nearly frowned. *How does he know that?*

I'm guessing his source *told him*, Cam replied, his interest piqued. However, he remained silent as his brother pulled up Emine's profile on the computer.

Cane selected a button beneath a fuzzy image of

Emine and said, "Activate lethal force for the unknown vampire."

"Lethal force protocols activated," the system returned.

My blood went cold.

Oh, shit...

The profile turned black, a countdown starting. "Ten, Nine..."

Cam, I started.

But he was already reaching for the same button. "Deactivate lethal force for the unknown vampire." His English tones sounded exactly like his brother's, the two of them far too similar for comfort.

"Lethal force protocols deactivated," the system replied, clearly agreeing that their voice signatures were the same.

Or maybe Cam already had administrative access.

Unless that wasn't required at all in this mode.

"What the fuck?" Cane demanded. "She can't be allowed to enter."

"She should absolutely be allowed to enter," Cam returned. "I want blood samples before you kill her. And I want them taken from a live source."

Cane stared at him, his jaw clenching.

Cam merely gazed back at him, that arrogant eyebrow of his arched upward. "She's an excellent test subject."

"I already perfected the immortal blood bags, brother."

"That remains to be seen," Cam replied flatly. "I'll need time to test your product. Until then, I want the slayer alive in case she can be of use to us. Surely your system has some way to detain her?"

I swallowed, both fascinated and mortified by the inner workings of Cam's mind.

His strategic processing of the situation was practically immediate, his ability to handle his brother and counter his words bordering on extraordinary. Especially the way he'd ended his response by essentially daring his brother to prove his system's capabilities.

But the reason Cam was so good at this verbal sparring match was founded in his deep understanding of Cane's goals.

A part of Cam respected his brother's desires, even partially agreed with his choices.

Keeping Emine alive made sense to Cam, and not because of any ties or loyalty he felt toward Khalid, but because her existence intrigued him.

Which meant he'd been telling the truth about wanting her blood. Or, at the very least, thinking about what he could do with it in a research setting.

Thinking about something and acting on something are two entirely different actions, Ismerelda, Cam murmured into my mind. *Just because I have an inkling to do something, doesn't mean I actually want to do it.*

He was right.

But I certainly didn't enjoy hearing those ideas in his head.

However, I preferred to know than not to know. To be included in his thought process instead of locked out. To maintain an open dialogue and have an opinion on how we proceeded rather than being left behind for my own "protection."

"Yes," Cane finally said. "The protocols allow for a variety of responses. I'll show you."

Cam waved him on. "Please do. But keep her alive."

Cane considered him for another moment, then conceded with a nod. "Fine. But I want to be the one to end her."

Cam shrugged. "I don't care how she dies. I just don't want to waste a potentially useful product."

The careless tone caressing Cam's words seemed to pacify his brother, because he nodded a second time.

And the room... appeared to relax as well.

I hadn't realized it, my attention more on Cam's mind than on the other vampires, but everything had gone quiet while the two men had been speaking.

Cam had noticed, but he'd been more focused on his brother than on the others. Although, now I could hear him scoffing at Cane's earlier comment about how everyone had wanted to *observe* his experiment.

They're not here to welcome me as their leader. They're here to make sure I'm on their leader's side.

What happens if they find out you're not? I wondered.

Only time will tell, he replied. But his mind was already identifying all the potential responses, and most of them were deadly. *He invited them all here for one of two reasons—to host a celebration or to host an execution. It can only go one way or the other.*

Thus, this was all a test.

A way to see how Cam responded to his brother's demonstration.

And the royals—as well as the one alpha present—were entertaining themselves while they waited.

But one wrong move, and we'd suddenly find ourselves facing off with some of the oldest supernaturals in the world.

I wouldn't stand a chance against them. Not as a human. Not even as Cam's mate.

His offer to turn me rolled around in my thoughts as Cane rearranged all the video displays. I'd meant what I'd said a bit ago about accepting Cam's proposal to make me a vampire.

It would afford me a semblance of independence,

something I'd never truly experienced in my very long existence.

I'd be free of my ties to Cam's immortality, able to survive on my merits, and become my own person. Live for me and no one else.

Then I could *choose* my future. Become a better version of myself. *Embrace this Cam as my mate.*

You won't be a better version, Ismerelda. You'll still be who you are now, just more durable. You're perfect. But I also need to focus, Cam whispered via our bond, his palm finding my thigh beneath the fabric of my dress. *And you're distracting me, my queen.*

Sorry. I hadn't realized how loudly I'd been thinking, or how much I'd distracted myself.

Because Cane was in the middle of a full-on demonstration, his video showing a clear view of Khalid and Emine as they headed into what appeared to be a tunnel.

He also had a second image up of Ryder and Willow, the two of them cautiously climbing to the top of a building. Knowing Ryder, he was going to use this as a teaching moment for Willow.

But this wasn't the time for a training exercise.

However, Ryder wouldn't understand that.

Because he has no idea what Cane's capable of, I thought, dread causing my stomach to tighten.

Cam squeezed my thigh subtly as he asked Cane something about a neutralizer.

What neutralizer? I wondered, nearly shaking my head. I'd been so lost in my inner musings that I'd clearly missed a hell of a lot.

"It's similar to what was used on you," Cane explained. "Only it doesn't require as much fine-tuning, as it's a temporary destabilizer rather than a long-term healing tool."

Healing tool, Cam repeated mentally, his tone telling me how he felt about the term his brother had coined for the weapon he'd used to subdue him.

"It'll activate automatically if the rebels reach a certain point in the tunnels. Or we can manually flip the switch now." Cam selected a box that brought up a panel display. "What's your preference?"

"How far into the tunnel do they need to go for it to initiate?" Cam asked.

"Another half mile, which won't take them long if they—"

The screen turned red, an alarm sounding from the device in his hand. Or maybe it was coming from his watch. I couldn't tell. It wasn't a loud blaring noise so much as a subtle beep, like a timer alert.

It seemed rather gentle in nature and quite at odds with the scene unfolding on the display—a scene I could now see very clearly. Because the red film had disappeared and a high-resolution video was left in its place.

Khalid and Emine grabbed their heads, their lips parted in clear agony.

I fought the urge to react to the visual, my stomach clenching even harder at the sight of them running from the invisible assault on their senses.

No, not running. *Phasing.*

Because they were moving far too fast for it to be considered a standard run. However, the camera seemed to be following their movements with ease.

This technology was terrifying.

But not nearly as terrifying as watching Khalid go to his knees.

He was one of the oldest beings of vampire kind. Just like Cam and Ryder and all the vampires in this room.

To take him down... My throat worked. *Cane wasn't lying when he said this* neutralizer *is similar to the weapon he used on you.*

"So you've found a way to incapacitate multiple vampires at once," Cam said, a note of intrigue in his voice. I knew from his mind that it was a false note, one he'd manufactured to appease his brother.

"Vampires *and* lycans, yes," his brother murmured. "It's a sound frequency that quite literally blows the mind. But with how fast we heal, it can be challenging to maintain. Which is why we do this..."

He flipped some sort of switch that revealed a wider view of the tunnel, one that allowed us to watch as four figures arrived at the scene. All of them were dressed from head to toe in black body armor, their heads covered in opaque helmets.

Each of them drew a gun, their barrels pointed at Emine and Khalid.

Cam opened his mouth to speak, but the weapons fired before he could comment.

Khalid and Emine instantly dropped to the ground.

My lips tightened as the cloaked figures swooped in to retrieve the bodies, their movements abrupt and without care as they picked up Khalid and Emine.

Then they all promptly disappeared from the scene.

Cane pressed a finger to his ear, the concealed technology reminding me of the silent device in my own ear. "Take Khalid to suite seven," he said. "The slayer can go to dungeon three." He glanced at Cam. "I'll give you a proper tour of the area once we're done."

"How much of the compound have I actually seen?" my mate asked.

"Approximately half. Your elevator was originally programmed to only display certain floors. Once we're done determining our future, we'll reprogram your access."

Cam stared at him. "What is there to determine?"

"Where you want to stay." Cane finally looked at me, his hard gaze glittering with dark anticipation. "*Who* you'll stay with." He returned his attention to Cam. "She just needs to live for you to maintain access to her mind. Nothing more."

Cam's palm slid up my leg, his fingertips brushing my inner thigh. "Oh, there's definitely more, brother." His tone and action made his insinuation clear.

"Hmm, but that more can evolve, and that's when things become dangerous. Perhaps I should demonstrate."

That sounded ominous.

But Cam simply cocked his brow. "Isn't that the point of all this? To provide a demonstration?"

Cane grinned. "Indeed it is. And on that note…" He called forward one of the surveillance feeds, this one showcasing only one heat signature.

A heat signature that the system identified as Cedric, according to the profile hovering beside it.

"Seems he's heading to the airport," Cane mused. "Must be expecting company."

"Or maybe he's trying to reach Damien," Cam replied.

"Perhaps." He studied the video for a moment. "We'll deal with him in a bit."

"Is that what you said when I left?" Cam asked him. "That you'd handle me later? Because obviously you could have stopped me before I reached the city's perimeter, and likely even then."

"Yes, I could have, but I hadn't realized you'd left until you were already acquiring a car. This system only activates when we're expecting a security threat. That protocol wasn't engaged when you left."

"And if it had been engaged?" Cam pressed. "What threat level am I noted as? Lethal force? Neutralize on sight?"

Cane scoffed at that and clicked his device. "Show King Cam's profile," he instructed the system.

"King Cam's profile," the feminine voice replied. "Status: administrator. Authorization: full system access."

Cam scrutinized the information. "So you would have let me leave."

"Of course."

"Yet you kidnapped my *Erosita* to force my return." Cam's flat tone masked his agitation. "Seems extreme."

"Some might consider it a valuable test."

Cam grunted. "To what? See if I'm cured or not?"

"Yes." Cane brought up the third feed showing two other heat signatures. "And I'm going to demonstrate why."

CAM

I drew my thumb along Ismerelda's inner thigh as I observed my brother's presentation.

Ryder and Willow.

They'd scaled the side of a building near the compound and appeared to be engaged in some sort of sniper lesson.

I yawned, bored.

"All I see is Ryder engaging in his version of foreplay," I deadpanned. "I'm not much of a voyeur, Cane. That was always your preference, not mine."

Hence the playroom, I thought to myself. This was exactly the kind of space my brother would enjoy.

Because he could watch the others fuck.

Cane's lips twitched. "I'm just waiting for the mutt unit to confirm they're ready."

"Mutt unit?"

"The lycans you saw earlier," he explained. "The ones who grabbed Khalid and his bitch. They're the mutt unit. They're like glorified guard dogs who also know how to retrieve."

When I didn't comment—mostly because I was processing that information, as well as the derogatory tone my brother had just used—he told the system to display the mutt unit.

"See," he said, pointing to five bare-chested men on the screen. They appeared to be pulling on black bodysuits. "Those collars control them. They also create a protective helmet, one I'm waiting for them to engage before I continue our demonstration."

"Are these the lycans Thida and Jenkins brought with them?" I asked, recalling what my vampire driver had said.

Cane snorted. "No. Those mutts need to be broken and tamed. And only a few of them will be given the privilege of joining the mutt unit. The others will go to the labs."

Jenkins visibly stiffened in my peripheral view, the dark-haired alpha obviously overhearing my brother's crude words.

However, Cane appeared to be oblivious to the lycan's outward response. Perhaps because it could have been the result of the female on his lap. Or, more likely, because my brother just didn't care.

Cane clearly believed lycans were lesser beings. While they weren't immortal like vampires, they certainly possessed their own strengths and abilities. To attempt to *break* or *tame* them was a mistake.

Alas, engaging in that debate with Cane would only distract him at this point.

And I really didn't want to prolong this *demonstration*.

I needed every detail he could give us in regard to his

security schematics. Primarily because he'd just essentially informed me that Izzy and I couldn't simply leave.

He'd know. And while the profile he'd shown me might have depicted me as a system administrator, I strongly suspected he could change my status with a simple command.

"Yes, you're free to engage," Cane said, his finger at his ear as he watched the wolves on the screen touch their collars. "Capture, not kill. Affirmative."

Helmets materialized out of thin air, the opaque material covering their faces.

"What's it made out of?" I wondered, curious about the technology.

"It's similar to these displays, only more durable," my brother explained as he flicked away the video of the wolves and pulled up Ryder and Willow once more. "Think of it like an electronic shield that also happens to be bulletproof. Very useful. All the mutts have them. Particularly for this reason, though."

He pressed a button on the bottom of his console, the action bringing up a series of command keys. I quickly scanned them, my eyebrows lifting. "These are all attack codes."

"Yes, they are," my brother murmured, selecting the one labeled *Neutralize Lycans*. "We have underground shields that protect everyone from these frequencies, but above ground…" He trailed off as he minimized the command console to show Willow cringing on the rooftop. "Above ground, they're not protected."

Ryder hovered over his mate, his concern palpable as he attempted to determine the cause of her distress.

He lifted her into his arms in the next moment and jumped off the roof, then phased.

The camera followed him the whole way, the

impressive technology streaming the events in real time. It almost felt as though I were phasing right along with them.

It absolutely rivaled Khalid's technology, yet my brother taking the royal into custody proved Khalid wasn't the source. *So who is?* I wondered as Ryder hunkered down with Willow.

She seemed to be coming to her senses. Or she was at least in less agony than before, anyway.

My brother pulled up the control panel again, selecting a volume-like icon that he slid upward. "This expands the radius," he said as he moved it about halfway up.

When he showed Willow and Ryder once more, it quickly became evident that she was experiencing the *neutralizer* again.

"What exactly is it doing?" I asked him.

"The electronic pulses attack the group psyche section of a lycan's mind. The frequency creates a sound that echoes in their heads, making movement and thought impossible. It debilitates them, thus *neutralizing* the threat." He glanced at me. "It's similar to what I used on Khalid and his bitch, only designed to impact lycans instead of vampires."

"I see." So he'd created a weapon to *tame* all of lycan kind.

Jenkins was still stiff in my peripheral vision, his jaw clenched. This time, I was certain it had nothing to do with the woman on his lap because she wasn't moving at all. In fact, I was pretty sure he'd already killed her. She was too still. Eerily so.

If he doesn't approve, then why is he here? I wondered. *What benefits is my brother—*

"See how distracted he is?" Cane asked, interrupting my thoughts. "He's so focused on Willow that he hasn't even noticed the approaching mutt unit." He gestured to where the lycans were creeping up on Ryder via a nearby alleyway.

In the next moment, Ryder phased, almost as though he'd heard my brother.

Only it'd obviously been him sensing the lycans.

However, it hadn't been enough of a distance, because a gun fired a second later, the bullet piercing Ryder's skull and sending him to the ground.

Cane shook his head. "One of the oldest of our kind and he's taken down by a trained dog. Why? Because he was *distracted*." He looked at me. "*This* is why having a mate is a weakness, brother. I realize she's your connection to your past, but that's all she can be. We can't afford to have you distracted anymore. Not if you want to lead."

"I never said I wanted to lead," I told him flatly. "But I concede your point." Because he wasn't wrong. Ryder should not have been so easy to defeat. Same with Khalid. Although, it remained to be seen what Emine actually meant to him.

Still, my brother was playing with fire.

He had no idea how impactful a mate bond could be or how violent Ryder—and possibly Khalid—would be once they regained consciousness. Fury was a strong motivator. And possessive instincts made that fury burn so much hotter.

A furious royal was a dangerous one.

Same with a furious lycan, I thought, noting Jenkins again. He still hadn't moved.

Yet no one seemed to notice.

He was an insignificant being in this room full of vampires. A lost piece of the puzzle.

"Take Ryder to suite seven to join Khalid," Cane said, presumably to his *mutt unit*. "The hybrid can go to dungeon four."

Hybrid, I thought, repeating the term. *I'm assuming his source told him that, too.* Because I highly doubted Ryder had made that information public.

Cane minimized the screens on display with a click of his finger, the space around us no longer littered with technical specs and surveillance feeds.

"The hybrid should make for interesting research," he informed me. "Far more interesting than the slayer."

"We won't know until we conduct our studies," I replied, easily playing his game. My brother had always been a strategic genius. However, he possessed one fatal flaw—his desire to impress me.

It made him easier to read.

He might be cold inside, but his eyes lit up whenever I uttered phrases that suggested I was his ally rather than his enemy. *We. Us. Our.* They were all just words that placated his ego, confirming I liked what he'd created.

And part of me did.

I could admire the brilliance of his scheming. He'd not only enslaved humankind but also convinced the lycans to partner with him. All while actually treating the wolves as second-class citizens.

The way he'd devised the annual Blood Day celebrations to give equal resources to both lycans and vampires was also well crafted. He'd essentially presented us all as equals, yet our kind were the ones benefiting the most from this arrangement.

However, I suspected he hadn't put much thought into how the lycans might react to this discovery. Sure, he'd developed a weapon that might protect the city, but for how long?

It was a temporary nullifier.

"How do you plan to neutralize the lycans? And do we know how many are coming?" I asked him, wanting more details on how this weapon of his would operate against this pending attack.

"It's a funny thing, actually," he murmured after flicking his fingers together to grab a nearby blood slave's attention. "During the test phase, I upped the volume to max capacity and left it there for about an hour. The lycan lost his mind. Quite literally."

He chuckled at the memory, like it was an entertaining moment from his past.

"He had to be put down," Cane went on. "It seems that messing with supernatural wavelengths, like the *Erosita* bond and pack psyche, can cause permanent damage." He winced then, glancing at me just as the female blood slave arrived. "Like memory loss."

This time, I let him see some of my anger, just with a singular focused look. "You're saying you damaged my head like you did the lycan's. How fortunate that you didn't have to *put me down*."

"I was trying to cure you, brother. They're very different practices, I assure you. And I used the utmost care when handling your mind."

"How comforting," I deadpanned.

He sighed and grabbed the blood slave's slender arm in a bruising grip, then sank his fangs into the woman's wrist.

Charming, Ismerelda muttered.

I squeezed her thigh, letting her know I heard her.

The female trembled as my brother continued to drink, his intention clear. "Stay standing," he told her, compulsion underlining those two words.

If he was trying to elicit a response from me, he'd have to do something a lot worse.

Humans died every day.

To do so cruelly was just part of this world he'd crafted.

The woman's skin turned ashen as sweat beaded across

her brow. I watched with disinterest, giving my brother the attention he craved, while proving to him that I didn't care.

He'd wanted to cure me of my humanity, and I was letting him believe that he had.

But this had never been about *humanity*. It'd been about Ismerelda. She was my heart. My soul's anchor. Without her, I'd cease to care about anything at all.

Which meant the *cure* was her death.

And I suspected my brother knew that. I'd managed to thwart him by claiming my desire to obtain her memories, but that reason would only last for so long.

Who knew what kind of time limit he'd put on it? A day? An hour? A week?

I couldn't just sit here and wait to find out.

I also couldn't simply take Ismerelda with me and flee.

My brother had proved his intentions, his desires, loud and clear. He wanted me to lead alongside him, and if I wouldn't, he'd find a way to force my hand. Or at least attempt to. And *that* was the problem.

He had to be stopped.

We can't go on like this, I thought. His actions against the lycans would reflect on all of vampire kind.

The last thing I wanted was an army of wolves as an enemy.

Because not only would they blame vampires, they'd blame *me*. Cane was my brother. My *blood*. The wolves wouldn't want to punish just him, but everyone and anyone affiliated with his actions.

That included me.

And through me, Ismerelda.

Unacceptable, I thought, my jaw threatening to clench. *Cane has to—*

"Princess Hazel," Michael announced, causing my gaze to fly to the room's entrance.

And instantly lock with the familiar royal.

Because I'd just seen her hours ago in a room full of allies.

A room full of allies she's been betraying, I realized. *By informing on them to my brother...*

IZZY

HAZEL IS THE SOURCE KEPT REPEATING IN MY HEAD.

It was my only thought.

At least until I realized she wasn't alone.

Lily... I fought the urge to clasp my hand over my mouth, my mind instantly whirring with horror. Because Hazel had brought Lily here. To Cane's lair. *To a room full of sadistic royals.*

Oh, God... Cam... If they... I couldn't finish the sentence, my heart hammering in my chest.

Cam drew his thumb along my inner thigh, his body far more relaxed than I felt. He acted as though he wasn't surprised at all to see Hazel or Lily, his expression a perfect depiction of boredom while Cane stood to greet the other royal.

The human he'd been drinking from remained frozen on her feet, her head bowed, her limbs trembling.

I hate him, I thought. *I fucking* loathe *him.*

Cam didn't reply, his thumb still stroking my skin. He didn't echo my hatred. But he did seem to be contemplating this change in events, analyzing what it could mean and how best to proceed as Hazel started toward us.

Lily walked beside her, the picture of demure with her eyes cast down and hands loose at her sides.

"I would say I'm surprised by your arrival, but I'm not," Cam drawled. "Although, I am impressed by your acting abilities. You seemed genuinely shocked to see me the other day."

"Because I was," she replied with a smile, her gaze flicking to Cane. "*Someone* hadn't informed me that you were awake and roaming."

"I'd been a little busy, darling," Cane murmured. "But I'm so glad you're here now. Together, we should be able to set Khalid back to rights."

"Yes," Hazel agreed, appearing relieved. "Cedric, too."

Cane nodded, his gaze going to Lily. "I'd kill her now to make a point. Alas, we need her as bait."

"Bait?" Cam repeated. "Is this why you didn't send your pet lycans after Cedric?"

"Yes. I figured he would serve as my final presentation on why having a mate is a weakness. He's about to attempt to infiltrate a compound he knows nothing about—to save a human." He openly scoffed at the concept, like he couldn't fathom a reason anyone would do such a thing.

"Is your goal to convince me to kill my *Erosita?*" Cam asked, his thumb still caressing my inner thigh. "Because I thought you were trying to show me the security protocols you built, but it seems like you're more focused on what I intend to do with Ismerelda."

"I'm attempting to accomplish both, brother." Cane collapsed on the couch beside Cam again, his movements knocking the human female over in the process. He glanced down at her with disgust. "Michael."

"Yes, My Prince?"

I'd forgotten all about Michael until he spoke, his presence immediately sending a shiver down my spine. Fortunately, he was standing beside Hazel, so I couldn't see him.

"Take care of this blood slave for me." Cane gestured to the quietly sobbing female on the floor. "She's obnoxious."

"Of course, My Prince," Michael replied. His eyes caught mine as he appeared, his glittering emerald orbs promising violence.

I returned the glare.

Because fuck compliance.

I wasn't a *pet*.

And anyone who expected me to act like one had better think again.

Cam had told me to play the game. However, Cane had essentially just admitted that his goal was to have me killed.

So fuck whatever the hell this was supposed to be.

Cam's thumb paused against my leg, his palm squeezing slightly. *Your anger is intoxicating, love. But we're not ready to act yet.*

He was right. I knew he was right. But I wasn't sure how much longer I could just—

A sudden *snap* sent a shiver down my spine, the human limp on the ground. "Fond memories," Michael murmured, his gaze still on me as he lifted the now-dead human into his arms.

Cane chuckled.

Cam's hand tensed.

"Are you threatening my *Erosita*, Michael?" he asked, his voice low. "Because I wouldn't recommend it."

Silence fell, the others clearly listening to every word spoken in our area of the room.

"I don't know how many times I need to explain this, but she's the only link to my memories," Cam went on, his focus shifting to Cane. "Memories I can't access because of your *cure*. Until I'm done using her, she's not to be touched by anyone other than me."

"No one is touching her, brother."

"No, but you've made your position clear—my link to Ismerelda is a weakness. However, your actions are the reason that weakness needs to remain intact. So while I appreciate what you've shown me, it's a moot point. She's not my mate; she's my link to the past. She's also a good fuck."

Cane studied him for a beat before looking up at Hazel. "Thoughts?"

She lifted a shoulder. "From what I've observed, he's not the old Cam at all. As I mentioned to you already, he told the others he had no interest in leading their little rebellion. And he's been almost silent during their meetings."

That wasn't true.

Well, it was true. But it wasn't the full truth. Cam had denied his place the first day. Then he'd made it clear he would lead... for me.

However, Hazel had left that part out.

Why would she do that? I wondered.

"So why did you stay?" Cane asked, his attention back on his brother. "Why not come back here?"

"Come back to what, exactly?" Cam returned. "After gaining access to Ismerelda's memories, I learned I wasn't the liege and that everything was a fucking lie. So I stayed with the others to learn more about the last one thousand years of my life. How would I have even known to return here?"

All while Cam spoke, his mind was busy analyzing Hazel's intentions. *Is she trying to coax me into a lie? Playing a word game of some kind? Or is she playing Cane? Why offer him all the other details, but not this?*

Cane considered him for a long moment. "I suppose that's fair." He looked at Michael. "Is there a reason you're still standing here? I thought I asked you to remove the trash."

"Apologies, My Prince," Michael murmured. Then he bowed a little haphazardly with the dead woman in his arms and left the room.

"I suppose if he was all I knew from the compound, I wouldn't return either," Cane muttered to himself before shaking his head. "I apologize for how I've gone about this, Cam. I truly wanted to help you, not hinder you. But I realize now that I made some errors in judgment."

"Apology accepted," Cam replied, his body seeming to relax a little beside me even while his mind continued processing everything around him. "I assume we're waiting for the next phase now?"

"Indeed. Once Cedric arrives, we'll secure him with Khalid and Ryder and begin the process of curing them. Perhaps seeing the methods in action will give you a better appreciation of what I went through to fix you."

Highly doubtful, Cam thought. However, aloud he said, "Perhaps."

Cane smiled. "Good. You should stay and observe as well, Hazel. I know you're eager to help Khalid move on from this slayer mess."

Hazel snorted. "I thought it was bad when it was just a vampire fledgling. But to learn she's actually a slayer, too? That..." She trailed off, her jaw visibly clenching.

"Yes, I know," Cane growled. "We'll fix it, though. And once my brother finishes gathering his blood samples, we'll end her just like we ended Aurelia."

Hazel blinked. "Blood samples?"

"For potential experimentation," Cane explained as he glanced down at his wrist. "Cam suggested..." His brow furrowed, his words vanishing as he studied his watch.

Hazel glanced at her own wrist in the next second, her eyebrows also coming down.

The rest of the room seemed to do the same as well, even Jenkins.

"You scheduled an alliance meeting for thirty-six hours from now?" Robyn asked, her elegant tone a false representation of her character. "I thought we agreed on next week?"

"I didn't schedule anything." Cane enunciated each word clearly and concisely, his gaze narrowing with irritation. "This is obviously a prematurely sent message." He stood, his hand going to his ear. "Mira?"

It's starting, Cam whispered to me, his gaze locked on Hazel rather than his brother.

"Mira?" Cane repeated, a note of agitation underscoring her name.

"My Prince," Michael said as he ran into the room. "We have a problem."

"No shit." Cane started toward him. "A communication was sent—"

"The mutt unit hasn't returned," Michael interjected before Cane could finish. "And the system can't find them."

"What?" Cane clicked his device to bring up his array of screens. "Surely—"

The room went black, cascading silence over everyone and everything.

My heart skipped a beat.

Vampires and lycans could see in the dark. But I couldn't. Something Michael knew, as did every other predator in this room.

"Cam, if you can hear me, take Ismerelda and run," my twin suddenly said in my ear. "The lycans are coming. And they're not in a kind mood."

The hairs along my arms stood on end, fear choking me not because of my brother's words, but because of the very real potential that someone else had overheard them.

It was too quiet. Too *still*.

Until suddenly it wasn't quiet or still at all as growls echoed through the compound.

My neck prickled for an entirely different reason now.

My brother had said the lycans were coming.

But he was wrong.

The wolves are already here...

CEDRIC

Several Minutes Earlier

TALK TO ME, LITTLE FLOWER. IS CANE PROPERLY DISTRACTED?
I asked Lily as Damien dumped a bucket of water on
Ryder's head.

"I enjoyed that more than I probably should have,"
Damien mused, the royal unconscious at his feet.

If there was one thing I'd learned in the last five
minutes, it was that Damien clearly had a death wish.

Yes, Lily replied, my attention instantly returning to her.
He and Cam are discussing Ismerelda's fate.

Good. That meant he wasn't focused on Lily, which was
part of the plan.

A plan I'd conceptualized with Khalid and Hazel.
Only, Lily hadn't originally been part of it. That change
had been a concession for the lycans.

While Khalid had met with Ryder earlier, I'd hunted
down Luka.

"You're a hard wolf to find," I'd told him near the airfield. "But we need to talk."

The look he'd given me in return had said he'd rather shoot me instead.

However, I'd captured his attention when I'd added, "Khalid knows the truth about Mira. But she's not the only one pretending to support Cane's rule. Hazel is, too."

The former served as a way to inform Luka that Khalid and I knew a lot more than the others did.

And the latter was a truth Hazel and Khalid had given me permission to share. One that represented a peace offering of sorts.

Because Mira would likely know about Hazel's connections to Cane. He'd purposely arranged for the territories around Italy to belong to his allies. He'd been protecting his pet project.

Only that pet project had grown into something Hazel couldn't stomach.

She'd understood his need to kill slayers, as she'd apparently been there when Aurelia had betrayed him. But she felt he'd taken his quest for global domination too far. His treatment of the lycans was her primary sore point. She saw it as a betrayal to the species, and she couldn't forgive it.

Of course, she hadn't been pleased to learn about Emine, especially since Khalid had waited until this week to reveal that information in front of Hazel and the others.

But she was very familiar with Khalid's proclivity for testing loyalties and reading reactions.

He'd needed to be sure of Hazel's truths, and her response to Emine had proved she could let go of the past —something Cane appeared to be incapable of doing.

Luka hadn't asked me to elaborate on any of that, though. Instead, all he'd done was say, "I'm listening."

I hadn't bothered with formalities or long-winded speeches. I'd told him my plan, laying out every detail. Including the fact that Khalid was in the process of recruiting Ryder. "But he's not telling him everything. Khalid doesn't trust easily. He needs to see how Ryder performs first."

It was a penchant of his—like his loyalty tests—that irritated the fuck out of me. But I couldn't deny how well it worked.

"Your plan has a flaw," Luka had finally said after several minutes of processing my idea.

"What is it?" I'd asked, open to suggestions.

"What's your stake in all of this?" he'd countered. "I get Khalid's stake—he and Emine are likely going to be captured. Perhaps Ryder and Willow, too. That gives them something to fight for. But you're just going to what? Find Damien while Hazel waltzes into the underground with a wire?"

"It's not a wire but a transmitter," I'd corrected him. "It'll allow us to hack into Cane's mainframe, something I need to do with Damien outside of the compound. Which means I can't join Khalid and Ryder."

"No, you can't," he'd agreed. "But your *Erosita* can."

I'd blinked at him. "Excuse me?"

"If you want us to cooperate with you, we need to establish trust. Which means we need you to have a stake in this—a stake we can all understand and appreciate. That would be your mate."

"You're asking me to put my mate in danger… as some sort of loyalty test?" I'd demanded, furious at the very concept.

"Yes."

No elaboration.

No room for deliberation.

Just an emphatic *yes*.

Lily had sensed my fury, her mind instantly caressing mine as she'd whispered, *I'll do it.*

Like hell you will.

But when I'd regrouped with Khalid and relayed the terms to him, he'd nodded and said, "That's actually brilliant. We know Cane has eyes everywhere in the city, which means he could potentially stop you before you're able to reach Damien. But if Hazel tells him she's coming with Lily, he'll leave you alone. Because he'll turn her into bait."

"Or he'll just kill her," I'd stressed. "Which isn't acceptable."

"He won't kill her," Hazel had interjected. "He's too much of a showman for that. I agree with Khalid—he'll use her as bait. But let me call him first, give him our latest update, and say that I'll have Lily. Then I'll offer to finish her off on the jet first and see what he says."

Khalid and Hazel had ended up being right because Cane's immediate response to Hazel had been "Don't kill her. Bring her here. We'll use her to motivate Cedric. It'll double as a valuable lesson for my brother, too."

I'd finally conceded to the plan, mostly because it'd been the smart play. But that didn't mean I liked it.

Fortunately, my Lily was good at blending in and keeping her head down.

She was living proof that appearances could be deceiving, something she might have the opportunity to showcase today.

Damien brought over another bucket, the water from inside the airport hangar—where we had over a dozen hostages strung up and knocked out, thanks to the lycans.

"Now you're just being lazy," Damien drawled, his words for the royal on the ground.

"Maybe..." Willow trailed off. "Never mind."

"We don't have all night," Luka said. "If you can't wake him up, we'll go without him."

I checked my watch. "The others will be here in fifteen minutes."

He grunted. "We don't need them."

"No, we don't," I agreed. "But they're coming anyway."

Deirdre had found a jet for them to use—one she'd ordered from a nearby city—thus allowing the remaining vampire and lycan rebels to join us.

"The meeting invitation is ready," I added, trying to pacify Luka's growing impatience. "We just need to hit Send. Then it'll only take a few minutes to cut the power." Primarily because I'd already hacked into the system via Hazel's transmitter—it'd given me the backdoor access I needed to take the whole damn network down.

Security feeds, which I'd already subtly altered to hide our current activities at the airport.

Communication.

Watches.

Door locks.

Lights.

Collars.

Sensory weapons.

Everything.

Damien dumped the second bucket on Ryder, causing the royal to finally stir. "It was one fucking bullet," Damien told him. "One. Uno. Solitary. Sure, it went in your head. But you're fucking ancient. Wake—"

Ryder blurred into motion, his fist connecting with Damien's jaw a heartbeat later.

"What the fuck is going on?" Ryder demanded, his dark eyes searching for and landing on Willow. He immediately knelt beside her, his intense stare taking in every inch of her lithe form.

I understood that look.

Primarily because I'd given it to Lily countless times.

Cam just forgave Cane, Lily whispered, concern vibrating through our bond. *He also said he's using Izzy for her link to his memories and that she's not his mate.*

I considered that for a moment, my mind automatically placing myself in his shoes. *He's protecting her.* I knew that because it was what I would do in his situation. *He doesn't want Cane to know how much she means to him.*

I don't know, Lily said slowly. *He was pretty believable.*

Vampire politics are all about riddles and games, I reminded her. *You can never trust anyone's word.*

You trust Khalid.

Do I? I mused. *Or do I tolerate him?*

"We need to go now," Luka said, interrupting my mental conversation with Lily.

"Go where?" Ryder demanded. "Someone had better start explaining, and soon."

Damien touched his jaw, his golden irises swirling with amusement. "We've apparently partnered with the lycans to take down the compound. Welcome to the party."

Ryder's eyebrows shot up. "How long was I out?"

"Too fucking long," Damien drawled. "But these arrangements were made before the lycans shot you."

"Cane's pet lycans," I clarified before Ryder could react to that last bit. "Luka and the other alphas took out the unit that assaulted you. They're all tied up in the hangar. It remains to be seen whether or not their minds can be saved. That's also a conversation for another day." I looked at Luka. "Is your team in position?"

"Yes."

"Then we should begin," I agreed. "Damien?" His technical skills were superior to mine, something I openly acknowledged. I'd merely had the benefit of playing with Khalid's tech before—which I'd used to spy on Damien and the others. But now that Damien had access to the same instruments, we were playing on even ground, where he easily proved to be the expert.

"Who made these arrangements?" Ryder asked as he stood, pulling Willow up along with him.

"Khalid and Cedric," Damien replied, his gaze now on the computer schematics rather than on Ryder. "Message sent."

"What mess..." Ryder trailed off, his gaze flicking down to his wrist as said message scrolled across his watch. "This is related to all the crap you spewed at the meeting earlier?"

"The plan I presented to Jace and the others?" I rephrased. "Yes. But we've since escalated it."

"You mean you always intended to escalate it," Damien countered before looking at Ryder. "They only presented the political part of the idea to the others. Meanwhile, Cedric went to talk to Luka, and Khalid recruited you."

"He failed to mention we would be working with the lycans."

"Is that going to be a problem for you?" Luka asked, his tone indicating his annoyance. "Because I'm happy to leave you here."

"My problem is, I was not fully informed on the true nature of this mission," Ryder replied, his tone uncharacteristically flat. "As for the new objective, I'm absolutely not sitting this one out."

"Then stop complaining and let's go," Luka fired back. "You can take the nuances up with Khalid later."

"Oh, I will," Ryder said.

"Just as I imagine Jolene will take all of this up with you," Damien murmured, his words seeming to be for Luka.

Because apparently Luka hadn't informed the other alpha of our joint plans. From what I understood, he'd done it so Edon and his mates wouldn't find out.

It seemed there was a bit of a rift happening between the Clemente Clan triad and the other alphas. *Trust* was the heart of the issue, something I gathered was a result of Edon's mates having close relationships with the vampires.

Ironic, considering Luka himself had chosen to align with me and Khalid.

But I supposed he didn't want to risk anyone else finding out before we were ready to reveal our allegiances —temporary as they may be.

Because I wasn't naïve. I knew this alliance between us was short-term.

As soon as we completed this assignment, we would part ways. Indefinitely.

They know Ryder and Willow are not in custody, Lily told me, a hint of urgency in her tone.

"Time to go," I said before repeating what Lily had just said. "Cut the power."

Damien didn't comment, his gaze focused as he typed in the requisite commands. "All systems are officially offline. It'll take them hours to reboot."

"Let's move," Luka growled, his impatience evident in his tone and in the way he started toward the waiting truck —one he and a fellow alpha had commandeered from the human Vigils.

"Toys are in the bed," Damien informed Ryder as he followed the huffing lycan. "I'll give you first pick, see if that improves your attitude."

"I don't think my *attitude* is going to *improve* until I've killed a few people," Ryder bit back.

"Good thing we're heading into a bloodbath, then," Damien drawled. He pressed a finger to his ear and said, "Cam, if you can hear me, take Ismerelda and run. The lycans are coming. And they're not in a kind mood."

"Neither am I," Ryder growled.

"When are you ever in a *kind mood*?" Damien returned.

Ryder pressed a palm to his heart. "I'm kind to Willow every day."

Willow snorted, causing Ryder to look at her.

"Have something to say, pet?" he asked her.

I tuned out her answer, my focus instead shifting to Lily and the growing tension underground. *Are your contacts working?*

Yes, she whispered back to me. *The night-vision lenses are allowing me to see.*

Good, I replied. *Can you get close enough to Ismerelda to hand her the glasses?* Khalid had left a pair for Lily on the plane, the plan for her to try to get them to Cam's mate if she could.

We'd known Cane wouldn't even think to check Lily for any contraband, and even if he did, Hazel would just make a comment about Lily being human with poor eyesight.

Cam has her tucked into his side, Lily told me. *But I'm going to try.*

Good girl, I murmured. *Keep your head down, though. The lycans are coming.*

I can hear them.

Those are the test subjects Mira is working with, I told her, aware that Luka had been mentally communicating with his mate and keeping her apprised of our movements. *They're going to be vicious.*

I know where the grates are, she promised me. *I can see them.*

She also knew where to look because Mira had supplied us with the schematics of the room prior to Hazel and Lily venturing into the underground. She'd also provided similar details of the dungeon, but had Lily been sent there, Damien would have freed her with the unlocking of the cell doors.

Just like he'd already freed Emine.

And Khalid.

Everything was unlocked. Every door. Every entryway. Tunnel access. The stairwells. All of it.

Cedric… Lily's unease crept through our bond. *The wolves…*

They're not after you, I told her, my voice firm as I understood the trajectory of her thoughts. *You're not at the breeding camp, Lily. You're in the compound. They're coming for the vampires, not you.*

But they sound just… just like…

Focus, I commanded her, my mental tone leaving no room for her to even consider following someone else's orders, including her own. *Give Ismerelda the glasses, then find a place to hide. I'm coming for you.*

And if not me, then Khalid and Emine.

Lily's hesitation melted beneath a wall of determination as she forced herself to take charge. *I am* not *a weak flower.*

No. You're my *flower,* I told her. *And my flower is only delicate in appearance. She regenerates. She fights for her life. She's strong and she survives.*

I survive, she echoed. *I'm a survivor.* Resolve underlined her tone. *I can do this.*

You can, I agreed. *Now give Ismerelda the glasses and find the grate. It'll be unlatched.* Because that, too, was controlled by Cane's network.

While his system was impressive, he'd manufactured it

based on technology that Hazel had given him—technology that Khalid had purposely provided to her.

Which made us familiar with the security parameters and what could happen with a complete shutdown.

Khalid had backup plans in place for that.

Cane did not.

And he was about to learn what happened when one relied on a single method for protection. Just as he was about to learn what happened when you pissed off a wolf pack.

Or, in his case, *several* wolf packs.

The truck came to a stop just outside the old Vatican City walls. "Time to make it pour," I mused, my gaze catching Damien's, as I knew he would understand the reference.

"Blood rain," he murmured, his golden irises swirling with amusement. "My kind of party."

"Good thing you're invited to join this time."

"Good thing," he echoed, hopping out of the truck bed. "Let chaos reign…"

"Cheers to that," I agreed, following him. *Ready for a little hide-and-seek, Lily?*

Only you would turn this into a game, she muttered back to me.

You hide. I seek.

And then?

I didn't answer her. She knew what would happen next. I'd *claim*. Because no one took my mate from me. Least of all a mad royal with a mating complex.

Lily was mine.

I'd find her. I'd protect her. And I'd kill everyone in my path.

Howls reverberated in the evening air, dusk having fallen over the city.

But those howls weren't coming from outside. They were coming from the earth. Because the battle below had started.

This is the beginning of the end.
May the Blood Alliance fucking burn…

IZZY

Goose bumps pebbled down my bare arms, the howling growing louder with each passing second.

I couldn't see anything; I could only *hear*.

Growls.

Claws against metal.

Grinding echoes.

Damien's voice lingering in my ear.

I shivered. He'd been so loud. So clear. *Did the others hear him?*

No, Cam whispered back to me. *I couldn't hear it, so the vampires didn't either. I'm not sure about the lycans, though.*

I nearly sighed in relief at knowing Cane hadn't heard it. Except the last part of Cam's response wasn't comforting. *If—*

The slamming of a door cut off my mental reply, my entire body jolting in response to the sudden sound.

It'd been close. *Too* close.

Because it was the door to this room, I realized half a beat later.

Fuck. Being blind messed with my senses, leaving me unnerved. Every sound caused me to quiver. Every movement nearly made me jump.

We need to get out of here. My brother had told us to run. But where would we go? How would we leave? *We're trapped in a room full of ancient supernatural beings…*

"We need to build a barricade," someone said into the darkness.

Robyn, I guessed based on the elegant tone.

"Stack the couches and kill the humans," she went on. "We need all the weight we can gather."

"Surely Cane has a backup plan, yes?" a male voice countered, the thick accent likely belonging to Ayaz. He didn't normally communicate in English, his preference for Farsi well known.

"Does it look like he has a backup plan?" Robyn snapped.

"How long will it take the system to reboot?" Cane asked, ignoring them both.

"It depends on what's been done to it," Michael replied, his voice sending a chill down my spine. "Our previous difficulties were contrived; this is real."

"Contrived?" Cam repeated, picking up on the same word I had.

What does he mean by "contrived"? I wondered. *That the technical issues—the ones he'd blamed on me and Damien—were a lie? Was it just a way to weaken Cam's faith in me even more?*

"It was part of our experiment," Cane replied, his tone dismissive.

I could almost picture him waving it away with his hand, like it was no big deal.

Asshole, I thought. *You're a fucking monster.*

"Michael," Cane continued, completely oblivious to my anger. Because why would he care? I was a *human*. An *inferior*. A means to an end. And there was absolutely nothing I could do to change his opinion. "You need to go find Mira and figure out what's going on."

"But, My Prince, the wolves..." Michael trailed off, then cleared his throat. "Right. Yes. Of course I'll go."

"Then why are you still here?" Cane asked him.

"Apologies, My Prince," Michael said, his tone lacking his usual reverence.

Yet the door opened and closed, confirming he'd obeyed his master's orders.

I hope a lycan finds you and shreds you, I thought at him.

"The technical issues were fake?" Cam pressed, not dropping that part of the exchange. "All of it was a lie?"

"We'll discuss it later," Cane returned.

"Yes, preferably after we come up with a plan," Robyn interjected. "Such as *barricading the door*." Her tone turned to a screech as she uttered the words.

"Jesus Christ," one of the men muttered.

A scream followed.

Then another.

Furniture shifted.

Wind stirred through the air, causing my hair to tickle my ears.

Vampires phasing, I thought.

All of it was happening too quickly for my mind to process.

Seconds flew by, the room being rearranged at rapid speed. I could feel it, not see it, the sensation leaving me dizzy and nearly tumbling me to the floor.

Only for my arm to be caught in a vise, a hand ensnaring my neck.

My world froze.

Then I *did* fall.

Down... down...

My knees crashed into the ground, sending a harsh shock up my spine.

"*Fuck*," I wheezed, my throat aching from being squeezed. Fortunately, though, I could still breathe.

A furious growl reverberated around me, the sound almost as feral as the lycans approaching. Yet it came from a different sort of beast.

It came from Cam.

"Do not touch her," he snarled at whoever had attempted to choke me.

"She's human," someone replied.

Jenkins, maybe?

No, *Helias*, according to Cam's thoughts.

"She's mine," he bit out.

"Calm down, brother," Cane said, his tone underlined with a hint of demand. "We need her body. She'll wake up like the others. It'll be—"

A deafening howl pierced the air, the sound forcing me to cover my ears.

Because it was *loud*.

So loud that I swore it came from beside me.

Snarls swiftly followed.

Then liquid suddenly splattered across my face, making me gasp.

Warm. Wet. Sticky.

Blood, I recognized. *Oh, God...*

The world spun as someone—*Cam*—grabbed me by the waist and phased me elsewhere in the room.

Stay down, he demanded, releasing me.

I almost protested, mostly out of confusion, but something crashed over my head in the next instant, forcing me to remain.

Trembles traversed my spine as angry noises filled the room, words spewing in foreign tongues, accusations seeming to fly, and a very pissed-off Cane bellowing, "Quiet!"

"*No*," someone replied. "I'm fucking done being *quiet*." A low, rumbling sound caressed those words, betraying the identity to my senses. *Lycan.*

Jenkins, Cam confirmed.

Jenkins howled, I reiterated, the reality of that statement sending ice down my spine. *He just told all the lycans where we are in the compound.*

"You've spent twelve decades leashing and controlling my kind," he grated out. "Your reign ends today, Cane."

My lips parted. *Jenkins isn't Team Cane.*

No. It seems he's Team Lycan, Cam replied.

"Have you lost your fucking mind?" Cane demanded. "I've given you everything you've asked for, and you dare attack a royal? A fellow leader?"

Ayaz, I heard in Cam's mind. That'd been the source of the blood splatter.

"I granted you every privilege," Cane went on. "And *this* is how you thank me?"

"I *paid* for your version of a privilege by giving you members of my pack. What did these royals do to earn their *privileges*?" Jenkins demanded.

"They've supported my rule. Upheld the Blood Alliance. Kept my secrets." Cane's exasperation was a stifling presence in the room, one that seemed to create an undercurrent of palpable tension.

"As did I," Jenkins returned. "Yet I also had to give up

lycan lives. Watch you belittle them. Listen as you referred to my species as *mutts*."

"We all make sacrifices for greatness," Cane told him.

"You mean lycans make sacrifices for vampire greatness," Jenkins countered.

"So you make a point by throwing a tantrum and attacking a royal?" Cane demanded.

"No," Jenkins replied. "I'm going to make a point by killing one."

A crack disturbed the air, the abrupt sound followed by a loud thud.

Cam's mind told me what he'd just seen, yet I could barely believe it. Primarily because it was too insane to even imagine.

The *crack* had been Robyn's neck.

The *thud* had been her head falling to the floor.

The lycan had just ripped her apart in a blink, his claws easily slicing through her skin and his strength *snapping* her bones as though they were brittle shards.

"And I'm about to kill another one," Jenkins growled.

A roar followed, the source of it unknown. But it caused every fiber of my being to fire with alarm.

Chaos ensued, snarls and feral curses creating a savage cacophony that chilled me to my very core.

I felt trapped.

Alone.

Lost in the darkness. Defenseless. *Weak.*

And I hated it. Hated being human. Hated being unable to stand beside Cam and fight. Hated being *useless.* If only—

Something grabbed my wrist, causing my pulse to pound in my ears.

No, no! I thought, trying to yank my hand away.

Only, the person had a steel grip.

Shit!

I half expected to be jerked out from under the couch, but instead the offender pressed something into my palm.

"Here," a soft voice whispered, giving me pause.

Wait... Lily? I nearly asked. *What...?*

I felt the wirelike item in my hand.

Uh, no, not wire. A... a plastic stick that unfolds and has... Oh. It's a pair of glasses...?

My brow remained crinkled until I slipped the item over my nose. Then my eyebrows shot upward.

Because I could *see*. Not exactly as clearly as I could with the lights on, but it was enough to make out Lily's features.

I'd played with night-vision goggles before.

These were something else entirely.

Except I couldn't see beyond the couch.

"We need to go," Lily said against my ear.

"Go where?" I mouthed back at her.

She canted her head toward a nearby wall, making me frown. I didn't understand.

Follow her, Cam urged in my mind. *She and Hazel obviously have a plan. That's why I put you there—I saw Hazel phase Lily into that corner right as Jenkins attacked Ayaz.*

I'd been too lost in the abrupt motion to understand why he'd done it. Then I'd been too distracted by Jenkins to even question it.

Everything felt so discombobulated and intense. And it was all happening so *quickly*.

Ismerelda. Go with Lily, Cam demanded.

Wh-what about you? I asked as howls rent the air. It sounded like the lycans were right outside the door now.

I need to handle my brother.

What are you going to do to him? I asked.

Kill him, Cam answered flatly. *It's the only* cure *for his madness.*

While I agreed, I could also sense Cam's hesitation. This was his brother. A being he'd spent thousands of years with. His *blood.*

It's what I have to do, Cam added, a hint of finality in his tone.

I swallowed, his thoughts confirming how he'd come to this conclusion.

This wasn't about saving humanity or avenging the lycans. This was about doing what he needed to do to protect me. To protect *us.*

I'm not altruistic, Ismerelda, he murmured. *So don't think of me as a hero, because I'm not one. But I am going to do what I need to do to ensure Cane never touches you again.*

There was no hesitation in his decision, his mind made up.

Now go with Lily. Hide. I'll hunt you later, lioness.

Those final words sent another shiver down my spine but for entirely different reasons. *That sounds like both a threat and a prom—*

A crash cut off my mental reply, the ground shaking beneath me.

Lily's nails dug into my wrist as she tried to pull me toward the wall. I started moving willingly, my pulse thudding harshly in my ears.

Our coverage from the couch ended about three feet away from the wall she'd gestured to, but that didn't stop her from darting forward toward some sort of grate. Her fingers pried it open while I looked right, my lips parting at the sight of wolves pouring into the room.

Cam...

Go! he shouted as he punched a lycan in the snout.

Shit! I scrambled after Lily, heading toward the floor

duct she'd just crawled into. *This is insane. I can't believe I'm doing this. Holy crap, what the fuck is even happening?*

Vibrations rocked the cold surface beneath my palms and knees as I joined Lily inside, the world echoing off the metallic walls.

Animalistic sounds.

Vampires hissing.

Grunts.

Curses.

More growls.

It was all mingling together in a reverberating wave of violence that left my stomach churning.

"This way," Lily said, the confidence in her tone startling me.

"You know where we're going?" I asked as I followed her.

"Sort of. I studied the grid well enough to get us to where we need to go," she replied. "Just keep moving. And don't... don't panic."

That last part seemed to be more for herself than for me.

But I accepted her advice anyway because I was absolutely about to panic.

Cam's fury didn't help, his anger hot and fierce via our bond. From what his mind told me, the attacking lycans were from the labs, all of them recognizing him as an assailant, not an ally.

Because of Cane.

He'd groomed Cam to be the face of the organization, the one who showed up in the labs most recently to oversee their experiments.

Or maybe it was the fact that they looked so much alike, shared the same bloodline, and supposedly desired the same outcome.

Regardless, it left Cam in a predicament, one he was currently trying to fight.

He couldn't afford to go easy on the lycans attacking him now. They wanted him dead; thus he had to respond with equal force.

Some might shy away from that, try to save their lives and detain them until they could work out the misunderstanding.

Old Cam might have done that.

But new Cam was too smart to even accept that as a possibility.

He struck them down with superior force, killing without remorse. This was about survival, not taking over as king or being the hero everyone wanted him to be.

My Cam was a villain.

A dark heart.

A predator with a penchant for practicality.

He wouldn't bow. He would slay.

For himself. For me. For *us*.

We would survive this.

We would persevere.

We will move forward.

I kept that mantra playing in my head as I followed Lily, her swiftness in the vents suggesting this wasn't her first time crawling through an obstacle course like this one. If we weren't in the process of fleeing for our lives, I would have been tempted to ask her.

The growls and snarls in our wake grew quieter with each passing second.

We slowed as we reached a cross section of the vents, Lily glancing left and right as though uncertain of which way to go.

She eventually chose left, then paused about ten feet down by a grate. She peered through it, her brow furrowing. The space was too small for me to join her. We were lucky that we fit in these vents. Cam would have struggled to follow me, which explained why none of the lycans had bothered to try.

Of course, Lily and I weren't their intended targets in this fight.

Or I didn't think we were, anyway.

We would just be collateral damage.

"This is one of the royal suites," she whispered to me. "Looks like the lycans have already ravaged this room..." She moved out of the way to let me see through the grate.

And yeah, it'd definitely been destroyed. "Jasmine..." I trailed off, noting the female's horror-stricken expression. Her head was on one side of the room. Meanwhile, her mutilated corpse was on the other, the claw and teeth marks making it clear that she'd been mauled by a wolf— perhaps multiple wolves.

"Yeah," Lily said, moving forward again. "We need to find an empty one."

"Then what?" I asked her.

"We wait," she replied.

My brow furrowed. "Wait for—"

A hand curled around my ankle, yanking me backward and out of the vent I'd just been peering through. My lips parted on a scream that ended on a choke as my shoulder blades met the wall.

It was all so quick.

Rough.

And unexpected.

Knocking the air right out of my lungs.

Leaving me...

Fuck.

Cam's voice was in my head, demanding to know if I was okay. But I was too busy trying to see to answer him.

The glasses were still on my head, yet everything had turned black.

Can't… breathe… I realized, my fingers clawing at the palm clamped down around my throat. *Let… go!*

"You're mine now," a voice said.

Michael.

Cam roared in response.

I wasn't even sure where Michael had come from or how he'd tracked me. "Why… can't… you… just… be… dead?" Each word was silent, my lips moving to form them. However, I didn't have the air to *voice* them.

My back hit the wall again as Michael shifted his grip, my head ringing from the impact.

Hate, I thought. *I fucking… hate… you.*

Cam said something in response, but I couldn't hear him over the roar flooding my senses. It was loud. All-consuming. *Deadly.*

I refuse… to die… like this, I thought dizzily as Michael's free hand went to my dress.

"I'm going to fuck you. And then I'm going to kill you," he said against my ear. "Say goodbye to Cam, Izzy. You're about to lose him once and for all."

CAM

A Few Minutes Earlier

FUCK.

These lycans were rabid, their goal clear—*kill*.

Hazel phased around the room, her movements an attempt to avoid being mauled.

Ayaz was already dead.

Helias was fighting three feral lycans.

And Jenkins seemed hell-bent on taking down my brother.

I knocked a wolf off my arm, ignoring the searing pain his teeth left behind in my torn skin, and punched another in the snout.

Trying to talk them down would be impossible. These were lab wolves, ones that had been in cages for gods knew how long. Poked and prodded. Experimented on. Controlled via whatever technology my brother fancied.

No, there would be no reasoning with these animals. I wasn't even sure if they could shift back into their human forms.

My fist connected with another snout, a growl growing in my chest.

This felt like a distraction. A way to keep us all busy until the real trouble arrived.

Damien had said to grab Ismerelda and run. Clearly, he knew what was coming.

The lycans, I imagined. Not these feral wolves but the clear-headed alphas.

Fuck, I raged again. *Fuck. Fuck. Fuck!*

Ismerelda was lost in a vent somewhere. Hazel was still flying around the room. Helias was losing his battle— something I didn't mind at all.

And my brother...

Just killed Jenkins, I realized as Cane dropped the lycan's heart on the ground and crushed it beneath his boot.

He phased to my side to snap the neck of another lycan. "Come with me," he demanded, leaving the room.

I shared a look with Hazel, then teleported after him into the hallway, where six more lycans were clawing their way across the floor. It seemed they were all coming up— or maybe down—via the stairwell.

Cane took off in the opposite direction, his speed superior to the wolves'. I chased after him, not because I intended to hide with him, but because I needed to end this. To end *him*.

He was too far gone to be saved. Too jaded to be reasoned with. It didn't matter how many times I explained Ismerelda's importance—even in a practical manner regarding her memories—he still wanted her dead.

That much had been clear when he'd so easily dismissed her life moments ago after Helias had attempted to snap her neck.

Using humans as a barricade, I thought. *Fucking pathetic.*

Once I finished off Cane, I'd come back for Helias. Assuming the wolves didn't eat him first.

Cane slipped into a room and moved with purpose to a nearby closet. I arched a brow as he slid open what appeared to be a hidden door inside. "This seems pointless with the system shut down," I told him. "The lycans can simply pull the door open like you just did."

He snorted and stepped through the threshold. "I'm not proposing we hide, brother."

Frowning, I followed him and arched a brow at what I found. "Guns?"

Cane hummed, his focus on a box in the corner. "Not everything requires a network connection," he mused as he put something in his ear. "In fact, most of my weapons don't link to the mainframe at all."

A blistering sound seared my skull, causing my knees to give out beneath me.

Fuck!

I pressed my palms to my ears, my entire body jolting beneath waves of electric pulses that seemed to radiate from my fucking brain.

What the hell is this? I wanted to demand, my eyes squeezed shut. *What the fuck is going on?*

A low pulse of heat vibrated my spine, sending me sideways to the floor. It was like being fucking electrocuted. Only it all appeared to be in my head.

Ismerelda's concern spiked via our bond, her fear hitting me straight in the heart.

Can she feel this, too? I wondered. *Is she in pain? Do I need…?*

That last thought trailed off, my brain blanking for a moment.

I'd just considered cutting her off from the agony.

Is that what I did before? Built a wall to protect her from the pain?

It'd been my instinct just now, my need to ensure her safety superseding everything else.

But that hadn't worked before. It'd nearly destroyed us. *I can't do that again. I* won't *do that again.*

Another jolt hit my spine, causing me to arch on the floor, my nerve endings suddenly on fire. I could barely process my need to breathe, let alone see or move.

And then it all ended.

"Portable neutralizers," Cane mused, his voice an echo in my head. One that made me growl deep inside.

Because it reminded me of something.

A past I couldn't quite recall.

Yet my body seemed to remember it in vivid detail because my muscles locked as though prepared to fight.

"Well, not exactly. This one is designed specifically for you. But these…" He trailed off as another high-pitched noise rang through my head. "These are for everyone else. Combined, I imagine, they're fairly painful. I'd apologize, but you won't remember it anyway."

Can't… breathe… Ismerelda rasped into my mind.

Because of the neutralizer? I asked her.

Let… go! she shouted in response, making my heart stop.

Are you…? Are you asking me to rebuild the barricade? I asked her. Because that didn't feel right at all. In fact, it felt downright wrong. *Ismerelda—*

Michael, she interjected, her mind linking to mine in a way it hadn't before, her reality blending instantly with mine and making me realize that she wasn't in pain from me at all.

She was in pain from *Michael.*

He had his palm wrapped around her throat.

I roared internally and externally, furious at both him and my brother.

The intense sound increased in volume, causing my roar to end on a gasp, the pain unlike anything I'd ever experienced.

Fuck. No wonder I'd lost my memories… He's frying my godsdamn brain!

"This is for the best, brother," Cane informed me, a hint of sincerity in his tone. "I thought perhaps the microphone on your shirt was a fluke. But when my surveillance caught Ismerelda placing that piece in her ear, I knew it was purposeful. You're not ready to reign by my side yet."

The disappointment in his voice was almost real. *Almost.*

"There were other signs as well, of course—your attachment to your *Erosita* being the primary indicator. I could see it in the way you went from fucking her without remorse to basically making love to her. Couple that with the fact that you won't let anyone touch her, and, well, it's clear your link to her is a problem."

My teeth ground together, the blaring alarm in my skull making it impossible for me to speak. But if I could say something, I'd tell him that *he* appeared to be the one who was obsessed with my *Erosita.* Almost like he couldn't stand the concept of me having someone else in my life.

Obviously, it went deeper than that.

He feared my connection to her because it threatened his plans.

"At least I know how to proceed," he went on. "Your

rehabilitation was nearly perfect. But Ismerelda ruined everything. She has to die, brother. It's the only way to fix you."

He knelt, his palm stroking my head as one would a pet.

"This will hurt, but you won't remember any of it when you wake next time. And I'll ensure you never learn the truth, too. That's my gift to you, brother," he murmured, his phrasing making it sound like he actually believed he was doing something kind for me.

A shot of unadulterated terror fired through my bond with Ismerelda, the shock of it reminding me of when she'd nearly been raped.

I instantly tuned in to her mind, needing to know what was happening, and felt a similar jolt scorch my veins.

Only mine wasn't *terror*. It was *rage*.

Michael had pinned her to the ground, his hands hiking up her dress.

And he was fucking *exposed*.

Ismerelda screamed beneath him, her voice hoarse as a result of him abusing her throat. But she was a fucking wildcat, her terror having melted into a wrathful wave of vehemence. She scratched his face. His chest. *Anywhere* she could hit him as she writhed furiously beneath him.

But it wouldn't be enough.

I knew it in the way he was staring down at her.

Knew it because he was a vampire… and she was a human. *My* human. *My* mate. *My Erosita*.

Michael was about to take her from me. To ruin what we shared. Tarnish what was left of our bond.

And my brother is going to ensure I forget all about it.

No, I thought. *Fuck. That.*

I refused to forget.

I refused to block her out.

I refused to let this fucking happen.

My eyes flew open, the alarm still splintering my skull. But I pushed past it, my mind linking to Ismerelda's to give me a semblance of peace. To be able to *breathe*.

Because *she* couldn't hear anything.

She felt none of my pain at all.

Instead, she experienced the agony that was Michael. His touch. His growl. His nefarious intent.

My brother said something, his words no longer loud in my mind. I could barely hear him at all.

I was consumed by Ismerelda. Focused entirely on my female. *My queen.*

Her fight became my fight, her determination bolstering my own as I curled my hands into fists. My brother thought he could best me with his penchant for technology, this weapon he called a neutralizer. He wanted to cure me. To *change* me. To mold me into his perfect king.

But I was already content with my role in the world.

Pleased to be Ismerelda's Cam.

Her villain.

Her partner.

Her king.

I bowed to no one else but her. Served at her throne, not his. And I was fucking *done* with Cane's game.

A growl rumbled in my chest, and I sprang to my feet, my brother's eyes widening in shock as I grabbed him around the throat. The volume escalated, the vibration nearly bringing me to my knees once more.

But Ismerelda held me steady.

Her mind *anchored* me.

"You're wrong," I told him, my voice a snarl of a sound. "Having a mate isn't a weakness." I squeezed, my hand cutting off his ability to breathe. "It's a fucking *strength.*"

I snapped his neck before he could reply.

Because there was nothing he could say.

He'd made his choices. Dug his grave. And now it was time to ensure he fucking slept in it.

For good.

I stomped on the weapon he'd used against me, my mind instantly at ease.

Then I grabbed an ax from the shelf holding an array of sharp objects.

"Goodbye, brother," I said, hoisting the deadly item in the air.

And swung down toward his neck.

His head rolled, his green eyes staring up at me with a permanent expression of shock.

The look would forever haunt me. *My brother's dead.*

It'd been the only way. No amount of sleep could have helped him. Not even his fucked-up version of a cure.

He'd been too inhumane to save.

Too *lost*.

Cam! Ismerelda screamed into my mind, her struggle causing the air to leave my lungs in a whoosh as I dropped the ax and grabbed a gun instead.

I'm coming! I shouted at her. *Don't stop fighting!*

Cam, she sobbed via our bond, her body seeming to be caught beneath Michael's. *I can't—*

Her mind fell silent.

No, I thought. *No!*

I couldn't be too late.

I'm going to fucking kill him! I raged, tracking her scent. *Don't you dare die on me, Izzy! Don't you dare fucking die!*

Lycans paced the halls, a few of them stepping into my path.

"Your quarrel isn't with me," I growled at them. "*Move*."

"Where's Cane?" someone asked.

Thida, I recognized, glancing over my shoulder at him. "*Dead*," I snarled. "Tell your pack to move, or I'll be forced to kill them, too."

The alpha's eyebrow inched upward. "You killed your brother?"

Fuck this. I didn't have time for a discussion.

Rather than comment, I phased *through* the wolves. My actions probably knocked a few of them out, maybe even killed them, but I didn't spare them a second thought.

Because fuck them. Fuck this. *Fuck everything.*

Ismerelda, I whispered. *Talk to me.*

Nothing.

Fuck!

I tracked her scent, her blood a beacon to my senses.

A beacon that had my heart stuttering in my chest. My stomach churning with fear. *True* fear.

Izzy, I breathed, phasing to the doorway of a room boasting a sight that stole all the breath from my lungs.

I fell to my knees.

My gun dropping to the floor.

Oh, Ismerelda...

I couldn't speak.

I couldn't move.

I could hardly think.

There was just one thought rolling through my mind. One that held me captive on the ground. A realization that made my heart fucking stop.

I didn't make it in time...

IZZY

A Few Minutes Earlier

CAM! I SCREAMED, MY HANDS CAUGHT BENEATH ONE OF Michael's palms.

I'm coming! he shouted back at me. *Don't stop fighting!*

I squirmed, my lower half pinned by Michael's, his groin pressing against mine.

"I hope you've said goodbye, little blood whore," he said, his sinister gaze making me want to vomit. I almost wished he would have knocked the glasses off my face during the skirmish so I didn't have to look at him.

Yet I could see him clearly.

Every dangerous *inch* of him.

Cam, I said, my voice coming out on a sob. Because there was nothing else I could do. *I can't—*

Michael cursed as something slammed into his head, the unexpected impact causing my mind to blank. Because I wasn't quite sure I'd seen that correctly.

Am I dreaming?

Am I already dead?

Did Lily really just…?

"Fuck!" Michael cursed as she hit him again with what appeared to be a metal pole.

I scrambled backward as he released me, his attention on Lily as he charged her.

Only for a gunshot to stop him in midstep.

And send him to the ground.

Where he lay on his side. Lifeless. Mouth parted. Blood beginning to ooze between his unfocused eyes.

I gaped at the doorway as Mira entered, her gaze narrowed on Michael's body. "A shot to the head isn't going to permanently kill him," she said. "You need to slice off his head."

I blinked, my brain struggling to process everything that was happening. "I… what?"

"A knife, Izzy," Mira snapped. "Cut off his fucking head."

Why…?

I coughed, my mind still not fully functioning or understanding.

Mira was evil.

She'd betrayed me.

She'd given me to Cam. The evil version. The one who had nearly destroyed me.

And now… now she wanted me to… slice off Michael's head?

Why are you helping me? I wanted to demand.

But it didn't matter. Not yet. Not right now. Not with Michael's unconscious body a few feet away.

He needs to die, I thought, my brain hyperfixated on the task. I couldn't hear Cam. Couldn't feel him. Some sort of door had been closed when Michael had been about to fuck me.

I couldn't figure out how to reopen it.

All I could focus on was ending Michael.

Destroying him.

Ripping his fucking head off.

A knife appeared in my peripheral vision, Mira having stepped up to my side.

I didn't acknowledge her. Didn't look at her. Just took the blade from her palm and crawled over to Michael's prone form.

This man was fucking evil.

A monster.

A vampire who needed to *die.*

I rolled him to his back and drove the knife into his throat. Then I began to *saw.* It wasn't efficient. But that didn't matter. He could fucking suffer.

I moved my hand up and down, side to side, destroying his neck one stab and slice at a time. Until finally there was a *pop.*

And his head lolled to the side.

I stared down at him, my hands covered in his blood, my dress stained from my efforts. His pants were still undone, the sight of his waning erection making me sick to my stomach.

He'd been so close. *Too close.*

A sob ripped from my throat, my mind instantly connecting to Cam's as he whispered, *I didn't make it in time...*

I met his gaze in the doorway, my heart suddenly in my throat.

I didn't make it in time to see you kill him, he said, completing his thought. *I… I missed it.*

I almost laughed.

Because of all the things Cam could be disappointed in, it was in not seeing me kill Michael. I pushed away from the floor and ran toward him. He caught me as I fell into his sturdy form, his knees on the ground taking the impact of me collapsing into him.

Then I kissed him.

Hard.

My mouth devouring his without regard for anyone else around us. Mira. Lily. Dead Michael. The growling lycans. Shouting vampires.

I didn't care about any of them.

Only Cam.

My Cam.

His fingers threaded through my hair as he held me to him, the two of us on our knees on the ground while we feasted upon one another for everyone else to see.

I love you, I told him. *You. My Cam. This version. The one you've become. The one you always were. My mate. My king.*

I love you, too, he whispered back to me. *You're my heart, Ismerelda. My soul. Building that barrier between us was the biggest mistake of my existence. Without our connection, I lost myself entirely. It was you who helped me defeat Cane, Izzy. He was wrong. You're not a weakness; you're my strength.*

Tears filled my eyes with his words, his mind telling me how much he meant each one.

Our souls belonged together. No barriers. No hiding secrets. Just a pure, open connection.

Together, we were one. A unit. An unstoppable force.

King and queen.

But we weren't monarchs who were meant to rule a

kingdom. We were monarchs who were meant to rule one another.

"Fuck, that's not… that's not what I want to see at all," my twin muttered from nearby.

"What did you do, Izzy?" Ryder asked me. "Mutilate Michael with a fork?"

Only Ryder would interrupt a moment by evaluating my killing method.

I pulled away from Cam, my gaze holding his as I replied, "I used a dagger."

"Seriously? There isn't a single clean angle or slice anywhere on that neck. Are you sure it wasn't a butter knife?" Ryder asked.

"I didn't have an ax," I muttered, finally looking at him. "You're the one who taught me to always improvise. I improvised with the knife…" I trailed off, my gaze searching the room for the one who had given me said knife.

Only, Mira was nowhere to be found.

I frowned. "Where'd Mira go?"

"Probably to find Luka," Damien replied. "She's been working with him the whole time."

My eyebrows rose. "*What*?"

"She's been playing double agent, just like Hazel," Ryder explained before tousling my hair like one would a little sister. "Keep up, Izzy."

I swiped at him, causing him to jump back with a chuckle.

Would you like me to kill him? Cam asked, his mental voice serious. *I'll happily do it.*

I gave him a look. *You can't kill Ryder.*

I assure you, Ismerelda, I can.

Perhaps physically… he could. Or it'd be a pretty even match.

But that was beside the point. *I don't want him dead,* I told Cam.

He shrugged one shoulder. *If that's your wish.*

"Your fellow rebels have just landed," someone behind me announced, the English accent familiar.

I glanced backward to find the owner of that voice —*Cedric*.

He had his arm around Lily, her big blue-green eyes taking in the violent room.

Seeing her had me jumping away from Cam and running straight for her.

Cedric instantly stood, his posture defensive.

Probably because I'd just charged his mate like a bull.

"You saved me!" I exclaimed, feeling like an idiot for not checking on her sooner. I darted around Cedric, something he obviously allowed me to do because he could have absolutely stopped me if he'd wanted to.

Lily looked up at me with a small smile. "I did what I could."

"You did more than that," I told her. "You could have kept running."

She considered that for a moment. "Maybe. But it was nice not to run this time."

Cedric growled behind me.

Lily simply smiled.

And somehow I ended up pulled into Cam's side again, like he couldn't stand being away from me for more than a few seconds.

My brother rolled his eyes at the sight. Then he shared a look with Ryder. "I suppose we should go greet Jace and the others."

"Why the fuck would I want to do that?" Ryder demanded.

"Because *you* are the one who ran off with Khalid and

Cedric without telling Jace. I don't want to deal with that bullshit again."

"Then don't deal with any of it. Ignore him. It works well for me," Ryder told him.

My brother sighed and shook his head. "It's a wonder Ryder Region survives with you in charge."

"It survives because you run everything for me," Ryder replied. "You're the politician, Damien. I'm just the talent."

Damien rolled his eyes again. "Pretty sure I'm both the politician *and* the talent," he said as he stalked off toward the hallway.

Only for him to then back up several paces as Luka, Mira, Thida, and a handful of other alpha lycans entered the room.

They took in Michael's corpse, as well as Jasmine's remains, then looked at Cam.

"You really did kill your brother," Thida said to him. "Along with a few of my wolves."

My eyebrows lifted. *You killed Cane? And Thida is Team Lycan, too? Like Jenkins?*

Yes, Cam replied, answering both questions with his single-word response.

Aloud, he replied, "There seems to have been a misunderstanding regarding my involvement in my brother's antics. I won't claim to be innocent in all this. But I will say that his choices are not *my* choices."

Thida and Luka both studied Cam, their expressions giving nothing away.

However, Mira smiled. "I knew Izzy would bring you back."

I glared at her. "You're a bitch." The words just sort of slipped from my mouth. Yeah, she'd given me a knife. But she'd also lied to me and brought me to hell.

To be with me, Cam murmured into my mind.

Sure. But... I trailed off, not wanting to rehash everything that had happened.

Because in the grand scheme of things, it no longer mattered. He was *my* Cam now. The past was simply history.

"But thanks for the knife," I added as an afterthought, my words for Mira.

"You might not understand my motive, but I did what I had to do," Mira told me. "I wanted to prolong lycan life. Cane and Lilith took that objective in a direction I didn't agree with, one I probably should have seen coming. Alas, by the time I realized their true intentions, it was too late to stop them. So I did what I could to salvage the situation."

My teeth ground together. Primarily because I understood her motive. However, that didn't mean I could forgive her for what she'd done.

"The lycans will pursue justice where appropriate as far as Mira is concerned," Thida announced.

"Actually, I think that topic, among several others, should be addressed at the Blood Alliance meeting set for..." Khalid trailed off as he entered the room, his focus on his glowing watch. "Roughly thirty-four hours from now, give or take thirty minutes."

Emine slipped in behind him, her expression bored despite her blood-streaked clothes.

She'd clearly killed a few vampires. Maybe some lycans, too.

However, Khalid looked like he'd barely broken a sweat, his all-black suit crisp and clean. Just like Ryder's dark jeans and long-sleeved shirt.

I highly doubted either of them had held back in the chaos below. They were just *neat* when it came to their lethal natures.

Unlike me, I thought, glancing at my blood-soaked hands. *I really need a shower.*

"I realize the lycans and vampires are at odds, but we need to allow all of our brethren—vampire and lycan alike —to join us here before we make any more rash decisions," Khalid went on. "Your lycans are free. The vampires involved with imprisoning and experimenting on them are dead. And we all know Cam wasn't truly behind it. He was never one of Cane's allies. The same cannot be said about you or Mira."

That last sentence was delivered directly to Thida, Khalid's gaze hardening as he spoke.

"You know, I'm starting to think you might make a better king than Jace," Ryder drawled, breaking the tense silence. "And obviously you'd be a better choice than Cam."

"Who says anything about having a *king*?" Thida countered. "And in what world do you think lycans would ever bow to a vampire after all that's been done?"

"Yet another topic for the meeting," Khalid smoothly interjected. "Let's take thirty-four hours to calm down, and then we'll regroup."

I flinched as the lights popped back on, my glasses lighting up like a firework. Cam swiftly removed them from my face as I rubbed my eyes, the unexpected change leaving me dizzy.

My nose crinkled as I realized I was spreading blood all over my face.

Shit.

I dropped my hands, wincing at my soiled state. It was bad enough that I still had Michael's imprint all over me. And now I had his blood *in my damn eyes.*

"Thirty-four hours," Cam echoed as he scooped me up into his arms. "We'll be back then."

"Hold on—"

"I wasn't asking, Thida," Cam bit out. "Just like I wasn't asking you all to move before. You saw what happened then, and I'll happily do it again."

The lycan grimaced, his jaw tightening.

But Luka merely laid a hand on the other man's chest and forced him back a step. "Just let him go," he said. "Khalid's right. Save it for the Blood Alliance meeting."

Cam didn't wait to discuss it more, simply stalked off into the hallway and went directly to the stairs.

Do you have any idea where you're taking me? I asked him.

Back to the room we occupied earlier, he replied. *Where I'm going to worship every fucking inch of you with my tongue.*

I shivered. *Can I shower first?*

Yes. A flat answer, yet the intention behind it was underlined with possession.

He wanted to scrub Michael's essence off my skin and replace it with his own.

Then he would claim me.

Bite me. Fuck me. *Love* me.

Then, when he finished, he'd do it all over again.

Because he could.

Because I was his.

And he was *mine*.

For better or worse.

For eternity and beyond.

CAM

Thirty-Four Hours Later

"You're seriously still going on about this?" Ryder demanded, his attention on Kylan as Ismerelda and I entered the room. "Khalid chose me because he knows I'm the better shot."

"How does he know that?" Kylan returned. "I don't recall ever testing that theory."

"It's not a theory. It's a fact."

"It's a theory," Kylan tossed back at him. "One we're going to test just as soon as we're excused from all this political bullshit."

"Aww, look at you two planning a date," Damien drawled as he collapsed into a chair beside Ryder. "That's adorable, really."

"You know, I think I just decided who we can use for

our little *test*," Ryder said conversationally, his attention still on Kylan. "Damien loves playing dodge the bullet. He'll make the perfect target for our game."

Kylan's dark eyes lit up. "That does sound entertaining."

"Oh, it will be," Ryder murmured, smiling as he rotated toward his second. "Won't it, Damien?"

Ismerelda's twin simply stared at the royal. "I'll only play if I'm also given a gun and allowed to return fire."

Ignoring their continuing banter, I pressed my palm to Ismerelda's lower back and led her deeper into the room.

It was an open space, one clearly meant to host large parties. But it was all centered around a circular stage rather than a table.

The royals had begun selecting chairs, as had several alphas and a trio of Blessed Ones.

A trio that was currently glaring daggers at me.

Sota and Troph, I understood. Fen, I did not. I hadn't even known he was awake. But perhaps the other two had told him what I'd done to them.

Of course, my actions had been a result of Cane's manipulations, something I knew they'd been informed of over the last thirty-four hours, but they clearly hadn't forgiven me.

That was fine.

I could handle being their villain.

Several of the lycans gave me similar looks, their disgust palpable. But they appeared to be staring at all the vampires in the room in that manner.

Which explained the clear divide around the stage— one side was taken over by wolves, while the other was claimed by the vampires and the Blessed Ones.

I took a chair next to Jace, my focus on the single cluster of wolves and vampires sitting nearby. Either

Willow and Rae were tired of listening to their mates banter, or they were trying to convey a point to the room.

Jace followed my gaze and said, "It seems Rae, Willow, and Silas are making their stance clear, and Silas's mates are supporting that statement."

I hummed, intrigued yet bored.

Politics didn't interest me. But I was here because I had to be here. *For Ismerelda.*

She sat beside me, her expression amused as I glanced at her. *I didn't make you come.*

Ah, but you did, my queen. Twice today.

Her cheeks reddened at my change in subject. *That's not what I meant.*

But you have to admit it's a far more enticing subject than this meeting, yes? I asked her.

I don't know. The meeting hasn't started yet.

I sighed. *And yet we already know exactly what will be discussed.*

Darius and Jace had stopped by more than once in the last day and a half. The first time had been to check in on me and Ismerelda, as well as to express frustration over how everything had gone down. And the second time had been to discuss a plan for today's meeting.

I'd listened more than anything else, letting the two of them determine our path forward. Ismerelda had added her own thoughts, which were all I truly cared about.

When they'd left, Ismerelda and I had made our own decisions. Specifically one involving her future as a vampire.

I placed my palm on her jean-clad leg now and gave her a subtle squeeze. *You're going to make a beautiful vampire queen.*

So you keep saying, she replied.

It's a fantasy of mine, I murmured. *I can't stop thinking about everything I'll be able to do to you after you've turned.*

You can do most of those things to me now.

True, I agreed. *But I am going to enjoy testing the boundaries of your immortality.*

Something you already do…

In a very different way, I promised her. *You're not fragile. You're strong. Becoming a vampire will just make you indestructible.*

She leaned in to brush a kiss against my cheek. Then she settled once more and watched as Hazel entered with Keys. He'd apparently chosen to become her shadow rather than mine.

From what I'd gathered, he'd flown in with Hazel and the others, then she'd left him on the plane while she'd played her role as double agent.

"This place…" Juliet's whisper drew my attention away from Hazel and to my progeny's *Erosita.*

"It's where it all began," Darius replied, his green eyes meeting mine for a brief second before refocusing on his mate. "You stood right there." He pointed to the center of the stage. "And I was in that chair." He gestured to the one Ryder sat in now.

Juliet visibly shivered. "Item seventeen…"

"Is a twenty-two-year-old Caucasian female with mahogany hair and chocolate-colored eyes," Darius continued, clearly reciting something from their past. "Human is five foot seven, one hundred and thirty pounds, and speaks English, Spanish, Japanese, and German. Her other intellectual aptitudes are detailed on page nine of your guide."

He brushed a lock of her dark hair away from her face, her big eyes radiating affection. "I only saw your shoes."

His lips curled. "And I saw *you.*"

He pulled her in for a kiss, one that caught the attention of several other royals and alphas in the room.

They're not used to open affection, Ismerelda whispered via our bond. *Darius hasn't been allowed to show it since the day he bought her from this Coventus.*

I see.

This place held special meaning to them.

Because it was where their story had begun.

He chose her as a distraction, a way to prove his allegiance to the Blood Alliance, Ismerelda added. *But it was all a charade. And that simple exchange—that* kiss*—has just let everyone know the truth. He never conformed to their rules.*

I wonder how many others played a role in this world that they didn't truly admire, I said to her. Vampires were all about maintaining facades, and it seemed the Blood Alliance might be the biggest facade of them all.

Khalid and Emine were the last to enter the room, Cedric and Lily having preceded them by only a few seconds.

With the final vampires in attendance, everyone sat, the tension thick in the air.

Jace cleared his throat. "I believe by now that everyone has been brought up to speed regarding recent events," he said, his gaze going to Luka. "Yes?"

The lycan nodded. "We've informed the various pack leaders in attendance, as well as the ones who couldn't be here in person." He glanced at the screen where three alphas stared expectantly at the room, their video presence the only way they could make the meeting in time.

Yulian, Jenkins's son, was one of the faces on the screen. The death of his father had probably created some chaos back home, likely making it impossible for him to journey from former-day Siberia to Rome.

The other two alphas were also from distant locations.

"We've brought all of the vampires up to speed as well," Jace commented, referring to the other royals in attendance. "And, as promised, we've detained Cane's remaining ally."

Sofia, I thought, aware of the agreement Jace and Luka had come to yesterday regarding her known affiliation.

My brother had kept meticulous records.

Records that were now public.

Which was how I knew that everyone in this room was aware of what he'd done to me and how I'd been manipulated by my brother.

I'd skimmed over a few of my brother's notes. Any guilt I might have felt regarding his death had diminished after reading his crude analysis of my *cure.*

Immortal insanity had definitely wrapped its deadly fingers around my brother's brain, leaving him irrevocably broken.

I'd miss him. But I wouldn't mourn him.

I rested my arm over the back of Ismerelda's chair as Luka and Jace stared one another down, neither of them submitting to the other.

"What will be done with her?" Luka finally asked, referring to Sofia.

"I believe that's up to you and your fellow lycans," Jace replied, causing several vampires in the room to straighten.

"Well, I believe that should be up for a vote," Sahara interjected. "A royal can't just be *given* to a lycan for retribution."

"Even if we did vote, the lycans are the majority party present," Naomi murmured. "Besides, she made her bed when she decided to keep some of Cane's failed lycan experiments as *pets.*"

Several lycans growled at the notion despite having

already been made aware of that information from my brother's detailed records.

"But if you think we need to *vote*," Naomi went on, "then feel free to initiate it. However, I personally vote that we not waste any more time."

"Indeed," Jace agreed. "What Cane did was inexcusable. The lycans have more than earned their right to deliver whatever retribution they see fit."

"And what should we do with the rest of you?" Brandt demanded, the Calgary Clan Alpha clearly agitated. "We obviously can't trust you."

A few lycans grunted in agreement.

"We're not asking you to," Jace replied. "In fact, we don't expect you to at all." His gaze drifted across the stage to a burning pair of turquoise irises. "Khalid?"

"Hmm," he hummed, silent for a long moment.

Then he hopped up on the stage.

"I think our solution is a fairly easy one," he informed the group as he held up one of his fancy little devices.

Screens appeared throughout the room, causing several lycans to jolt in surprise. But I was becoming used to his parlor tricks, the display before me one I'd almost anticipated.

"Once upon a time, we met as an alliance to design our future," he said, indicating the detailed map unfolding before us all. "We divided ourselves into eighteen regions and seventeen clans, the regions going to the vampire royals and the clans going to lycan alphas. It worked for us then. But this is no longer that time."

The map began to change, names being crossed out by an invisible marker.

Silvano was replaced by Ryder.

An *X* marked out Lilith.

Helias, Ayaz, Jasmine, and Robyn soon followed suit.

677

Khalid glanced at the lycans, the demonstration seeming to pause. Then a line formed across Sofia's name.

And a note appeared beneath Tómasson Clan denoting Yulian as the new clan alpha.

"So much change," Khalid mused. "So much left unsettled."

My name appeared then at the top with a question mark beside it.

"We need to create a new map," Khalid went on. "And we need to decide if we want a global alliance governing all of the territories or if we want to simply govern ourselves."

Several of the lycans shared glances, while some of the vampires arched their brows.

"How will blood and human lives be regulated without a global governance?" Claude asked, his eyebrow arched. "What will happen to the Blood Universities? To the Coventuses? And what about the immortal slaves?"

"The same could be asked about the breeding camps and moon chases," the Stella Clan Alpha muttered.

"We'll divide the human assets evenly among all the regions and clans—or whatever we create with the revised map—and close down the universities. Blood and human life, as well as the activities we use humans for, will be regulated amongst ourselves rather than dictated by an alliance," Khalid explained.

"It'll be similar to how the humans used to govern themselves, only with far less politics," Cedric added from his seat. "At least in certain regions and clans."

"The humans had global governance," Claude pointed out.

"That they solely used when it suited them," Cedric returned. "And it was only utilized by certain governments. Others ignored it entirely. I imagine we'll form similar allegiances—however, between like-minded regions and clans."

Khalid nodded. "Yes, we can trade, share resources, and allow border crossings, as well as everything else that comes with allying ourselves with another clan or region. But we won't be required to adhere to one specific set of rules."

"Rules created by the Blood Alliance, you mean," Luka clarified. "You're suggesting we dismantle what we've built and go our separate ways."

"I'm suggesting we move on from what we built and focus on our independent nations for a while," Khalid rephrased. "We all have different wants and needs. Why are we conforming to a single set of rules?"

"To keep things equal," Sahara told him. "To ensure our resources are not squandered. To *share* our food."

"Equal?" Brandt scoffed. "The system was designed to benefit vampires. None of this has ever been for the benefit of my kind."

"Agreed," Thida echoed. "Cane never wanted to create immortal lycans, which was the only reason I'd aligned myself with him and Mira. But all of his notes revealed the truth—he only ever cared about immortal human slaves."

"Blessed Ones," Sota interjected, his voice gravelly. "He used the bloodline of *Blessed Ones* to create *food*."

A few vampires glanced at him, their mouths tightening in response.

Because these were our *fathers*.

And my brother had experimented on them almost as harshly as he had the lycans. The only difference was the Blessed Ones hadn't endured the torture for long.

Meanwhile, some of the lycans had lived through it for over a century.

"Regardless of what he did or how he did it, his goals

were clear. None of it was for lycan kind," Jolene said, his tone ringing with a finality that momentarily silenced the room.

At least until his grandson cleared his throat. "I'd argue that includes the establishment of the universities, breeding camps, and the moon chase."

Several lycans turned to face Edon, some of them arching brows.

"We don't need humans to procreate," the young alpha continued. "And the moon chase was a pastime developed for morbid entertainment; it was a way to take out our anger on humankind for what they'd attempted to do to us. Yet now we know Cane orchestrated all of it. So what's the point?"

"He's right," Jolene murmured. "Our clans have never needed humans for anything. We lived alongside them in peace for millennia. We can do it again. But with a few extra precautions in place."

"You're suggesting we give humans back some of their rights?" Sahara asked, the incredulity in her tone telling me exactly how she felt about that prospect.

Jolene's dark eyes traveled across the stage to where Sahara sat primly on the edge of her seat. "I'm suggesting we consider Khalid's idea and govern ourselves. Your needs are different from ours."

"Obviously," she muttered.

The conversation continued, the focus around current human assets and what should be done with them.

As Jolene and Edon had pointed out, the lycans didn't have as strong a need for mortal lives as the vampires did, thus suggesting the notion of evenly splitting the existing resources was flawed.

"The vampires need blood," Sahara kept stressing.

"You mean *you* need blood," Claude retorted. "You've

been gluttonous, and now you're lacking in resources. I don't see how that's anyone else's problem other than your own."

A few vampires agreed. Lycans, too.

But eventually the group came to an agreement that the mortals within the Blood Universities would primarily go to existing vampire regions.

Which led Khalid back to redrawing the boundary lines.

"It makes the most sense for those of us still alive to maintain the land we already own," Jace said, speaking up for the first time in several minutes. "That applies to both royals and clans."

Several of the alliance members nodded, agreeing with him.

Which primarily left former vampire regions up for claim.

"If we want to remain even in our distribution, those territories will need to go to another vampire," Naomi murmured. "It will also allow for a more fluid transition. Otherwise, we'll have to find new homes for everyone in those regions."

"It is possible for lycans and vampires to live together," Rae said, her irritation palpable. "This doesn't have to be an *either-or* conversation."

"For the intents and purposes of this discussion, and the allocation of power, it does," Khalid replied. "But once the land is divided and the leadership is confirmed, the royals or alphas in charge can decide how to run their own territory and who to welcome within their boundaries. That's the beauty of being independent."

Rae fell silent after that, her focus going to Kylan.

After a beat, he nodded, which seemed to make her shoulders relax a little.

Willow and Ryder appeared to be having a secret conversation as well. But rather than nod, he merely tilted his head to the side, causing Willow to glare at him. However, it seemed to be a playful glare more than an angry one, something her twitching lips gave away.

"Cam?" Khalid prompted after another thirty minutes of debating—a debate that ended in everyone agreeing with the assessment that the vacant seats in the various regions should be claimed by vampires. "You're the oldest of our kind. Is there a territory you wish to claim?"

I gazed at Ismerelda, her green eyes shining. "Yes," I murmured. "We'll be staying here."

The room fell silent.

"In the compound?" Jace finally asked, his surprise evident.

I pulled my focus away from my queen to address my cousin. "Perhaps not *in* the compound. But in Rome. We want Italy."

"Italy," he repeated. "Only Italy? Or Sofia Region, too?"

"Helias Region?" Khalid added. "That could also be a possibility."

"Just Italy," I murmured.

"But there are very few resources in Italy," Jace said slowly. "The country has been abandoned."

"Thus giving us an opportunity to grow in our way," I told him. "However, we'll be keeping any of the humans who wish to stay, including the immortals my brother created. The lycans can go to whoever wants to attempt to rehabilitate them. And, of course, the Blessed Ones will continue to rest here."

Several lycan alphas offered to take the *mutt unit* survivors into their territories, making that an easy concession.

However, my claim on the *immortal blood bags* sparked a whole new debate, with Sahara pointing out the unfairness of me being the only one with access to the blood slaves my brother had created.

But Jace was quick to point out that I didn't have any other humans in this territory aside from the Vigils, thus saying it was a fair allocation of resources.

"He has all the blood virgins, too," Sahara hissed.

"We've already decided that those will be evenly distributed among vampire kind," Khalid reminded her. "Just like the humans enrolled in the Blood Universities."

She sputtered and drummed up a few more excuses, but in the end, she lost.

"Italy is now Cam Region," Khalid said after a nearly unanimous vote.

"Izzy Region," I corrected him.

He glanced back at me, his eyebrow arched. But he smartly didn't comment and instead retitled the area on the map.

The discussion moved into a list of potential royal candidates, the priority assigned by birthright.

Darius was at the top.

He declined a region, saying he was happy to remain in the northwestern United States with his *Erosita*.

His progeny were also on the list, as well as several other older vampires with ancient bloodlines.

"We'll need to meet with them to decide their desire and placement," Khalid said. "Until that happens, the vampire regions will remain under the control of their existing sovereigns. Similar to how the clans fall to their alphas' next of kin."

Luka and Thida dipped their chins in acceptance, as did several other lycans.

A deal was then drawn up regarding the human

resource distribution, roughly ninety percent of which was allocated to vampire regions.

"The lycans will keep any and all existing humans within their clans. Should you choose to continue breeding them, or devouring them at the moon chase, that's your choice," Khalid said. "But you will not be given more, unless it's done so via a trade with another clan or region."

More nods rippled through the room.

Khalid stared at the map he had pulled up in the center of the stage—the image matching the one on all of our screens. "I believe… that concludes our business."

Silence fell, everyone exchanging glances as though this might be the last time we'd ever see one another.

No one said a word for several long minutes, the lycans and vampires taking in over a century's worth of history. One hundred and eighteen years of brotherhood.

All founded on a lie.

"It's been an experience, ladies and gentlemen," Jace murmured, his chin notching upward. "To the future."

"To the future," several others echoed.

This was it.

The final meeting.

And then the Blood Alliance adjourned… for the last time.

PART III

FOREVER BITTEN

CAM

A Little over a Month Later

I LEANED AGAINST A LIMESTONE COLUMN, MY GAZE ON THE corner staircase. My queen had wanted to play a game, one where she was the prey and I was the predator.

When I caught her, I would devour her.

And then… I would turn her.

We'd wanted to wait for the proverbial dust to settle before making this move. Mostly to ensure there were no unfortunate surprises waiting for us in our chosen kingdom.

Fortunately, all had been quiet.

The Coventus was closed.

The Blessed Ones were asleep.

The compound labs were vacant.

And the catacombs were beautifully silent.

Except for the soft pitter-patter of bare feet.

My lips curled.

I hear you, little swan, I murmured, using her old nickname on purpose.

Her excitement sweetened our bond, her feet moving faster over the stairs. She wanted to run. To play. To make me chase her.

No, it was more than that.

She wanted me to *hunt*.

Which was precisely why I didn't phase to her as she appeared. Instead, I gave her the opportunity to flee. To lose herself in the catacombs and to hide.

I counted, ensuring she could hear every number via our mental link.

And when I reached a hundred, I started to prowl. *I'm going to destroy you when I find you, love,* I warned her. *There will be no limits. No holding back. Just a predator ravaging his prey.*

Her arousal heightened, her mind easily seducing mine. But it was her scent I tracked now.

That sweet, addictive aroma curled around me in warm welcome, hardening my cock and driving my inner vampire mad with want.

I let her feel that desire. Revel in it. *Fear* it. Because I hadn't been lying to her. Human or not, I would not go easy on her.

This was our last time as vampire and *Erosita*.

As beast and mate.

Oh, she'd still be mine after this. But everything would change, too. *In the best way possible*, I mused, my mouth practically salivating for our future.

Biting her as a vampire would be so fucking sweet.

Because she could bite me right back.

Fuck, those delicious fangs were going to sink into my

godsdamn cock while I exploded down her throat. That would be my first request.

Well, perhaps my second.

Because feasting on her pussy would always be my favorite way to enjoy her.

Your thoughts are going to make me come, Ismerelda moaned through our bond, her need a beacon to my senses.

Are you touching yourself, sweet swan?

Yes, she whispered, her response making me growl.

Because *I* wanted to touch her. Lick her. *Fuck* her.

You're supposed to be running, I reminded her.

I am, she promised, the sound of her pants confirming she'd told the truth. Because I could hear her now, her bare feet slapping against the cold floor, her fragrance an invitation in her wake.

I didn't run after her.

I walked.

No, I *stalked.*

This was a game, one meant to escalate our need, and my throbbing dick proved it was working.

There would be no foreplay when I found her. Just a brutal *taking.*

She picked up speed, her heart rate singing in the silent catacombs. My lips curled as I paused, my back pressing up against a nearby wall as I waited.

Lost, little one? I whispered into her mind.

N-no, she stammered. *I…* Fear was taking hold of her, the emotion adding an intoxicating flavor to our game. She wasn't truly afraid, just anticipating being caught.

And she wanted to prolong it.

But she'd lost her way, the catacombs a maze of tombs and limestone chaos.

I closed my eyes, her natural perfume swirling around

me as she ran, her steps taking her closer rather than farther away.

Poor, sweet swan, I taunted. *Lost in the lion's den…*

I leapt forward to catch her, only to have her strike me across the face with her nails. "Then it's a good thing I'm a fucking lioness," she returned before jumping up and wrapping her legs around my waist.

Her mouth claimed mine before I could even begin to react, her twist of events unexpected and absolutely accepted.

Because *fuck*, this woman was the perfect mate. And I told her as such as I possessed her mouth with my tongue.

She clung to me as I phased us through the catacombs, my mind set on a single destination. One I'd created specifically for her.

A crypt.

The place where she'd be reborn as a vampire.

But first… I needed to be inside her.

I set her on the coffin, her thin white dress nearly translucent in the candlelight around us. "You're stunning," I praised her, loving her ethereal appearance.

She resembled a bride—innocent and sweet and ready to be corrupted.

Only, a goddess stared up at me, her power intangible yet overwhelming in nature.

"Take off your dress," I told her, pleased that she obeyed without question.

This was our dynamic.

I kneeled for her. But she also kneeled for me.

Equals.

Eternal soul mates.

I kissed her as her outfit fell to the dirt floor, my mouth hungry against hers.

She was naked.

No lingerie. No layers. Just hot skin and ready female.

Free my cock, I said into her mind.

She grabbed my belt, unfastening it with nimble fingers before popping open the top button and pulling down the zipper.

My shaft pulsed as she fisted it, my body more than ready to take hers.

Guide me, my queen. Put me where you want me.

She hummed, her mind vacillating between acceptance and teasing.

But in the end, need overruled all else.

She wrapped her long legs around my hips again, her heels digging into my ass as she forced me to align my groin with hers.

Then she angled my head toward her entrance and said, "Fuck me, my king."

Lust licked a decadent path down my spine, my abdomen flexing.

"As you wish, my queen." I thrust forward and forced her to take every inch of me. Her hot cunt spasmed in response, her lips parting on a gasp.

Then I silenced her with my tongue.

Hold on to me, I told her as I began my sensual assault. *I'm not going to stop until you've come at least twice on my cock.*

Which wouldn't be hard since she was already on the verge of detonating now.

She grabbed my shoulders, her nails sharp even through the fabric of my dress shirt.

I caught her hip, my hand angling her to the place I wanted her most, my opposite palm going to the back of her neck.

"Cam," she breathed, arching into me.

One of her palms fell away from my shoulder to brace

herself against the coffin, her lower half rising to meet my movements.

It was so fucking hot.

So *exquisite.*

And yet not enough.

But it would never be enough.

This woman was mine. My heart. My past, present, and future.

I loved her despite my inability to love or care for anyone else.

She was my humanity.

My link to the world.

My reason for being.

I let her feel the power of my love. The intensity of my claim. My very real need to possess every inch of her over and over again for the rest of our lives.

She clenched around me, her pleasure bordering on euphoria.

I held her there, right on the precipice, my pace slowing.

Then I slammed up into her and forced her off that cliff.

She screamed, the sound music to my ears as she squeezed my shaft with her slick walls.

So good, I told her. *So fucking good.*

She moaned in response, her words unintelligible as I continued fucking her.

Her nails bit into my shirt again, only to drop to the buttons and rip through the fabric altogether.

I arched a brow, surprised by her violence.

And she responded by yanking the shirt down my arms. I released her only to let the fabric fall, then reaffirmed my grip and took her even harder.

She used her heels to tug down my pants.

I kicked them off along with my shoes, amused by her nonverbal command.

Then I recaptured her mouth and issued a few silent demands with my tongue.

Demands I echoed with my hips against hers.

Thrusting.

Fucking.

Owning.

She braced herself again, her body keeping pace with mine despite her blissed-out mind. It was automatic. *Primal.* A need our souls understood almost as well as our very beings.

I bit her tongue.

She bit mine.

Blood pooled in our mouths.

A vampiric kiss.

And fuck if it wasn't intoxicating.

I fisted my fingers in her hair, my need to hold her close overriding everything else, even my pace below.

Then I palmed her tit with my free hand, my thumb easily finding her rosy nipple.

Fuck, Ismerelda. I pulled out to the tip and drove back in. *Keep choking my cock with that hot cunt. That's it, love. Dominate me with your pussy.*

I growled.

She was so fucking tight.

But I needed her to come again.

Only then could I join her.

Fuck me, Izzy. Push yourself up off of that coffin and fucking ride me.

She shuddered, her body following my commands and forcing her hips to move. Each thrust upward caused her clit to meet my base, our bodies practically glued together now from mouth to groin.

Because she'd more than pushed herself up. She'd practically climbed me with her arms wrapped around my shoulders and her legs encircling my waist.

I pushed her back down, laying her almost flat out on the coffin, and I fucked her hard.

I knew it hurt.

But she took it.

And then she fucking started to *come*.

Because my queen liked my savagery. She enjoyed the darkness. Reveled in my beast's proclivities and let me see hers in kind.

I kissed her while she fell into a euphoric state, my cock relishing her spasms until I couldn't take another second of it.

I growled as I released myself inside her, my cum possessing every inch of my mate's pussy. Filling her. Claiming her. Branding her as *mine*.

"Now," she panted. "*Now*, Cam."

I knew what she meant, what she *needed*.

And I obliged, my fangs sinking into her neck as I pulled her essence into my mouth. Her delicious flavor elicited a groan from my chest, her blood so fucking *good*.

It would change after this.

But it would become better.

Even more addicting.

Because it would taste like immortality.

She climaxed again as the endorphins from my bite coaxed her into a rapturous tailspin, her wet heat clamping down around my still-hard shaft.

I'm staying inside you while I turn you, I told her.

Yes, she whispered. Not that I'd phrased it as a question, but she'd consented anyway.

I took another deep swallow while she writhed on my cock.

It was fucking perfection.

I nearly came again from her shock waves of pleasure.

But I had to focus. To *listen*. Because this was the vital part of the siring process. Waiting for her pulse to weaken to just the right point.

A point that proved to be more elusive because of her ties to my immortality. Her body wanted to regenerate. To *heal*. But I had to force her into this state.

Her shudders eventually began to lessen. Her limbs going limp beneath me.

A memory of me killing her before lingered in her thoughts. But she quickly dismissed it.

Because she trusted me.

Her Cam.

Her mate.

And she refused to let the past taint our future.

She sighed, her head lolling to the side, her pulse barely existent now.

I imbibed a final sip, then pulled away to bite my wrist.

Her lips parted on a final exhale as I pressed my bloody wound to her mouth and compelled her with my mind to drink.

She instantly latched on, her body clearly ready for this next phase of her existence.

You were born to be a vampire, I mused. *And not just any vampire, but a vampire queen.*

We still had a lot to conquer in our new territory. Humans and vampires and immortal beings to govern.

But I had faith in our ability to rule.

We would prosper.

Together.

As King Cam and Queen Ismerelda.

My heart stuttered, indicating that I'd given my *Erosita* just a little too much of my blood. But I would be fine.

It was she who needed all the strength she could borrow to ensure a smooth transition.

"I love you," I whispered against her lips. "Forgive me."

I snapped her neck before she could consider a response, her life ending right in front of me.

I studied her for a moment, my naked queen.

Then I pulled out of her sweet heat and carefully lifted her broken form into my arms.

When she woke, it would be with me by her side.

Underground.

In the coffin I'd crafted for this very purpose.

I lifted the top, my gaze roaming over the cushioned bed I'd created for us.

It was luxurious. Sensual. *Vampiric*. A symbol of our lives to come.

"Sleep, my love," I whispered as I settled us inside the velvet interior. "Tomorrow we'll rise, and the future will be ours."

Darkness settled over us as I pressed a button to lower us into the earth, the casket door closing.

I shut my eyes, my mind seeking hers. *When I feel you start to stir, I'm going to fuck you into awareness.*

Then I'd kneel before her.

And worship her for eternity.

EPILOGUE

IZZY

MY THIGHS CLENCHED AS SOMETHING THICK AND HARD SLID in and out of me, my insides blazing with an inexplicable fire.

Everything *burned*.

I groaned, my lower half writhing against a hot, muscular form.

My Cam, I thought, delirious from his sensual assault.

My Ismerelda, he returned into my mind, our bond sparking to life.

Something about that felt… strange. Or perhaps not.

It wasn't wrong.

It… was definitely *right*.

However, it felt deeper somehow. More ingrained. Like our souls had reached a new level of bonding.

I arched as he hit me particularly deep, my body

coming alive before I could even open my eyes. Everything was dark, the atmosphere around us chilly.

Yet I was still on fire.

So hot. Too hot.

My nerve endings were sizzling.

My core was clenching.

Oh, God… I'm coming…

Stars exploded in my mind, my brain short-circuiting as I fought for clarity. For *understanding.*

What have you done to me? I asked dizzily. *Where are we?*

"In a coffin," he said against my ear, his body a blanket of masculine heat above me. "Underground."

I shuddered. *Underground?*

"In the catacombs, love." He bit down on my earlobe, causing me to jolt, my eyes opening in a flash.

"Wh-why…?" I trailed off, my eyes blinking in the darkness.

Except it wasn't that dark at all.

I could see the ornate decoration etched into the wood above Cam.

A coffin, I repeated to myself. *We're… we're in a coffin.*

Mmm, he hummed in confirmation, his amusement trickling through the bond. *Fucking… in a coffin.*

I gasped as he slid deep, his cock filling me completely.

"*Cam,*" I breathed, arching up into him.

"Ismerelda," he returned, his lips ghosting over my neck. "My vampire queen."

Vampire… The word reverberated in my mind, my world beginning to materialize. It was… murky. Like wading through dark water, searching for a light.

However, all I could see was Cam.

So clearly.

So *vividly.*

And not just because he was on top of me.

But because he was *inside* me. His soul married to mine. *We're still mated.*

We are, he murmured.

That shouldn't have surprised me. Kylan and Rae had already proved that was possible. Yet, to experience it… I shuddered. *This is so intense.*

Yes, he agreed. *Fucking amazing, too.*

Yes, I echoed, arching into him once more. *I can feel everything.* Not just him, but the world around us. The *earth.* The catacombs. The air.

It was as though my senses had finally awoken.

Like I was experiencing *life.*

I wrapped my arms around him, my movement surprisingly strong and quick. Then I flipped him so I could be on top. Only the coffin lid made it impossible for me to sit up.

Growling, I shoved against it.

And it flew upward.

Cam whirled us, causing my back to hit the cushion beneath as he rotated to catch the lid before it could crash back down on top of us.

My eyes widened.

He chuckled.

Then he tossed it to the side of the crypt and leaned down to kiss me. *We'll work on mastering your new talents,* he murmured into my mind. *Let's start with you fucking me as hard as you can.*

The world spun once more as he placed me back on top, my mind whirring for a quick second before almost immediately settling.

It was unnerving how natural that'd felt. How *exciting* it was.

I pressed my palms to his chest as I seated myself more firmly on his cock.

His mind told me I should be starved right about now, yet the only one I wanted to feed from was him.

And it wasn't his blood that I wanted, but his body. His pleasure. His *growls*.

"It's my turn to destroy you," I taunted him.

"Do your worst," he replied, his lips curling. "Break me. Make me *bleed*."

I scratched my nails down his chest in response, the motion causing him to bow off the cushion beneath us.

His eyes narrowed, his hands finding my hips as he thrust up, the action nearly stealing my breath. "Fuck me like the vampire goddess you are." He sat up, his fingers suddenly fisting my hair. "And don't hold back."

I kissed him, my teeth—no, *fangs*—sinking into his bottom lip.

He returned the favor, our embrace turning violent.

Yet beneath it all was a hint of carnality. A sensual promise between souls. A love no one could ever touch.

Because this male was mine. And I was his.

Once upon a time, a royal vampire mated a mortal, I mused to Cam. *She was his swan and he was her hero.*

But this is no longer that time, he whispered back to me.

No. We're in the future now, I replied. *A future where there are no heroes. No swans. Just us.*

Just us, he agreed, his tongue tracing my lower lip. *We choose our fates.*

Yes, and I choose you—the right *Cam.*

He smiled. *I choose you, too, love. My vampire goddess.*

My vampire king…

Thank you for reading the final book in the Blood Alliance series!

ACKNOWLEDGMENTS

Wow. This book nearly killed me (or maybe that's a result of writing it while pregnant and then caring for a newborn!), but I'm so proud of how it ended, and I hope you enjoyed it, too!

I would not have been able to complete this monumental task (specifically at this stage of motherhood because *yawn*) without my team.

First and foremost, to my husband, thank you for keeping me sane. For loving me despite my long hours and penchant for daydreaming, and for ensuring I sleep and eat like a regular human.

To Vicki, thank you for all your love and support. You're one of my best friends, and I love you so much. Thank you for all that you do for me and Luka. <3

To Laura, thank you for all of your love and support as well! If I could make you immortal, I would. When I figure it out, I'll let you know ;) Love you!

To Amy and Yuli, thank you for taking such good care of Luka for me when I'm lost in my writing cave. You're both amazing and a welcome addition to the "Foss Clan."

To Bethany, my editor extraordinaire, you are the most amazing human in the world. If you lived in the Blood Alliance future, I'd make sure you ended up in a harem with your favorite vamp or lycan! Seriously, though, thank you for everything. You're the reason I'm able to do what I do (and set stupid deadlines…).

To Jean, Katie, Heather, and Erica, thank you so much

for following along with me while I battled this book, and for ensuring it's the best it can be.

To Louise, Diane, and Erica, thank you for being my rocks when I'm deep in the cave. You three constantly keep me afloat when I need it most, and I love you guys!

To Chas and Candi, thank you for all your support, and for marketing my books via the platforms I don't know how to use! One of these days, I'll learn... or not.

And to my readers, thank you for motivating me every day. I love your messages, comments, and emails. They keep me moving forward.

USA Today Bestselling Author Lexi C. Foss loves to play in dark worlds, especially the ones that bite. She lives in Chapel Hill, North Carolina with her husband and their furry children. When not writing, she's busy crossing items off her travel bucket list, or chasing eclipses around the globe. She's quirky, consumes way too much coffee, and loves to swim.

Want access to the most up-to-date information for all of Lexi's books? Sign-up for her newsletter here.

Lexi also likes to hang out with readers on Facebook in her exclusive readers group - Join Here.

Where To Find Lexi:
www.LexiCFoss.com

Printed in Poland
by Amazon Fulfillment
Poland Sp. z o.o., Wrocław

33146202R00409